CASUALTIES OF PEACE

Mir thought he heard the boy scream as the hundred-meter flame wrapped him up. It could only have been the superheated air blasting free of his lungs. His brain was cindered long before the message of intolerable pain reached it from vaporized nerve-ends.

In the Landing Detachment they said of being well and truly burned-down that it reduced you to your bare essentials. Zorich had become a skeleton, bulked slightly by an armature of char, and glazed like a ceramic pot, black enamel of tissues fused by sunheart heat. Mir dropped to his knees beside him, and at once jammed a hand over his own mouth as the sweet roast-pork stink of burned human meat struck him in the face.

The blackened corpse stirred. Mir reared back like a frightened horse, squealing through his nose. *Is he still* alive? *Universal Spirit, don't let him be!*

CLD

COLLECTIVE LANDING DETACHMENT

VICTOR
MILÁN

AVON BOOKS • NEW YORK

CLD (COLLECTIVE LANDING DETACHMENT) is an original publication of Avon Books. This work has never before appeared in book form. This work is a novel. Any similarity to actual persons or events is purely coincidental.

AVON BOOKS
A division of
The Hearst Corporation
1350 Avenue of the Americas
New York, New York 10019

First AvoNova Printing: September 1995

AVONOVA TRADEMARK REG. U.S. PAT. OFF. AND IN OTHER COUNTRIES, MARCA REGISTRADA, HECHO EN U.S.A.

Printed in the U.S.A.

RA 10 9 8 7 6 5 4 3 2 1

For Raina

Down in the Engine

Prologue 1

THE CELL WAS remarkable only in its sterility. The cement walls, the solid featureless door, the ceiling of translucent polymer which absorbed sound and emitted light, and the cover of the thin pallet that served as mattress, were stark white. The pedestal that upheld the mattress, and the half-meter-wide basin by one wall, with a pressure plate above that elicited a stream of tepid water from an aperture in the wall into the basin, were of a silvery alloy. The light that fell from the ceiling had the constant subliminal jitter of fluorescents, which after a time seemed to get inside one and vibrate in the teeth and marrow, and green and blue undertones which turned once-healthy skin the color of a week-old corpse. The light pervaded everything; it seemed at once to blur the featureless walls—turn cement into swaddling that confined without providing stability or security—and to shimmer from the metal fittings like heat mirage off pavement on a sunny day.

In all, it was a setting fit for an examining room—or a morgue. Or what it was: a prison cell, to house a prisoner condemned beyond hope of appeal, built by a secret police ministry with pretensions to the therapeutic. The occupant of the room understood that well; it was his Ministry, after all.

The man in the midst of this white-desert microenvironment, lying unmoving on his back on the slablike bed, was that element which did not fit. Amid all this immaculacy, he was filthy. The simple hospital-style smock that covered his shrunken frame was ragged and grey with the long accumulation of bodily secretions. His hair and beard were wild filthy mats. They were dark with rich veins of grey running through. He could tell this because his hair had grown long enough that he could pull it before his eyes with long dirty-nailed fingers, oddly bent from frequent imperfectly healed breakage, and see.

He was an embarrassment to himself. Each time he awoke he had to accustom himself all over again to the stink of himself. He had long since despaired of getting person or single garment clean in any meaningful way with the limp and lukewarm flow from the outlet; he had no means of shaving or barbering himself, unless he cared to pluck out hairs by the roots. He was still using the basin for other purposes; he had not yet descended to shitting in the corner like an animal, or simply fouling himself wherever he happened to be when the urge struck him.

He reckoned it was just a matter of time. But he resisted, if for no other reason than pride. And perhaps that Particularity justified the treatment that had been given him.

In this context, it sometimes struck him, the Ministry for Communal Values was working an act of grandmotherly kindness by denying him a mirror. Kindness formed no part of the design intent, he knew. It was simply that, as a man who had betrayed the Collective and, therefore, the manifest will of the Universe itself, his features were unworthy of being looked at, even by himself.

He had made the transition back to awareness some indeterminate time before. To find himself here in his white-walled box was something of a relief, because when he was asleep the dreams came: dreams of recollection, of the things that had been done to him since the smiling men and women came into his large and comfortably appointed office; dreams of speculation, in which he saw the things which might—or must—have happened to his wife, his daughter, his son.

Indeed, the smiles had informed him, after the body behind one had shocked him from his chair to his knees with an electric bludgeon, his daughter Yirina's treason was the reason for his arrest. *No leaf falls far from the tree where it grew,* the smile reminded him.

Values was very fond of nature metaphors. It was one of

the things which marked them as superior to their bitter rivals in the Ministry for Continuing Revolution, who had an unhealthy and thoroughly Devolutionary obsession with mechanism.

Of course he understood that it was his daughter who was the uninvolved victim of his misfortune, and not the reverse. He must be removed to make room for another to become Values supervisor for the Santander District. He had been careful to keep his own behavior above reproach—one didn't rise as high as he had in service to the Historic Process without some skill at intrigue—but ambition is resourceful. His rivals had found an alternate route of attack.

—He might have made some estimation of his interval of consciousness by listening to the heartbeat in his ears, the only sound the room's acoustic insulation admitted except for the white noise whisper of ventilation from the narrow whitepainted slots set just below the ceiling. He had taught himself to ignore the metronome of his pulse. To listen to the beats was to become aware of the vast number of seconds which had fallen into ruin here in this white wasteland, like the leaves of dead trees; and to make himself aware of the awful imminence of the infinity of seconds poised above him to drop, one by one, until they crushed him beneath their accreted weight.

He sat, rubbed the back of his neck, which was stiff from sleeping without a pillow. His stomach made a small protest. There was no day or night in here, of course, but if Values' standard confinement procedures were being followed, every twelve hours the slot in the base of the door would open to admit a grey polymer tray of food-paste, of a slightly lighter grey. That was every twelve hours of the Stellar Collective's standard twenty-four-hour clock, based on the rotation period of long-lost Earth, and without reference to the local diurnal period, which was a hair over twenty-seven standard hours.

The food had some lumps in it, for texture, and, while tasteless, was plentiful enough to fill his stomach. Of course, whether it was enough to keep him alive was another matter. It was a synthetic mix, and the actual nutrient content was variable at the will of his jailers. Should they have decided the Universal Will demanded that this miscreant be starved to death, it might suit Values' noted compassion that this be done without the subject experiencing the anxiety of hunger pangs.

He found himself listening with extended senses for the minute sound of the panel sliding open in the door, and the tray sliding forth. Aside from the no-sound sound of the ventilators, it was the only sound he heard which he did not make himself—that and the weekly noise when the top of his bed was rotated by hidden mechanisms to bring up a fresh pallet with a crisp and spotless cover. Aside from nightmares, it was all the company he had.

In his isolation. At odd intervals, though, they came for him. And then he knew he was in for all the company he could stand, and more.

The lodestone of his existence was the chief torturer: a pock-faced stocky devil with a nose like a blade, whose never-changing affable smile displayed pride of craft, not pleasure in the pain he inflicted on his subject's body. And even more, his mind and soul. In sessions shared over months of confinement the torturer had learned the contours of Mir's being more thoroughly than any lover.

Adept as a master gardener was the torturer. He knew exactly how to nurture each seed of hope within his subject, germinate it, bring it along. Then, when it pushed its green sprout head above the surface, he would pluck it out by the roots with firm dispassionate fingers.

—Instead of the furtive small-animal scrabbling of the food tray at the slot, the captive heard more definite and weighty sounds: the locking mechanism of the door itself. His pulse spiked with anticipation. He had come actually to look forward to the infrequent torture sessions—there was no pretense at *interrogation;* the contents of his brain had long since been read directly from the chemical configurations in which memory was stored by unspooling drugs. Even torture was a break from monotony, was human contact, was input for starved senses. And he got to watch a master at his work.

Or perhaps they had simply decided it was time for him to leave his silhouette on a wall. *I don't want to die,* skittered through his brain like a tiny frightened animal. He should have welcomed death as release. Somehow, somehow, he could not, would not, though resistance would be futile even if he had the wherewithal to try—

The door slid aside into the wall. Customary procedure

called for a pair of attendants to be standing there, faceless and inhumanly bulky in masks and padding, shock bludgeons in their thick gauntleted hands. They would advance on him, shock him to make him docile, and lead him forth to a wheeled dolly waiting in the corridor outside. Unless today they had decided to drag him, so that he could enjoy the full benefit of stairs.

Instead a solitary woman stood there, wearing a white therapist's smock over the neutral-colored clothing appropriate to a middle-rank custodian of Values. She seemed in early middle age. Her hair was greying, and severely cut.

She looked at him. "Supervisor Albrekht Mir?"

He blinked. The lids seemed to scrape across the balls of his eyes, as if lined with abrasive coating. It had been an eternity since he had heard his *name*. Much less the title he had once enjoyed.

He moistened his lips with a tongue fat as a foot. He tried to speak, but the parts of his throat seemed to rub together like insect mandibles. He could produce no sound, but must swallow hard to summon spittle and try again.

"I am he," he said.

She nodded. "Come with me, if you please."

If you please? Wildly he looked around, wondering from which direction the trap would be sprung. This much he had learned, in his younger days when he occupied himself with the more *executive* functions of his Ministry: it can always get worse.

"What—what's going on?" he croaked.

"You are rehabilitated," she said.

Prologue 2

THE SHIP WAS a cold-blooded thing. He liked to come down here and listen to its dead heart beat.

The bulkheads were painted greyish brown, with an undertone hint of red. His fatigues were the very same color. Much of the Stellar Collective was painted that shade, carefully standardized according to specifications drawn up in labs on Praesidium. He had grown up surrounded by that color.

Painted on the bulkhead in blue broken-block letters was AIR RECIRC #6. Six great air pumps, gleaming pale-alloy mounds arranged in parallel rows of three, sucked waste air into exhaust vents throughout a large section of the joyboat carrier *Beria* with a constant bone-driving throb, forcing CO_2-rich gas through blue-gleaming polymer conduits thicker than a stout man over racks of blue-green algae in a recycling compartment and onward through ionizing scrubbers.

He liked to sit in the midst of this space, surrounded and hidden from view by the humped throbbing housings. On a ship in space there were no open bodies of water to sit beside to try to soothe the turbulence inside like cool water rinsing a wound, no shining path of light on water with its unrequited promise of escape. Deathbirds were lucky to get enough to drink and sluice their bodies clean with; the latter because their unhappy hosts of Kosmos Force didn't want them stinking up their ship, the former because it was the Universal Will that they be delivered as healthy as possible to a place where they would have the opportunity to die for their crimes.

The young man and his comrades, a regiment worth of them, jammed into the compartments of a ship whose outer hull was crusted with Assault Boats, armored like scorpion young, were CLD. Collective Landing Detachment. The condemned cutting edge of the Engine of History.

From a pocket of his utility blouse he took a butterfly knife with pierced matte black handles, whipped it open with quick grace. He laid his right arm, sleeve rolled to elbow, across his thighs, pressed the blade against the soft skin of the arm's inside, just below the elbow, applied pressure till red welled around the knife tip. Then, tongue tip protruding slightly between his lips, he began to cut.

His grandmother, back before they took her away, used to like to say, "Spaces are just as important as places." It always made anger flare inside his skull, because it made no sense that he could figure out.

Then he would swallow his rage, burning down his throat to burst in his belly like a clammy-damp bomb. He could not be mad at his grandmother. She was all he had.

Later, though—when the expectation that anything *did* make sense had been squashed out of him—he began to wonder. Began to feel he understood what his gran had been saying. In the Stellar Collective you were always surrounded by people; it was designed that way, their constant locust friction rubbing away at your ego until you were exposed and formless and ready to be shaped to fit the Universal Will. Down here in Air Recirc #6 he could find *space* amid the chill and isolation.

Round and down he drew a line, twining his forearm like a red bead strand. When he reached the wrist he stopped. He held his arm up to the light from the overhead grille, admired the smooth glistening purity of the blood in its domes and trails. Blood dripped on the legs of his trousers, on the grey natural-fiber nonskid mat that covered the deck beneath him.

He whipped the blade out of sight between the handle halves, laid the knife down. From beside him he took a 25mm launchable grenade. He twisted off the rounded projectile head, set it carefully beside him. What remained was a little can of chemical propellant about twenty-five millimeters high with a cannelured base. Carefully he salted the dark tiny pel-

lets into the raw wound, from wrist to elbow. The chemical
stung on contact, hit him fresh and bracing, like icy water in
the face or the day's first hit of Zone.

He piled it on, until a little ridge of propellant ran along the
cut, caking with blood-ooze. He set the grenade's base aside
and from a pocket took out a spark initiator. He held it near
his wrist and touched it off.

Hissing, white light and smoke, a spark that climbed his
arm like a glowing writhing serpent. His nostrils filled with a
familiar sweet-sharp smell. He was flamer man for his squad.

When the burning was done he held up his arm again. The
wound was cauterized and nicely charred. If the shocked-out
Reclamation scout with the thousand-parsec eyes and the
thumbprint whorls of scars on his cheeks had told him true,
they should scab over nicely, and become raised scars.

If he wasn't . . . the young man was just going to have to
eat his disappointment. Because the scout had wandered drunk
and singing bitter songs out of the off-limits bar into the humid
Hovya night. And Dauber terrs had caught him and left his
skin hanging from a lamppost. *Just like a dumbfuck scout,* the
young man thought with sudden savagery, *to think he was safe
just 'cause he wasn't hanging his ass in the breeze of some
unknown turdball planet beyond Realized Space.*

It didn't matter. He had served in CLD for six years. He
knew about scars, and reckoned these would shape up right.
And if they didn't, they were going somewhere he'd have
ample opportunity to share his pain.

He whipped his knife open again, a figure eight caracole to
keep his wrist supple. Then he worked over his forearm until
he had a nice pattern of longitudinal cuts serpentining around
his arm, turned into red latticework by thin blood-trails.

He had taken up the base of the purloined launch grenade
again when a voice said, "Ho! What have we here?"

The voice was like a boot in the face. He looked up, cheeks
burning at the intrusion. Tears pressed the backs of his eyes.

There were three of them, thick-necked and thick around
the middle in their Black Gang coveralls, midnight to mask
stains. Foremost was a short broad one with a black beard
fringing the lower half of a round face. He grinned down at
the young man. He was missing an incisor.

A tall blond man leaned over his comrade's shoulder.

"Looks like we found a stray deathbird piece of shit."

The bearded man grinned wider. "Well, now. Imagine that. You're out of your country, deathbird."

"He's a pretty one, ain't he?" asked the third, whose brown hair hung in his eyes in longer-than-regulation bangs. "But hey, shit, he's all over blood."

"Look at that little knife," the blond said. "He cut himself."

"Ugh!" Brown-Bangs said. "That's sick! You deathbirds make me want to puke."

"You go right ahead and puke, then, Schull," Black-Beard said, "somewhere else. Kotkin and I have better plans."

He reached out and stroked the young man's head. The youth's hair was short, just grown out enough to lie down into a soft, sleek black pelt.

"Destroying Collective property's a serious offense," Black-Beard said. He took the butterfly knife from the young man's hand. The young man did not resist.

Black-Beard held up the butterfly. "My, my. Possession of an unauthorized weapon. You could be in a world of trouble, boy. Unless you care to be *nice* to us."

He tossed the knife away. It fell with a clatter, off among the great humped shapes.

The blond man rubbed the backs of two black-nailed fingers down the young man's cheek. "He's blushing," the blond man said. "Isn't that sweet?"

The hand drew back, then slashed backhand across the young man's face. He fell back against cool solid mechanism housing, felt the rhythm of the ship's breathing through his back.

"What'd you go and do that for, Kotkin?" asked Schull.

Kotkin laughed. "I treat all my bitches like that. Woman or man, they got to learn to appreciate my dragon."

The young man wiped his mouth with the back of his hand. No blood. Beyond progressive paling of his blue eyes he showed no emotion.

The engine room crewmen took his lack of response for passive acceptance. "Bend him over, boys," said Black-Beard, who wore petty officer's stripes on his coveralls. He began to undo the fly. "Rank hath its privileges, you know."

"*Klad,*" Schull said in disgust.

"Of course. It's what makes the Big Wheel roll. That's the Universal Will."

Lips peeled back from the brown-haired man's teeth. His eyes flicked apprehensively around, at the great air pumps, at the snake dance of colored polymer conduits twisting overhead.

"Watch what you say, Gund," he muttered. "Never know who's listening."

Black-Beard guffawed. "It's nothing they haven't heard before. If it is, it's high time they lost their cherry. Besides, you said the forbidden word first. If anybody's going down, you're first."

Kotkin shook his blond head. "I don't fancy winding up like him," he said, nodding at the young man they hemmed against the air pump housing. "To be sentenced to death, then have your ass shipped off to Process knows what Spirit-forsaken shitball world to get it shot off by slimy autocs."

"You worry too much," Gund said. "Enough foreplay. Get his trousers down."

Hard hands gripped the young man's biceps. They turned him around and slammed him against the housing. The alloy was cool, smooth and hard against his cheek, and the ship's vibrations entered into his bones.

He let his mind, pleasurably fuzzed by the hyacinth he chewed before drifting down here, float back to the first time he had been raped by a woman, back when he had been sentenced to the Detachment but not yet sent to the training camp. Not the first time he had been raped, of course; his older, larger fellows took care of that when he was sent to orphanage after his grandma went away. It was his first by a woman, though, who performed the deed with a mop handle while male guards, laughing, knelt on his wrists and ankles. Afterward they took their turns with him, too.

His fatigues were standard two-piece, distinguished from a common soldier's utilities by yellow stripes on the arms. The shipmen's jumpsuits took a lot longer to get off than his pants normally would. But as Schull and Kotkin held him pinned against the pump housing he writhed just enough to slow them pulling down his trousers without earning more than a couple additional cracks to the side of his head.

In a few fumbling moments he heard a sigh from Gund and

a rustle as the jumpsuit dropped around the petty officer's ankles. His bruds were still struggling with their victim's pants.

Preoccupied, Schull was a little slack in his grip on the captive's left wrist. The youth was left-handed. He snapped his arm abruptly back and in, driving against Schull's thumb. His hand popped free.

The young man whipped the hand downward. A second butterfly knife slipped into it from a sheath concealed in the sleeve, fluttered open blade down, and stabbed the brown-haired man in the crotch.

The blade didn't go in very far, perhaps two centimeters through coarse fabric, skin, and meat. Enough to make Schull shriek and jump back, clutching at the stain spreading rapidly across his groin.

From the shallow stab it took no time to wrench the knife blade free. His right wrist still pinned against the housing, the young man ducked beneath the arm that held it, pivoting clockwise, slashing the tip of the knife across Kotkin's belly. The cut was even more superficial than Schull's stab, but bloody-painful-unexpected it made Kotkin let go and jump back, too.

The young man turned to find the petty officer standing behind him with his jumpsuit around his thighs, dragon in hand, and a look of stunned surprise behind his beard. His chest was matted in black fur like an animal's pelt. Beneath it his skin was pale, bluish in the subliminally flickering overhead light.

The young man slashed the rampant penis smartly across the head. Gund screamed shrilly and doubled, trying to cover himself with his hands. He tried to back away from his assailant, but his jumpsuit tackled him. He fell backward, penis pulsing blood like red ejaculate, spattering grey fiber deck matting and spotless pump housing.

Schull lay on his side sobbing and clutching his bloodied belly as if holding in his guts with his hands. Kotkin stood hunched against air pump, pallid and shocky. The young man sprang forward to straddle Gund's black-pelted chest. Kneeling on the petty officer's biceps, he began methodically to slash at his face.

A jarring synthetic blare, half-ring, half-buzz. Kotkin had

recovered from his stab wound sufficiently to stagger to a hatch and slap the mutiny button with his palm. In a matter of moments the pump station would fill up with Kosmos Marines.

The young man tucked his knife away. Grabbing Gund's bearded cheeks, he bent down and kissed him full on slashed bloody lips. Then ran.

PART ONE

Dropped

"HEY!" THE YOUNG transfer cried. He was dabbing at the fiber mat that covered the deck between the bunks with a push broom. "Hey, you karls! Take it easy. I can smell your farts!"

"That's just Balt," said Jovan without turning his head from his game of cards.

"Watch your yob, pig farmer," a burly man with one black eyebrow spanning the front of his head growled from his bunk. "I don't take noise from a hayseed with shit between his toes."

Jovan turned his head. He was a tall lanky man with straw blond hair hanging down above green eyes. His hands were big and hard. As with most of the men in First Section, scrubs included, the fingers were crooked from poorly set breaks. It was a sort of badge of honor in CLD.

"And I got no use for a greasy urban snot-glob." He grinned. "Wanna dance?"

Balt grunted and looked away. Jovan was less inclined to start trouble than just about any deathbird in Section. But no man in the Detachment was readier to finish it. Balt, though squatly powerful and a fearsome infighter—as was anyone who had survived a combat tour in CLD—seldom showed much eagerness to mix it with anybody who might actually lay hurt on him.

"Well, well," Loki said. He had an end of the mattress of the top bunk of a three-deep rack peeled back and was rum-

17

maging beneath it with pale spider fingers. "What have we here?"

Most of Section's new transfers were huddled in the after end of the compartment. There were ten in all. The Realization of Hovya had taken its toll on First Section.

"Hey!" a transfer yelped when he saw what Loki was up to. "That's my bunk!" His hair was still cut so close from the Grinder that it was barely a shimmer around his round knobby skull. He tried to hurl himself forward.

Well aft by *Beria*'s conventional-space drives, First Section's compartment seemed crammed in as an afterthought among polymer conduit tangles. The passage between sharp-edged metal bunk-racks, painted blood khaki like everything else, that ran along either side of the narrow compartment was so tight that a strongly built man couldn't walk it with shoulders squared. A booted foot stuck out of a bottom rack, and the boy went sprawling.

He fetched up hard against a bunk on which a square unremarkable man of medium height lay on his back with blunt fingers laced behind his head. His face was one shade of red, short hair of another. He had diagonal sergeant's stripes on the sleeves of his BK fatigues, above the three horizontal yellow bumblebee stripes that marked him as Detached. He raised his head and looked down at the boy.

"Somebody just saved you a beating, boy," he said. "Or worse."

"But Sergeant Stilicho," the youngster wailed, "he's in my *stuff!*"

" 'But Sergeant Stilicho, he's in my stuff,' " mimicked Loki, who was blond, mildly tall, and specter-thin. His face had a chiseled kind of beauty, except for the nose, which had been broken repeatedly and most recently set so that the tip skewed off true. His eyes were green, and set at a slant above prominent cheekbones. "This is the Stellar Collective, scrub. You are allowed to *have* no stuff; that's Particular, don't you read your Book?"

From the scrub preserve at the compartment's ass end, a boy with a head sticking up like a black-tufted white tuber from the neck of his sweat-stained BK tee shirt exclaimed, "I won't hear anyone make fun of the Book!" His own copy of *The Communality*, which Dependents of the Stellar Collective were supposed to keep with them at all times, was hung around his neck on a braided cord, so imposing it pulled his skinny upper body down into an oldster's hunch.

"Then don't listen, you shriveled little trouser-weasel!" Starman told him.

The boy popped to rigid attention. "I am Lander 234-444-523-115-11111. I confess and apologize for my crimes against the Stellar Collective, which manifests the will of the Community of All Life and the Universal Spirit!"

"Shut up that noise!" roared Black Bertold. He was a sergeant, second-in-command of Second Squad, and normally one of Section's more amiable members. He had brilliant blue eyes and a full bristling beard that gave him his name. He had been a Kosmos Marine before being Detached, and since CLD was nominally part of the Collective's space navy even though it almost invariably fought under army command, Landers were allowed facial hair. "And slap that useless abortion next to you. He's starting to disgust me."

The useless abortion in question lay on a top bunk next to Gollob, facing the wall, a husky youth with dark blond hair. He was new transfer Chyz, who had instantly been nicknamed Chyz the Jizz, the Mad Wanker. He was busy justifying the sobriquet right now, left elbow pumping away.

Loki honked laughter. "The starship trooper's jealous our fresh-faced new colleague won't let him lend a hand! Unhappy in love is our Sergeant Bertold."

Bertold's impressive black brows clamped down above his startling eyes, and he showed teeth through his beard. It was rumored he had just been jilted by a gunner's mate, an apple-cheeked blond boy from the Core World of Trotskiy.

"Go ahead and push, my fine roughnecked friend," he said with apparent mildness. He was only 169 centimeters tall, but big through chest and shoulders, with short powerful legs and long arms that ended in outsize hands with great cancerlike scar-wads for knuckles. He was a rush-and-grapple infighter, who matched up well with the much taller but skinnier Loki. He knew tricks he claimed came from Brazil on lost long-ago Earth that enabled him to immobilize even Big Bori, who was well over two meters tall. "You might find you get to sit out tomorrow's assault."

"Ha!" sneered Loki. "You'd have to kill me, and you're

too much the super-trooper for that! Even if you broke every
bone in my poor body, they'd drop me in the first wave with
contragrav generators strapped to my R&R unit. Deathbirds
always go in first. Say, what's this?''

As he taunted Bertold he continued to rummage through the
few forbidden effects hidden under the scrub's mattress. He
came up with something stuck on his hand. It was a sort of
doll or puppet made from a rag-stuffed sock. Smiling eyes and
mouth had been crudely drawn on it in black marker. Tufts to
either side of the top had been tied off to resemble nub ears.
"Hello," Loki said.

The bunk's owner uttered a despairing wail. "Mr. Bun!"
Stilicho tried to hold him, but he broke free and flew wildly
at Loki.

Loki stiff-armed him in the face and dropped him to crack
his coccyx hard on the mat-covered deck. "Mr. Bun, is it?
Scrub Henriks has a *toy*. Isn't that sweet?''

"Give him to me!" screamed Henriks. He popped up trailing pennons of tears and clutching frantically.

Loki lofted the sock-toy over his outstretched hands. Starman unreeled a long arm from his bunk and snagged it from
the air. "I believe it has little ears," he said, tugging hard on
the nubs. Henriks lunged at him. Starman fended him off with
one hand, grinning ferociously.

For a scrub to lay hands on an ancient, as Landers were
called when they had survived enough frontline savagery to
be accepted as comrades rather than liabilities, was almost
unheard of. It invited a thrashing or worse. But Henriks was
almost out of his mind.

"My mommy gave me that sock!" he screamed. "I made
him myself; I've had him all along. Please!"

"Please. Now, I call that nice. A scrub who knows how to
be polite." Starman held the doll out. Henriks snatched for it.

Starman wrist-flicked it over the boy's head back to Loki.
Then his hand darted in a quick jab that set the boy down
hard on his bottom with blood starting from his right nostril.
"Not nice to grab," the black Senior Lander taunted.

Aft a tall blond scrub stood up. "That's enough," he said.
"Why don't you give it back to him?"

"*What's it to you, you miserable dog-smeller?*" the black
Senior Lander screamed with vehemence that rocked the

husky new transfer back from three meters away. Starman was mercurial at the best of times. Space flight made him moody, alternating between quiet spells and screaming rage-fits. "Pull your sharp nose out of others' business, before we chop it off and shove it up your ass."

Henriks bounced up and stumbled to Loki. "*Please!*" he wailed. "My mother—"

Somebody else tripped him. He fell hard onto his face. Moaning, he crawled forward.

"I'm surprised they left your family alive," said Stilicho. "Usually when they Detach you your whole tribe leaves silhouettes on a wall."

"Doesn't your mommy know it's treason to care what happens to traitors?" Starman asked.

The boy groveled at Loki's knees. Loki held high the improvised stuffed toy, drew his long thin-bladed knife. A few quick slashes, and Mr. Bun was fluttering around Henriks's prominent ears, like Preservation-approved biodegradable confetti at a Direktor's Birthday parade.

Henriks screamed. "*No!* Mr. Bun! *Mommy!*"

"Your mother's a whore." Loki spit and put the knife away.

Balt's bellowing laughter rang off the bulkheads. Henriks jumped up, fists pummeling for Loki's face. "You bastard! Your mother's a whore too!"

Loki fended the blows with casual forearm shifts, not deigning even to take offense. "This in fact is true," he said. He drove a stiffened forefinger into Henriks's solar plexus, doubling him over. Then he put the heel of his hand against the crown of the boy's head and pushed him back. The boy almost flew, even in the ship's artificially maintained one standard gravity. There was surprising strength in that attenuated frame.

"My mother was a whore, and my father, too. Offering whatever orifice fell handy to whoever had the *klad* to pay."

The scrub who had spoken out for Henriks came forward and assisted him to his feet. He was Zorich, tall, handsome, robustly built, the golden boy among the new transfers. A natural soldier, he bore up under the most brutal hazing with such unflagging cheerfulness even the ancients gave him grudging respect.

"Come, sit by me," he told the helplessly sobbing boy,

steering him to a vacant bunk next to Stilicho. It belonged to the Dancing-Master, the senior sergeant in command of Second Squad, who was off somewhere with Junior Lieutenant Mir, the Section CO, and his second-in-command, Senior Sergeant Kyov. "Don't mind them. They're trying to toughen us so we have a chance in our first battle. We all survived the Meatgrinder, but even that's not the same as the real firing line."

"But I want Mr. Bun!" Henriks sobbed.

"If the boy brought the toy through the Grinder, he did damned well," remarked the White Rat, perched on a top bunk looking like his namesake about to clean his whiskers. He was an albino, from the radioactive slag dumps of Primus, the heavy metal world where the survivors of Jochen Stahl's New Red Army, fugitives from a war-shattered Earth, had first made planetfall two and a half centuries before. The Rat was tiny and wizened and weak as a child, but no one offered him hurt, not even Balt or Loki. He was the finest scrounger in all of the 523rd Regiment, CLD. If you had skills like that you were an invaluable survival asset in the Stellar Collective, to say nothing of the Detachment. "It's more than most can do to make it through with their lives."

Loki shrugged and turned away. He had lost interest in the game.

Big Bori had been lying sprawled on a bunk alternately dozing and watching Jovan play cards with Rouen and Dieter. The others always tried to dissuade him from joining play. He was easy to beat even when the others didn't cheat, and when he lost he didn't react well. Now he sat up with a troubled expression twisting his vast face.

"You hurt that boy's toy," he said, half-wondering, half-accusing. "You wouldn't hurt *my* toy, would you?"

"You can bet to that," muttered Jovan. "A vacation in the R&R tanks has its points, but getting all your bones broken first isn't my idea of a picnic."

Bori stared at Loki. "Why did you do that, Loki?"

Everybody caught his breath in his teeth. Loki and Poet and Starman formed an unholy alliance often referred to as the Usual Suspects. The brain-damaged giant usually aligned himself with them; he had bonded to Loki in particular like a puppy. In turn Loki handled Bori with his usual edge artistry.

But every once in a while Loki pushed it too far. Such occasions were half-dreaded by Section and half-eagerly anticipated. They *did* dispel the tedium of a long space flight.

"He was a bad boy," Loki said with paternal sadness.

Bori nodded, eyes huge. "I'm not a bad boy, am I?"

"Not right now. You're a very good boy. But"—he held up a long finger, ticked it back and forth—"watch yourself!"

Bori nodded and subsided.

Stilicho pushed a sour chuckle up from the base of his throat. "You're a total fool, Loki. You'll swing someday."

Loki put back his head and emitted a ringing macaw screech of laughter. "Of course I shall! And who's the fool? We're all sentenced to death, you quill-hog! All that's wanting is the proper autoc to carry out the sentence of the loving and compassionate Communal Court!"

That sucked in a brief clammy silence like mist beneath the conduits. To be Detached was indeed to be under sentence of death. And the joyboat carrier *Beria* was at that moment hurtling them toward yet another possible place of execution.

The scrubs clustered together around Loki's victim, who was holding his face and weeping—trying to keep it muted, so as to save himself a beating from the ancient. "It was terrible what he did to poor Henriks," said Nau, the former star computing student. He had light brown hair, dark brown eyes, a mild rabbit face. "Isn't there anything we can do?"

The question was directed at Stilicho, but sidelong. Nau had an insatiable need to know, but was intimidated by the ancients.

The sergeant rolled his big jaw around. "You could steal something of his and destroy it."

"But he doesn't value anything!" burst out redheaded Florenz.

Stilicho shrugged. "Who told you the Universe was fair, boy—or that there are always answers?"

He tried to slip in unnoticed. It was hopeless, of course, even for a scout and alley-skulker of his experience. There was no concealment between the bunk-racks, in that jittery incessant light from the overhead that turned all faces to those of the moving dead—appropriate enough. The nerves of Section's ancients had been scraped and drawn like animal skin on a drumhead by prolonged exposure to danger. They could feel a man *move* in this close, stinking air—air from which no amount of filtration, scrubbing, or reconstitution could remove the traces of every set of lungs which had contained it, air whose staleness was accentuated by the stinks of sweat and feet and that peculiar musty smell Collective battle dress gave off even when clean and particularly when new—the smell of lubricants and farts and diseased gums, of illicit alcohol and various other forms of chemical release from the joys of service to the Historic Process—air so dense with odor that it seemed to leave small room for the twenty-some human bodies to fit in with it.

Loki was first to spot his condition, of course. He planted his specter-thin carcass directly in the young man's path, put hands on hips, and said, "So there, you are, Poet. You were out having fun. And you didn't invite *me*."

Loki was frequently Poet's partner in crime. Just as frequently they tried to kill each other. Poet was in no mood for banter. He muttered something and tried to sidle by.

Stilicho rolled himself up onto one elbow. "What in Process's name have you been up to? You're a hell of a mess."

Poet held up his arms, showing the raw cuts which wound around his right forearm, and the blood-lace that overlaid them. "Cutting."

Loki laughed. It was a jarring laugh, that struck in among the nerve ends and rattled around. It was intended to be. He held up his arms, which were twined with angry red welts, scarcely healed over.

"Imitating your betters, are you?" he asked.

The hatch hissed open behind him. Senior Sergeant Kyov came in with the Dancing-Master behind him. He stopped.

"Poet, look at you," he said. He had hazel eyes, brown hair, a face that seemed to have been weathered into contours of concern. He was probably in his late thirties, though the way the Landing Detachment put its stamp on you, he might have been twenty or sixty just as easily. In most units of the Engine of History, whose embrace men and women generally fled as quickly as Collective law would let them, he would have been a creaking ancient. In CLD, from which there was never a muster-out, the only thing remarkable about him was surviving so long. "You're blood all over."

Poet said nothing. He gazed down at his boots. The usual defiant scruffiness they would have exhibited down in the dirt planetside had been replaced by a shine that cast his features distorted back up into his eyes. That the Collective Landing Detachment belonged nominally to Kosmos Force and not the Engine of History at all cut little sausage in either direction; but the space navy had you utterly in its power when you were out there in the Big Empty. Kosmos had its ways of making you toe the mark.

"What happened to you?" the older man asked in that gentle, persistent voice of his. He laid a hand on Poet's shoulder. The young man made no move to knock it away. He hated Kyov—commander of First Squad and father to all—hated his never-ending solicitude, hated him for his quiet authority, which he never pressed, never insisted on, and yet was part of him, intrinsic as the smell of his own sweat. Yet Poet, too, depended on the soft-spoken noncom, for the solidity he provided, for his unquestioning acceptance of all those placed under his care. Not even Loki, defiant braying Loki, enemy of peace and order and decency and most beings that chanced across his path, would stand up to Kyov for long.

"Was down in Recirc 6," Poet said, scuffing a foot on the seaweed-fiber mat. "Had some trouble."

"You slut!" Loki shouted. "Waltzing with the Black Gang, and didn't think to invite your friends." He scanned the shorter man critically. "Not all that blood is yours, surely?"

Before Poet could answer he was seized beneath the armpits and lifted straight off the deck. Huge hard hands turned him around in midair like a recalcitrant puppy. Big Bori's face stared at him like a moon of scars.

"Little friend," the giant boomed. "Little friend, did they hurt you? Say the word, and Big Bori will make 'em weep."

He let go of Poet with one hand to ball it into a gigantic misshapen fist for emphasis. He had no trouble keeping the dark-haired youth suspended with one arm.

Poet's cheeks flushed. "Put me down, you giant lump of ling shit!" he screamed. He kicked the big man in the belly, hard.

Big Bori looked confused. "What's the matter, little friend?" He looked at the others, who were beginning to gather round in hopes of hearing a lurid tale of combat with the hated Black Gang—and not impossibly, scoping a little real-time internecine battling as well.

"What's the matter with him?" Bori demanded. "I didn't hurt him? Did I?"

"He just wants you to put him down, Bori," Kyov said. "There's a good boy."

The giant promptly set Poet back on his feet. "I am a good boy," he announced. Poet shook his head and muttered obscenities beneath his breath.

"So what went on?" a voice asked from the back of the mob crowded in between the cliff face bunks.

Heads turned. It was Kobolev, leader of a trio of new transfers who did not fit the standard scrub profile. They called themselves the Bold Originals. They had all known each other since childhood, had enlisted in the Engine of History together, been busted together, and somehow managed to keep together through the hell of Detachment training. They were older than the rest of the current scrub crop, more self-assured, and physically more imposing. They refused to associate with the other scrubs and refused to be identified with them. Their solidarity and size allowed them to get away with it.

Kobolev—himself the eponymous Bold Original—was a big man with blue eyes bright and hard as glass, good-looking in that stuffed-sausage way garrison life in the Engine gave you. He sported a black beard that outlined a wide jaw and sent a probe up his chin toward his lower lip. He and his beefy bruds had been consigned to the bunks nearest the hatch, second in order of undesirability to those crammed at the compartment's far end.

Poet stared at him. He was still feeling aftershocks of the anger that hit him when Bori picked him up. He had cooled off enough for calculation, though; and he wasn't clear in his own mind yet whether it would be better to have the new arrivals as friends or foes.

"Brought some putes to Now," he said.

Kobolev and company looked expectantly at him. Poet could be pretty talkative, but he didn't feel that way now. He pivoted and walked toward his rack near the aft end of the compartment. His bunk was a top one, which he insisted on; the conduits pressing almost down on him gave him at least an illusion of security and even privacy—and the *actuality* was forbidden even to honest Dependents. Despite his appearance—and he wasn't that much older than he looked—he was one of Section's veterans of long standing. He took what he liked and did as he pleased, though that was a product more of savagery and a wolverine eagerness to display it than seniority.

The other Landers eased back to give him room. In a group in which casual brutality was normative behavior, he had a Reputation.

He brushed by the cleaning-happy scrub, who had resumed pushing his broom once the skirmishing ended. "Hey!" yelled the new transfer, whose name was Sturz. "You're dripping blood on the mat!"

Poet gave him a dead-eyed look.

Most men's shit would have turned to water at that point. Sturz persisted. "What if Lieutenant Vyacheslav sees that?" he demanded.

"Who gives an autoc's green-warted dragon?" Starman said. "What will the Kosmos pinprick do, Detach us?"

The White Rat perched on his bunk, hunched half over to keep his head off the conduits above, gnawing a chunk of purple *tuva* root. "They can't shoot us," he said. "Only approved enemies of the Stellar Collective have that privilege. These Kosmos crotch-grabbers have to deliver us hale and whole, and like it!"

The young transfer went ballistic, squalling about detention, punishment drill, and stim—the torture where they gifted you with straightshot pain-to-the-brain. Big Bori sat up.

"Why are you making so much noise?" he asked mildly.

"Because you're making a mess!" Sturz screamed. "And I can smell your farts!"

A hand attached to an arm as big as most men's legs and some men's bodies extended and fell heavily on top of the scrub's sandy-haired head, dropping him in a heap on the deck.

"Now you don't," Bori said, and absently rubbed his knuckles.

2

THE PASSAGEWAY OUTSIDE the Community Center was wider and brighter than the rest of the corridors that wound their way through the *Beria*'s guts. That fit; the CC was the biggest single space inboard, as well lit as the bridge. It imposed a huge overhead on life-support, and rendered the rest of the warship even more cramped than it otherwise would have been. But in the eyes of the Stellar Collective it was the most important space inboard, no matter what the bridge crew or Engineering thought. All warcraft massing more than five-hundred tonnes had to have dedicated CCs; on smaller vessels the general mess served the function. The whole purpose of the Collective was to foster community: the community of all sapient life in the Universe. The military whims and exigencies of Kosmos and the Engine had to yield to that.

Stragglers filed through the main entrance to join the two battalions of the 523rd Regiment gathered in the amphitheater. Back among the passageways that served the main galley, beside the entrance that allowed speakers to reach the podium from behind without mingling with the audience, a young Kosmos junior captain, immaculate in crisp naval whites, stood waiting with poorly concealed impatience.

"Colonel Danilov? A word with you."

The officer commanding the 523rd Regiment, Collective Landing Detachment stopped. He was a head shorter than the junior captain, but probably had him by a few kilos, mostly in the chest and shoulders, and little of it excess lipids. His head was broad, its squareness emphasized by his grey flattop. His face resembled a collection of well-used knuckles. He looked at the naval officer with uncompromising blue eyes.

Not far away, a small figure with a bandaged right forearm lurked in a side passage. Poet had a DNA-deep aversion to front entrances.

"Captain Borchardt sends his compliments, Colonel, and requests your presence in his compartment at your earliest convenience," he heard the ship's officer say.

The expression Danilov showed him was to a smile what winter-bare trees were to July. "Since I am leading my regiment in a combat assault some fifteen hours from now, I'd say that's liable to be when the campaign is over. My compliments to the senior captain." He turned to go.

The junior captain reached for a sleeve of his background-adaptive battle dress, which was set to neutral, meaning blood khaki. Before contact was made the colonel turned. The look in his eyes made the naval officer draw back his finely manicured hand without touching him.

"I don't believe the colonel understands."

"I understand that, should I not be present and prepared to lead the landing on the planet we're orbiting tomorrow, such of my family and friends as remain Outside will shortly leave their silhouettes on a wall. As, for that matter, I will as well. Your captain will have to wait."

"But it's urgent!"

Danilov frowned but stayed. "What is it, then?"

"One of your men," the junior captain said. "He assaulted some of our crew."

"Indeed? How many?"

The naval officer showed the tips of upper incisors, raked them quickly across his underlip, and looked down at the deck. "Well, three were injured."

Colonel Danilov raised his eyebrows. "So at least three of your men were involved in a set-to with one Lander. Odd. I haven't heard of any of mine going on hospital report." He smiled.

"Colonel, this is a serious matter! At least two crew were unfit for duty."

"That's certainly serious. What do you propose I do about it?"

"Surrender the guilty party at once."

"With an assault about to commence? Absurd!"

The junior captain nipped his lip again. "Sir, the captain is prepared to accept your court-martialing him."

Danilov uttered a bark of laughter. "Even if I had time for such nonsense, what would I do? Throw him in the brig? Do you think that's *punishment* to a man who'd otherwise be going into battle?"

"But he's armed!" the young officer said breathlessly. That was his big gun; for anyone who wasn't military or police on actual duty to possess arms was a capital offense. The Stellar Collective was committed to preventing violence.

The colonel laughed again. "If he's not now, he will be shortly."

He turned to go. "You can't cover for his crimes!" the junior captain cried in a passion. "You'll be court-martialed!"

"And what can they do? Sentence me to death?" He shook his head. "Too late, by five years. Now go back to your captain and tell him that my Collective duty requires that every fit man take part in the coming assault, and *that* overrides even his wounded vanity."

"I can't tell him that!" the Kosmos officer gasped.

"Then tell him what you will; I've no more time to waste." He shrugged. "And who knows? Perhaps the enemy will do his part, and carry out the sentence of death the Communal Court has already passed upon the guilty man."

The young Kosmos officer gaped at him a moment longer. Danilov stood impassive as a basalt statue, and every bit as pliable. The junior captain turned and scuttled away.

The little deathbird colonel watched him go. Then, as if by chance, he swept his gaze across the place where Poet lurked. Without his expression flickering he turned and walked into the CC.

Poet let go a long breath. He shook a red Zone tab into his palm from one of his hidden stash points, popped it, and hurried into the amphitheater.

"So I hear you carved your initials in some dog honkers who were trying to take you for a walk behind the barracks," said Rudi, whose bulk was squeezed into the seat next to Poet's.

Warrant officers from regimental HQ, wearing yellow brassards, circulated through the Center, barking numbers and shining laser pointers to guide latecomers to seats. Poet followed the dancing dot to one beside the fat fixer and sat with his head sunk into the collar of his chammy battle dress.

The *Beria*'s class of joyboat carriers was built to accommodate a theoretical full-strength battalion of twenty-five companies. The 115 had only twelve. The Collective was committing a vast number of troops—some said an unprecedented number—to the impending assault. The invasion fleet had been assembled in great secrecy behind the frontier along which the Collective and the Strahn Hegemony had been locked in stalemate for almost a decade. Transport was at a premium. Accordingly the 115th Battalion, the 800th, and regimental HQ were all jammed together in the ship.

"They say you cut off one's dragon and stuffed it in his mouth," Rudi continued, with relish glistening on his fat lips like grease. He was a fat bald man stuffed into his battle dress like a sausage in its skin. A fixer he was, a former deathbird from Section One who had wangled transfer to the HQ staff.

"That's slotted by me, Poet," Rudi said. "Any hurt you lay on those stuck-up Kosmos bastards is only what they deserve. They treat us like ling shit."

He patted Poet's thigh with a plump hand. Poet would not hold back from traffing his own body; he'd done it often enough, after they took his gran. But Rudi didn't want that; he didn't like boys, or girls either, so far as anyone could tell. He was just being friendly in his greasy-gauche way.

Poet did not take readily to human contact; he eyed the hand—black hairs clustered over the back of it like miniaturized wiring harnesses—and thought about flipping free a hideout blade and pinning it to his own thigh. It would be worth it to see the look on Rudi's fleshy face. Poet was indifferent to his own pain, but he'd learned how to relish others'.

But no. Reluctantly he put the thought from his mind. He needed Lullaby if he wanted to sleep tonight, and he had no intention of facing the assault itself without being armored in the buzz of Zone. For those comforts he needed Rudi. He was no mean fixer himself, but security was tight on a Kosmos vessel under way. In all the 523rd Rudi alone managed to maintain the proper lines of supply.

A fistfight broke out somewhere off to the left. Rudi took his hand away and craned to watch. Poet quit perching on the end of his seat like a frightened cat and tried to relax.

With a shake of his blond head Junior Lieutenant Haakon Mir let himself back down in his seat. The fracas didn't involve anyone from First Section, thank Process. Six Universal months on the firing line with First Section had taught him that the most useful command technique in CLD was the blind eye. Since he hadn't gotten them killed the first time or two autoc ergs in whatever form began to curdle the air around them, the deathbirds had come to accept him, after a fashion. But he knew full well that to assert his authority too often was not to risk having it challenged, but inevitably to cause it to be. Here beneath Colonel Danilov's eye he could not afford to ignore an outbreak among his own.

The Collective actually thought it was doing him a *favor*, when it permitted him to keep his commission even after he was broken and Detached.

He sighed, looked warily around. Arranging seating in the CC was as demanding a process as assembling the invasion fleet without alerting the paranoid Strahn. Landers were a suspicious, clannish lot, prone to feud and random irruptions. The 115th and the 800th battalions could not be allowed to mingle more than overcrowding made inevitable, or fighting would break out ahead of schedule.

But that was only prelude. Mir's own First Section was at war with Three, and had to be kept apart. The other three Sections of 1st Company were buffered-in between them. Section Two, First's ally, was closest. Sandwiched between Two and Four was Section Five, made up entirely of scared-looking scrubs—the newly Detached, raw as a wound, and all of them strangers to the Company. Fifth Section had been wiped out in the brutal campaign on Hovya. Rumor insisted that the few survivors were so battle-shocked they had to be gassed.

Just a year ago, officer cadet Haakon Mir would have dismissed the story as a treasonous canard against the Stellar Collective. Now—he suspended judgment. Whatever the truth was, everybody was *really looking forward* to going in the shitter next to a whole cherry Section. They were erg-magnets and no mistake.

At least First Section had been seated along one edge of the auditorium, so that instead of an alien and possibly hostile unit to their left they had only a bulkhead covered in molded BK acoustic panels. That meant the only major risk was that his turbulent command might get bored with the briefing and just decide to desert *en masse*. Marines canned in body armor and armed with shock bludgeons stood by all the entrances against just such a contingency. Deathbirds wouldn't necessarily back away from hassling even them, though anybody zapped by the bludgeons would ride down to dirt tomorrow with muscles still cramping uncontrollably. But the presence of the guards did serve to raise the stakes beyond what mere wandering interest would justify.

Two of his men were conversing loudly for the benefit of the Marine guarding the nearest side entrance. "Remember how the Daubers treated our tin can boys on Hovya?" Loki asked.

"Damned right I do," Starman replied. "Tumbled their gyros with shoulder-launched rockets, then built bonfires beneath them where they fell."

"When they tried to right themselves the autocs would knock their hands from beneath them or push them over with long poles. Tricky bastards, but that's Anton."

"I'll never forget the way the power armor heroes bellowed," said Starman with a grin. "Took 'em a good twenty minutes to die."

The marine glowered at them, but through his faceplate Mir saw sweat shine on his forehead, between brows and helmet.

They were two of the worst troublemakers in the entire regiment, that pair. They were also two of the best men. That was CLD.

The lieutenant drew in a profound breath, sighed it out. He was a handsome man in his early twenties, with features so regular that only the battle fatigue tracks around the blue eyes and the lines of stubborn humor around the mouth rescued it from insipidity. He was by nature a decent and earnest young man, devoted to doing the right thing. Which had become rather problematical now. He was still mystified, after the manner of a hurt child, by exactly how one who had grown up with no thought but to serve the Collective and the Historic Process had wound up *here*.

His eyebrow itched; he scratched it, instinctively keeping elbows to his sides. To jostle one of his men was to invite immediate retaliation regardless of his rank. He almost had to smile at the irony of it all. The son of a District Values supervisor, one of the most powerful men in the whole Santander Stellar District, set in command of a collection of psychopaths and derelicts whose only reason for continued existence was to die for the Historic Process.

—He choked back the impulse to tumble into a chaos of giggling, then wondered, *Why do I even* bother? He was a traitor, by reason of being a convicted traitor's brother—as if Yirina, wild as she was, was any more capable of disloyalty to the Collective and its ideals than he was. By everything he had been raised to believe, he was now mere criminal scum, the lowest of the low, a Devolutionary monster who had dared place his Particular desires above the Universal Will. *What's the point?*

But he would maintain. Perhaps for his men, for whom in spite of everything he felt responsible. Perhaps for the memory of his sister, whom he still loved, though he knew that in itself was treasonous and unnatural. Perhaps even for himself, though that was the highest treason of all.

And maybe it was that, in six months of brutal training and six more months of constant combat, he had not broken. He had seen others break, seen others die; the Detached were beyond mercy and beneath compassion.

He had held himself together in the face of all, and he was damned if he would let go now.

At the focus of the half-dome space Colonel Danilov mounted the podium. "Men," he said. It signified the unusual regard in which the colonel was held that the hubbub diminished perceptibly as he spoke.

It came back up when a second man, taller and younger, with yellow hair, walked out to stand a step behind him. The renewed murmuring had a hostile cast. The newcomer seemed not to notice.

"Scope this," said Jovan, nodding toward the second man.

"Red shoulder tabs. That's Values. Most community advisors I've seen are Revo."

"Who gives a flying rat's ass?" demanded Starman. He was unique in the regiment, and for all anybody knew in the entire Stellar Collective: his skin was brown so deep as to be almost black, lustrous as the polished wood of some exotic tree. It was rumored that there had been many people like him back on lost, legendary Earth. In the modern Collective he was as exotic as any autochthon, and tended to draw crowds of the curious, eager to rub his skin to see if his unearthly color would rub off.

Sometimes he took such attention with grinning good humor. Sometimes he attacked. There was no predicting.

"I do," Jovan said, sitting back and folding his arms. "How often do we get an explanation of what we're about? I'm a man who likes explanations, and there you have it."

From behind him Loki honked a strident laugh. "As if it matters! Everything they tell us is lies, anyway. And the final destination's death. Where's the difference?"

"This is treason!" shrilled Gollob, the scrub with the big Book. He jumped to his feet. "Lander 234-444-523-115-11111 takes full responsibility for his crimes against the Collective. I apologize—"

"Sit *down*, you half-wit!" hissed Stilicho. Heads turned. Starman stiffened his fingers and speared them into the new transfer's kidneys.

Gollob gasped, bent over in pain. Hands dragged him back into his seat. He struggled frantically to stand and speak his piece despite the hands his squad mates were stuffing in his mouth and buffeting him with. Finally, with the air of a man bestowing a great mercy, Stilicho leaned over and stunned him with a hammerfist blow to the temple.

"Tomorrow," said the colonel, "you will land upon the planet we call the Rookery. Since we have mouths instead of beaks, we can't pronounce its true name."

That shook loose a few chuckles. Behind him a world sprang into holographic being, six meters across and slowly rotating. It looked a lot like most worlds: mainly water, with three big continents and various other land masses of greater or lesser consequence. The land showed green and brown through swirls of clouds; white ice capped the poles. To the veteran Landers that told a lot: it was at least a comparatively congenial world to human life, neither too wet nor too dry, too hot or too cold.

Only the foolish felt more than qualified relief. The rest understood how much scope that left for Hell.

"You will take part in a gigantic operation," the colonel continued, "perhaps the largest of its kind ever executed. A mighty war fleet circles the Rookery. At jump-off five million men will land at once, dispersed among all settled regions in a planetwide strike.

"The sheer magnitude of the operation is expected to collapse the enemy's will to resist. By defying the Stellar Collective the autocs have placed themselves in opposition to the Universal Will, and, as all life is one, on some deep level they must certainly realize that. That will undermine their determination at the very start."

A few guffaws answered that. The CA from Values glared fixedly, then hauled out his notepad and began to dab furiously at its keys with a fingertip. The audience roared; he was too far away to take names.

"But the best news," Danilov said, laying his voice over the outburst like a heavy hand, "is this: the Rooks—the autocs—are pre-Objectives, with a very young technological base."

The rotating blue sphere vanished, and was replaced by a creature like a man-sized bird, with brightly colored feathers and huge eyes staring out above a great hooked yellow beak. The being stood on splayed yellow talons, clutching a flintlock to its chest with serious-looking claws.

"Their most advanced weapons systems," said the colonel, "are based on black gunpowder—"

"What's gunpowder?" whispered Florenz.

"Shut the shit up," Starman said without heat. Nau turned to whisper an answer in his brud's ear.

He's a boy with lots of answers as well as questions, thought Poet, measuring the scrub to see if he needed trimming to size. *We'll find out if any of his answers are the right ones.* Poet laughed to himself. The Zone had just hit, with a niacin burn in his cheeks and a rush that turned his veins to liquid fire. The two scrubs were limned in sharp lines of black and color.

Behind him Loki was softly singing "Strela Girls" and cleaning his nails with his two-edged battle knife. "Stop that," the Dancing-Master hissed. "I want to hear. This is important."

"Go frig yourself," Loki suggested, "if you can find a tweezers and a microscope."

The Dancing-Master gave Loki a hard look. He let it go at that. The Dancing-Master had been a commissioned officer and more before he was Detached. He was too good for this sordid flock of deathbirds, as he seldom tired of reminding them, and he had no taste for the intramural violence which was their daily fare. It was beneath his dignity as a natural leader.

"—lack any form of planetary communications, or indeed means of long-distance communication more rapid than the animals they use for transport," Danilov was saying.

"They use animals for transport?" Big Bori said in a thunderous whisper. Heads turned. "They better watch it, or their MAE will give them trouble!"

"I don't think they have a Ministry for Animal Emancipation," Stilicho said.

"That's why we fight," said Gollob, who had recollected his wits. "To teach them how to care."

Loki tapped him on the nose with the tip of his blade. "Shut up," he suggested, "or you'll preach compassion through a second mouth."

"If they're so primitive," a voice sang out from over in 2 Company, "why are we bothering with them?"

The CA scowled. The colonel drew his head back. Then he nodded.

"That's a fair question," he said. The community advisor looked scandalized that Danilov would lower himself to answer anyone Particular enough to question the Collective's orders—not to mention use a Devolutionary word like *primitive*. "And one I am in a position to answer. You know, for the last ten Standard years we have been deadlocked with the powerful Strahn Hegemony. Now our Direktor and Praesidium have lost patience. If the Strahn will not hear our gentle persuasion, then let them feel our force!

"The Rookery lies outside the plane of the Galaxy, and likewise beyond both Hegemony and Realized Space. When we seize it, we shall have at a stroke turned the Strahn flank. It shall become a dagger aimed at the heart of the Devolutionary and obstructionist Hegemony.''

The proper response was thunderous applause. The actual was slab silence. The CA shook his head and muttered.

Danilov surveyed his command. ''I shall land with you, and I shall fight alongside you. The Historic Process is inevitable as the Galaxy's slow rotation, but still it demands of us our greatest effort. I shall give my utmost to discharge my duty to the Collective and the Universal Will. I expect you to do the same.''

He nodded and stepped back. No waves of applause broke over him like surf; he expected none. His deathbirds did not jeer him, and that was all the accolade an officer could hope for—more than most of them ever got. Even a colonel had to adjust his expectations in the Collective Landing Detachment.

The community advisor from Values now stepped forward. This drew a few catcalls and whistles, but these were quickly stilled. Revo—the Ministry for Continuing Revolution—operated both the most visible of the Collective's various secret police agencies, the Monitors, as well as the Stellar Guard, a parallel military formation that sought to rival the Engine of History in scope. Like most members of the armed forces, Landers tended to think of Revo as The Enemy, and hate them above all—certainly above the wretched pre-Objective autocs they were generally called upon to squash. The more sophisticated recognized that the lower profile of Values' secret police formation didn't necessarily mean it was weaker than Revo. Values' shadow subtlety was in some ways more terrifying than Revo's heavy hand.

The CA bobbed his head and cleared his throat, a noise which the electromagnetic field surrounding the podium picked up and spit out at the audience as a terrifying blat of noise. It made him wince and duck, but he recovered quickly and held his head up into a shower of jeers.

''Men,'' he said, ''you are all criminals. Traitors to the Collective, Devolutionists and Obstructionists and even Autarkists, who in your Particularity have sought to impede the Historic Process and flout the will of the Universe Herself. You have, one and all, been sentenced to death for your crimes against State and Nature.''

He gripped the lectern with thin pale hands and blazed his gaze around the amphitheater as though his eyes were laser bores to drill through skulls and reveal corruption. The crowd sank into toad-squatting silence. Few if any Landers had seen this specimen before, but they knew him: knew those eyes that stared unblinking approval as you writhed to the music of electricity blasted through alligator-jaw clips clamped on your nipples and genitals, the thin mouth that smiled as the guards stamped on your scrabbling outstretched fingers. In the Collective the community was all, the individual nothing; and here was the Everyman of secret police zealots in the skin.

He blinked sky-pale eyes and smiled grandly. He knew they knew him. Their fear hit him like a drug.

"But rejoice!" he cried. "In its mercy and its wisdom, the Stellar Collective has found a way for you to redeem yourself and expiate your crimes! Live the Collective!"

He waited, seeming to poise on the balls of his feet. After a moment, a surly "Live the Collective" rattled from a few throats. The advisor blinked, taken briefly aback by the lack of enthusiasm. But he had plenty for everybody.

"Ours is the glory of service and sacrifice. I salute you— yes, justly condemned scum that you are. And in a way I envy you.

"Men of the Collective Landing Detachment, redemption and triumph await you! The autochthons of the Rookery have few weapons and poor ones, and no will to fight for the masters who enslave them, and who obdurately refuse to yield to the Universal Will. When this is done you'll hardly know you've been in a fight."

That produced a ripple of cheers and applause, almost exclusively from the new meat. Scarred ancients glanced at them contemptuously and held their peace.

"We have banished individuality and greed forever!" the community advisor caroled. "All that remains is service to the Collective. Now go and share the benefits of our oneness with the beings of this planet, in all love and humility!"

Under the visored gazes of the marines, the Landers filed from the CC. First Section moved in a packet of hostility, discrete amid the flow.

The Dancing-Master was rubbing his hands together. "This is going to be cake. Cake."

His brown eyes shone with the bright promise of unanswerable force: of an overwhelming planetoid mass of energy weapons, full-automatic projectile support weapons, on-call artillery from shoulder-fired grenade launchers to massive 300cm rocket batteries to glide bombs launched from beyond the horizon; armored vehicles, tracked and floating on contragravity fields; air support; and a panoply of nastiness poised up in O, from simple chunks of metal that could be dropped like meteorites on the heads of the hapless autocs to particle beams. It was a monumental picture, difficult for the mind to grasp, even for one who had firsthand experience of the Engine of History's terrible might. For the autocs of the Rookery, unsophisticated and unsuspecting—who may not, indeed, have been aware of all this crystallized death floating above their heads—it would seem as if the Universal Spirit Herself was descending from the sky wielding a blazing Sword of Retribution.

Starman sneered. "Nothing's a piece of cake," he said, "unless it's one made with shit for flour."

"Your cynicism only shows how scared you are," the Dancing-Master said. "Afraid of a few autocs with muskets!"

Starman laughed wildly and spat. The two were separated by half a dozen Landers; the gobbet went wide and struck the back of the neck of a Standard from the 800th battalion. He wheeled and threw himself into the knot of First Section, to be greeted by an overhand right to the forehead from Stilicho's piston fist that dropped him drooling to the mat.

The two Sections went for each other in a whirl of arms and obscenities. Electroamplified shouts announced the powersuit marines coming to break the dance up. First Section hurled their antagonists into the marines' armored faces and fled laughing through the narrow wind of *Beria*'s guts.

They stopped well clear, laughing and wheezing and clutching their knees.

"Let's get stinking drunk," suggested Stilicho, always practical. And so they did.

3

"I LOVE COMBAT landings," Jovan said sourly as the joyboat began to buck. As atmospheric turbulence took the little craft and began to shake it like a bean in a bowl, the new transfers began to vomit in unison, even two of the haughty Bold Originals.

"Look on the bright side," said Dieter above the howl of air tortured by the penetration of the joyboat's hull. He was sunk well down in his acceleration couch across the aisle from country boy Jovan. "At least Gollob has found something better to do than apologizing for his crimes."

"The little ling snot didn't spatter *you*," Jovan said.

"Shut up, you!" howled Big Bori. "Your jabber makes my head hurt!"

A chorus of groans from the ancients answered him. As a favor to his good friend Loki—arch joke *that* was!—Rudi had contrived a deal with certain ratings from the *Beria*'s life-support crew who were running a still in Hydroponics Section. Illicit starship alk was pretty much of a kind, on any vessel you happened to be riding, a colorless fluid known as White Death, whose main merit was that it shocked the taste buds senseless before you got a chance to appreciate how truly vile it was, on its way to blowing out the back of your skull. Landers had long ago—maybe generations ago, since deathbirds had no written history—discovered that mixing it with Ling Piss, the insipid cerise generic fruit-flavored soft drink generously provided the Coggies by the Engine of History, made a passable drink. If your main aim was to go ballistic in the shortest possible order.

The *drawback* was, the morning after a White Death binge, your head rang like a sun.

From the back couch of the passenger section Haakon Mir surveyed his tiny command and tried not to sleep. For some reason he always became almost uncontrollably drowsy before action. The fact that the padded acceleration couches were so comfortable didn't help. Comfort wasn't a common feature of Detached life. It wasn't common for most of the Collective's trillions, either, but Mir came of a social stratum that wasn't exactly conversant with such details.

Of course, the couches were only comfortable because they *had* to be; any source of discomfort, like imperfect lower back support or an arm or leg with no place to go, could translate under the stress of high-gee combat maneuvering into an injury that took a man right off the line. The Engine of History took notice when it came to bodies being unfitted for combat. The triumph of Historic Process was inevitable, but no one said it would be *easy*.

Otherwise the joyboat was not going to be confused with the luxury-class accommodations to which the Mir family's Service had entitled them when Haakon was young. The compartment was lit dimly by a fluorescent strip running overhead between polymer nets that made the Landers' rucks fast to the hull. It stank of the fear-sweat and puke of countless previous assaults, and the disinfectant Kosmos used to try to cover it up, so harsh it tore at the membranes of the nose like tear gas. Worse, the couch had shifted ever so slightly when Mir strapped himself in, hinting that the bolts which secured it to the deck might not all be dogged as tightly as they could be. And he had heard blood-splashed barracks tales of what happened when those bolts sheared during the twisting, turning run-in to a contested landing. *I'm glad the Rooks lack antiair.*

But then, even aboard the liner *Malthus,* which had carried Mir's family to its new home on Santander, capital of Santander District, when he was six, there had been things you didn't want to inspect too closely. Life in the Stellar Collective was like that. Even for Custodians as exalted as a District Values supervisor for the Ministry of Communal Values and family.

—He felt his eyes mist at the corners, forced himself not to think about family or childhood. Made himself concentrate on the immediacy of command.

Twenty-seven men entrusted to his care. And perhaps the greatest testament to his command abilities, such as they might be, was that only a few of the certifiable bad actors—Loki, Balt, Poet, the unpredictably dangerous Starman—were actually liable to put a blade in his back if they thought they could get away with it.

It was an achievement. He was Detached himself, it was true, but even deathbird officers were on limited sufferance under the Traditions, that handful of laws the Landers had made for themselves, the only laws in the Universe they respected. An officer right down in the bogs with the cogs—as Mir was—found himself in a particularly tricky position. Because his actions had instantaneous bearing on the unit's survival, he had one or maybe two mistakes' grace and then: Sanction Withdrawn. Which meant a blue bolt in the back of the head in his very near future. Or worse, abandonment on deadly ground.

Still, still . . . he shook his head. He cared for his men, brutal and hostile as they were. And maybe that was itself Devolutionary, further evidence of his own treason: to care for those who had offended against all that was good and true and inevitable. The community advisor from last "night's" briefing would certainly have called it that.

A smile, private and bitter. The promising cadet Haakon Mir of a year ago would have said so too, no doubt. But that was another life. That person was dead already, though execution of the sentence passed upon his flesh still pended.

He thought of Yirina, found himself hoping, again, that she had died quickly. The starkness of the thought still appalled him; but after what he had gone through, it was the best thing he could imagine to wish her. She had not been Detached, he knew—and the fate of those whose crimes were judged too heinous for them to be thrown into the ever-hungering maw of the Landing Detachment, the striking tip of the Engine of History in its eternal war for Universal peace, did not bear imagining.

And my mother and father—no. He would not think about them.

He looked around the joyboat's compartment again. Such of First Section's gear as wasn't netted overhead was stowed aft of the padded couches, restrained by cargo nets. The new transfers, having exhausted their stomachs of that morning's hurried breakfast—which had been plentiful and good; Kosmos despised and resented the fosterling deathbirds wished on it by the Ministry of Struggle, but was too proud not to feed them well—were producing an enthusiastic chorus of dryheaves grunts and moans. He felt sorry for them; his own stomach twisted at the sour-sweet reek of their puke, and he had been veteran-cagey enough to eat only a little. Scrubs always vomited on their first hot landing. Even those accustomed to spacing.

His ancients were acting strange, too, seeming subdued and misery-sunk. He chalked it up to hot-drop nerves. You never got over them, really.

Because there was something special about dropping for the first time onto a strange planet, where that personal executioner appointed you by Universal Will might just be waiting.

"The part I like," Black Bertold said, rubbing his hard hands together, "is that nobody's shooting at us. It hardly seems like a combat drop at all."

The other veterans glared sincere bloodshot hatred at him. He had slammed spiked Ling Piss as enthusiastically as any of them the "night" before, but he never showed any aftereffects.

"It'll seem a real holiday," Loki said, "when the autocs cut off your eyelids, stake you out in the sun, and start dribbling what passes for honey hereabouts over your balls."

Bertold just laughed. He was always eager for a fight, or at least did a good job of pretending. A vigorous thrusting man, he had been a combat-tempered veteran long before he was Detached, making scores of combat landings as a Kosmos Force Marine. Mostly he let Loki's nasty humor roll off his back. But when Loki really wanted to make him mad, he could. Loki was a master at knowing where to put the needle in.

"You really think the autocs got no flak?" asked Jovan, who had his head back and his eyes closed.

"Of course not," Dieter said. "They're too young-tech." He was a dark-haired youngster who had been with Section long enough that the others had begun to treat him as an actual being, rather than an animated lump of nothing very useful that was mainly liable to sod up and get killed along with whoever was unfortunate enough to be near him at the time. A doctor's son from the Core World Lenin, he'd lacked the *klad* to avoid conscription but had enough to wangle a nice safe job in the rear with the gear as an Engine QM clerk.

Unfortunately, his superior officer was diverting stores to Particular use, and her daddy had not just *klad* but Service, being a District-sized circuit in the Ministry of Guidance, which was the bureaucracy in charge of bureaucracy. A scapegoat was clearly required, and the horns just happened to fit the ever-cheerful Dieter. Like all Landers he'd been busted up, buttfucked, and sentenced to die, but he never lost his fixed-grin optimism, not in the Grinder, not down in the midst of the shitstorm.

"That's what the colonel said, my boy," Bertold affirmed heartily. When he was guyed for combat he was as giddy as Dieter.

"You can tell he's a marine," Loki said, getting up on his knees and turning to leer back at the black-bearded man. His couchmate, the scrub named Nau, sat with both hands pressed over his mouth and his eyes starting out of his greenish face. Loki had cheerfully informed him that if Nau puked on *him*, he'd sew his mouth shut. "His heart just thrills at the whiff of an officer's discharge chute."

Bertold laughed again, brittle-bright. "Colonel Danilov is a good man," Kyov said quietly, from his couch in the back, across from Mir. "He's Detached, same as us. He cares about us."

Loki's eyes, which seemed constantly to change color, flicked away from the older Lander with the dabs of grey like random paint on his beard. "He's an officer," he said in a less ebullient voice, "and they're all swine, no matter what suit you dress them up in." Like Poet, he seldom attacked Kyov directly.

"Would you rather some red-ass Engine Regular?" asked

Stilicho. Though he himself seldom acted up, he was one of the Usual Suspects, ally to Loki, Poet, Big Bori, and Starman. Some strange attractor drew the Section's steadiest man into an orbit with those who prided themselves on being its wildest. Perhaps it was that, like them, he was impressed by nothing, but had a different way of showing it. Stilicho was one of the few men in the Section who dared argue with Loki. "Somebody who'd spit on us in barracks, and spend us like a sailor just into port, throwing *klad* after whores and cheap wine by the double handful?"

Loki produced a sniff of excellent disdain. "It's all the same, one or the other. The Brass tell him, 'send these sniveling wretches where they can die most promptly, and quit gumming up the gears of the Engine of History.' And the officer bobs his head and says, 'Yes, at once, most glorious manifestation of Universal Will!' And reaches out and flushes us down."

"At least Danilov doesn't piss on us first," Stilicho said.

Jovan shook his head, an act he repented with a moan. "How can anybody not at least have missiles?"

"The technology level of the Rooks," the Dancing-Master announced, "approximates that of the Napoleonic Period on Earth, about two hundred years before Stahl and Lo led the Originals on their Hegira."

"*That's* useful to know," Loki sneered. "Rubbish about Earth, which nobody's seen for three hundred years—or is it three thousand?" In fact nobody really knew how long the humans who formed the nucleus of the Stellar Collective had been gone from Earth, owing to certain problems with the primitive Lo drive which had enabled the stolen starship *Red Phoenix* to flee Earth faster than the light of her yellow sun.

"Knowledge is power," the Dancing-Master said primly, "which is why I can humbly and without Particularity assert that I'm more fitted to hold responsibility within this sorry excuse of a unit than certain others I could name." He meant Kyov, who not only came from Dependent stock but had been a common laborer himself, loading wet-bottom cargo ships on the docks of New Havana on his homeworld Cienfuegos before his second career as a workingman's philosopher got him Detached. The Dancing-Master was stuck subordinate to two men he felt were his inferiors in rank and education, and the fact ground him like gear teeth.

"All those facts," said Loki, clucking and shaking his shock of blond hair. "When some autoc bullet comes whizzing along and sucks your brain out the back of your skull, it makes so much diffeŕence how many facts are stuffed into it, as it lies there on the ground."

"I know, for example," the Dancing-Master said, ignoring him, "that not only don't the Rooks have antiair, they don't have *air*, or any powered transport but what animals provide them—and wind, for their ships at sea. No communications beyond riders and some kind of crude semaphore. No weapons but muzzle-loading projectile weapons based on chemical reaction—I tell you, no way do they stand for so long as a day against a million men of the Engine of History—which, do I need to remind you, is the greatest fighting machine in the history of the human race, not to mention one whose victory is assured by the inevitability of Historic Process?"

"Then we have nothing to worry about," Dieter said happily.

"I can tell you one thing they have that we don't."

Heads turned to Poet, who was drumming his fingers rapidly on the back of the couch in front of his. The young man smiled. He was wound tight on Zone—which, while it was intensely illegal, at least came close to using the drug for its intended purpose, since it had been developed by the Collective to prime troops for risky assaults. The Stellar Collective officially denied using drugs for any such purpose, of course.

"And what does your extensive military knowledge tell you that is, Poet?" the Dancing-Master asked.

"Food."

He chuckled then, and seemed to go away from behind his childlike blue eyes.

"Go on, Poet," Kyov urged gently. "Tell us what you know."

"He's passing wind through the mouth," rumbled Balt from up front.

"If he was, you'd be first to be back to smell it," said Loki, still draped over his couch back. "Come, my child. What have you learned?"

"Talked to some naval scrubs on cargo-handling detail,"

Poet said, leaving unstated the obvious fact that the conversation had come in the course of some illicit transaction. Kosmos personnel were forbidden to fraternize with the deathbirds in their midst, which didn't break many hearts on either side. "Told me they were stowing extra tonnes and tonnes of rats in the joyboats."

"And why would that be?" the Dancing-Master asked.

" 'Cause this is a left-hand world. And our sugars got a right-hand twist. Our bodies can't burn the shit. Plus the local proteins won't bond to ours, so our bodies won't take them up." He shook his head and laughed. "What we don't bring, we don't eat."

"That's ridiculous."

Mir found himself glancing across the aisle at Kyov. This was the first he had heard that men could not eat native foods. Landers loved rumor, the wilder the better. But Poet was a scout, and actually took the job seriously. His information was usually dead-on, or at least close to the mark.

Kyov nodded. "It's true," he said.

Mir swallowed. He relied heavily on his soft-spoken Section Sergeant. It was a major reason he had survived this long, he knew. Since the only way out was in a polymer bag, CLD, unlike the regular Engine, had many experienced noncommissioned officers in its ranks.

And Landing Detachment NCOs had an intelligence network that was *much* more efficient than anything boasted by Engine, Kosmos, or even the Ministry for Struggle itself.

That woke Jovan from his torpor. Skinny though he was, he was a man who loved his meals. "Then where the hell *is* our grunt?" he demanded, drawing fearful strangled yawps from the scrubs. "We got but two weeks' rats stowed!"

"In Second Section's joyboat," announced the White Rat, who sat in front of Kyov.

Everybody looked at him. "We got the heavy equipment for the two Sections," he said, enjoying the attention. "Two got the food."

"That's crap," yelled Jovan.

"That's typical," said Stilicho.

The Rat shrugged. "That's how Kosmos loaded it out," he said. From somewhere in his battle dress, which fitted like a tent that had just blown down on top of him, he produced a yellow apple and began to eat.

Kobolev, having recovered enough to put his head down for brief consultation with his two bruds van Dam and Eyrikson, got up from his couch near the front and walked back along the aisle. It was a strict violation of regulations, not to mention a chancy proposition as the Assault Boat, Section, Armored got down to some serious bucketing in the thickening atmosphere. Neither Mir nor his noncoms said anything. Trying to make Landers stick too close to the manual made one accident-prone.

"Now that we're dropping into it," Kobolev announced in a booming brass-edged voice that he probably thought signified Command Presence, "it's time we got a few things straight—"

The joyboat struck a turbulence-roll and shot a hundred meters straight up. Kobolev fell across the lap of scrub Henriks, who reached deep down and found a few stray contents of his stomach to disgorge upon his hapless fellow new transfer. Alone among the scrubs Kobolev had not vomited. He remedied that omission now.

The boat dipped as abruptly as it had risen. Loki sailed up to crack his head on the butt of somebody's pulser netted to the bulkhead above. He fell back, clutching his head and waving side to side in rage.

"Ow!" he screamed. "I've broken my skull!"

"Sorry about the little bump back there." The elaborately cheerful voice of the Kosmos copilot fell like spring rain from overhead speakers. "These things happen, you know. Problems negative, if everybody was strapped in like a good little boy." He chuckled, confident *somebody* hadn't been.

"You *bastards!*" Loki shrieked. "You did that deliberately! When we get off this shitball I'm going to hunt you down and whittle your love handles down for you—and your mothers have already been complaining they were too small to satisfy them!"

The joyboat gave another fantastic lurch, cracking Loki once more against the overhead. His bruds laughed and jeered at him. The flight crew stayed silent; the 523rd hadn't been inboard *Beria* that long, but already the carrier's crewfolk understood Loki was perfectly capable of carrying out the most extravagant threats.

But the pilot wasn't cutting capers. The craft was bashing a thunderstorm, jumping wildly in three dimensions. Thunder reverberated in hull and bones and made loose bolts rattle.

A wail rose like a space-raid siren from the middle of the compartment. Big Bori was hunched over, clutching his huge head in his hands and weeping flamboyantly. "The gear, the gear," he moaned. "It's gonna break free! We're all gonna die!"

Those Landers who weren't curled into fetal balls or locked in now-dry heaves looked nervously back at the nets which constrained their and Second's heavy gear. The ancients had seen what happened when a crash landing or even sometimes a rough approach made cargo nets give way. Cleanup was accomplished mainly with high-pressure hoses . . . a job gene-engineered for deathbirds.

But the joyboat passed safely through the storm and steadied into smooth flight. "If you're not buckled in," came the copilot's voice, "you'd better get that way. We're approaching your assigned insertion site. Landing in two hundred seconds."

Dieter looked all around with a manic smile. "See? Everything's fi—

His eyes bugged from their sockets, and a pink stream of spiked Ling Piss and breakfast shot out to strike Big Bori full between the eyes.

4

WITH A WHISTLE-SCREAM of thrust reversers cutting into air-breathing jets, the joyboat came to an almost-gentle rocking halt. Then it settled down to Rookery surface on its contra-gravity floater field.

The Landers were on their feet already, breaking personal gear—what the Stellar Collective called "dispersed," to avoid use of the forbidden term "individual"—out of overhead stowage. The ancients laughed and grab-assed like Lyceum boys. The very fact they had been ordered to buckle in for final approach was a good sign. Coming in on a hot landing zone, they would have been up and under packs, ready to spill out as quickly as possible while the craft hovered on its floats. If the LZ was hot enough, the joyboat might just burn out of there without waiting to let them unload the heavy stuff.

But the pilot had brought them down as if they were landing in the midst of the biggest starport on Praesidium. That showed what Kosmos Force thought of the locals, with their muzzle-loaders and transport beasts.

"Section Sergeant Kyov," ordered Mir, trying to get his helmet of rigid bonded polymer bundles, scoop-shaped and covered in background-sensitive chammy fabric, to balance properly on his head with its visor raised. "Secure LZ and deploy First Squad in a defensive perimeter. Two and Three will off-load."

"Ah, you spoiled darlings of privilege!" jeered Loki as

51

First checked its weapons and prepared to go out the hatch. "You get to lie on your bellies while we slave."

Poet snarled something wordless at him. His slight frame was bent beneath the unwieldy air-compression/ionization unit strapped to his back. The edge that Zone gave him on the trip down was turning into an ugly sizzle of rage at the backs of his eyes and along the still-fresh wounds on his arm.

"We get to die first if the autocs hit us, you mean," Stilicho said equably.

" 'The word "privilege" is inapplicable to servants and executors of the Universal Will,' " declared newby Gollob shrilly, quoting a passage from *The Communality*. He still had his copy hung around his sprout neck. Not even the hardened deathbirds scanted the rule that every sophont of the Collective must carry a copy at all times, but the others' were in microdot form. "I, Lander 234-444-523-115-11111, confess and apologize for—"

Bent well down beneath the overhead, Big Bori cuffed the boy, then grabbed the front of his battle dress and lifted him onto his toes.

"Shut up and carry, or I'll give you something to be sorry for, you'll see." The giant spoke quietly, gently almost, but when he released Gollob the transfer slumped to the decking mat as if he'd been killed.

Loki gleefully kicked the scrub in the ribs. A moment, and Gollob's fellow newby Sturz came up and gave him an experimental boot from the other side.

Instantly Loki hopped across Gollob's prostrate body and flung himself on Sturz, hammering his face with looping swings of his bony fists. Sturz cried out and fell back across Dieter, who was trying to get out of his gee couch. Dieter's right eye was beginning to swell shut from the clout Bori had given him for vomiting on him, and his affability had slipped off true. He cried out in annoyance and pushed Sturz off. The newby fell with his head in a pink pool of puke.

"You can abuse the fresh meat when you've been shot at alongside the rest of us," Loki declared, grinning down. "Right now you're no better than he is, you fart-sniffing freak."

He raised a fist for a fresh shot. Golden Zorich thrust himself between the ancient and his victim.

"That's enough," he said softly.

Loki's eyes flared up killing-bright. The blond-haired handsome scrub held his ground.

Sturz raised his head from the reeking puddle and waved his hand before his face. His nose wrinkled. "Phew! This stinks worse than farts!"

Something went visibly out of Loki. He laughed. "A fine collection of loose nuts they've gifted us with," he said.

"So what else is new?" Starman asked with a laugh that crackled like static.

Since the flight crew had spotted no sign of opposition on the way down, the pilot popped the big side hatch, by which the joyboat was attached to the carrier's hull for interstellar Lo-space jumps. A hiss of escaping gas, and the hatch slid up and over, letting in a rush of cool air and Poet's first glimpse of the planet men called the Rookery.

The position of the deep yellow sun made it afternoon. The smells that hit his Zone-honed nose as he unassed the landing craft were unfamiliar, but something in them and the temperature of the velvet air suggested it was spring. The joyboat had put down atop a low mammary of hill beside a river that meandered through a broad valley. It was an excellent spot for visibility; First Squad had an uninterrupted field of fire in all directions as it spread out around the hilltop, keeping well clear of the reentry heat beating off the lifting-body joyboat. The only sight obstacles were stands of feathery pinkish and lavender trees down along the river, and the nearest of those were five hundred meters off. The somewhat higher hills that defined the valley came no closer than a klick on either side.

Poet went to ground behind the big ceramic nozzles of the drives. The joyboat hull gave off creaks and pinging sounds as it bled friction-generated heat. The ground cover was an ankle-high tangle, yellow shading off to pale green here, orange there. Wildflowers tickled Poet's hands and cheek with tiny white spike-petal halos as he surveyed the terrain across the stub social-work end of his flamer.

The mat was redolent with a softly spicy aroma. It was so soft beneath his skinny body that if he hadn't been vibrating to Zone's clandestine rhythms, he might have nodded right off.

He saw no sign of sophont presence on this world. Nothing

moved in his field of vision, and he saw no signs of artificial structures. That pleased him strangely. It wasn't that he feared attack; it was that he hated the thought of alien presences intruding here. He wished the others would go away, too, and leave him all alone on this world.

When he was a child he had always feared being alone. That was what Gran had always threatened him with when he was a bad boy: that if he caught the eye of the Authorities, they would declare her unfit to care for him, and take her away and leave him all alone. And they had taken her one day. So she left. Him. All. Alone.

Alone.

Several klicks away in what the display laser-painted inside his visor told him was local south, the uniformity of broad patches of chrome yellow to either side of the river suggested cultivation. At that distance a slight haze fuzzed seeing, making it impossible to be sure.

He caught the smell of woodsmoke, though, just a tang at the back of his palate. Even straight his senses were keen. Like most of his bruds he had a thoroughly urban background, but he had a natural knack for scouting. That task didn't fit too well with the bulky flamer he was assigned to carry—and which he liked well enough, for the terrifying effects its plasma jets had on an enemy. But at need he was happy enough to shed the beast and go sliding off through the bush with just a knife and maybe a few grenades for emergencies.

And now he lay here, body quietly humming, to watch the distant river, and listen to the sound of the breeze in the ground cover, and his own blood in his ears.

"It's *beautiful,*" Junior Lieutenant Mir breathed, standing in the open hatchway. He spoke quietly, fearing he'd draw ridicule for such fine sentiment from the Landers scurrying around him; they had few inhibitions about disrespect for officers, he knew too well. But most in earshot were new transfers, who after the fashion of scrubs had still not divested themselves of the notion that they *still had something to lose*—an idea so madly optimistic not even Dieter entertained it any longer. Of the veteran Landers with souls like boot leather, only Stilicho was nearby. The redheaded man briefly caught Mir's eye, and then he moved on, leaving the lieutenant to wonder, *Was that the hint of a grin he gave me?*

He jumped down. The soil and ground cover gave beneath his boots. They seemed to have just the right combination of firmness and resiliency, like a perfect mat in an exercise room. Perhaps it was relief after the reek of the joyboat's confines, but the young lieutenant's spirits floated so buoyantly in the crisp spring air that he had to grasp them firmly so they wouldn't sail off toward the horizon like a toy balloon.

We haven't even been shot *at yet!* kept playing in his mind. His first combat landing had been savagely resisted, the carrier itself coming under fire from orbital platforms as soon as it shaped orbit. Though he couldn't see—the joyboats lacked portholes to permit the human cargo to see out, for just this reason—the three craft nearest his had been destroyed as or shortly after they broke contact with the mothership. Proximity-fused missiles peppered the armored—but lightly so— hull the whole way down; on final approach a ground-mounted laser knifed through the hull, slicing off a veteran Lander's shoulder and the upper corner of his rib cage as he lay snoring, oblivious to the ruckus, right next to Mir in the couch between his and the hull. The final two beats of the man's heart had cast great washes of blood over the then-scrub Junior Lieutenant. And the first thing he had seen when Section spilled from the landing craft into a hail of small arms fire was another joyboat coming apart in midair, a whole Section and flight crew gone in a tumble of yellow flame.

Despite the numbing fatigue of combat, he had been unable to sleep for a week, even during the lulls. Every time he shut his eyes he was gripped by that sense of utter and absolute powerlessness he had known on the way down. He still had nightmares about it, as often as he had about his arrest and early detention—as many even as he had about the Grinder.

He shifted to one side to clear the hatch for the scrubs, who were scurrying in and out like worker ants, bent under crates of pressed synthetic fiber or natural wood, while the veterans stood about and whipped them on with roared abuse and the occasional slap. Mir hated to see new transfers hazed, but actually they had it worse among the Engine Regulars, who began their conscript stints as strangers and generally ended them the same way, without the love/hate glue of a common death sentence that bound the Detachment together. He had also long

since learned the worse-than-futility of issuing orders that
would not be obeyed; and so he held his tongue.

To set a good example—and because he was a combat veteran, too, and distrustful in his DNA of even the most apparently peaceful enemy terrain—he made it a point to carry his
pulser unslung, with sliding stock extended. As he walked the
perimeter First Section had dropped into he kept his right hand
on the rear pistol grip and his left lightly grasping the similar
second grip he had installed beneath the stub barrel, in pref-
erence to the more standard rifle-style forearm.

Section Sergeant Kyov was just easing Nau into place behind his pulser, on the far side of the joyboat from the cargo
hatch. At the junior lieutenant's approach he stood up and saluted briskly. There were times when Kyov's punctilious ad-
herence to the military courtesies most officers of the Engine
of History took utterly for granted made Mir want to weep
with gratitude. He found it ironic that only gentle Kyov,
whom Mir had never seen enforce an order with his fists and
whose voice was seldom raised, of all the men in First Section would *dare* treat Mir with the respect formally due an officer.

Mir returned the salute and the two men turned to survey
the river valley surrounding their hilltop. "It's beautiful," he
said again, for he felt no misgiving at expressing such sentiments in front of Kyov. "So placid, so serene."

"It feels as if we're intruding, sir," Kyov said, nodding
slowly.

"It feels as if any hint of ugliness or menace would be an
intrusion."

Kyov looked at him with his calm hazel eyes. "That's always when it's most dangerous, isn't it, sir?"

Mir grunted. *Yes, isn't it?* he thought. *And what a delicate
way you have of making sure my mind is focused on the things
that really matter.* Resentment spiked through his gratitude
like a laser through fog; he hadn't needed the gentle nudge.
But without such deft solicitude from his Section sergeant he
never would have survived his first floundering months of
command.

He did scan the countryside a second time with an entirely
different set of referents. "Kosmos picked a good spot. De-
fensible, good visibility."

"Yes, sir. But that means we can be seen, too."

Mir nodded. "The men are well disposed." That First Squad's four scrubs were distributed evenly around the hillside, properly prone and with weapons pointed in the right direction, was testimony to Kyov's skill. The ancients knew what to do with themselves.

A comforting amount of firepower encompassed the hilltop: Poet's flamer, short-ranged but terrifying, Stilicho winding the mainspring to his grenade launcher's drum magazine, Rouen with his Bitch—an ancient soldier's nickname for an electromagnetic rifle firing needlelike projectiles at three thousand meters a second—modified for use as a sniper's weapon, and Balt lying behind a second Bitch, heavy shrouded barrel supported by a bipod, which was set up to fire full-auto as a squad machine gun.

Beside Balt, almost dwarfed by the fat ammunition canisters strapped to his back, lay his quiet little scrub A-gunner—what was his name? *Hynkop, that's it.* Names were officially denied the Detached. In a universal—and universally futile—gesture of defiance, the deathbirds insisted on being known by names of their own choosing. Which the scrubs had not got round to picking out for themselves yet.

Overlooking all from a little turret popped out the top of the joyboat was a 60mm Gatling gun which fired depleted-uranium slugs, a very effective weapon anywhere from orbit downward. Section wouldn't enjoy its coverage any longer than it took to unload the supplies, though.

—A flick of motion caught the edge of his peripheral vision. He spun around, heart jumping into his throat: *Is this it? Have the autocs found us?* But it was only Balt, backhanding poor Hynkop.

Mir's mouth tightened. Balt's cruelty was gratuitous and extreme even by Detachment standards. Balt was brutal, a simple sadist to Mir's way of thinking, and without Poet's quiet cunning or Loki's flamboyance.

He was especially out of sorts today, and nursing his own black eye, thanks to a ritual the transfers had witnessed wide-eyed the night before. After lights-out, when he was goggle-eyed on Ling Piss and White Death, the ancients of First Section had one and all descended on him, thumped him groggy, and bundled him into the showers, where they

scrubbed him raw with deck brushes beneath scalding jets of
water.

Landers were anything but fussy about hygiene—usually.
But Balt cultivated a majestic grunge, an odor of feet and
armpits and fetid crusted crotch that torqued the sinuses of the
toughest veteran. The old guard claimed that, after they'd been
on campaign a spell, they could smell him over week-old
corpses on a hothouse world. Whenever they came in from
the field they gave him an enforced bath, and again before
they went out, to give themselves as much respite as possible.
It was flat impossible to convince him to wash on the battle
line.

Apparently casual, Kyov ambled over to the stocky, single-
browed Lander. He knelt, murmured something to him. Beside
them Hynkop lay staring straight out across the valley as if
they didn't exist.

Mir heard Balt growl something, felt his stomach clench.
Balt had no respect for Kyov; there could be trouble. Then the
lieutenant saw Balt's beetle-browed glare slip past the sergeant's shoulder.

Mir followed it to where Loki stood, chivvying back scrubs
teetering to the weight of crates, who kept trying to stack them
aft of the joyboat. Standard procedure called for the landing
craft to rise well clear of the ground before lighting off the
fusion drives. But in an attack the joyboat jock would torch
off any which way, incinerating anything within a hundred
meters of the ceramic nozzles.

Loki was staring at First Squad's Bitch gunner with a fixed
smile. It wasn't that he and the rest of the Usual Suspects
respected Kyov's authority, though they seldom defied him
openly. It was that they were all eager for an excuse to murder
Balt. Balt stretched the envelope of Sanction farther even than
they did, and besides, Mir suspected he had tried to cheat them
in certain Black deals. He was unquestionably the Suspects'
main competitor in Section at traffing contraband.

Balt scowled but nodded. Kyov smiled encouragingly at
him, touched Hynkop on the shoulder, then rose and moved
on to the next man in line, as if all he'd ever intended was to
make sure the Bitch was ready for action.

Two years ago, Mir thought, *I wouldn't have deigned to
glance at Kyov if I passed him on the street, even before he*

was Detached—and after, I'd have spit on him as traitorous scum, unworthy of the mercy the Collective showed in permitting him to live.

Now I can only watch him and hope I'll one day absorb half his knack for command.

He started to follow the sergeant along the perimeter. And a Klaxon blared from the joyboat, blasting the valley stillness to fragments.

5

IT WAS GOLDEN boy Zorich, most promising of scrubs, who bit the tit of the Universal Spirit. Maybe that was inevitable.

"Clear the drives!" Mir shouted. "Emergency takeoff!" He saw Poet rolling rapidly the other way, ran toward Nau, who had sat stone upright and was frantically pointing his pulser this way and that, looking wide-eyed for enemies to shoot. Mir grabbed the bewildered transfer by the collar and dragged him bodily to the side, away from the joyboat's line of thrust.

Landers dropped burdens and spilled out the big hatchway, which was already biting shut. The ancients bolted downhill away from the craft, even those on the perimeter. Joyboats had been known to fishtail on crash lifts.

"Come here, you fool!" At Loki's cry Mir looked up from where he'd thrown Nau and himself, down among the yellow weeds. On the thrusters' far side stood Loki, gesturing frenziedly. It was Zorich the promising, Zorich the natural, who held a crate of antitank-rocket reloads by the rope handles, and who had frozen right in the eye of the engines. "Get out of there, damn it!"

The air around the drive nozzles shimmered away from quick heat. "Process, *no*—" Mir screamed.

What erupted from the drive was nothing more than Rookery air, flash-heated by the joyboat's fusion lamp and projected out the nozzles at a minor but measurable fraction of lightspeed. Unassuming air—nitrogen, oxygen, carbon dioxide, and your so-called noble gases—blazed into a yellow plasma tongue like Poet's pet flamer amped up a millionfold.

Mir thought he heard the boy scream as the hundred-meter flame wrapped him up. It could only have been the super-heated air blasting free of his lungs. His brain was cindered long before the message of intolerable pain reached it from vaporized nerve ends.

In flame and roar the joyboat spiked a hole in the turquoise sky: *gone*. Mir dropped face to arms against the wash of drive heat and the stinging barrage of debris thrown up from the exhaust. Then, with wind surge and thunderclap, the air that fled the touch of flame rushed back to fill the space where the craft had lain.

Before the localized windstorm died off Mir was on his feet, dashing the few meters to where Zorich lay on his back with his arms and legs raised as if he were trying to crawl on the sky.

In the Landing Detachment they said of being well and truly burned-down that it reduced you to your bare essentials. Zorich had become a skeleton, bulked slightly by an armature of char, and glazed like a ceramic pot, black enamel of tissues fused by sun-heart heat. Mir dropped to knees beside him, at once jammed a hand over his own mouth as the sweet roast pork stink of burned human meat struck him in the face. *If I puke on the poor boy, I'll never sleep again.*

The yellow mat had been burned in a swath, crisped and khaki at the fringes. It still smoldered around Mir as he beat his palms on the ground in an agony of grief and uncertainty—quickly joined by actual agony as he scorched his hands on the hot ground. The heat drove up through the insulated ballistic fabric of his trousers and into his knees like spikes.

The blackened corpse stirred. Mir reared back like a frightened horse, squealing through his nose. *Is he still alive? Universal Spirit, don't let him be!*

But it was only some vagary of thermal mechanics, uneven cooling of calcined variegated organic ruin. Zorich's right arm split away at the shoulder. The back of a black claw hand fell against Mir's knee, leaving a charcoal smudge. Mir turned away and puked.

A hand on his arm. "Come away, Junior Lieutenant. You'll melt your pants to your knees." The firm voice and firm touch belonged to Stilicho; Mir looked up, almost surprised, and then looked around at the faces of his men, floating like pale balloons above the ground cover. *Do they blame me?*

"Damn you, damn you, *damn you!*" Loki raged. But not at Mir. The gaunt blond corporal lay on his back, hosing blue-green pulser bolts after the joyboat, though it was no longer even a speck against a fluffy white cumulus pillow in the sky. "You filth, you dragon-biter! When we get off this shitball I'll hunt you down and have your ball sac for a dice bag, you shit!"

Mir raised his head, tossed his head to clear a stubborn strand of vomit from his lips. "Why do you care?" he demanded in a ragged voice. "He was just a scrub."

Loki turned him a gaze blue and hot as drive core flame. To his amazement Mir saw tear tracks glistening on his cheek. "He was *ours*, Lieutenant! He was one of us. And the bastards didn't care. They think they can burn us like drums of shit, and never a comeback!"

"They've abandoned us," called Poet, rearing up on his knees out of the mat. "Buggered off and left us." He laughed, as if that were rarely funny.

"Come on away, Lieutenant," Stilicho said again. "*Max nix.* Landers die. It's what we do."

A shudder rippled through Mir's body. He drew a deep breath, through his mouth so as not to smell, nodded. Rose.

"Senior Sergeant Hovalesko," he said, using the Dancing-Master's real surname, "see to the body. Bury it at the foot of the hill; that's close enough we can support the detail if trouble comes. Everybody else will dig in, Squads One and Two forming a perimeter, Three on the hilltop in reserve."

The Dancing-Master was nodding importantly, as if he were being consulted instead of ordered. "And what about the supplies, sir?"

Mir began a frown, planed it off and gave his head a little wet-dog shake. No point letting the Dancing-Master get under his skin, even when he acted as if he were still an officer-instructor at the prestigious *Akademiya Stahl* on Praesidium, and Mir a not–particularly promising cadet on a field exercise. The broken officer gave far more grief to Kyov, and the sergeant let it all roll down his back.

"I'll inventory them later," he said. "What we managed to

get out. Right this moment I want to know what the *hell's* happening. Ovanidze!''

First Section's chief technician and communications man stood by with his mustard yellow bangs hanging in his eyes, making no move to join the rest of the unit burrowing like ticks into the flesh of the hill. "Sir!"

"Try to raise Captain Doorn." Ovanidze bobbed his head and knelt by the pack that held his commo gear. Mir took his tac display from the pouch at the small of his back, broke it open, and brought up a map of their landing site and surroundings.

The yellow circle of their designated LZ was centered perfectly on the blinking white crosshair indicating the position of the beacon built into Mir's own Dispersed Radio, Tactical; they had been delivered right on target, give those tight-assed Kosmos bastards that much. The map display showed them in a shallow river valley about five klicks wide and running roughly north and south. Except for a dust of what he took for farmhouses, there was no sign of habitation closer than a town thirty kilometers northwest.

The TD gave him the option of switching back and forth between map and actual overhead imaging. He hoped that indicated extensive advance satellite recon. However, even though the power of computers and software was kept carefully limited by special picked teams of systems analysts, to avoid a replay of the circumstances which forced the Originals to flee Earth in the first place, Military Intelligence or the Ministry for Outreach or whoever had conducted the remote sensing used inferential mapping expert routines to produce detailed maps from images taken on a hurried sweep in big low-resolution gulps. Bitter experience had taught him "inference" was a buzzword for "guesswork," and was all the more aggravating because you never knew when it might actually turn out to be *right*.

He called up Section Two's landing site. It was about eleven klicks away, a hair north of west, indicated in yellow. Three had been due to go in roughly south-southwest, so that the three units formed an equilateral triangle. On the map.

"No luck raising Company, sir," Ovanidze said. "Not even a carrier wave." He shook his head. "I'm getting a lot of noise. Mainly atmospherics, but it seems like maybe the primary's acting up.''

Nau licked his lips. "Could it be maybe that the primary's always like that?''

Ovanidze gave him a flat-pebble gaze. Nau recoiled. "Sir!'' he added quickly.

Ovanidze gave his head a peremptory shake. "No sir,'' he said, repeating the ancient formula. "I work for a living.'' He let it go at that; he wasn't the sort to pound on scrubs. He looked to the lieutenant.

The skin of Mir's face was starting to feel dry and tight, as if he'd suffered a bad sunburn. Perhaps it was from the heat of the drive flame—or something worse. Supposedly the neutron flux from the drive was focused straight back, but you never knew. He almost laughed; he wasn't likely to live long enough for accumulated radiation doses to matter much.

"Try Battalion, then,'' he said.

"Already did, sir,'' said Ovanidze. His cheeks had a doughy puffiness to them that threatened to swamp his water blue eyes. It gave him a false appearance of pudginess; he was actually gaunt as a scarecrow. "No joy.''

"Regiment—?'' Ovanidze was already shaking his head.

The yellow sun was swollen huge and dropping perilously close to the western line of hills; they had landed later in the local day than he had first thought. The light spilling over the hilltop was deepening to a butter color that poured noticeable shadows off even the men lying prone. Soon it would be dark. He felt a crawling itch in his groin and at the back of his neck, that sense of something gone terribly wrong. It was no stranger to anyone who had seen combat in CLD. But this time—

"What about Second Section?'' That was an overriding consideration; they had the food, on this world where men could find nothing to eat.

Ovanidze worked his keyboard. "Nothing,'' he said, without even looking up.

"Third? Anybody?''

Ovanidze put his hands up. "Sir, if there is any signal traffic originating anywhere on this planet, the SC-50 won't show it to me.''

Mir sat back on the heels of his boots. Aside from the other two Sections of 1st Company, he had no frequencies outside his own chain of command, and that no farther up than Regiment. His premission data dump contained no LZs for anyone but his companion Sections. Thank the Engine of History's flaming passion for security, combined with the sanctity of *hierarchy,* as mandated by Universal Will: a lowly Section leader had no business talking to anybody farther than three steps above him, and really no higher than Company except in emergency.

"Get out the satlink antenna," he instructed. "See if you can pull in anything from orbit."

The words seemed to drop like pebbles to the base of his stomach and lie there, cold and hard. *Anything from orbit . . .* For there *not* to be anything was unthinkable.

Ovanidze dug in his polyfab pack, brought out the dome-shaped phased-array antenna and set it on the ground. The men had mostly gotten themselves foxholes gouged from the hill. They were muttering complaints, some loud enough to overhear should he choose to, but *max nix*: they meant nothing and he knew it. The scrubs were too intimidated to talk back to an actual officer—*give them time!*—and the ancients knew full well how useful mere holes could be in keeping beams and bullets from intersecting their hides.

And the digging wasn't bad. The soil here was soft, a brown so dark and rich it looked as if you could eat it with a spoon. Its nuances of smell were unfamiliar, but there was that which was common to most human-habitable worlds: base crumbled-rock dirt, mingled with organics and moisture. Scents which brought back farm summers in the wine country of Santander, before he went for a soldier boy, eyes bright and full of promise.

"A lot of traffic upstairs," Ovanidze said abruptly, and Mir was grateful at being hauled back to the present before nostalgia started eating his gut like cancer. "It's all scrambled, of course, and we don't have the key; nothing meant for us. *So* far." He frowned and rubbed his round chin. "Call me crazy as a zong in rut, but it seems to me somebody's pretty worked up about something."

"Lieutenant! *Look!*"

Mir caught up his pulser from the mat beside him, came around and up to one knee with the weapon pointing toward the cry but high, so the line of fire safely cleared the squaddies' heads. Necking one of his own with a blue bolt AD was approximately the quickest way a Detachment officer could find to get himself laid lengthwise.

It was the keen-eyed White Rat who raised the alarm, but the bone white hand sticking out of the end of his chammy sleeve—now yellow to match the predominant background—wasn't pointing at a horde of autocs screaming up out of the bottomland. It was aimed straight up.

Way up where the sky had gone indigo, a bright white light was unfolding like an accelerated-motion flower.

6

"THAT'S A SHIP dying," said Starman, looking stricken. He hated Kosmos, but both loved and hated its ships of space.

"I hope that dragon-mongering joyboat pilot was on it," snarled Loki from the hilltop's far side.

Mir found himself standing, staring up at the flare as it expanded, began to cool into yellow and fade. His throat was dry.

"What does it mean?" Florenz, one of First Squad's scrubs, asked forlornly. "What does it mean?"

"There's another!" Lennart cried, pointing. This one hung low in the north, like an evening star. "God's mercy on you."

"What if they're enemies?" asked Nau. Lennart shrugged. He was a man who wept for unsaved souls, even as he separated them from autoc bodies with precisely aimed needles from his sniper-Bitch.

"Those are our ships," Kyov said.

"Now, how do you know that, dock-walloper?" asked Loki, standing up beside his hole and placing his hands on hips in one of his trademark stances. "Do you have telescopes for eyes? Or do you noted working-class intellectuals just *know?*"

"Who else is up there?"

"Might be enemies," Jovan retorted. "Like the boy said."

"In that case," Black Bertold said, "the ships we're seeing blow are likely to be ours as theirs."

"Who gives a speck of ling shit?" Loki asked, making a flicking gesture with the tips of his long slender fingers. "Not I, I assure you."

"They're our comrades," said Kyov.

"Puffed-up Kosmos toads and butt-born Engine Regulars?" Loki said. "No comrades of mine."

"What if our own boys are still up there?"

"More to the point," Jovan said, "what if our *food* is still up there?"

Mir snapped out of his trance. "You men on perimeter watch, keep your eyes on the ground! If the autocs are out there waiting to hit us, now would be a fine time."

He sat back down on the resilient ground. For a time he stared at the sky. It was just like a meteorite-watching party in the countryside in his youth: the cry would go up, "There! There's one!" And hardly had that ball of expanding ionized gas begun to dissipate than another would appear, until the night's face was dotted with fading patches of light like skin cancers.

"Is it the Strahn attacking?" Florenz the redheaded scrub asked, voice quavering.

"Could be," said Stilicho.

The boy's skin went green-pale beneath his freckles. "What if they drop a rock on us?"

"You could run out and try to catch it," Ovanidze suggested. He was monitoring the traffic from overhead, though he'd taken the headset off. He complained that the static bursts when a ship died were enough to pop his eardrums.

Florenz huddled in his hole and shook.

"Are those all ships blowing up?" asked Nau, getting his nerve up again.

"Some of them are missiles," Kobolev stated, in the manner of a man who knows much and does not care to be overlooked.

"Ling shit," Starman sneered. "You don't know what you're talking about. You couldn't see a missile go off in orbit. Not unless it was a megatonner."

"And how do you know they're not?" Kobolev demanded. "I remind you I'm a Standard. I don't like the tone you're taking, Senior Lander."

Starman cawed laughter. "So you're a baby noncom! That

makes you just a pimple on my black ass. Wait'll you're an officer—at least then you'll be a boil."

Eyrikson growled and started to come out of his hole. "Stand easy, Lander," Kyov said.

The young transfer was big-shouldered and athletic. He scowled at Kyov through shaggy white-blond bangs hanging almost in his eyes in defiance of regulation, then glanced at Kobolev. The Bold Original waved a hand. Eyrikson eased back into his hole. He gave Starman a look which said, *We'll settle this later.*

Starman laughed.

"Well, if those *are* ships, and they *are* the Strahn," said Nau, "what if they land troops?"

"Then we fight," Kyov said, with more than a hint of sadness.

"But we're—I mean—we're supposed to face autocs with muskets," Nau stammered. "The Strahn have modern weapons!"

"So they do," Stilicho said, "and plenty of them."

"But—"

Loki trumpeted laughter through his often-broken nose. "Now the scrub is getting Particular indeed! He had his heart set on dying with a musket ball through his empty head! What a grave disappointment, if a centaur blue bolt carries out his sentence instead!"

"What's a centaur?" Big Bori asked.

"The Strahn," Ovanidze said. "They're like centaurs."

"Oh," the giant said. "So what's a centaur?"

"They're like half-man and half-horse," said Jovan. He had grown up around horses, a major form of transport on agro worlds like his native Steiner.

"Oh," said Bori. "What's a horse?"

Jovan threw up his hands. "Don't trouble your empty head," Loki said. "If you see something that isn't human, you just make bang-bang until it falls down."

"Or even if it is human," Starman said. "Might be some spare Big Circuits wandering about out there, as lost as we are."

Bori nodded as if receiving vast wisdom.

"There's nothing much to worry about, you know," Dieter said to Nau. "Even if it is the Strahn, they'd hardly waste time on us. We're just a Section, out here in the midst of nowhere.''

Loki gave a death's-head grin. "Now we're doomed for sure.''

After half an hour the aerial display peaked. By that time it was all but full dark, with no more left of day than puddles of amber light in the hollows between hills to the west. Mir sent men out in the heavy dusk to place infantry radars and heat sensors around the hill's base. Then he motioned Kyov to his side.

"It's getting near time to eat," he said quietly. "After the meal, gather up everybody's rat packets. We don't know when we'll get more.''

The older man nodded. "Whom shall I put in charge of the rations once they're taken up?''

The lieutenant thought a moment. "Poet and Loki," he said. "They care about a lot of things more than their stomachs. And send the White Rat to do the collecting; the men will have their work cut out for them, holding out on him.''

Kyov smiled, saluted, and started away. "Look!" somebody shouted.

It was a dot of yellow light off in the west, planet-bright. As Mir looked it grew brighter and larger, but not in the manner of a ball of hot gas expanding in O. As if it were getting . . . nearer.

"Process!" Florenz screamed. He erupted from his hole and came running loose-limbed back over the top of the hill. "Oh, Universal Spirit, it's crashing right into us!''

Starman stood up out of his own hole as the transfer came galloping past, held out his right arm straight from the shoulder. Florenz clotheslined himself neatly, ran out from under himself, and fell to earth with a thump and a *whump!* of expelled breath like the sound of spilled benzene taking light.

The glow was growing large now, taking on a sense of form, of great onrushing mass. "If it hits within a klick of us," Black Bertold remarked, "Jovan won't have to worry where his next meal is coming from.''

"Even as a cloud of disassociated atoms," Jovan drawled, "I'll wonder.''

"It won't hit us," Starman said, and vanished back down his hole.

The fireball resolved itself into a great ship, hull ablaze with friction glow. Sheets of plasma or plain flame gushed from huge rents in its side. Glowing fragments were breaking away as it swept overhead with a head-crushing, howling roar, lighting the hilltop brighter than noon and sending those on the surface flat on the ground and those in holes to the bottom to cower.

"Chunk hit in the river, about three hundred meters downstream," Poet called when the stricken monster's passage scream had dwindled enough to let him be heard. "Pretty."

As the doomed ship vanished over the eastern horizon, Mir looked off in the indicated direction. He thought to make out a grey cloud of steam. He just had time to feel the skin at the back of his neck bunch up at the closeness of *that* call, when a flash behind the eastern hills lit their own.

"Down!" he yelled, as a yellow sphere rushed up the sky in the east, drawing a column of dust and smoke up after it. There was a perceptible delay as the fireball dimmed and was surrounded by cloud. Then the rolling overpressure hit, with enough force to bulge eardrums inward and tumble stacked crates.

"And *that's* what you call catastrophic decontainment of your fusion bottle," Starman announced.

"Ah, the many ways to pull a cat," Loki murmured reverently.

"Catastrophic *decontainment,* catastrophic *deresolution,* catastrophic *superimposition,* catastrophic *reentry. . . .* "

"Generous is the Universal Spirit, to gift us with so many cats!"

A stirring and squeaking from the bottom of Gollob's hole, as that scrub started up to protest this latest blasphemy. But then, "I'm blind!" screamed Sturz from the east face of the hill. "Process, Mother, I can't see!"

"Your shit-scoop has fallen over your eyes, you simple fart-sniffer," Big Bori said.

The scrub raised quavering hands to his head, found the rough polyfab cover of his helmet, shifted the helmet back up on top of his head. Then he popped out of sight down his hole like a burrowing animal, to the Section's jeering laughter.

"The light show looks over," Stilicho said. No new bursts of incandescence were elbowing stars aside.

"Whoever we have to thank for it knew how to put on a criminal finish," Loki said. "I applaud them."

Mir decreed a cold camp, which brought some grumbles. "Shut your yobs," Bertold said cheerfully. "We've woes enough without giving the Rooks a beacon to find us by."

"Let them come," Loki said. "Maybe plucked and cleaned, they'll be fit for roasting over the fine fire we'll build for the purpose."

"That isn't possible," Gollob said. "Nothing on the planet can nourish us. Weren't you listening about the left-hand sugars? It is Particular and irregulationary not to pay attention to information pertinent to the success of the mission—"

"It's also treason to spread rumors," said Balt. "It wasn't no officer who told you that, it was a bung-sniff corporal. MTJKs or Engine Guidance would neck you in a hurry, death-bird or not, was someone to drop a bug in their ear." His thick saliva-glistening lips twisted in a smile. "So unless you wanna be *communal*—"

What little color there was in the boy's face dropped down through his collar; even in the starlight they could see him blanch.

"Pay no attention, boy," Stilicho said. "We got no narcs in CLD. They have a way of not lasting." He looked carefully at Balt as he spoke. The heavyset man's thick brows lowered until they almost hid his eyes, and he turned away.

"I don't roast a bird for its sugars," Loki told Gollob. "And learn to keep your tongue in your head before I decide to roast *you,* with your Book for fuel."

"You mustn't talk that way!" Gollob shrilled, pressing hands over ears and jumping up. "I am Lander—"

Lennart kicked his feet from under him. "If you keep up that apology shit," said Poet softly, from right beside the boy, "you'll do it through a mouth beneath your chin." Starlight skipped along the blade of the knife that had appeared in his hand with scissors sound.

Gollob got big-eyed and, blessedly, quiet. The others looked away from him. They understood better than they cared to let on what had made him this way: the Meatgrinder. CLD's test-to-destruction training camps, designed to approach theoretical Hell as closely as possible. That he survived at all meant he had unlooked-for toughness, resilience undetected beneath his unprepossessing surface, but undoubtedly real. Because, of those consigned to the mercy of the Grinder, only a minority made it out alive.

Compassion was not a big item in the Landing Detachment. But despite themselves the deathbirds understood pathetic Gollob: when they took you up, what could be broken in you, they broke. Every Lander knew that in his bones. In the bones of his fingers, say, the breaking of which was as ritual a part of the debasement of the prisoner as rape; and even if you got injured in such a way that they R&Red your hands, you still felt phantom pains forever after in the regenerated bones, in those dreams from which you woke in a shaking-cold sweat, with a brud's hand pressed over your mouth to keep your cries from drawing Anton. . . .

But intolerance was a short leash in CLD, and not a sturdy one. Gollob would learn. Or he would die and be forgotten.

But then, that's the lot of us all, thought Junior Lieutenant Haakon Mir. The others must have shared that thought; for a time they grew quiet, there in the dark, at the bottom of a sea of alien stars.

7

"WHAT DO YOU think went on up there?" Jovan asked, spooning up self-heating rats from a flimsy polymer container. You had to be careful with the rat packs in the field; they had a tendency to make a crinkling sound, which could draw unwanted attention.

"A space battle," Ovanidze said, and looked knowing.

"Everyone knows that, you pasty-faced proton pusher!" Big Bori roared. "Don't tell us what we already know. We are serious men!"

Ovanidze didn't even glance at the giant. Bori was just parroting what someone else said; he didn't have much notion of what a proton pusher might be. Or maybe he did. He had been an engineering student on Lumumba before the Revo took him on suspicion of treason. The chemical unspooling he'd been subjected to had been clumsy, reeling most of his knowledge and a good part of his intellectual capacity out his mouth for the edification of interrogators from the Ministry for Continuing Revolution's secret police, the Monitors. But who knew what scraps and shards of knowledge remained in that big shaggy head, slipped down into cracks or abandoned in unknown alcoves?

"It's electron pusher, if anything," Ovanidze said without heat.

"If anybody has answers," Stilicho said, "it's you. And you're just dying to tell us."

The tech shrugged. "I can only speculate—and I don't want to outrage our scrubs by rumormongering."

He paused, half-smiling, to let the snickering die down. "But if you insist on hearing speculation"—cries of, *Get on with it or we'll thump you!*—"I'd say we've been abandoned. There's no traffic in O that I can pick up, not a scrap. And starship commo runs off fusion bottles; they could burn through all the ionosphere noise."

Jovan squinted at him through the dark. "You mean not even bad guys? The Strahn or whoever?"

"It might be that the Strahn aren't considerate enough to use wavelengths my setup can detect," Ovanidze said, "but what I get is: nothing. Zed, zilch, zot."

Mir caught himself on the edge of a sigh. He did not want to give the men a glimpse of how he felt.

"So the bastards ran on us," Stilicho said with matter-of-fact finality.

"They wouldn't!" burst out Nau. Then he looked sickly repentant.

Ovanidze gestured at his communications rig. "You've got some technical training. Try for yourself, if you think there's anybody still up there."

Henriks, who'd had little to say since the untimely demise of Mr. Bun, stood up and began to scream. Mongoose-quick, Poet whipped a bedroll over his head. With less-expected speed Stilicho stood up, clubbed the boy down with a hammerfist blow to the temple, and sat on him. It was all done without discussion or rancor; they'd all seen it before, and ceased even to be annoyed by it.

"So what happens to us?" asked Chyz.

"You give your long-suffering dragon a rest, would be a start," said Loki.

Mir was staring off to the north, where a faint auroral glow hung like rose pink curtains before the stars. *Odd that we should see the planet's aurora borealis this far south,* he thought.

"At least no one's come down to attack us," Kyov said.

"Leaving us," Loki said, "to take on an entire planet alone, for all we know."

"You old-timers," Kobolev said, appearing out of the dark. "You must all have had your balls shot away for you long

ago. What's a planet of primitive birdbrains to us? Even
though you deathbird scum can't hold a candle to the Engine
of History.''

The ancients uttered harsh clacks of laughter. "The Engine
of History!" Starman jeered. "Going into battle they sniff our
bungholes. But when it's time to flee, they make certain to
return the favor!''

"Engine Regulars," Poet said, clutching his drawn-up
knees and rocking back and forth. "Last to fight, first to flee.''

Mir gave the transfer a hard look. "What are you doing off
the line, Standard?''

Kobolev shrugged. "It's time for us to be relieved.''

"That's for me to say. Now get back to your position.''

For a moment the big, black-bearded transfer stood with
hands on hips, as if tempted to defy the lieutenant. Then he
looked around.

Loki had produced a knife with a long, slim blade and was
ostentatiously cleaning his fingernails with it. "When it comes
to *balls*, scrub," Starman said, "spare some thought for your
own.''

"Insubordination!" Kobolev choked out.

Ovanidze giggled. "Welcome to CLD," he said. "Now
back to your post before we spank you.''

Third Squad came off the perimeter and was replaced by
First. The remaining ration packs were collected. The men
bitched, but it was nothing they hadn't expected, and all had
been conditioned to obedience long before they ever got Detached.

Kobolev and his two companions sat in a sullen cluster and
cast dark looks the lieutenant's way, but when it came their
turn they surrendered their rat packs without a fuss. It might
have had to do with the way Poet stood by, smiling quietly
and making brief brilliant jets of fire squirt out the nozzle of
his flamer, or the way Loki practiced balancing his knife by
the tip on each of his fingertips in turn.

Mir inventoried the supplies they had managed to get off
the joyboat before it took off. To his disgust he founds crates
of replacement copies of *The Communality*, and enough un-
derwater rebreather masks to outfit Section, but much was actually usable: communications and sensor gear, antipersonnel

mines, power cells for small arms and other equipment, NDOs—Networkable Dispersed Ordnance—such as expendable antiarmor missiles and Overload projectors and surface-to-air missiles. The AT rockets would not be wasted—bunker-busters always came in handy—but the lieutenant wasn't sure whether including SAMs were an example of obtuseness or miraculous foresight on the Brass's part. That would depend on the Strahn.

There were even a few precious medical supplies, which had probably been swiped from ship's stores by the White Rat or Loki or Rudi's gnomes, and hacked into the loadout charts in *Beria*'s database. The regular armed forces, army and Kosmos, prided themselves on the availability of medical care for their personnel, especially emergency care. Health care for civilian Dependents of the Collective, on the other hand, was hard to come by, entailing a long wait when treatment was forthcoming at all—anyone seeking medical attention had first to pass a review board to decide whether his or her worth to the Collective justified bestowing tightly rationed care. When it was available, it wasn't necessary *desirable*. "You go in hospital like you go in CLD," an underground aphorism held. "In order to die."

Klad, of course, changed the equation, as it always did. Those who had enough needn't worry about being found unworthy of healing—and could count on receiving the best in terms of competence, facilities, potency and purity of drugs. Which, however, left a great deal of room for a crapshoot. That was the way of *klad*: it offered no guarantees, just better odds.

The Collective Landing Detachment was from a standing start lucky to do as well as the hapless Dependents when it came to medicine. Despite the Engine's desire to keep its convict-soldiers functional and on line, regular quartermasters and medical officers often found better uses for supplies slugged for the deathbirds, such as diverting them to their own uses. So the Detachment had to look out for itself. Which was nothing new—and the reason the Rat enjoyed such esteem.

What was lacking, of course, was food. *Two weeks,* thought Mir, shaking his head.

There was nothing he could do about that, so he went to bed in a shallow trench he had scooped for himself on the river face of the hill. The snugness of cool moist walls, smell-

ing at once strange and familiar, gave him the illusion of security. Life since his arrest had taught him that all security
was illusion; but it had also taught him to take what he could
get. He felt almost safe as he fell quickly into sleep.

Second and Third Squads prepared to bed down. Kobolev,
van Dam, and Eyrikson hung off to the side muttering among
themselves. As the others were ready to turn in they came
forward, gesturing the brothers in close.

"Now that the lieutenant is out of the way," Kobolev said
in a low voice, "we need to set some matters straight."

"Straight," echoed Eyrikson, bobbing his blond head. He
and van Dam wore pulsers at waist level, at the end of their
long issue slings.

"As the real soldiers in this lot," the Bold Original said,
"we'll naturally run things. We know how things go in the
Landing Detachment. The officers are mere figureheads. Real
power reposes among the men; and what could be more Universal and communal?"

"You know a lot about life in CLD," said Black Bertold.
He sounded amused.

Van Dam bobbed his head. "That's right," he said. "We
learn quick."

Kobolev showed a carefully measured grin. His teeth were
fairly even and white, betraying his origin comfortably within
the Custodian class. "I hope you lot learn quickly as well.
From here on, what we say goes, and all prior arrangements
are out the window, as might be said."

Eyrikson tugged at his sleeve. "Get to the part about going
out behind the barracks," he said.

Kobolev brushed his hand away. "Well, yes. That is one
point to be raised. As all know, we're men without the benefit
of women, but men we remain, if you catch my drift."

Loki was squatting down on slat haunches, next to Big Bori,
who sat spraddle-legged like a great gauche idol. He looked
up at Kobolev. Starlight gleamed on his angle-set eyes.

"You'd better grow accustomed to picking feathers from
your pubes, then, eh?" he said. Beside him Bori chuckled, a
sound like a pile of granite boulders shifting to a temblor.

"Heh-heh," Kobolev said. "He's a funny one, isn't he,
bruds?" Eyrikson and van Dam laughed hugely.

"We'll not be taking advantage of the local talent," the burly noncom said, "at least until we've scouted what kind of holes they have. In the meantime"—he shrugged—"the Universal Will is that all share. You'll just have to see that our needs are met, and there you have it. It's nothing you haven't done before; you shouldn't find it any too onerous."

"So you're saying," Loki said in a voice of silk, "that you expect us to spread for you on demand?"

Eyrikson giggled. "Of course," Kobolev said, "since the Universal Will is so clearly that we lead. Natural leaders, we are, and for making the sacrifices leadership entails, we're entitled to certain, shall we say, returns. That's the heart of Service, and Service is *klad*, and *klad* is the way the world works."

Eyrikson nudged his ribs. "So when do we start?"

Loki tilted his head toward Bori. His eye caught the giant's.

Big Bori leapt to his feet. "Red-ass ling pimps!" he roared. "We were bringing autoc scum to Now while you were still pulling at your mothers' tits!" He dealt the startled Kobolev a roundhouse buffet on the side of the head that laid the erstwhile Engine Regular full-length on the ground cover.

Eyrikson tried to bring his pulser to play, but it had gotten around behind the small of his back, and he got tangled in the sling as he tried to haul it around. Loki sprang at him from his heels, laying a shoulder into the young scrub's muscular midriff. Eyrikson was driven backward by the force of Loki's lunge—and tripped immediately backward over Poet, who had crept from his foxhole on the perimeter to station himself on all fours, right behind him.

Realizing he and his mates had badly overplayed their hand, van Dam turned and tried to bolt. Big Bori caught him by the back of his battle dress tunic, plucked him one-handed into the air, and slammed him down on his side. As the transfer lay gasping for breath the big man began to stomp mercilessly on his ribs. The other ancients of Second and Third Squads piled on the fallen Bold Originals, kicking and punching, as Gollob and Sturz stood by staring in gape-mouthed amazement. Only Standard Narva, who really *was* an ancient and known as the Oldest Living, hung back. That was only because of his age; he squatted on the sidelines beating bony fists on his thighs and cawing toothless laughter.

Having brought down Eyrikson, Loki flung himself astride Kobolev's chest, struck him six rapid blows in the face, then grabbed his ears and pounded the back of his head on the ground while his mates played merry hell on the transfer's rib cage with fists and boots.

"You *sow*," he hissed. "Sport your wedding tackle at us, and we'll cut it off and sew it on your face in place of that cancer you call a nose!" And for emphasis he flattened Kobolev's nose with a hammerblow.

Months on the firing line had made Junior Lieutenant Haakon Mir a light sleeper. The commotion brought him quickly awake, sitting up with his pulser in his hands and the safety off.

The Rookery's single moon had not risen. Through the dark Mir could make out a flurry of action on the hill's far side. There was no Bitch snarl; no blue-green directed-energy pulse flashes lit the night. That meant the action was strictly intramural.

For a moment Mir sat there, as if he'd just come awake in his own grave. Instinct and training urged him to bound out and restore order.

Every instinct except *survival*. If he intervened he would die, if not on the spot, then as soon as action produced a convenient context for him to catch a stray bolt in the back of the head. The best he could practically do was rely on the Tradition: *We don't neck our own.*

He slipped his pulser back to safety. *It isn't cowardice,* he told the righteous idealistic cadet he once had been. *What good could I do?*

Feeling queasy, he lay back down into the comforting grave embrace. Despite the muffled sounds from the far slope, and the gnawing of his conscience, he was soon asleep again.

The Bold Originals were duly pulped and left beside the stacked stores for a quiet communal bleed. Second and Third Squads took to their bedrolls with the sense of a job well-done, and the day's fear, frustration, and anger well vented. Poet slipped back to his hole and took up his flamer, thin cheeks flushed.

Quiet descended. Small creatures sang to each other from

the night, and a cool breeze sniffed around the alien intruders clustered on the hilltop. It seemed to find them offensive, left them alone to settle down to ruffling through the feather-trees down beside the river, raising a soft chaotic susurration.

After a time Balt grunted, let himself settle down away from the receiver of his electromagnetic machine gun to sit on the floor of the extralarge foxhole he'd commanded Hynkop to dig. He studied the boy a moment through the dark. Hynkop gazed back, eyes wide and round but no more so than usual, his unremarkable young face placid. Balt made a decision, and grunted again to mark it.

He reached down, undid the fly of his battle dress trousers, unshipped his dragon with a grimy-nailed hand, thickly pelted on the back with tangled black fur.

"Time you learned the rest of your duties as assistant gunner," he said in a low voice.

Expressionless still, Hynkop bent forward and opened his mouth.

The Rooks hit them at dawn.

8

AFTER DARK SECTION customarily stood two-hour watches by squad. When the long local night ended and grey dawn light began to seep like spoiled milk between the eastern hills, First Section had been on its second rotation for just over an hour.

Poet saw them first. He had refreshed himself with a jolt of Zone when the White Rat woke him for his watch by squatting four meters away and cautiously chucking pebbles at him. His senses were whetted down so fine that the smell of dew on the yellow mat was like fine Praesidium brandy, and the first hint of daylight struck the colors of the river valley and made them ring in his eyes.

They were wading along the near bank of the river, where the boles of lavender feather-trees masked them from Section's ground radar: a party of riders, tall and slender, bent over the long necks of riding beasts covered in colorful feathers, with beaked heads and clawed feet and backs that sloped pronouncedly from withers to croup, such that all the saddles had high cantles to keep the riders from sliding off behind. The riders carried long slim lances with bunches of feathers tied behind the heads, and stubby projectile weapons slung across their backs. Whether they wore uniforms or whether the splashes of crimson and blue they displayed was their natural coloration, Poet couldn't see at this distance. Where bright colors came into play, Zone tended to blur detail, as though you were looking through binoculars with a faulty chip.

"Autocs," he said into the slim spar of microphone curving from the headset built into his helmet. "Coming up from the southeast along the river, six hundred meters out. Forty–fifty riders, mounted on silly-looking four-legged birds."

A moment later and the lieutenant was lying on the moist ground cover beside him, adjusting focus on his binoculars. Kyov joined them, moving with quiet confidence.

"Looks like they're scoping us out." Poet said, tapping fingers on the hard polymerized-ceramic mountings of his flamer. The autocs were still way too far away for his weapon to reach.

Mir grunted. Suddenly the ground radar sent up a brain-piercing electronic yammer, and from the far side of the hill a shrill young voice screamed, "Process, there they are! They're coming!"

"Combat positions! Hold fire!" the lieutenant shouted, rearing up and around to look to the east. A mass of infantry had appeared along the crenellated rampart of hills, black stilt silhouettes against the rising sun.

As they came down the valley walls the enemy force resolved itself into three tightly ordered phalanxes of what Mir judged company strength, arranged abreast behind a double line of skirmishers. The infantry were as colorful as the cavalry sneaking up the river. A different hue predominated in each company: red on right, blue left, yellow center. The skirmishers wore green. Each formation carried a bright standard of its own color.

Roused by the alarm and Florenz's frantic cry, the men of off line squads were slipping into holes on the perimeter. Had First Squad been Engine Regulars, indoctrinated to think of themselves as having no existence except as part of a group, they would have had to squeeze themselves together in a lump along one arc of the perimeter to allow the other squads to fit in—exposing two-thirds of the circle to enemy attack. Death-birds, they just stayed put while Two and Three interspersed themselves among them, executing without command or hesitation a maneuver that would have reduced a like number of Regulars to an inchoate herd.

Mir himself lay on the crest of the hill, shielded by crates where he could see in all directions. He had his visor up. The helmet had vision-enhancing capabilities, but unless it was dark or ergs were flying, he preferred, like most, to rely on his own eyes.

"Dirt check," he said into his microphone. "Sound off by number."

Everybody's radio was functioning. *That's a relief.* "Stay low and hold your fire until I give the word," he said.

"What are those shiny things on the ends of their guns?" Chyz wanted to know.

"Those are spears, not guns," said Kobolev. The Bold Original sounded subdued this morning.

Starman laughed, a discordant noise. "Spears my bleeding piles! Those are bayonets."

"What are they for?" Chyz asked.

"To ram into your belly when Anton gets close," Stilicho said. *Anton* was the generic soldier name for autoc forces.

"You're joking!" Chyz exclaimed. Stilicho laughed.

Kyov slipped up beside the lieutenant. "Sir," he said, pointing beyond the advancing Rook infantry. "Look behind the infantry."

Mir had already noted what he took to be resupply wagons, big-wheeled and segmented, being drawn by feathered dray beasts down the slope in the enemy's rear. Through his binoculars he was startled to see dark grey tubes mounted on the rear segment of each wagon-serial.

"Those are guns!" he exclaimed softly.

"I think so, sir."

With his teeth Mir took hold of the flesh inside his mouth, just below his lower lip, and worried it. Frantically he tried to recall his Earth military history. Like most history of the long-lost human homeworld taught in Stellar Collective schools, it had mostly been a litany of abuse and exploitation. A few concrete details had crept into the mix like raisins in batter, though; he was trying to sift out a few concerning Napoleonic-era technology.

"They're deploying," Kyov said.

"They're still a good kilometer off," the lieutenant said. "If they're really equivalent to early nineteenth century guns, they're smoothbores, and smoothbores shouldn't reach *nearly* this far—"

White smoke gusted from a gun already unlimbered to fire above the heads of the advancing foot soldiers. A few heartbeats and the report reached them like a giant ax biting into wood.

A moment more, and something moaned overhead, seeming so low Mir instinctively ducked down among his ramparts of Universal Law and rebreathing gear. A flash, a crack, and a ragged grey smokeball appeared in midair thirty meters beyond the hilltop.

Kyov showed a world-weary grin. "Snaked again," he said.

"Process! They're got proximity fuses!" yelped Nau.

"NBL," said Loki, who was a self-made demolitions expert, or at least believed himself to be. "Not bloody likely. Probably just a fuse, period, set to burning when they light the beast off."

"How do they calculate when it's going to go explode?" Nau asked. Thinking of technics seemed to soothe him.

"They don't. They guess, and trim the fuse accordingly."

"Mark this date on your calendar, boy," said Black Bertold, who *was* trained in explosives. "For once Loki knows what he's talking about."

"I'll take that out of your hide with interest, bear-pogue," Loki promised cheerfully.

One thing the Rooks have, Mir thought grimly, *is rifled artillery.* "At least they're really muzzle-loaders, Lieutenant," Kyov said.

A crew was busy doing something at the muzzle end of the cannon which had fired on the hill. "I'm not going to give them a chance to guess lucky," Mir said, and cut himself into the command circuit.

"Rouen and Lennart," he commanded, calling on First and Second Squads' snipers, both armed with Bitch rifles and facing the enemy artillery, "start taking down the gun crews. Starman—"

Third Squad's sniper, laser-armed, was covering the river and the approaching riders. "Shift over and join them. The cavalry doesn't worry me."

"Four hundred meters, Lieutenant," Poet said.

"Men facing the river: if the riders charge, burn them down. Everybody else, on my command: hit the big infantry formations with everything you've got."

"Duty requires I point out that the skirmishers are closer, sir," the Dancing-Master radioed. Mir noticed that even at stone-toss range his voice was scrimmed with static.

Mir grinned. *The man most convinced he should have my job is the only man in Section who'd apologize for contradicting me.* "It looks like they put their faith in those big squares," he said, "and they're target-rich environments."

The infantry had reached the low ground between the valley-wall range and First Section's hill. The skirmishers were five hundred meters off, the mass formations about fifty meters behind—well within range of all of Section's weapons except the three flamers.

"Commence firing," Mir ordered.

He was watching the crew of the gun which had first fired. The spindly Rooks moved with what seemed to him deliberate efficiency; he guessed the reason they took this long to ready their piece again was uncertainty of how long to cut their fuse. He heard the chuff-*snap* of the two electros firing, and the laser's louder crack. Three gunners dropped, one seemingly about to fire the weapon.

Mir heard a grenade launcher go, four shots thud-thud-thud-thud with the cadence of a journeyman framer hammering nails, the tearing-canvas sound of full-auto Bitches, and then the squeal of air rushing away from pulser bolts, echoed in headphone crackles. He panned his binoculars down and, shedding magnification in favor of a wider view-field, swept across the Rook formations.

The infantry was being torn to shreds, polychrome brilliance drowning in red. The 25mm launched grenades were not as awesomely powerful as the entertainment sims portrayed them, but they could tear the leg off a foot soldier or an officer's beaked mount, and amid these crowded ranks each round could take down several. Snarling Bitch fire slashed through the Rooks like invisible scimitars, and even the most buck-fevered scrub, forgetting all the technique literally beaten into him during CLD training, could hardly manage to avoid finding a home for his pulser bolts.

Sickened, the lieutenant let his binocs fall from his eyes. Unassisted vision would show him all he needed to see of the one-way battle. And much more than he wanted.

* * *

"Here they come!"

The Rook cavalry, which had been hidden from view by a steep cut in the bank, burst over the top, their mounts' talons gouging wounds in the damp soil. They leveled lances and charged the hilltop.

Waiting, waiting, Zone-impatient yet not dissatisfied, Poet had been enjoying the pretty colors. Anticipation of inflicting pain and sensory input almost managed to mask the ugly muttering chaos undertones, the turbulence of terror running through the current at the center of his soul. No drug would hide the fear completely, much less stop it: Poet had tried them all.

What Zone provided was *distraction.*

Jovan's shout, raw with eagerness, seemed to toll over and over through Poet's mind like a great bell. He heard the blond bumpkin's hunger, and resonated with it. Here was the moment every Lander lived for, the window of repletion and requital through which he could reach to pay back every slap in the face, every cock or broom handle shoved up his rectum, the broken bones and bruised flesh and trampled hopes that had marked the stations of his progress through the guts of the Collective to CLD. In Poet, in Jovan, in every one of them, anger smoldered like a barely dormant monster.

Poet said nothing. His was a quiet frenzy. He simply let his fingers flutter-dance on the outside of his flamer's trigger guard, and the degrees by which his grin winched its way across his face, across the spectrum from amusement to pleasure to a bizarre *risus sardonicus,* marked the building of his anticipation.

Pulsers squealed. The lead rider, his natural crest augmented by a panache of scarlet and purple feathers, was brandishing a hooked sword. His mount reared, screamed, clawed air as bolts struck home, raising clouds of blue-green flare, blackish spatter, and pink steam. The leader's head exploded as he fell. His feather headdress, smoldering, was trampled by the talons of the mounts behind.

It was a little over two hundred meters from the point where the riders broke cover to Section's positions: two hundred uphill meters of unobstructed ground, every centimeter well within pulser range. Balt gave a lancer a protracted sizzling burst from his Bitch. Rook and mount came apart as if dropped from a great height.

The Rooks came on, beaks spreading wide to vent hawk shrills of fury. The bird-mounts ran with terrifying speed. Still, half were down by the time they came within the forty-meter effective range of Poet's Little Sister.

He had dialed the weapon for minimum dispersion to give him maximum reach. He aimed at the yellow blaze at the base of the riding creature's throat, fired.

Plasma spiked white-hot from the flamer. Like a heated needle it passed through the animal's neck, piercing the rider's torso as the beast's head blew off in a steam explosion. Mount and rider exploded into flame and fell in a blazing comet tumble, raising a great hiss and tentacles of steam from the dew-laden mat.

The Landers raised a great orgasmic shout of triumph. Poet smiled. The dragon's-breath flamer was more than even the dashing Rook cavalry was prepared to face. The handful of survivors turned their mounts' beaks back toward the safety of the trees. Poet's flamer reached out and turned another beast and rider to a reeking bonfire before they fled from range.

Perhaps half a dozen made it to river's edge and out of sight.

Something passed Poet's head with a droning moan. At first he thought it was an insect, but a white ball of smoke rolling lazily across the face of the hill told him a dismounted Rook had fired at him from behind the decapitated corpse of a riding beast. The carabineer was upwards of fifty meters away, too far for Poet to hit him with a plasma jet; the magnetic fields which channeled superheated stuff were unstable at that distance.

So much the worse for you, Anton, he thought. He fired. The plasma jet gave out eight meters shy of the target. What struck the Rook was the cloud of superheated air the plasma pushed in front of it.

The Rook caught fire. Uttering a brain-drilling shriek, it jumped up and danced away down the hillside, beating wings of fire, condemned to burn without the *misericordia* of quick plasma death. Florenz gave a cry to match the burning autoc's and jumped out of his hole, hosing his pulser full-automatic from the waist. By good luck one burst the Rook's chest, ending his pain.

A bullet hit Florenz in the midriff. The impact threw him

backward into the perimeter and left him in a writhing puking knot on the ground.

Balt turned his electro toward the telltale puff rising from behind another dead mount. He fired in brief methodical bursts, each one raising a spray of red like squirts from an airbrush, until he had sawed through the carcass to the sniper. A weird musical death cry skirled up the wind, and all was silent on that side of the hill but Poet's breath echoing inside helmet and visor, and his heart jackhammering so fiercely he could feel the veins pulsing in his eardrums.

After a splinter from a Rook shell that burst in air beside the hilltop laid his cheek open, Junior Lieutenant Mir took to directing sniper fire against the guns the autocs had deployed among the hills. That way he could narrow his focus to the more selective slaughter he was ringing down on the gunners, and avoid witnessing the mass butchery of the infantry, now broken and streaming back up the slopes in terrified confusion, their voices like a flock of seabirds startled by a predator's approach.

Cheers ringed the hilltop. Mir looked around to see his men's fire harrying the last of the Rook cavalry out of sight. "Fly away, you feathered buggers!" Big Bori screamed hoarsely, and cackled like a fool. Lennart was reciting the Lord's Prayer over and over.

A patter of thumps on the breastwork of crates around him, sounding like small boys pelting a sign with stones, told Mir that not all the Rooks had run off. The skirmishers had dropped into cover and begun to return a steady fire. So far their marksmanship hadn't been good enough to tag any of the Landers, hunkered well down in their holes. But the fact that they were able to bring their shots basically on target at four hundred meters told the lieutenant that Rook small arms, like their artillery, was rifled.

"Snipers," he commanded, "finish the gunners and keep watch on the skyline in case any more of them get bold. Everybody else, leave the mob alone and start taking down those skirmishers before one gets lucky and pops one of us."

He shifted his view down to a marshy patch of the valley floor in time to see a cluster of launched grenades raise a geyser of water and mud from a stand of tall purple-black grass above which hung a puffball of gunsmoke. "Lucky for us their weapons mark their positions so conveniently," he said softly, off the net.

"And unlucky for them," added Kyov, again crouching by his side.

Mir sighed and lowered his glasses. "Our fortune is somebody else's misfortune," he said, "almost by definition."

"If only somebody else's misfortune necessarily meant *our* fortune," the older man said with a sad, wry smile, "we'd be men of Service indeed."

Mir cocked a brow at him. "Would you really be able to take pleasure from that, knowing what you had was bought with the pain of others?"

Kyov shrugged. "The Detached life teaches one to take what one can get, Lieutenant."

Which didn't answer the question. Before the young lieutenant could decide whether to press the issue or not, he saw Loki's head snapped back against the rim of his hole by a resounding blow to his visor.

The lanky blond man dropped bonelessly from sight.

9

THE CHEERS AND jeers were chopped off. "Zero that sniper!" Mir shouted.

Quick on the uptake, the hidden Rook marksmen were already getting the idea that they couldn't snipe and hope to stay hidden from the terrible alien firepower. Firing from the bottomland was rapidly slackening as the skirmishers snaked out of there in a hurry. A dozen weapons converged fire on the Judas-puff of smoke betraying the sniper who had nailed Loki.

Big Bori came blasting from his hole like shellburst ejecta. "Little brud!" he screamed. "Little karl, are you all right!" Tears streamed paths through the dirt on his cheeks.

Despite continuing danger from bitter-enders in the bottomland, other Landers were crawling out of their holes to see. Even Poet, seeing no prospect for immediate flamer play, wandered over the top of the hill. They gathered around the fallen Loki's hole.

He lay at the bottom, a surprisingly small and childlike crumple. His helmet had fallen away. His fine features were wax-pale beneath a tracery of blood and his eyes were closed.

Bori wept uncontrollably. "Little brud," he moaned, dropping to his knees on the hole's brim. "Little brud, why?" He leaned forward and reached down to cradle his friend, his hands, great mauls of scar tissue and callus, surprisingly gentle.

Loki's eyes flashed open, staring white and blue from his

blood-painted face like the eyes of a terrible doll. He sat upright.

"I've come back from Hell to take you with me!" he shrieked. He reached up and grabbed Bori by his stubbled cheeks.

"*Aii*!" Bori screamed, leaping straight into the air. "Zombies! Zombies!" He turned and went lurching right out of the perimeter in a whirl of limbs.

"Bori!" Mir shouted. "Get back here, you idiot!" No more shots were coming from the Rooks, but that didn't mean there were no more snipers.

Ignoring him Bori raced gracelessly off toward the river, gibbering about the living dead. Laughing, Poet stepped to the side and sent a plasma stream crackling and roaring past the giant to blast a line of earth across his path. Where the superheated gas struck, the dew-damp ground cover dried, then burned.

Big Bori had a consuming fear of fire. Trapped between it and zombies, he collapsed to the mat and lay crying and moaning and covering his face.

"Kobolev, van Dam, bring that imbecile back!" the lieutenant roared.

"Get him yourself," Kobolev spit back. "There's snipers out there still."

"He brung it on himself," van Dam added.

The rest of Section pinned the Bold Originals with black-laser looks. Under most circumstances they likely would have said the same thing, but after last night they saw the Originals as outsiders. This refusal to assist a fallen comrade became another black mark on the three scrubs' collective ledgers.

That it was also refusal to obey a direct order, Mir reflected, seemed to interest no one but himself.

Kyov said, "Poet, Lennart, come with me. We'll fetch him back."

"Don't bother," Poet said. He bent over and tapped the muzzle of his flamer on the helmets of Chyz and the Fart-Smelling Man. "You and you, come with us."

Loki had emerged from his hole and lay beside it, laughing hysterically. The Section had no actual medics, as was not uncommon in CLD. Corporal Geydar, Bertold's second-in-command of Third Squad, had scavenged enough knowledge to fake it. He knelt beside the wounded man.

"Hold still," Geydar said sulkily. His eyes were red; as usual he had spent the battle crying uncontrollably. The rest of the time his weeping was more controlled. "If you're going to drop dead on the march, I want to at least know why."

The salvage party returned to the perimeter, each dragging the still-sobbing giant by a limb. Letting go a hand, Poet eyed Loki with interest. "If you're really going to die," he said, "will you tell me where your *klad* stash is?" Every man in Section, if not the whole battalion, assumed Loki had an enormous accretion of plunder secreted away somewhere.

"In your ass, Poet!" Loki shook his head, and tears of mirth diluted the blood on the sides of his face and streamed down over his temples. "Did you see that great buffoon? I bet he shit his pants when I grabbed him."

"He did," Poet said, "thank you so much."

"Thank the Lord," Lennart added, "that he's in *your* squad."

Geydar held up Loki's helmet. "The padding inside is all cross-linked and brittle," he said. "The bullet knocked the rim of his helmet into his forehead and gashed it." He sniffled and shook his head. "I don't see how they expect us to survive with such shoddy equipment."

"They don't, you sniveling pute!" Loki cried, sitting up and snatching his helmet back. He placed it precariously on his head and glared around, rolling his eyes madly behind his mask of drying blood. "Birds beware! The army of the living dead are upon you!"

Big Bori had begun to pick himself up. Now he flung himself down again. "Don't say that," he begged.

"Sodding well don't," said Poet with that sudden quiet intensity he had inside, that always took even his long-standing comrades by surprise. "It cuts too fucking close to truth."

Lieutenant Mir was taking stock of his situation. His fatalities were . . . none. Florenz's armor had been more than sufficient to stop the soft, unjacketed lead bullet, which was found beside him, a disconcertingly large grey lump. He had sustained a nasty bruise, and deposited the remnants of last night's cold rats into the low yellow foliage tangle. Dieter, Section's other ersatz medic, opined that unless he commenced puking blood within the hour, he'd probably survive.

Other than that there were four cases of shell fragment cuts, Mir's included, and Loki's wound, which included a sore neck and ringing headache that made him snarl and snap at his comrades as soon as the first rush of surviving—and catching Bori with his joke—subsided.

As the fact of the unit's not just surviving an attack at greater than twenty-to-one odds, but surviving intact, sank in, a manic mood seized the Landers. They began to backslap and hoot and break into fits of giggling for no reason at all. Small parties forayed out to peer at the Rook riders who had fallen near their position.

Satisfied that the last skirmishers had finally been driven off—or at least had lost any further interest in trading shots with the intruders—Mir followed one group out to see his first Rooks at close range. They were slender creatures, built basically like attenuated men, with clawed extremities, large eyes facing forward above hook-tipped yellow beaks to provide good depth perception—a predator trait, he remembered from his nature classes. Their bodies were covered with brightly colored feathers, with some individuals displaying marked similarities of color and pattern. Whether that signified subspecies, clan, or family distinctions, he had no idea. The cavalry wore purple-feathered tunics of woven fabric.

"Take a look at this, sir," Nau said tentatively. He held up one of the cavalry weapons, a short, thick-barreled piece with a wooden stock.

Mir accepted it. Its lightness surprised his hand. He turned it over, noting that it used a friction system involving a piece of shaped flint clutched in jaws at the end of a spring-driven arm, which evidently snapped backward to scratch sparks off a metal striking surface. The striking surface was attached to the hinged cover of the pan, which held the priming powder in such a way that the primer would be protected from the weather until the act of sparking it also uncovered it.

"Clever bit of work," he admitted. As a Custodial-class youth he had been taught to respect the achievements of less–technically mature peoples. They had a purity to them, a harmony with nature—the Universal Will—which was sacrificed by those who lived more by machines. Or in this case, more sophisticated machines. That was a sacrifice the men and women of the Stellar Collective, as the chosen implements of the Historic Process, were taught to make gladly. One day, their teachers assured them, when all the cosmos was Realized and brought in tune with Universal Truth, then all creatures could put aside their technotoys and live in perfect harmony with Nature and each other. Until then, duty required the sophonts of the Stellar Collective to make use of whatever tools were necessary to forward the Process.

"More than that, sir," the scrub said diffidently. He didn't look at the officer as he did so.

"How do you man, Nau?"

"It isn't metal, sir."

Mir frowned at him. "Oh, the firing mechanism is, other parts probably. But the barrel—feel it, sir."

The barrel was brown, but when Mir ran his fingers along it he realized at once that the scrub was right. Whatever it was felt more like hard plastic than metal. It had a slightly corrugated feel to it.

"My guess," the transfer said, "is that it's made of long ceramic rods or fibers, bound together by some sort of matrix, like resin."

From nearby came a croak and the muffled noise of a flurry of kicks meeting flesh. Mir glanced up. One of the downed riders had proven to be still alive and wounded. A circle of half a dozen Landers surrounded him. Mir hurriedly returned his concentration to the object in his hand. It was hard to get deathbirds to take prisoners when there was a *point* to it. There was no use interrogating Rooks; they and humans shared no language.

Of course humans and newly discovered autoc species *never* shared a language. But usually Reclamation or Engine Intelligence or somebody would have specialists who could interrogate captives and disseminate propaganda—which in Mir's experience the autocs ignored—and sometimes even provided local phrase books for the cogs in the bogs: *Where are the bandits who oppress your people? Please give us water. Dig a trench and stand facing it, hands behind your head. We're from the Collective; we're here to help you.*

Here they had nothing. To dilute the risk of alerting the paranoiac and *very* technologically mature Strahn, it looked as if Kosmos and the Engine had done nothing but a quick flyby, made a couple passes in O to photomap the surface, and blown out-system on the solar wind. It brought home to him with cold-stone-in-the-gut immediacy just how far out in the Void they'd been hung.

And now we've been dropped . . .

The sodden thud of metal-shod boots on flesh jerked him back to reality. He was almost grateful for the sounds.

"Why doesn't the pressure of the propellant burst the rods apart, then?" Mir asked.

Nau's eyelids fluttered in momentary terror. "I—I don't know, sir. Maybe if I could cut one apart—"

Mir shook his head. "Don't worry about that. I doubt we'll have time. Do you derive anything from this information, Lander?"

Nau shook his head. "Only that the Rooks must be pretty advanced with ceramics, plastics, and polymers, sir."

Mir nodded slowly. The planet was comparatively low density, such that its gravity was lower than Earth Standard—or at least, what Collective science said Earth Standard was— even though its diameter was somewhat greater than the human homeworld's. That meant fewer metals to work with. It made sense that to mature as far technologically as they had, the autocs would have had to develop a disproportionately sophisticated nonmetallic materials science.

—He couldn't see where that might lead, either, other than that, like the rifled weapons his men had been faced with, it showed the autocs were more tech-mature than Danilov's briefing had led him to expect. That made him chuckle. He could imagine what Poet or Loki would say if he voiced such a thought: *"What else did you expect? When have they told us anything true?"* The jeer would be followed with a remark about officers, to the effect that they had about as much sense as Big Bori, without Bori's excuse.

He returned uphill to stand surveying the stacks of supplies. *We have a problem, here,* he knew. There was far more equipment here than his men could reasonably carry, even counting only the usable stuff.

"We're going to have to cache this," he announced.

"Can't do it up here, sir," Stilicho said. "Autocs'll be all over this hill as soon as we're clear."

"Leave nix for Anton," Jovan said.

"We can use some of our demo charges to blow a few holes down among the trees and bury the stuff there," Dieter suggested. "We can seal it with ground sheets against seep from the river."

"The snipers can sweep with their scopes on IR, make sure none of the birds're spying on us," Stilicho added.

Mir nodded. "Very good. Section Sergeant Kyov, distribute the medical supplies among the men. Fill out their packs with antiarmor NDOs and antipersonnel mines. Loki, you and the Rat take four men for security and go down by the river. Find a good place for a cache and do start blasting."

It took two hours to get the supplies Mir judged worth saving toted down to the river and buried, with Second Squad pulling security. That left almost half of what they'd managed to get off the joyboat piled atop the hill.

"Blow it," Mir commanded. The sun wasn't yet halfway up the pale turquoise sky. The young lieutenant kept casting nervous glances at it, as if it were some giant distant eye, which would surely see them if they lingered too long.

"You can't do that!" the Dancing-Master protested. "That's Collective property!"

"So are we," Rouen said, "and that don't stop 'em pissing us away."

Kobolev glanced at his two bruds. Like everybody moving crates, they had stripped off their blouses, preferring coolness to the protection the ballistic fabric gave them.

"I must agree with our brother, here," the bearded transfer said. "A serious matter, wasting Collective resources."

Mir looked at the erstwhile Engine Regular and felt his cheeks get warm. "We have to get moving before the Rooks come back in force. We don't have time to bury the rest."

Eyrikson put back his blond head and guffawed. "What a laugh! If they come back, we'll wipe 'em out, just like we did this lot!"

Despite the Bold Originals' unpopularity, that drew nods from some of the Landers. "Why should we worry about these scrubs?" Henriks asked, forgetting that word also applied to him. "They don't have anything that can hurt us."

"Nothing but numbers," Kyov said. "A whole planet worth."

"Blow it," Mir repeated. He looked back at Kobolev. "If you can get me shot for wanton destruction when we get out of this—*if* we get out—you're welcome to."

Without waiting for a response he turned to Ovanidze, who had the housing off his big commo unit and was fiddling inside. "Anything?"

Without even glancing up from his work, the tech shook his round blond head. "There's other traffic on the planet, but I can't get a fix on it. Your sun up there is an active son of a sow, and there's some background crackle I swear has got to come from residue of a supernova blowing off somewhere in the neighborhood. We're not alone down here, but as to where we're gonna find friends—" He shrugged.

"I don't see what the hurry is," the Dancing-Master said. "We have a good position up here—"

"Good and exposed," Stilicho said.

The Dancing-Master hunched an impatient shoulder. "The autocs haven't shown any sign they can hurt us. We can fort up here and wait—"

"Until our food runs out," Kyov said. "Second Section has the rest of our grunt."

That quieted the Landers down. Jovan stooped down and shouldered his pack. A pair of grey polymer one-shot Overload projector tubes jounced atop it, secured by straps. "That settles it," he declared. "Let's go find Two."

"Just a moment," the Dancing-Master said. "Where *is* Second Section? We've heard nothing from them."

"We know where their LZ was," Stilicho said. "Let's hump the ten klicks and see what's happened to 'em. Likely their commo's just futzed."

"Yeah, that's it," Jovan said, licking his lips. "Goes out all the time, even without all this noisy sun shit."

"Corporal Loki," Mir commanded, "blow the surplus. The rest of you, get ready to shift. Police the area and up packs."

Loki's thin face shone fresh-scrubbed beneath his helmet; blood drying on his face had begun to itch him, and he had washed up in the river. The bottom edge of the *khlopok*-gauze patch taped to hold his forehead together showed under the helmet rim. Red was already seeping through.

"We can't leave now!" he exclaimed. He took in the eastern hill, whose lower slopes were strewn with bodies like wildflowers, with a flinging sweep of his arm. "What about all them?"

"They're dead," Mir said. "Leave them."

"There must be plenty of wounded left out there to play with," Poet said with a shy smile, flicking a knife open and closed in his hand.

"And handsome souvenirs to gather too, I warrant," Loki added. "I wonder if these fools have feathered nut sacs? A District Values supervisor's maiden daughter would let you bugger her in front of her whole Evolutionary Youth Cohort's biweekly self-criticism session for a play-pretty like that!"

Mir glared at him and started forward, hand raised. His father *was* a District Values supervisor, and Yirina had been his daughter, if not "maiden" since she was sixteen. And what had happened to her—sweat starting, mouth drying—

"Ho, Lieutenant," Loki said, taking a step back and raising hands palm outward. "I didn't mean to yank your fuse!"

Mir stopped dead. *These men are getting to me.* He had actually been advancing on Loki, raising hands in anger. An act so uncharacteristic it took the Lander by surprise, disarming what would have been his usual reflex, of happily seizing an opportunity to trade blows with an officer. Mir took a deep breath and turned away.

A whistle brought heads around. Bent beneath the weight of his ruck, grenade launcher hanging by its sling before his hips, Stilicho was pointing off toward the crest line of the eastern hills. A small party of riders poised there, feather panaches quivering from lance heads.

"They'll be doing the fuse-pulling if we hang about working our jaws too long," the ancient said.

The hot survival/murder/victory flush had ebbed, and with it the initial ecstatic conviction of invulnerability. Adrenaline-high letdown had begun, and it was one of the worst comedowns of all. Though Balt sent the riders whirling out of sight with a burst from his Bitch that threw sheets of upflung debris in their beaks, the Landers ducked heads deeper into collars and felt stomachs go sour with fear.

Luckily Two's designated landing site was to the west, in the opposite direction from which the enemy main force had come. Section set off down the hill. As they passed the still sprawls of color that were the fallen cavalry, Florenz shook his head.

"Pross," he said, taking a pull from his canteen. "We must've brought a thousand of the putes to Now."

Poet skinned out of ruck and flamer pack and slid forward, soundless across the ground mat. He came from where the downward sweep of the scrub's helmet formed a blind spot, struck him a sudden blow on the side of the neck that dropped the redhead to the ground.

Poet began to kick the scrub in the ribs. Florenz shook his head to clear it, then pushed off as powerfully as he could with arms and legs. That was a mistake; it only rolled him onto his back atop the bulk of his backpack, stranding him with his limbs waving ineffectually in the air like an over-turned roach's.

Grinning close-lipped, Poet kicked him in the face. Then he drove a heel hard into the middle of the transfer's already-bruised belly.

"Poet," Kyov called. "That's enough."

Poet halted with one boot poised above the supine boy's stomach. Then he pivoted, set the foot down on the mat, and walked away. Florenz managed to roll over onto all fours, where he threw up the water he'd taken in since his last spell of vomiting brought on by the Rook bullet.

The other scrubs in First Squad were staring big-eyed at the quiet little Lander as he returned to his place in the formation—except Hynkop, who never seemed to react to anything.

"Why'd you do it?" Nau asked. "Why'd you trash him like that?" At once he shut his mouth, realizing too late as usual that he might have just targeted himself for Poet's sur-prising temper.

But Poet only shrugged. "He made me mad, that's all," he said.

10

THEY SAW NO more enemy on the march to Section Two's LZ. They crossed the river at a shallow spot half a klick upstream from their original hilltop fort and climbed the long easy slope to the west.

They marched through a realm of soft contours and mellow colors: ochers, ambers, yellows, pale oranges, light greens. As the long day grew warm the sun raised sweat on their faces, but the heat was mild. As the soil warmed, the smells of earth that was not Earth and growing things rose up around them like unseen mist.

To Haakon Mir, the smells and yellow-earth tones of the Rookery were beginning to seem right and natural. It was more than just that he was making a natural accommodation to his new environment, he thought, as he drove himself along on legs inured to up-and-down kilometers by brutal forced-march training, bent beneath the weight of his ruck—not carrying his own burden was another excellent way for a CLD officer to run lethally afoul of his men, whereas in the Engine of History no officer would think of toting a pack. It seemed to him as if he somehow fit here, more closely perhaps than any world he had known, whether it was Novy Utrecht, where he was born, or Santander, where he had grown to maturity, and where he had been an officer-cadet at the District *Akademiya*. Certainly it felt more, well, *homelike* than any planet he had served on before. Deep down he found himself wondering if even semilegendary Earth could seem more right.

Is such thinking too Particular? he wondered. *Or even Dev-olutionary? After all, we evolved on Earth, to fit Earth's environment and no other, and that evolution is a manifestation of Universal Will. Is it a crime to feel this way?*

Then he raised his face to the warm soft touch of the alien sun and laughed. What could it matter if his thoughts were crimes? The age-old refrain of CLD came home to him: *What can they do? Detach me?*

For the first time since his own arrest and Detachment he fully felt the liberation of the damned. He laughed again, louder still. The men marching near him shot him sidelong glances and edged away. Unexpected behavior might presage a snap, violent or even deadly; fingers were slipping into trigger guards, just in case. He didn't care.

—He found Kyov beside him, matching his pace though the Section sergeant's legs were shorter than his. When Mir glanced at him Kyov met his eyes and the grizzle-bearded lips sketched a smile. *He understands,* Mir thought, with a rush of comrade feeling for a subordinate that was as deviant, in the Collective scheme, as his sense of belonging on this foreign world.

They paused to sit and breathe and guzzle water from their canteens atop a long low ridge that ran away northeast and southwest. Water, at least, was plentifully available. Away from the river beside which they had landed, the countryside was veined with small streams. Some of the men looked hard at Poet, Loki, and Stilicho, who had been ordered to split up their own burdens in order to carry the Section's rations; hunger was beginning to stir its millipede legs in bellies. But nothing was said.

Momentarily shut of the weight of his pack, new transfer Nau stood up on his toes, stretching out his arms and legs and weary lower back. "What a beautiful planet," he said, looking around the easy-rolling landscape. Haze was beginning to soften the distances. Apparently this was natural, not pollution; aside from the woodsmoke smell that had greeted them on landing, and the powder tang of that morning's battle, the men had detected no artificial odors they didn't bring with them.

Poet sneered. "It's just rock and gas," he said.

Nau looked at him with a stricken expression, then sat

down, drew up his knees, and curled his arms around them. That was the thing about the scrubs: it was not that they were unprepared for combat; when they got out of the Grinder they were in effect seasoned veterans already, who had proved they could function under battle stress. The ones who couldn't died. But they had learned well to fear authority, and more, to fear the human predators into whose ranks they would come as strangers. Since childhood they had been conditioned to thinking of the Collective Landing Detachment as the scum of the Universe, inhumanly depraved and vicious. Now they found themselves at the mercy of the bogeyman—and had not internalized that now they were bogeymen *themselves*.

Some couldn't take it, in spite of all they had endured in training—or maybe because; maybe the cumulative weight of stress and fear broke them at last. In their first days with a unit, especially in a combat zone, they could behave almost as erratically as any Engine conscripts. They had force-learned to contain their inborn dread of battle and its dangers—but not the fear of *the new*, which the experience of being Detached had instilled in them.

The phenomenon fed upon its own tail: the ancients, who knew the cost of breakdown on the firing line, regarded the scrubs with the same fondness they lavished on unexploded munitions. They shunned them when they could, and otherwise treated them even worse than they did each other, until the transfers had not just shown that they could maintain without doing something bizarre that would get their bruds killed, but had shown some serious *class*, which meant they were ready not to claim but to seize their place in the outlaw fraternity of CLD.

Sitting on the ridge's western face, Mir shook his head and sighed. He had been raised in the belief that, while an individual meant nothing in and of himself, he could still make a difference, and that therefore his duty to his community—and the Universe for which it stood—was to make such a difference as he could. Yet Mir had long since run up against the cold unyielding fact that he could make no difference; he couldn't change the way the vets treated the scrubs any more than he could change the way the rest of the Engine of History treated CLD.

Any more than he could change what had happened to him. Or Yirina, or their mother and father.

Kobolev had shed his pack and sat with hands on thick thighs. Walking had worked some of last night's knots out, and some of his arrogance back.

"Why do you call him *Poet*, anyway?" he demanded. "He's damned near inarticulate, and he's got no poetry in his soul."

"Never ask why, cog-dog," Starman said, so close behind him the Bold Original jumped. "You could catch your death."

"Let's go," Mir called, rising to his feet. He was disgusted, and he didn't know why. "We don't even know if Second's going to wait for us. We *know* the autocs won't."

"Snake the autocs," growled Kobolev. Though he and his two bruds were by far the most robust of the transfers, they weren't moving any too briskly today.

"After you've been here a while," Rouen remarked, "that won't seem so outlandish an option."

"And it's your only one," said Jovan with a big country grin.

Kobolev gave Rouen a dark look. The veteran looked at him through straw-colored bangs and smiled a flat smile. He held his sniper-Bitch easily in patrol position before his hips. There was in the easy poise of his stance that which suggested he would not hesitate to use it on much of any pretext. Kobolev spat and turned to bend creakily down to shoulder his own pack. Section resumed its march to the northwest.

The first they saw of Section Two's joyboat was marks of its passage. Nearing the LZ marked on Mir's map, they came to a ridgeline with a ten-meter-wide gouge taken out of the yellow soil of its top, and much of a stand of brush burned down cold.

"Rough landing," Stilicho said.

Jovan's cheeks collapsed toward his pursed mouth. "This doesn't look good," he said, rubbing his belly. "My stomach is already quaking at what this is gonna mean."

"Then it's going to leap out your mouth and run all the way home when it gets a load of this," Starman called from the top of the cut's shoulder. "Look here."

He pointed west and south of the route they had been following. First Section crowded up beside him to look.

A kilometer away, a hilltop had been split open as if a giant had kicked it. The gouge seemed to line up with the one they were standing by.

Mir felt momentarily light-headed, as if a swarm of the tiny insects that periodically rose up around them had invaded his skull. "Come along, men," he said. "Let's keep moving. We won't learn anything just standing here."

They found the joyboat several hours later, when the sun had rolled over the top of the pale green-blue sky and the light suffusing the countryside had taken on the warm mature tones of afternoon.

"I'd like to know," Jovan said in loud exasperation, "just how in Process's name you can auger in on an unopposed landing?"

"Kosmos is ever-resourceful in failure," Loki said. He stood atop the rear assembly of a joyboat's main drives, three white spun-ceramic nozzles in an equilateral cluster, lying in the midst of a plowed field beside a long groove cut in the planet like a wound.

"You mustn't say that!" shrilled Gollob. "They're our comrades in service of the Universal Will!"

Preoccupied with implication, no one even bothered to cuff him. "Now, can we *really* be sure this was really Section Two's boat?" black-haired Dieter suggested cheerfully.

For answer Ovanidze held up a fragment with lettering on it in white. It was unmistakably a piece of wrapping torn from a standard-issue rat pack. He let it flutter free down the freshening afternoon breeze.

The land had widened and flattened. They had passed through fields showing unmistakable signs of cultivation, and orchards of trees exploding all over with colorful blooms, which showed Mir a carefully tended look. While they had encountered constant flocks of tiny colorful wild birds, they had seen no more of the native sophonts.

A stone farmhouse with a high-pitched thatch roof stood eight hundred meters southwest, beneath feathery, purple-leafed trees squatter than the trees by the river, with spreading black limbs. Rouen lay across two furrows, scrutinizing the structure through his own binoculars, which had belonged to an officer of Kosmos Force's elite Pioneers, the combat engineers. Back on Hovya the officer had taken violent issue with several boys from Section over whether it was appropriate for Landing Detachment deathbirds to frequent a field brothel intended for loyal servants of the Universal Will. He wound up floating facedown and naked in a latrine, tragically lost to service through some unexplained mishap.

The sniper, country-bred like Jovan but much more taciturn, had traded Poet two packs of reefer and a dozen prepackaged Zone injectors for the glasses. Loki still ragged on Poet for letting such a valuable item go cheap, but Poet was strapped at the time.

"Don't see nobody," Rouen reported. "And if they're there, they ain't been long enough for their body heat to seep through the walls, or done any cooking since last night. I don't get Hanni on infrared. Death cold."

"I can creepy-crawl the place," Poet said.

Mir shook his head. "Let's keep following the wreckage trail," he said. "Maybe we can find something salvageable."

Loki caught Poet's eye and grinned. "Officers," he said.

"It must've fallen from orbit," Black Bertold announced authoritatively across the surprisingly sturdy wooden table in the kitchen of the stone house.

"If they did that, they wouldn't have hit anywhere within kilometers of here," Starman said with a sneer. "The mathematics are all wrong."

"It hit damned hard," Stilicho said. "Must've gone skipping over the surface of the planet like a stone, the way it scattered wreckage all over Hell and everywhere."

"And not so much as a stale crust of bread to be recovered," Jovan said morosely.

Mir had kept them following the joyboat track and it became painfully obvious, two and a half klicks beyond the abandoned farmhouse, that craft and contents were destroyed beyond retrieval. By that time the shadows were getting long, the presunset breeze beginning to freshen. To fortify the morale of men stunned by the loss of their comrades—and their only known source of food beyond the rations they carried on their backs—he had ordered a return to the autoc dwelling for the night.

Or maybe he wanted to shore up his own shaken spirit with walls of grey smooth stone.

The house was surprisingly large, with an airy feeling to the spaces inside despite solid construction. Rook chairs resembled sawhorses swaybacked to fit the curve of Rook bodies when they sat straddling them, some padded comfortably and covered with durable tanned hide, others just bare wood, polished to gloss by body oils and the friction of feathered keels and bellies. If you turned either kind sideways, it made a passable stool. Several actual three-legged wooden stools had been found in the kitchen. Those who didn't have them sat cross-legged in the dried streambank reeds that covered the floor.

"Maybe the throttle got stuck open," Starman suggested. "Maybe the butt-boy Kosmos jock panicked and drove right into the planet to escape the Strahn. The mechanics are all wrong for a free fall from orbit."

"Have you done them? Or are you just blowing smoke out that black ass of yours?" Bertold said.

Light from the single oil lantern, turned low, that sat in the table's center gleamed off the balls of Starman's eyes. "I may blow smoke out my ass," he said, "but you shit through the mouth, soldier-boy."

Bertold jumped to his feet, knocking his stool over behind. "You can't talk that way to me, convict!"

Starman's response was a diving tackle that took Bertold around the knees and brought both men thudding to the floor, which was some kind of stabilized mud or earth beneath the reeds. Bertold was a touch taller than Starman and more heavily built, but Starman had the wiry strength and energy of fury so long in building it could never be discharged to compensate. They rolled over and over among the reeds, gouging and kneeing.

Scrubs jumped up and away from the table, staring at the battle with wide frightened eyes. "Kill the pute," Jovan suggested without heat. "He's starting to talk like that zong Kobolev."

"Which one?" asked Loki, sitting by one wall with his knees drawn up chewing on a dry reed. Big Bori hulked beside him, head lolled on one broad shoulder, snoring and drooling over his collar.

"Bertold," Jovan said. "Sodding cog-dog thinks he's better than the rest of us deathbirds. Whereas he's neck-deep in the same shit as the rest of us."

"True," Loki said, nodding. He tilted back his head and pitched his voice to ring like a trumpet. "The course of duty's clear, Brother Starman, and I can only trust you to act in full accordance with the Universal Will!"

Junior Lieutenant Mir appeared in the doorway, apparently drawn by the sounds of strife. Loki flicked his pale eyes to the young officer. The other ten or so men crammed into the spacious kitchen never looked away from the rolling, cursing tangle of limbs on the floor.

The young officer's mouth dropped open in a look of surprise. He started forward. Loki began to hum tunelessly to himself.

From beside the table Kyov rose and moved to intercept the lieutenant. "Sir," he said quietly, "perhaps we should make the rounds of the place, make sure the sentries are alert and everyone else has settled in."

Looking past the sergeant's shoulder, Mir saw Starman catch Bertold by his black-bearded chin and rap his head sharply against the corner of the square brick oven jutting from one wall. Bertold sagged. Starman got a better grip on his head and began to pound it against the oven in earnest. The spectators set up a rhythmic stomping in time.

"Sir—" Kyov said.

Mir made a mouth and, yielding to the soft pressure of Kyov's eyes, turned away. *He won't* really *kill him,* he told himself. *It's the Tradition.*

With Kyov in tow he wandered back through the house. Most of it was two big open chambers that ran the length of the main structure and were separated by a bearing wall of dressed stone. He knew a little about engineering, enough to be impressed by the span of the ceiling; it was well supported by wooden posts, peeled, polished, and oiled, with buttresses springing like branches from the tops of them. The two chambers were furnished with rows of what the lieutenant could only think of as nests, ranging from mere bowl-shaped heaps of feather-filled cushions and straw at one end of each room to cushioned shallow baskets at the other. There were a few chairs, and tall wardrobelike cabinets along the walls.

No passageways communicated between the dormitories; they might have been two different buildings. Both had doors which opened directly to the large kitchen, however. Mir theorized that however the occupants had been segregated—by sex?—they must be allowed to socialize in the kitchen. Where, presumably, they could readily be monitored by seniors.

The floor was thickly strewn with reeds that crunched underfoot as Mir and Kyov walked through. The reeds were dried but clean, apparently fresh. Though the dorms were well ventilated—through windows which were narrow, set high in the walls, and equipped with massive wood shutters, all of which seemed to indicate the thickness of the walls wasn't just a structural consideration—the air was thick with a strange, rather sour smell. At first the Landers had complained of the stink. Now those men who weren't on watch or gathered for the kitchen bull session were sacked out in the Rooks' nests, snoring peacefully, and Mir realized he himself had grown rather accustomed to the odor. *It's really not unpleasant at all,* he thought, *once your nose gets over the shock.*

The place looked as if a whirlwind had been through it: those cribs which weren't occupied were overturned, and feathers from cut-open cushions lay everywhere like particolor snow. A rumor had started among the men that the Rooks used gold currency. Such was among the most precious forms of *klad*—highly portable, highly concealable, highly concentrated wealth. Wealth which it meant death to possess, of course—much that mattered in CLD.

Out on the stone steps before the house Poet sat, while above him clouds mustered like a hostile army. He had taken the bandages off his forearm and by the light of a rising fingernail moon was examining the barely scabbed-over wounds he had made.

"Sutt, you son of a bitch," he was murmuring to himself. "Why'd you have to go and get yourself scragged?"

Mir started to touch him on the shoulder, thought better of it. Sutt had been senior sergeant in charge of Second Squad of Section Two.

"You mourn his loss?" Mir said, surprised to find Poet grieving, and over a noncom at that.

Poet looked up at him with wide innocent eyes. "Pute owed me a twelve-pack of Zone hypes!"

"I . . . see," the lieutenant said. He moved on.

The guards were settled into four holes dug around the farmhouse, ten meters out. Kobolev and Eyrikson were walking perimeter watch. Mir did his best to make sure everyone was awake and alert.

Coming back to the house he skirted a single-story room that stuck off from the kitchen like the leg of a gamma. Its only communication with the outer world were those high, narrow firing–slit windows; a heavy door, solidly bound in rare iron, gave onto the kitchen. The stout lock had been left undone when the occupants fled, presumably in the wake of the terrifying joyboat crash.

Inside, the room was comfortably enough furnished with wickerwork nest-beds, chairs, and a wardrobe. The Landers had dubbed it "the Slammer" and generously ceded it to Mir. Mir found it hard to believe a structure housing what he took for a little over two dozen occupants would actually need a dedicated jail, and the annex was far more comfortable than any cell *he* had ever occupied, but he couldn't say what other purpose it might have served.

Down at the kitchen end of the house the White Rat was hunkered down examining a mound of some lumpy white substance, a meter and a half high, that was slumped against the wall. "I tell you," he said, "they just hang their feathered butts out the window and let fly."

Gollob and Sturz were his audience. They looked at each other. "You're kidding," Gollob said. The Rat was safe to talk to.

The albino gestured up at the narrow window that let into the wall just below the roof. A flat board jutted out from it with a triangle brace at either end, like a perch. The stone beneath it was streaked with long vertical blotches of white.

Mir was becoming aware of a stark ammoniacal smell, like the general aroma of the house, but . . . more so. Sturz waved his hand before his nose. "Sure smells bad," he said.

"Of course it does," the White Rat announced. "It's shit."

"Why would they shit by the *kitchen?*" Gollob asked in disgusted disbelief.

The Rat shrugged. "They're autocs. Who can say why they do anything? Autocs're all zerk. *You'll* see."

Gollob elevated his snub nose. "I don't see why they fight us," he said. "They should be grateful we're bringing them into accord with Universal Will."

The White Rat laughed.

Mir and Kyov circled back around to the porch. Poet had vanished. They reentered the house on the right-hand side. A ladder next to the kitchen door led up; they climbed.

A spacious loft or attic ran the length of the house beneath the steeply pitched roof. In it the two found Lennart, sitting folded into the window with the perch, his sniper-Bitch cradled, playing with the thick-armed wooden cross he wore about his neck. He was keeping a watch out over the shadowed countryside, lips moving in silent prayer.

Lennart came from Palme, Poet's homeworld, but from a jerkwater agro district inhabited by Christian zealots. It was not illegal to be a Christian in the Stellar Collective, at the moment. It was merely safer not to be. Mir considered telling him what that particular window appeared to have been used for, decided against it.

The roof pitch was so pronounced that the lieutenant was able to walk upright the length of the farmhouse. The loft was furnished with a desk and chairs, a cabinet of pigeonholes into which documents of thick fibrous tan paper, rolled and tied with different-colored ribbons, had been tucked. These lay partially unrolled and strewn across the reed-covered floor like fallen leaves. The Landers had also thoroughly ransacked this place in search of valuables: jewelry, coins of precious metal, trinkets which might be swapped for drugs or favors. Mir's lips tightened at the vandalism. The Landers, him included, had no grasp of what these bird-beings might find precious. But the Landers had a DNA-level sense of what their fellow Coggies would value, back in the Collective.

He wondered what they might have found. He'd never find out, he knew.

At the far window Ovanidze squatted like a gargoyle over his communications gear. He had a long wire strung to a tent stake hammered into the farmyard below for an antenna, and was making adjustments to his set with the cover off.

"Anything?" Mir asked.

The technician shook his head. "A signal would have to be damned strong, to punch through the interference." He gestured out at the dense overcast. "Wasn't for the clouds, you'd see a hell of an auroral display. There's a *major* solar storm in progress."

"Any idea how long it'll last?"

Ovanidze shrugged. "Just between you and me and these stone walls, Junior Lieutenant, the Big Circuits neglected to file-dump me the specs for the primary, or how far we are from it. Just on the basis of how big and yellow the sun looks, I'd guess it's got a rotation of upwards of twenty-eight Universal days—maybe twenty-six of these outsize Rookery days. An outburst like this is usually caused by something localized, sunspots or a coronal hole. If that's true, somewhere within a half a rotation period the trouble spot will rotate around to the other side, so things might—*might*, if this overloaded chain of speculation doesn't give out on me—break in a fortnight or so."

Mir's heart weighed like a cannonball in his chest. "And till then we have no chance of communicating with our comrades?"

"Not unless they're close, or have a powerful transmitter. That's assuming, Junior Lieutenant, that there *are* any comrades on this world." He peered closely at Mir. "What if we're the only ones to reach the dirt alive?"

Mir sucked in a deep breath, charged with ozone. A sense of isolation beat down upon his shoulders like truncheons.

"I can't think that," he said. "Keep trying."

11

ALBREKHT MIR HEARD a door open—by hand; he preferred it so—and turned from the guardrail of the great house he had built on coming to this world.

His wife stepped onto the balcony. She stopped. For a moment they simply stood gazing at each other, with the mauve and old gold light of sunset tinting clothes and faces, and the warm sweet wind up out of the Nin Valley filling their nostrils.

Natalya Mir had been a highly placed Values official in her own right. As executive producer for CommuNews, the Values-run Communal News Network, she exercised a degree of control over the District's popular media—simcast, text, and voice—exceeded only by her husband's. And Albrekht Mir's involvement ran more to policy guidance than hands-on direction.

She had known power of her own, and suffered accordingly. The details were unknown to him; they had been arrested separately and denied all knowledge of each other's fates. Until his agent had reported locating her, he had not known whether his wife was even alive.

She was a tall woman, and Mir was pleased to note her suffering had not bowed her. Indeed, Natalya Mir stood straighter than he ever remembered seeing her stand, and her blue eyes seemed to glow more brightly, even against the confinement pallor of her face.

In recent years Natalya had been gaining weight, particularly in the hips and legs. Perhaps Mir had as well. Imprisonment had reduced both to essentials. Natalya's fine cheekbones seemed to threaten to cut through her facial skin like blades.

She came to him, then, all in a rush. They clung to each other till ribs creaked and shoulders twinged, while the white sun slipped behind a bank of deep purple cloud and was gone. She smelled pleasantly but powerfully of soap, as if she had just come from a shower.

Tree-climbing arthropods in the branches of lordly slim bilondras tried experimental trills up and down the scale. The DVS's official residence was of semisubterranean design, half-sunk into the crest of a hill looking south over the rich bottomland to either side of the Resistencia River. Its clifflike southern face was three stories of local wood, hand-shaped and fitted, and rammed yellow-earth blocks. The balcony where they stood, outside the master bedroom, was at the highest level. A security risk, Mir now recognized; hostile parties could simply walk across the hilltop-level garden terrace that roofed the dwelling and let themselves down over the overhang. He wondered, without much real curiosity, how he could have committed such an oversight.

He found himself stroking Natalya's hair. Once long and radiant blond, it was now a silvery near-white plush. He could not describe the reasons for the act to himself, and that disturbed him; he had left physical desire behind, on some gleaming alloy table with a drain at one end, and affection seemed trivial now. He had thought that during the empty captive hours he had scoured every square micron of his soul's topography. To find unexplained impulses, then, was an unwelcome surprise.

There are always surprises, he reminded himself. He smiled bleakly. *That should have been the very first lesson of my captivity.*

She stepped away from him, smiled, reached up to touch his eyebrow, feather-soft, then run her fingers down to limn the gauntness of his face.

"I feared for you, Albrekht," she said, voice husky with emotion. "Almost as much as I feared for our children."

He nodded, slowly, hoping she would take that as acknowledging the community of their fears.

She moistened her lips. "Our children," she said. "What— do you know what's become of Haakon and Yirina?"

He drew a breath down to his diaphragm. "Yirina is dead."

Natalya closed her eyes and turned from him. She paced slowly to the rail, placed her hands on the smooth, polished wood, gazed out into gathering violet night.

"It's for the best," she said at last.

Albrekht Mir nodded. Yirina had been the point of attack. The most that could be hoped for her, after she was taken up on false treason charges, was that her death come as soon as possible. This had come to pass, so Mir had learned through . . . discussions . . . with certain of his former captors. Whether by clumsy accident, design, or an undiagnosed weakness of the heart—sometimes these things slipped through, even with the medical procedures available to families with the Mirs' Service—Yirina Mir had died early under interrogation. Stories differed as to exactly why, but it was clear that, while she had suffered greatly, she had not suffered long.

And, indeed, that was best.

Only at the beginning of his reborn life had Mir participated directly in the processing of his rivals. The Santander District vice-minister for Communal Values—the Ministry's chief administrator, and Mir's nominal superior—had taught Mir an invaluable lesson in that regard. Watching him, Mir had discovered that he could witness his enemies' pain and remain unmoved, feeling neither pleasure nor disgust, triumph nor pity. It was a great liberation—or in the currently approved jargon, a Realization.

On the instant of revelation Mir had borrowed a pulser-pistol from a Shadow guard and bolted the vice-minister through the eye. Then he turned, tossed the weapon back to the guard, and strode from the room, leaving without a glance at the man who had destroyed his family and sought to destroy him, lying there with his brain, expanded by the water in its cells being turned to steam, sticking from his ruptured skull like cauliflower, and electrodes still pumping current to his dead genitals.

That the interrogations continue was required by the need for information and security; security likewise mandated the systematic liquidation of his foes. It was not for the new Albrekht Mir to reprise the singular fatal error committed by

Jochen Stahl. Henceforth, however, he would leave such matters to the professionals.

Perhaps unconsciously, Natalya Mir was scrubbing the fingertips which had brushed her husband's face with her other hand. "And Haakon?" she asked.

"Sentenced to the Collective Landing Detachment."

Relief and dread rippled across her face like shock waves. "Detached?" she whispered. Like most Dependents she had a vague understanding from the popular media—which in Santander District she and her husband largely controlled—of what CLD was about, and the terrible toll exacted by the realism of their test-to-destruction training program.

She could not know the full details; and Mir was glad, for it would have made her more emotional still. He himself had only begun to grasp the true enormity of what it meant to be *Detached* when he set his new special executive to search for his lost children.

CLD existed, his man reported, to solve two problems: first, what to do with the huge number of offenders, political and criminal, generated by the Stellar Collective's mechanisms of social control: the rival secret police agencies run by Revo and his own Ministry; the Peace and Order Compliance Agents, as the Ministry for Justice's civilian police were known; the enforcement arms of dozens of lesser Ministries, each quick to assert its power and importance by claiming victims.

The second problem involved the military considerations of, how can you create an ultimate elite fighting force without a training program so rigorously realistic that it kills more applicants than it passes? And once you have such soldiers, what do you *do* with them? It was a fabulous waste of resources to leave them on the shelf after so much effort was expended on their training; yet combat, especially on the cutting edge of battle, rapidly ate them up. It was extravagantly expensive to use special shock troops. It was extravagantly expensive *not* to.

If not a perfect answer to that dilemma, the Collective Landing Detachment was at least an answer. It still cost the Collective a mighty chunk of resources to train a Lander. But no one cared how quickly convict scum might use them up. And there were always more.

That left, of course, the delicate issue of how you *controlled* such men. But that was what the Stellar Collective was about, after all: control. Gifted men such as Albrekht Mir, and gifted women such as Natalya, had devoted lifetimes to perfecting the art. So far it had worked; at least, Mir's man could find no record of large-scale revolt by Detached troops. But then, history was a highly plastic medium in the Collective, as a District Values supervisor knew better than any.

Natalya Mir did not grasp all of what CLD was about. But she knew enough to realize that her son had been consigned to Hell.

At least, for the moment, it was *living* Hell.

"Is he alive?" she asked, after visible self-struggle.

He nodded. "He survived the training camps." He refrained from sharing with her what the Landers called those camps.

"*Thank Process.*" Her shoulders slumped. For a moment he thought she would clutch him for support, but she did not.

"Beyond that, I've not been able to trace him. Yet."

Natalya Mir straightened her spine, squared her shoulders, drew back her head. "We have to *do* something, Albrekht. We have to get him out."

"That will not be easy. The Ministry for Struggle has small love for Values."

"Values has agents in the armed forces!"

"Indeed. We have agents everywhere." He shook his head. "But not even a District Values supervisor has access to many assets at that level."

She nodded, as if accepting a challenge. "Then we have to get that access. Whatever it takes! We've got to free Haakon— and take our revenge."

He nodded. "It will take power, my love."

Her eyes blazed up like beacons, and she stretched to kiss his cheek. "Albrekht! You've begun already."

"I have."

"I shall do my part. Never doubt that, my love." She was nodding, eyes no longer focused on him, already laying her own plan of attack.

It came to him that he had not seen her this animated since before they were married, when they were both idealistic activists, setting out to bring the cosmos into tune with Universal Truth and Will. *We became bureaucrats,* he thought, *comfortable and complacent. But no more. No more.*

He took her by the hands. "I rejoice to see you well and free, Natalya," he said. "But I must go. I've an appointment with my former case officer."

The term was a Values in-house euphemism for *torturer-in-chief*. Her smile was an acid-dipped blade, eyes fires of anticipation. "I won't keep you a second longer, my love," she said. "I understand completely."

She did not. But he did not choose to enlighten her.

12

THIS NIGHT WAS cooler than last. In the kitchen the Landers used wood from a pile behind the house to kindle a fire in the brick stove, which was in the corner near the heavy door to the Slammer, offset so the chimney wouldn't interfere with the crap perch. Sturz had found an apron, no different from what a human might wear, and put it on. It had taken threats of violence to prevent him from sweeping the dried reeds out the door with a straw broom. He was huddled about himself off to the side, grumbling from time to time about the smell.

As it tended to, the conversation had wandered into women and mired there like wheeled transport stuck in a marsh. Starman bragged. Loki dropped the odd elliptic hint of epic and Byzantine encounters. Jovan even forgot to think about food.

Bori was stacked in a corner playing with two dried seed-pods of some sort, which he was pretending were a man and a woman, filling in both halves of the conversation in a little boy voice. He was eager enough for sex when it was presented, and when the urge jumped on him it was wise to steer clear; but he had little use for abstract discussion of any sort. From across the room Henriks watched with a certain puffy-eyed resentment. When Bori played with toys, they clearly ran no risk of sharing the fate of Mr. Bun.

Sitting cross-legged on the reeds with his back to the Slammer door, Poet likewise ignored the conversation. He had little interest in women, and no more in men.

Sex had always been one of two things for him, or both: a source of discomfort, and a source of *klad*. He had managed to keep himself alive for a time, after Gran was taken, by selling whatever aperture or appendage anyone was willing to buy on the rain-slick streets of Stavanger. He had been used by the elder larger boys at the official orphanage, after the authorities took him up; and when he finally fought back with a metal spoon he had swiped from the commissary and sharpened against cement walls, it was he who was punished for noncommunal behavior. Later, of course, when he got arrested for real, he had been raped repeatedly by his keepers, men and women, with a sort of impersonal brutality; it was an undocumented but universal, indeed, Universal policy, that nothing broke down the Particularity of any who might dare commit the crime of considering himself—or herself—to be an individual, like rape. That much had been the common lot of every man here, every Lander anywhere, male or female: there were female deathbirds, or rumored to be, though Poet had never seen one; few women currently served the Engine in combat capacities.

He occupied himself flattening his hand upon the floor and stabbing downward between the fingers with the tip of his hideout knife, in random pattern and with ever-increasing speed. His sensitive juvenile face had a pinched look, a warning to his seasoned mates not to approach him or try to include him in the general banter and horseplay, unless they were in a mood to face a genuinely homicidal onslaught.

Rain was coming, he knew by the smell. He hated the rain, the cold. It reminded him of nights sleeping under bridges in Palme's largest city, watching the rain dimple the black oily canals. It made him feel small, alone, lost.

Tick-tick-tick, went the knife tip ever faster, against the hard maroon surface beneath the reeds. Poet's expression never changed.

Bertold had not been killed. He was duly beaten to a bloody mass and rolled into the backyard. Starman, fine features puffed and lips swollen to greater than their usual size, sat at one end of the table with an air of quiet triumph.

The rain had come, and rustled like rats in the thatch overhead. With it had come lightning that periodically filled the room with blue glare from the high slitlike windows, and thunder like a 300mm rocket barrage. The sex talk had finally dwindled into edgy mutual-eyeballing silence. With the exception of the occasional rogue planetoid like Balt, intramural rape was uncommon in CLD, since lethal accidents were so easily come by. But there came a point where nobody was quite sure anymore.

At the far end of the table from Starman the Dancing-Master held forth. "It's clear we have an unprecedented opportunity spread out before us like a banquet. A veritable feast, I tell you."

Jovan scowled. "Mention 'banquets' again, and I'll give you that thumping you've long been hankering after."

"Ha," the Dancing-Master said, clearly not taking the lanky farm boy at his word. He still believed his former status counted for something now he was Detached. He had always taken himself quite seriously; and that was his problem. As an officer-instructor in History and Moral Philosophy at the Stellar Collective's most prestigious military academy, he had insisted on failing an obdurately lazy student, whose father, it developed, was a high official within the Ministry of Sharing. His head still spun at the rapidity with which he had been framed, convicted, and Detached for misappropriation of Collective resources. He had never yet regained his bearings, not really, and his pride was an unhealed wound.

He thumped fist on tabletop, making the lantern rock. "It's a glorious opportunity!"

"To do what?" Loki called from the corner. "Enlighten us with your superior wisdom."

"Very well," the Dancing-Master said. "You've all seen that the autocs have no way of hurting us in battle."

"They split Loki's head for him," Narva said in a voice like a rusty hinge, mushing his words. He had about three teeth left, and one of those was steel. Everyone turned to look; he was few-spoken, and none of the scrubs had heard him utter a word before. "And they made that young lad puke pretty brisk, though he may have survived, I misremember now."

The Oldest Living—Standard Narva—had been with the unit longer than anybody, longer than Kyov, even. He had long since given up trying to keep track of the new transfers. To his rheumy eyes they flashed by like meteorites. Only those who could hang on long enough to become ancients achieved any kind of reality for him.

"Yes, yes," the Dancing-Master said, with an air of humoring senile folly, "but they didn't do us any *lasting* harm."

"So what?" asked Bori, abruptly noticing a conversation going on without him and becoming truculent. "What's that got to do with anything?"

"Simply this," the Dancing-Master said, trying to hide his exasperation. "There's nothing to stop us conquering this world, if you think about it plainly."

Jovan cleaned prominent ears with his little finger, examined the tip for residue. "You must've had got your skull creased by a bullet this morning, too," he said. "That's crazy talk."

"Don't start talking crazy," Bori warned, "or I'll have to thump you."

"Will you *stop*, you great oaf?" the Dancing-Master cried. "You don't even understand what I'm talking about!"

Bori growled and began to rise. Loki grabbed his sleeve. "Wait until we hear what he has to say; *I* don't know what he's talking about either. After we find out, then we can thump him in perfect understanding."

Bori frowned—his understanding always fell far short of perfect—but he nodded heavily and sat down again. He trusted Loki, a situation which the smaller man flagrantly abused.

"It's simply this," the Dancing-Master said, relieved. Bori had the attention span of a gnat; the Dancing-Master was confident that by the time his disquisition was done the giant would have quite forgotten his intention to thump him. "Have you ever heard of a man named Cortez?"

Loki grinned. "Assume I have."

"For the benefit of you who might not be as erudite as the corporal, here," said the Dancing-Master, not to be denied a chance to lecture, "Cortez was an early colonialist, long ago on Earth—long before there was ever Lo drive, or spaceships of any kind, even."

"Like the Rooks are now," Dieter said.

"More or less, more or less. In any event, he conquered a great empire of native peoples—human autocs if you like— with only five hundred men."

"That's silly," Big Bori declared.

The Dancing-Master gave him a superior smirk. "And just why do you say that, Senior Lander?"

"Humans are humans and autocs are autocs," the giant said. "Everybody knows that."

The Dancing-Master's smirk got brittle and flaked away. "These weren't really autocs, they were *like* autocs. They had much less mature technology than Cortez and his men, and despite their numbers, Cortez conquered them."

He sat back and put hands on thighs, out of sight below the table. The fact that his hands were still gnarled and twisted from badly healed breaks made him self-conscious.

"That's my point, and even Bori ought to be able to see it: this world is *ours*. All we need do"—he extended a hand, shut it in a fist—"is reach out and *grab* it."

Loki shouted out a wild laugh. The Dancing-Master glared at him. "What do you find so funny, Corporal?" he asked in a low voice.

"You, Senior Sergeant, and if you call me a rank again instead of my name, I'll shove your own rank badges so far up your ass you'll taste them. Bori was right, in his own near-mindless way. It *is* silly."

The Dancing-Master's mouth tautened like a noose. "Display your superior erudition, then."

"With pleasure." Loki hitched his back up the raw stone wall. Overhead, rain began to sizzle in the thatch. "You forget an important detail, Dancing-Master, a small matter of the hundred and fifty thousand native allies Cortez talked into helping him. The empire you're talking about hadn't done such a very good job of making itself *popular,* you see."

He spread his hands. "Show me a hundred kay of birds willing to join us, and then I'll say you have a point. Till then"—he shrugged—"*I* say we've been left here to die, and die we shall, whether the birds get us, or starvation."

The Dancing-Master leapt to his feet and glared at Loki. "You have no understanding!" he said. He slammed his helmet onto his head and stamped out the side door into the rain. Loki's laughter followed him until the stout outer door closed on it.

"Is that really true?" Dieter asked. "What you said."

Loki raised a brow at him. "Would I lie to you?"

"Almost always."

"Another time I shall make you pay for that," said Loki, laughing—which the ancients knew did not negate the threat. "In this case I am telling truth in its most pristine form. Naturally such slugs as yourselves find it in your skimpy souls to doubt me, since you have no feel for truth."

Stilicho chuckled. "Imagine Loki, who hates all useless knowledge, coming up with something like that."

Loki sniffed and stuck his sharp fox nose in the air. "It proved quite useful," he said precisely. "It showed what a puffed-up fool the Dancing-Master is."

"*That's* something new and different."

The door opened. It was Balt, water running from helmet and rainslick. His assistant gunner stood quietly behind him, the heavy electro slung across his back.

"Had a nice trip behind the barracks, did we?" sang out Loki in a sweet voice.

"Get snaked."

"Ha! Unlike yourself, I have certain standards. I shall willingly plant my probe in women, men, autocs, and most animal forms, as circumstances and the stirrings of my personal Engine of History dictate."

Gollob covered his ears at the scurrilous reference to the Universal Army. Balt scowled. "What does that leave out?" he demanded. His voice had been well ruined by harsh reefer, raw barracks-brewed alk, and the occasional punch in the throat; it sounded like a collection of pebbles being shaken in a tin. Despite the rain and his recent scrubbing, the skin on his jowls was beginning to acquire a grey grime undertone.

"You, primarily."

Balt scowled more ferociously. His eyes flicked from lean Loki and his shadow Bori to Poet, still pecking his blade between his finger like a shorebird stabbing for bugs in the sand. Bori had subsided into snores, but Balt knew from bitter experience how quickly the giant could snap to roaring violent wakefulness.

Balt was a cruel man. Perhaps he was no more cruel than the members of the group someone had long ago dubbed the Usual Suspects, Loki, Poet, and the rest. But he was a bully, who saved his savagery for the meek. Unlike the Suspects, Balt counted the odds.

They were definitely against him now. He wasn't fool enough to count the new transfer he had battered into serving as his personal attendant and toy as a useful ally; any of the Suspects, including the deceptively soft-looking Poet, who was no larger than the new transfer, could swat little Hynkop like a gnat. If indeed the scrub would lift a hand to help Balt. Certainly he had made no moves to help himself, no matter how unreasonable his self-appointed master's commands. The ungrateful little pute would doubtless stand by and watch the Suspects carve their initials in Balt's cheeks.

That made Balt mad. He dealt Hynkop a resounding swat on top of his helmet. The boy rocked but said nothing, though his blue limpid eyes blurred behind water. Balt grunted and sat near the door to outside, as far as possible from Poet. The dark-haired youth was his least favorite of the Suspects, having burned all the skin off him with a brief broad-aperture burst from Little Sister when Balt pressured him to render the sort of services Hynkop was proving so delightfully pliant about. Balt had paid him back, dosing his rats with lye after returning to barracks from his own R&R stint. Since then they had hacked out a wary accommodation, which took the form of Balt avoiding Poet and Poet paying Balt no attention whatsoever.

The other scrubs stared at Balt great-eyed, as if he were a Kadfar tarkus which had just rolled its armored shell, brief temper, and powerful internal organic-chemical laser into the kitchen with them. With the possible exception of Gollob, they all knew what he was doing to Hynkop. It gave him a special horrified fascination for them.

"Wh-what did you get Detached for?" asked Florenz, his attempt to sound like a grizzled veteran spoiled when his voice cracked. "Are you Politically Unreliable?"

Balt turned a smoldering boar glare on him. Florenz went blue-pale beneath his freckles and flattened himself back against the wall. His fingertips scrabbled at the closely fitted grey stone behind, as if he were hoping to pull one free and slip through the hole if the veteran decided to leap on him and have his way with him.

"Is it Devolution?" the scrub piped. "Particularity? Even''—

he could barely bring himself to utter the word—"*Autarky?*"

In hopes of placating the veteran, Florenz had enumerated the worst sins he could conceive. In response Balt opened his mouthful of brown stumps and emitted a belch of laughter.

"Ha! *Politicals!* Runny smacks. I spit on the lot of them!" He did so, symbolically honking forth a glob of phlegm and depositing it in the reeds beside Hynkop. Green snot spattered the back of the transfer's hand. He didn't move.

"He's in," supplied Loki, "for murder."

"That's one thing," Balt said proudly, while the transfers tried still more fervently to become one with the walls.

He lowered his brows to glare at Florenz. A moment before the boy keeled over in a faint he switched his scrutiny to Henriks, Nau, the Geek, and the Fart-Smelling Man, each of whom quailed in turn. "Say," he rumbled, "what's the mortality rate in the Meatgrinder now?" *Meatgrinder* was the unaffectionate name by which any CLD training camp was known.

The scrubs looked from one to another. Unlike the Bold Originals, they had not come through together. "S-seventy-five percent," said Florenz.

The vets' heads all came around. "Seventy-*five*?" Jovan exclaimed. "That's next to nothing! We were at eighty-two."

"Eighty-five for us," Loki said.

Balt laughed again. "Coddled smacks," he said. "We were ninety."

"One wishes your class might have enjoyed a rate just a fraction higher," murmured Loki. Balt snapped an angry look at him, but clearly didn't quite get it. Loki showed him the blandest of smiles.

Kyov had slipped in quietly and stood with his back to the oven, steaming. He had been out checking the men on sentry-go; he could not stay inside dry and comfortable long knowing his men were out in the storm. His expression said his mind was light-years away—with his wife and daughters, perhaps, on Cienfuegos. In that he had been lucky. His stature in the community gave him a semblance of Service; his family had been spared when he was arrested.

Now he looked up. "They're getting desperate," he said softly.

Loki looked up at him, hands on thighs and ears coming to points. "Who? Speak plainly, old man!"

Kyov shook his head. "The Engine. The Stellar Collective. They despise us but they need us; and they burn us up like fuel alk. They lower the rigors of training when the Historic Process's hunger for our flesh and blood gets too great."

Even the veterans' mouths fell open: it was seldom anyone heard a word of anything but quiet encouragement from the Section sergeant. "No!" Gollob cried, struggling to his feet. "You can't mean that! The Stellar Collective would never do such things!"

A strange wild gleam came into Loki's eyes, and they turned almost white. "Don't you know?" he asked around an off-center smile. "Don't you know our living bodies form the pavement over which the Engine of History rolls to glory? Live the Collective!"

In a flicker he was on his feet. He seized Florenz, the nearest scrub, by the front of his battle dress. Though the transfer was at least five kilos heavier, he jerked him upright and slammed him against the wall.

"Sing!" Loki commanded. "All you scrubs, sing together: 'All Glory to the Stellar Collective!' Quickly, now! On your feet and *sing!*"

The new transfers gaped at the veteran, then scrambled upright. Standing to attention, holding arms stiffly by their sides, they began to sing in quavering voices:

> *"I live only for the Collective*
> *It is my flesh and blood—"*

while Loki conducted. The other ancients watched for a few moments, then turned away and began to converse in a mutter about the comparative merits of the operators in the field brothels they had known on Hovya, their last billet before the current assault.

Mir stood in the loft window at the far end from the latrine perch, boot on sill. The roof overhang kept the rain from him, but the chill air, thick as pudding with rain smell and the strange but pleasing scents of the Rookery, was like a bracing spray in his face.

Beside his foot Rouen sat with back to window frame and his sniper-Bitch propped nearby, studying the plowed fields and the woods beyond with his binoculars. After several intent moments he shook his head and lowered the glasses.

"Nobody out there," he said, as lightning lit his calm smooth face. "On IR, Birds ought to blaze like torches in this chill."

Mir worried a tag end of thumb cuticle with his teeth. "They should have pretty high metabolisms," he agreed. "But perhaps their feathers insulate them enough to mask their body heat. Or maybe they wear some kind of raincoats, to the same effect."

Rouen grunted and shrugged. He was a quiet, self-contained man, who went in little for officer baiting or the other boisterous pastimes traditionally favored by Landers. He had no greater interest in theory or abstraction than other deathbirds did, though.

He came from ranching stock on a world dominated by the environmentalist Ministry for Preservation. That Ministry held the spiritual descendants of the Gaians, ecoterrorists who came late to Jochen Stahl's New Red Army. Though never very powerful, Preservation was one of the most capricious blocs in the Collective, and still regarded every human—every sophont—but its own elite as cancer cells. As Rouen had discovered after he was caught poaching to feed his wife and children after a hard winter. They had been excised like diseased tissue before his eyes by Preservation Angels, the Ministry's paramilitaries. For some reason he had been spared to serve in CLD. If that was the word for it.

Mir felt a kinship with the quiet straight-haired sniper, by reason of shared rural background. It was multiply absurd, and he knew it; he would never dare hint at it to the man, for fear of ridicule—or, more likely and maybe worse, a flat stare of incomprehension. Mir liked to feel himself in tune with the land and peasant life—the most noble lifestyle short of Universal Realization, when all thinking life-forms could resume the hunting-gathering ways Nature intended them for—on account of having spent his boyhood summers on farms on Novy

Utrecht and Santander. A foolish affectation, he understood that, but he couldn't shake it.

Again the lightning fragmented the sky, briefly forming across the clouds a triple cross that hung in the eye as purple after the yellow flash subsided. Rouen chuckled softly. "Good thing Lennart didn't see that," he said. "He'd call it a miracle, sure."

"The lightning here is incredible," Mir said.

Rouen nodded, having delivered himself of more speech than usual. After a few moments Mir said. "It's beautiful here. Maybe this world is our death trap, but I don't think I've ever seen a lovelier place."

Rouen shrugged and rested his head against the weathered wood of the window frame. "Just as soon be home," he said.

A joyless laugh pushed up from the lieutenant's throat. "There's that," he said.

The kitchen door opened, admitting a gush of chill air and rain smell. The Dancing-Master clomped in. He shut the door and started to take off his rainslick.

Moving with surprising speed for his bulk and usual lethargy, Big Bori came off the floor, flowing to the Dancing-Master's side. Before the senior sergeant could do more than widen his eyes in a startled stare, Bori raised a giant hand and slammed it down on the top of his helmet.

The Dancing-Master went straight down in a steaming gleaming heap. "I promised I'd thump you later," he said, massaging his hand with the other.

"Yes," said Loki, who had tired of playing bandmaster and resumed his seat cross-legged on the reeds, "but do you recall *why* you were going to thump him?"

Bori's bushy brows pressed forward and downward until his eyes almost disappeared from the exertion of thought. The ancients leaned subtly forward in happy anticipation. When he tried to think Big Bori often got frustrated, and when he got frustrated, he got angry. Even sly Loki sometimes overplayed his hand with the behemoth, and on those occasions *he* got thumped. Even Poet and Starman looked forward to *that*.

Bori's huge face lit abruptly as a star shell in a night sky. "I know!" he exclaimed in an almost childlike voice. "I know why I was going to thump him!"

He looked happily around at the expectant faces. "I thumped him because I *promised* I would." He beamed. "I got to keep my promises, don't I?"

He looked around the room. No one said anything. His face began to fist up again, until Dieter elbowed Nau in the ribs.

"Yes, Senior Lander!" the transfer piped. "One must always keep one's promises!"

Bori smiled and nodded. "That's right," he said. "I'm a *good* boy." And he sat back down.

In his corner Poet's knife hand was a blur. The knife tip made stitching sounds on the now-pocked floor.

Suddenly he stopped, raised his outstretched hand. Blood beaded from a cut in the web between index and middle fingers. Without changing expression he put hand to mouth, licked the blood away, then turned his hand to suck on the cut.

The rain, blown horizontal by the rising wind, began to slap the walls with tiny fists. To Poet it felt as if it were beating against his adolescent back through the fabric of a windbreaker since grown several sizes too small, which his grandmother had given him for a birthday before his parents died.

A single tear rolled down his right cheek. *My gran loved me.* Taking his hand from his mouth, he transferred the knife to it. Then he splayed his other hand on the floor and began the game again.

13

IN THE MORNING, as they were filing north away from the farmhouse, a warning crackled in their headsets from keen-eyed Starman, who was keeping watch from the loft until Section was safely clear.

"Riders," he reported. The noise from the sun was a constant fat-frying sizzle in their earphones, but at least they could communicate at tactical ranges. "They just came out of the trees a klick south. Six of them."

Mir circled a forefinger in the air. The men began to scatter, stumbling a little on the plowed rows, which were now slippery-soft mud. Overhead the sky was mostly clear, still darkening from dawn's lemon yellow. Wisps of mist still hung out in low places and among the trees by the farmhouse. Flights of small yellow birds bobbed past as the Landers deployed into perimeter.

"Have they spotted us, Starman?" he asked.

"Oh, yeah. Bet to it."

No point dropping the men on their bellies in the muck if it's not necessary. The lieutenant signed for the men to drop to one knee with weapons ready.

"Can you discourage them?" he asked over his communicator—an exclusive channel to the sniper that the others couldn't tune to; no use causing dismay if the answer was for some reason negative.

Starman chuckled. "Does the Direktor make her lovers pee in her mouth?"

The stone farmhouse blocked Mir's view of the orchard from which the Rook cavalry had emerged. He moved laterally to get a look at them. He had just spotted the riders, their usual gorgeous plumage dark-cloaked, if only by haze and distance, when he heard the *hiss-snap* of a needle leaving the thick-housed barrel of the electro, driven to hypersonic velocity by a magnetic impulse.

One of the riders slipped to the ground. Its slant-backed mount bolted, dragging the fallen Rook behind. A few heartbeats, and Mir thought he heard a thin cry drift up the still-moist air.

A riding beast reared, clawing air with its talons. Another whispering crack from the Bitch, and its rider rolled backward *right now* over its tuft-tailed croup. At this range it took the 2mm projectile a tenth of a second to reach its target.

The other Rooks turned their mounts and sent them racing into the woods, spurred by the backward-facing hind toes of their own large-clawed feet. The Landers hurled catcalls after them.

"I've lost them off infrared among the trees," Starman reported in a few moments. "When last seen, they were headed in the right direction in a hell of a hurry."

"Good enough, Starman. Catch us up. Section, move out, and stay alert."

He caught corner-eyed some of the veterans giving him glances ranging from annoyance to something a lot like pity, as if to say, "We're all alone and neck-deep in shit on a hostile world. What *else* are we gonna do?"

I'm still on sufferance here, he realized, with the slight jolt that thought always brought along. *This is the third world I've led Section into combat on—in half a Universal year!—but I'm still an officer. And that means* enemy *to these men.*

As the saffron sun rose and the day grew warmer and the last of the mist burned out of the hollows the hills seemed to grow progressively higher around them. The impression was confirmed by the overhead imaging and maps loaded into Mir's tac display. They were not quite wandering at random through the wilderness—though "wilderness" wasn't truly applicable; even the uncultivated areas had a neat, mannerly appearance, and Mir could not quite guess whether it was managed by the autocs or merely another facet of the planet's pleasant nature. The TD showed a city about a hundred kilometers north-northwest, whose symbol indicating it fell in the 100–250K population range. By a quick comparison with the map of the large northern continent on which they'd been dropped, and then the world at large, Mir saw that made it a substantial hub; the Rookery's very biggest cities held fewer than five million. It was surrounded by farmland, and tiny villages like an unruly swarm of moons. Mir was startled to note, as he wound the map back down through the levels of scale, that the farmhouse they'd just left was marked with the symbol for a collective farm, not an autarkic freehold.

It made sense to him that Section had been landed as part of a general effort to isolate and seize the city. It lay on a large river, at the hub of a road network. In the, at least presumed, absence of more traditional military targets—fixed planetary-defense installations, giant rail or other transport yards, major communications nodes, factories—it seemed the only strategic center in the area. Unless, of course, the Engine of History had simply scattered its troops at random like handfuls of birdseed—which Mir was forced to acknowledge, with a rueful grin and headshake, was a real possibility.

His plan was to make for the city, designated *Tse*-745, while avoiding lesser settlements as much as possible. He would work on the assumption that whatever troops had actually landed in this region would make for it as the most obvious rally point. There were holes in that supposition he could have navigated the *Beria* through all by himself. But he didn't see that he had anything else to go on, at least until the solar storms subsided and Ovanidze could find him some friendlies.

As the hills rumbled up like disordered bedclothes around them, they marched into a zone of fewer farms and more grazing land. They began to encounter herds of four-legged grazers with muted, mottled plumage. Through glasses they were seen to have broad rounded bills for cropping the yellow ground cover mat. They seemed acutely attuned to intruders, bolting whenever humans came within half a kilometer.

Several times the Landers spotted herders accompanying the flocks. These were generally smaller and drabber than the soldiers they had fought the day before, which provoked a certain desultory debate among the few men who cared as to whether they might be juveniles or females. They always seemed to be alone, and fled at sight of the alien invaders.

"We should be careful," said Rouen, the erstwhile rancher. "They aren't driving the herds to new pasture, just keeping an eye on them. They bother doing that, means there's something to look out *for*."

"Like what?" asked Nau.

"Predators," the sniper said. "Or raiders."

"If the autoc armies can't touch us," Dieter said, "why worry about bad animals? We're safe as if we were at home in bed with some nice fresh smack."

"Safer," Loki announced. "I was myself in bed with three of the little darlings at the very moment when Revo kicked in the door. The girls fought like tigers to keep me from being taken, of course, but all in vain."

"I thought you got busted for punching a planetary marshal in the snout," said Dieter, hitching at the strap of his flamer pack.

"Or pinching his brandy," Jovan said.

"Or pinching his mistress's rat card," said Ovanidze.

"I thought you were Detached for spreading counterrevolution," Starman said.

Stilicho chuckled. "Looks like you need to keep your lies in a line, Loki."

Loki sniffed. "I decline to keep anything straight, except of course my lordly wanker, which maintains a constant state of quivering rigidity. A genius is never appreciated by the fools who surround him."

"Har-har-har-ha!" bellowed Bori, so loudly the scrubs ducked their heads down into their tunics.

"Shut your mouth, you huge oaf!' the Dancing-Master hissed. "You'll bring the whole country down on our necks."

Ignoring him, Bori kept laughing at full bore, as if Loki's quip was the funniest thing he ever heard. Then the mirth storm ceased, and he blinked at the smaller, slimmer man.

"*Which* fools, Loki?" he asked.

"Lean close," Loki said, "and I'll whisper the name of the foremost."

The giant bent down. "*You!*" Loki screamed so piercingly

that Bori jumped straight in the air and fell down hard on his rump.

He came up roaring wrath and swiped both-armed at Loki, who scuttled away venting loon-hoots of laughter. The giant gave chase. Loki ducked behind Eyrikson. Big Bori blundered into him headlong.

"Watch where you're going, you lump of ling shit!" Eyrikson yelled. He pushed Bori on the chest. At almost two meters himself, he wasn't two handspans shorter than the monster.

Bori stopped. His eyes focused on Eyrikson. His right hand ripped around in a haymaker that took the scrub beneath the sweep of the helmet and dropped him as if he'd been shot.

"So much for you!" he bellowed. Glaring around, he saw van Dam standing several paces behind his stricken comrade. Forgetting his grievance against Loki, Bori advanced on the Bold Original with fists upraised. "Do you want some too, you limp-dick zong? I've plenty to go around!"

Van Dam went pale and brought up his pulser. "Get back, you fucking ape," he snarled, face pale as sun-bleached bone. "Or I'll burn you where you stand!"

Abruptly Kyov was standing between them. "Fun's fun, Bori," the sergeant said, ignoring the fact that the Bold Original's weapon was practically prodding him in the ribs. "But don't you think you should settle down now?"

Bori blinked again, then slowly nodded. "If you say so, Kyov." He shambled off to his place in line.

"What do you mean pushing in like that, old man?" yelled van Dam. His face shaded down from white to mottled purple.

From behind him in line the White Rat cackled. Van Dam spun and glared at him. He noticed that the albino already had his pulser trained on him, as if accidentally, and wisely refrained from trying to bring his own to bear.

"Don't you know what Kyov has done?" the master scavenger asked. "Saved your useless life for you, is all."

"I'd have shot him!" van Dam shouted. "I would."

The Rat laughed. "Your first blue bolt would've spent itself on Bori's battle dress," Starman called. "The second would have been delivered by Bori's own finger, after he rammed the barrel a handspan up your ass. Saw him do it myself once, to a marine on Zwed."

"Hamjad," Loki said. He had stood by watching the whole show.

"Zwed, I tell you. I remember as if it was yesterday."

"All that background radiation on your homeworld addled more than your genes, then."

The Rat snarled and showed his big yellow incisors. Loki sneered. It meant nothing; the White Rat was nonviolent, and Loki seldom imposed on anybody that useful.

Black Bertold, the Originals' squad leader, had given the skirmish no more than a disinterested glance. Corporal Geydar, his second, looked studiously everywhere else. Kobolev came up to his brud, patted him on the shoulders and spoke a few low-voiced words to him. Then they assisted a logy Eyrikson to his feet.

They had to hustle to catch up to Section, which just kept walking.

The little bit of byplay with Eyrikson and van Dam occurred just as Mir was about to call a rest break. He decided against it; if the men had that much energy, it might be best to let them walk it off. As they crested a soft shoulder of hill rise and started downslope, skirting one of the dense stands of dark orange–leafed brush with maroon branches that filled the hollows between hills, he kept waiting for Kyov to drop one of his hints—so subtle that the touchiest junior lieutenant freshminted from a military *Akademiya* could take no offense— that it was time to fall the men out. None came, and as they splashed through a little stream Mir realized his action in delaying break had been approved. The fact pleased him absurdly.

An hour or so later they came to a thick wood, amber and pale orange. Mir called a break just below the crest of a ridge five hundred meters short of the forest. He put Starman and Poet, respectively the sharpest eye in Section and the most paranoid, belly down on the ridgetop to keep watch, and ordered dry "sustenance" rat bars broken up and distributed, one quarter per man.

Issuing the rats provoked another round of the ongoing debate as to whether the suss bars consisted of recycled Engine Regular boots, the processed bodies of Detachment dead, or densely compacted sewage from Realized alien worlds. The bars were a near-black brown in which some claimed to see red or purple highlights and others green. The Engine of History claimed that they were highly nutritive, and would not melt under any environmental conditions of heat or moisture. They might have added not in any human mouth or stomach, either; the only way to avoid having them go right through you like so many potsherds was to break off a tiny fragment, pop it in your mouth, and let your teeth and saliva gradually erode it. Which, however, gave a man something to concentrate on besides the hunger gnawing in his belly. It was the sort of Engine policy which Mir could never decide was idiot savantry, or just idiocy.

Loki sat on a torso-sized knob of weathered stone and opened the fly of his pants. His penis, flaccid and uncut, was not altogether proportional to his skinny body. "Don't wave that thing about," Stilicho said. "You'll frighten the new transfers."

"They may as well grow accustomed to its splendor," Loki said, prodding at the bush around its base, "since they might become more intimately acquainted with it if we're not rescued soon." As he spoke the member in question stirred and lifted slightly, causing the scrubs to back off in a hurry.

But Loki wasn't interested in any trips behind the barracks just now. He was examining the tiny red welts clustered around the base of his storied personal Engine of History. "I'm well chewed," he observed. "Puts me in mind of a certain red-haired lady official back on Primus . . . but I digress. The Rooks' nests are well tenanted with fleas, it seems."

"Tell us about it," Balt said, scratching under his arms.

Starman laughed. "Any bug that bites Balt is only poisoning itself."

Balt glared darkly at him. "For once it's not just Balt," Loki announced. He held up a tiny black speck between thumb and forefinger. "All my black travelers have up and died as well."

"No shit?" asked Jovan. He had his hand down the front of his own trousers, scratching away.

"None besides that between your toes and between your unwashed ears, pig farmer," Loki said. "You see? We have this world by the proverbial balls, my brothers. Even the lice can't touch us!''

Mir chewed the inside of his lower lip. ''You too, Loki? Last night I heard you being the voice of caution.''

Loki flicked the dead parasite imperiously away. ''That was last night. Today I am filled with a grand confidence. Consistency is for the drabs in the Ministries—and not even them, the way 'Universal Will' changes like the wind!''

''You can't say that—'' Gollob shrilled.

''Shut up,'' Loki said unemotionally. He made no move to enforce his command. He was already bored with banging on Gollob for his incessant apologies.

''Junior Lieutenant,'' Ovanidze said excitedly. ''I've got something! Somebody's transmitting on Engine freaks, not twenty klicks away!''

14

"CAN YOU MAKE it out?" Mir asked, trying to keep his voice from cracking like a new transfer's.

Ovanidze shook his head. "Scrambled," he said. "Security. But it's a company-level freak, and they *sound* excited."

"Let's load up and go," Mir commanded. "We can eat on the march." Which they would have done in any event, as long as it took to chew even the minute fragments of suss-bar he'd issued.

The men were already up, chattering with nervous energy. That they might be trapped all alone on a hostile world was grinding them more than anyone would admit. The prospect of contact with fellow humans—even a mere handful, as castaway as themselves—hit like a jolt of Zone.

Narva was having trouble getting his ancient joints to respond. Stilicho and Jovan motioned several scrubs over to them, turned them bodily around and began stuffing excess baggage from the ancient's packs into theirs.

Round-faced Chyz pulled away. "Hey! Why do we have to hump this?"

Without changing expression Stilicho punched him overhand in the face. He sat down hard, his hand to his nose, with blood pooling in the palm and running down the heel. Jovan continued sticking shitcans—the stubby cylindrical power cells that fueled most of their small arms—into his ruck.

Chyz shook blood from his hand, shook his head, struggled

to his feet. "Why?" he persisted. "You wouldn't do that for us!"

Stilicho gave him a bland yellow look. For a moment it seemed he would strike Chyz again, and the boy visibly fought the urge to cringe. Then Stilicho frowned.

"Of course we wouldn't, Wank-master. If you couldn't keep up, we'd shoot you."

The boy looked as though Stilicho had slapped him again. "But I thought Landers didn't kill each other!" Belief in the sanctity of the clandestine Traditions of CLD had helped pull him through the Meatgrinder. Now his worldview was getting kicked apart again.

"But *never leave a man behind* takes precedence," the older man said, not unkindly. "We can't carry you with us if you can't move under your own power, and there's no dustoff on this world, don't you see?"

"Better that way," Jovan said. "No telling what these Birds'd do to you if they caught you live. The shit these pre-Obs can come up with to *do* to a body—" He shivered.

"But don't worry," Stilicho said. "We'd leave you with an incendiary grenade in your hands. That way, when the autocs came to strip your body—*boom* and *whoom,* you're cremated, and you have an honor guard for your trip to Planet Hell."

The new transfer swallowed. He didn't look any too comforted. Nonetheless, the vets' forbearance in answering him with mouths instead of fists emboldened him.

"Then why do it for him?" he asked, gesturing to the old man, who stood placidly nearby, sucking his lips. His dentures, which were approximately as old and decrepit as he was, were stowed for safety in his pack. R&R technology was reasonably reliable, if not readily available to the masses, but his venerable gums were well beyond the point at which even Collective science could induce teeth to bud.

"We do it because we always have," Jovan said.

Stilicho shrugged. "He's one of us," he added. "He's a hundred years old. Gives the rest of us something to shoot for."

"A hundred?" Narva's hoot soared like a frightened bird from a bush. "I'm older than that. Oh, very much older!" And his laughter tumbled into turbulence in the form of diminuendoing cackles.

Chyz looked questioningly at Stilicho. The older man just shrugged: *Who's to say?*

The boy shouldered his now-heavier pack and took his place in line.

For the Collective Landing Detachment twenty klicks was an easy three-hour quick march—four, in this up-and-down terrain, but no more. Even the scrubs met the pace without difficulty. After all, if they couldn't quick-march under fifty-kilo rucks for twenty-four hours straight, falling out for ten every two hours, they'd have never survived their first month in the Grinder.

The radio signals grew louder as they closed the distance, but no more intelligible. The scramblers were built into the other units' communicators; the other troops could not have broadcast in the clear if they wanted to. Nor could Section. Lateral communication between units on the ground was considered a bad security risk—and also prejudicial to morale, in case one unit was getting stomped good and proper.

Which, Mir thought, was what it sounded like was happening to this one.

They were in a markedly hilly region now, dotted sometimes with stones with all the rough edges weathered away, ochers and ambers and rich shades of brown. Quick-marching up hill and down made thighs tremble and ache, but the sun warmed without stinging and the foreign scents quickened the air like spice.

Mir had Poet on point fifty meters ahead. Loki and Dieter walked flank, and Starman trailed. The sun had rolled halfway down the turquoise sky when Poet called back from a ridge covered in brush and a few trees: "I see them."

The men broke into a run. Mir called after them to be careful, so nervous that they might do something rash and so excited himself by the prospect of being rejoined to other humans that he forgot his full-Section circuit and simply yelled.

But survival was ground into the Landers' faces like mud from the first minute in the Meatgrinder—if not the first instant of the arrest that set them on the path to the Collective Landing Detachment. Even the thrill of knowing their isolation was almost over wasn't enough to overcome the imperative of *staying alive.* The column became a ragged surge up the slope, but well shy of the top the Landers flopped facedown in the orange-leafed brush and began to inch their way forward on their bellies, weapons advanced.

Something about the smell of the brush tickled Mir's nose with familiarity as resilient branches caressed his face. It reminded him of one of the spices his nanny used when she cooked lunch for him, away back on Novy Utrecht. She was a scaled autoc, warm-blooded, with mobile lips and huge purple eyes. His parents had been very busy indeed with their careers in Values, which of course superseded any desires they might have had to gratify their children's Particular yearnings for attention.

Tsatchka had been his heat source, her enfolding arms, the scales dry but softly pliant, his support; as Yirina, even more snub-nosed and blond than he, had been his playmate, confidante, coconspirator in youthful acts of Devolution for which the female autoc would sternly reprove and punish them, and then huggingly forgive.

He felt warmth on his right cheek. A tear; and a needle of fear stabbed through his gut. He was surrounded by hard men, unsentimental men, men whose souls were armored like hard-shelled dinosaurids on an early-evolution world—men who were constantly alert for any slight weakness in one another's armor. To find a weakness and drive a dagger in and twist, this was the favorite sport of the damned.

Poet was waiting for him, slid down just out of sight behind the ridgetop. The young man's face *looked* as if it should be highly expressive. Yet for the most part Poet stayed blandly impassive, possibly with the aid of the drugs he was forever dosing himself with.

By long observation Mir had learned to read the subtleties of Poet's expression. The sensitive mouth, under a downy wisp of nascent moustache, was set, and the pale blue eyes showed an unaccustomed glitter. Or maybe that was Mir's imagination; but there was little jubilation in the shrug that greeted the lieutenant.

"See for yourself," Poet said.

Mir slithered up. He didn't need the binoculars.

A ravine, perhaps two hundred meters across and a hundred deep, slashed across the hills right in front of him, the most dramatic terrain feature he'd so far seen. On the other side was clear and level ground for perhaps another hundred meters, and behind that a thicket. Farther back rose low hills.

Bursting from the brush, some throwing away their weapons as he watched, came men. Their battle dress had the same background-adaptive "smart" pigment as his own; it was changing from the thicket's orange and maroon to ground-tangle yellow as they ran. Something about their appearance keyed Mir, and he was unsurprised when Poet murmured, "Red-asses." Engine Regulars, not CLD.

But they're human! We're not alone!

"What's going on?" Kobolev said in Mir's ear.

The lieutenant jumped. "Shut *up!*" he hissed.

"No need to bite my head off," the Bold Original said.

Like a swirl of brilliant autumn leaves borne on a gust of wind, Rook cavalry blew out of the thicket in pursuit of the fleeing Regulars. A soldier dropped to one knee and shouldered his pulser, firing aimed shots. Two riders and a beaked mount fell.

A third rode up to the kneeling man, leaned from his saddle, and thrust a slim black lance into his chest. The head punched out between the man's shoulder blade, the feather panache a blood-sodden lump.

The other riders swept past. The Regulars who were slow or stumbled were ridden down. Half a dozen halted at the lip of the precipice, turned and raised hands in surrender.

As many others hurled themselves over the edge in panic. The Landers watched in shocked silence as their bodies struck, bounced, rolled in flopping disjunct tangles down to the stream that ran along the bottom of the ravine.

For a heartbeat the feathered riders halted, staring at the survivors with great yellow forward-looking eyes. Then one kicked his spur toe into his mount's side. Uttering a shrill caw the riding beast leapt forward. The rider raised a hooked sword. Yellow sunlight shattered on the blade and scattered fragments across the ravine; and then the sword came down and split the man's unhelmeted head.

It was a signal for massacre. The other riders crowded in, all but jostling one another off the cliff in their eagerness to finish their foes. One rider hauled back his reins, causing his mount to rear; the beast lashed out with a great taloned forefoot. Despite tough polymerized-graphite armor cloth beneath the Regular's chammy blouse, the animal's claws tore his belly open and spilled his intestines in a red-and-purple writhe upon the ground.

Screams, and then thumps and the sliding clatter of dislodged stones as the last few bodies were hurled down the ravine to join their comrades shattered at the bottom.

Loki was first to react. Uttering a wild scream of his own, he rose to his feet firing his hurdy-gurdy full-auto from the hip.

Grenade blasts blossomed among riders strung out along the rim gazing down in grim satisfaction at their handiwork. The rider who had gutted the Regular and his mount were both projected straight over the precipice by a burst close behind. Beaks wide in screams, limbs a bright futile whirl, they fell.

The other Landers opened up. Mounts and Rooks screamed and fell, their own viscera, orange and maroon like the foliage, rolling on yellow tangle already sodden with their victims' blood. In a stutter of heartbeats accelerated by fear and rage all were down, except for one rider bent low over his animal's neck, tailfeathers bobbing as he rode balls-out for the cover of the thicket. Gouts of earth, thrown up by blue bolts, grenades, and needles, converged on him from a dozen directions. Big Bori, firing his fifteen-kilogram Bitch from the hip, caught him first. As maroon blood misted about the Rook, the explosions arrived. Rider and beast vanished in a cloud of soil, smoke, feathers, and flesh.

The Landers stood, not caring if they were seen, breathing gape-mouthed and ragged as if they had run all the way from the farmhouse. From beyond the thicket came the thuds and cracks of battle.

"What about the others?" Dieter cried, voice shrill. "We've got to do something!"

"What do you suggest?" Jovan shouted back, his voice scarcely lower. "Flap our arms and fly? It didn't work for the fucking *birds,* but be my Process-forsaken guest and try!"

Dieter showed his teeth in a wild grimace, his usual giddy optimism peeled from his face like flayed skin.

"I can't raise them," Ovanidze said. He spoke calmly as always; and in the supercharged air his calmness was more violent than a shout, intrusive and almost obscene.

"What do you mean?" Mir asked, and he realized that he was shouting, too. *Control*, he told himself. *If you lose it here, we're all done for.*

Ovanidze shook his mustard-haired ball of a head. "I get nothing from them. No transmissions. Zot."

Mir shook his own head, unable to assimilate what the man was telling him. "What do you mean?" he asked again.

The tech pressed buttons on his set. The lieutenant's ears filled with dead-air crackle, violent with the storms erupting unseen from the primary's seemingly placid face.

"That's what I'm getting," Ovanidze said.

"Not even from dispersed—"

"Not anything. No thing." Ovanidze hesitated, and his lumpy cheeks fisted beneath his eyes. "Lieutenant, they're gone. Whoever was over there is dead now."

"Food," the White Rat said. "They'll have rat packs, dead or not."

"I didn't see any packs," Kobolev said.

"They're somewhere," Loki said. "We find a way across, kill the birds, and take them for ourselves. Simplicity itself."

"Not so simple," Stilicho said. "How many red-asses were in that lot, Ovanidze?"

The tech shrugged. "Don't have the means to count, exactly."

"Guess."

"It was a company-level transmitter. Might've been more. There was a lot of traff flowing by."

"Two–three hundred men," Stilicho said, "and maybe more, all brought to Now. Looks like these easy mark birds have found a way to lay some hurt on us."

"If your shit's turned to water, old man," Kobolev said, throwing out his big chest, "then let the real men go over and deal with it."

Stilicho just looked at him.

Like a pulled string, a whistle split the sky, and the world blew up in flash and smashing noise.

15

When Mir could hear again through the ringing in his ears, what he heard was screaming, attenuated through aftershock tone as though by distance.

He started to rise from the dark spongy earth to which he had thrown himself without remembering that he had done so, caught himself, stayed on elbows. He looked around.

Twenty meters to his left a section of tree bole had been smashed as if by a stroke from a giant hammer: a raw, two-meter wound of orange pulp and long, jagged splinters. As he took that in there was another flash, and a dirty white cloud materialized in air above the ravine. Report hit his ears like slapping hands, bulging the drums inward.

"Where are they?" he shouted. His throat rasped from the acrid gunpowder clouds which suddenly enveloped the ridge-top.

"Nowhere!" shouted Starman, lying flat on his belly scanning the ravine's far side through the scope of his sniper-Bitch. "Their guns are hidden, not firing direct."

"Arty! Get the arty!" the Dancing-Master shouted to Ovanidze. "We need counterbattery fire soonest!"

The tech stared at him. "From where, you dickwit?" Loki shouted. "Praesidium? We don't have arty, we don't have overhead, we don't have anything but the dicks in our pants!"

The Dancing-Master blinked. Another explosion crashed off high in the branches of a tree right over his helmet. Concussion pushed him flat as tiny fragments rattled fallen leaves around him.

The screaming went on and on, without seeming to pause for breath, as if it came from a wounded machine. "IR glows, back in the trees," Starman said. "Think it's the FOs."

He switched his weapon to full-auto. Sniper electros were not supposed to be selective fire. CLD was not noted for obeying regulations against tampering with Collective property. Starman started ripping bursts at the hidden Rooks, trying to whipsaw through the trees they were using for cover.

Another blast. Mir thought his head would explode from the noise. Or from the screaming, which not even shell thunder drowned.

"Back down, off the crest!" he yelled. "Reassemble fifty meters downslope."

By this time the smoke surrounded them like predawn mist, dense and white, sending acid tendrils up noses and down throats and gouging into eyes. Section erupted from the thicket like a flock of frightened ground birds, limbs flailing to hang on to gear and balance at the same time. Big Bori, bawling like a baby, tripped over a root and went tumbling downhill in a cloud of leaf mulch, a one-man avalanche.

At the foot of the slope, training and the dictates of longer-term survival reasserted themselves. None of the men was a stranger to being under fire-with-intent, not even the scrubs. Section dropped to its bellies in a line, weapons aimed uphill, and strove to become one with the rich dark soil of the Rookery.

"Young-tech?" bellowed Jovan, voice cracking with outrage. "Young-tech my aching *ass!*"

Starman lay next to Mir. He grinned at the lieutenant. His teeth were startlingly white against the darkness of his face.

"What's the shake, Lieutenant?" he asked. "I fried the forward observers."

A fresh string of blasts erupted along the ridgetop. Starman turned the color of ash.

"Space navy asshole!" snarled Balt, who lay nearby with Hynkop huddled against his side, clutching the pack with extra Bitch ammo hoppers to his chest. "They got the snaking *range*. Don't need no observers no more."

The screaming was still going on, intolerably. With a shock,

Mir realized it was coming from the top of the ridge.

"Somebody tend that injured man!" he shouted. "Now!"

As he voiced the command he feared no one would obey. As barrages went, this was mild, a mere spring freshet compared even to what they had all endured in training. But this sudden demonstration that the Rooks could indeed reach out and hurt them, combined with watching the Regulars massacred, had kicked the Landers' morning self-confidence upside down.

Should I go myself? He wasn't sure if it might fatally compromise his position, to start off now to accomplish what he had ordered others to do. After all this time with Section he still found himself getting stuck in the clefts of dilemmas.

Kyov had shed his pack and piece and was already starting upslope, hunched over as if bearing the entire burden of world on his shoulders, on that sturdy frame to which his spare flesh seemed to have been shrink-wrapped. Without a word Poet slipped the straps to his flamer pack and went after. A moment later Loki followed.

Another salvo flayed the hilltop. The skin of Mir's face felt as if it were trying to flee back away from the terrible noise, so that the hardness of his facial bones seemed about to split it across. Unpredictable and vicious as they were, Poet and Loki were two of the unit's most effective fighters, and Kyov was its backbone. To lose them all at a stroke—

They emerged from the brush, sliding downward on their butts, Kyov and Poet holding the arms of the wounded man, Loki clearing his feet when the heels caught against a bush or dip in the ground. It was Florenz, the impulsive scrub with the red hair dark as Santander wine. His face was a blot of red, and he struggled wildly to free his arms, as if to clap hands to his face.

The three got him down onto a poncho unrolled at the foot of the hill. Mir crawled to look, and instantly turned away, suss-bar fragments rising like pieces of glass in his throat. A splinter of orange hardwood had been driven side-to-side through his temples like a spike. Somehow it hadn't killed him. His eyes were red swamp ruins.

Dieter knelt beside the injured man. He reached for Florenz's head, then jerked his hands back. "For Process's sake, man, get that thing out!" the lieutenant said hoarsely.

Dieter shook his head like a man in seizure. "I can't. Shit, shit, shit. If I try to pull it out, I might drive a splinter into his brain. *Shit.*"

"He's right, Lieutenant," Kyov said. His voice was calm as always, but his cheeks were drawn and his eyes full of pain.

"What can you do, then?" Mir demanded, hands trembling with urgency. Part of him was shocked at how shattered he was by Florenz's injury. This was CLD; they were deathbirds, due to die; the only spaces the court left blank on the sentencing-forms were *where* and *when*? All had already seen more men killed out of First Section than were *in* it at any one time. And Florenz was a scrub, most expendable of the walking dead, with the life expectancy of fresh-hatched sea life struggling down an open beach to the surf.

But this was different, and he knew why. They had been cut off before; that was no uncommon situation for CLD, first in, last out. But they had never been this cut off before. Kosmos was *gone,* and when they would come back—or even *if*—no one could so much as guess. They were without support, resupply, reinforcement, even food to eat beyond the already-dwindling rations they carried on their backs. And the only other humans they had found on this so-pleasant world so far had just been butchered before their eyes.

He understood something now, which had puzzled him since gymnasium days when they taught him the history of the Originals and their long-ago flight from Earth. Jochen Stahl, their leader and still the guiding spirit of the Stellar Collective, had discovered that the former Gaians were plotting to overthrow his Steel Fist doctrine. But he let them live, though he had been notorious for sudden ruthless discipline as commander of the New Red Army, fighting across a Europe shattered by two thermonuclear exchanges and nearly a decade of conventional warfare.

They rewarded his forbearance by rebelling. The Gaians seized control of the liberated starship *Red Phoenix.* They put to death Dr. Richard Lo, creator of the drive which—after certain refinements—today enabled the Engine of History to spread the Universal Truth across the galaxy at many times lightspeed. During the brief time they held control, before their own internecine squabbling allowed the Steel Fist survivors to unite the other factions against them and tear them down,

Jochen Stahl himself vanished, never to be seen again.

It was rumored, of course, that he would return one day when his children were in their greatest need. It hadn't happened yet. Rationalist though he was, deep inside Mir was not altogether sure it *wouldn't*.

The Gaian ringleaders went out the air locks into the Big Empty. Yet the *junta* which succeeded Stahl was unable to make a clean sweep of it, eliminate all known conspirators. The descendants, physical and intellectual, of the Gaians thrived today under the rubric of the Ministry of Preservation, and they were *still* a pain in the ass.

Mir's instructors had mouthed a lot of platitudes about mercy and collectivist brotherhood, but even as the naive child of Values privilege Mir knew full well those sentiments didn't save the suspect *now*. Worse—though no one dared mouth such suspicions, and Mir had felt guilty-dirty at the time for harboring them—such forbearance was itself Particular: *repressive tolerance,* the catchphrase went. "Individual"—in the Stellar Collective, all legitimate uses of that forbidden term had quotation marks around them—guilt or innocence meant nothing; in the Collective view, some were guilty, so all were guilty; it was the endless dance of *communities,* and the Gaians had been cut out. So why had Stahl gone so fatally soft, and why had his avengers held back from total retribution?

Now he understood. Down in his intestines he realized why the conspirators weren't all killed: *because the Universe is huge, and dangers are many. And we are small and weak, and few. So few.*

Mir had fewer than thirty men to face a planet filled with inhabitants who were *not* turning out to be the quaint walkovers the briefing inboard *Beria* had promised. There was no such thing as *expendable*.

"Do what you can for him," he said. "And quickly. We have to move. Whatever the birds have over there, they managed to wipe out at least a company of Regulars."

He expected some jape about a CLD Section being easily worth a company of red-asses—which was perfectly true, in his experience—but somehow no one found it in him. He turned to see Poet sitting to the side with his compressor pack next to him.

"What you did was very brave," Mir said to him. Quietly,

for fear of embarrassing him before the others.

He longed to ask *why,* but he noticed Poet's cheeks were flushed, his pale eyes fever-bright, and that his hands were vibrating like struck tuning forks. He realized that Poet had just slugged back a dose of Zone.

Without changing expression, Poet shrugged. "*Max nix,*" he said. "Makes nothing I die here now, I die there-then. Either way I'm gone. Makes nothing." Then he smiled a dreamy smile.

Mir turned away, feeling something he could not name.

Kyov and Dieter poured antiseptic powders in Florenz's wounds, and dosed him up with self-pressurized hypospray ampoules—hypes—of anesthetic, both illicitly borrowed from Engine Regular stocks at some time in the past. Then they wrapped a bandage around his head, with the wood splinter still stuck in it, and said that had to serve.

Mir marched them double time away to the southwest, following the ravine, mainly to be putting distance between themselves and the known Rook concentration. Florenz stumbled along, shepherded by Nau and Henriks, who regarded him with constant horror, as if he had risen from the dead. The wounded boy was happy enough, muttering and singing constantly to himself. Along with the painkillers, some helpful brud had zapped him covertly with Max Nix, a clandestine mood alterant named after a favorite deathbird slogan; he still felt the pain, but now he didn't *care.* It was not so much an act of consideration as expediency. Florenz would slow them up less if he could move under his own power.

With a long afternoon and ample incentive, they covered a further twenty klicks of hilly terrain before the sun finally crashed and burned among the hills. They were among dense hardwood forest by that time. A bald knob of hill rose in front of them, with a spindly but extensive yellow stone ruin crowning it. Mir ordered them to fort up there for the night.

"I wonder what this place was?" the Dancing-Master asked as the men settled in to eat. Mir had ordered self-heating ration packs to be distributed, one per three men. The men needed the feel of hot food in their bellies. *Is it enough? Too much?* Mir had no way to judge. His only certainty was that any guess he made would be wrong. The mystery lay in whether it would be fatally so.

"Who gives a shit?" Balt demanded, digging at a brown gravy-smothered lump with his fingers.

"I think it was a cathedral," Mir said, mostly to himself— except for Kyov, nobody listened to him except for direct orders. He stood beside a buttress raised against nothing, raised his hand to run a finger over cool smooth stone. "It feels like a cathedral."

Whatever it had been, time had gutted it thoroughly, leaving only soaring pillars and bits of wall with ivylike creepers climbing up them from cracks in the sandstone flagging, an impression of high narrow vaults, of airiness, almost wispiness, belied by the tightness of the masonry work. It seemed to Mir that in its fullness this place must have been a paean to flight in stone, a memorial to that which the Rooks had lost at some time beyond racial memory, but which they must know, from watching their smaller cousins, they once possessed. And it struck him that it must be ancient indeed, for its workmanship was of a nature to resist time, despite the lightness of its appearance.

Mir wandered through the ruin and the deep twilight. Cool and the scent of moist earth and stone rose around him like a cloud. Tiny insects buzzed in profusion, but as if they had learned the lesson of Loki's crotch-crabs, they left him scrupulously alone. They were winnowed by dark birds who wove among the upright ruins on wings like scimitars, calling to one another in croaks that sounded tantalizingly like speech.

A wisp of darkness, silhouetted against indigo sky and the burnt-orange band of the horizon beneath a still-intact pointed arch. Mir froze, then pulled his pulser up by its long sling until he found the pistol grip and slipped his finger within the comforting confines of the trigger guard. He moved forward with all the stealth he'd learned in the Meatgrinder, where they ran infiltration exercises against sentries awaiting them with orders to shoot to kill.

"Good evening, Junior Lieutenant," the shadow said in Poet's voice.

Mir froze, then walked forward normally. He held his pulser in patrol position, and he didn't remove his finger from the trigger guard. It wasn't wise to take Poet for granted.

"It is a lovely evening, Poet," he said, standing beside him in the arched entranceway.

He couldn't help glancing down at the slight young man who sat beside him with knees drawn up under chin. He wasn't carrying his flamer pack, but his knives he had with him always.

The lieutenant wondered what went on inside that dark head. Did Poet sense the age and majesty of the place? Was the evening beauty so huge and undeniable it made something resonate within him? Or was he as dead inside as his eyes suggested, his only feeling the artificial buzz of pleasure imminence Zone imparted?

The young Lander said nothing. Mir stood next to him for a while, oddly comfortable in his silent company, as the light drained away and night fowl began to hoot mournfully at one another from the woods.

He turned to go. "They're out there, Lieutenant." A chuckle. "Just in case you're interested."

Feeling a crawling between his shoulder blades and in the skin below his eyes, Mir turned. "What do you mean, Standard?"

"The birds. The Rooks, whatever. They're out there, and they're watching us."

Mir squinted into the night as if his eyelids would squeeze light out of darkness. He saw nothing but the dark surrounding sea of trees.

"Do you know how many?" Poet shook his head. "Well, could you help Starman or Rouen mark them down, then?"

Poet laughed softly. "They won't see them, Lieutenant," he said. "Not with infrared, not with infantry radar, not with starlight. Not with human eyes, not with machine eyes. They know this world; they know how to use it. Autocs're like that. They don't let themselves be seen. But they're out there."

Knowing he was treading uncertain ground, Mir asked, "How do you know?"

A shrug. "I feel them."

Mir resisted the urge to grab the boy and shake him, knowing that would earn him a blade in the belly. "I'll raise the alert," he said.

Poet shook his head dreamily. He was coming down from

his Zone buzz, Mir realized, and may have taken his own shot of Max Nix to help him mellow off the high.

On the other hand, Poet fuzzed on drugs was a vastly more lethal creature than the clearest-headed Regular Mir had ever encountered. He had to take the boy seriously.

"Don't waste your energy, Junior Lieutenant," he said, clasping hands around his knees and beginning to rock gently. "They don't like the night, but they know how to hide in it."

"And how do you know that?" Mir demanded, too incredulous for caution.

A shrug. "I'm a scout. I've learned to read autocs. The dirt, the ground cover, the trees: they tell me what I need to know about the things that live here. I hear the planet talking."

He tipped his head sideways. "Don't you, Junior Lieutenant?"

Mir shook his head and walked away. He felt unreal. He didn't know which creeped him out worse, Poet's calm assurance that the Rooks were watching them, or Poet himself. He resolved to double the watches in any event.

When he got back to the ruins of the great chamber, where most of the men were gathered, he heard Eyrikson demand, "What's a Rook, anyway?"

"It's some kind of Earth bird," Kobolev said.

Loki crowed derision: "What's that I hear?" he said. "The sweet song of the Universal Chorus?"

Kobolev stiffened. The *Universal Chorus* was an official sobriquet for the Universum, the representative body which supposedly ruled the Stellar Collective from Praesidium, below the Direktor and the actual Praesidium itself. In truth it was a debating society and not much of that, whose main function was to applaud whatever action the Executor—who held the *real* power on the planet Praesidium, capital of the Collective—chose to take. "The singing of the Universal Chorus" was a common colloquialism for jackass braying.

"The voice of ignorance masquerading as wisdom," Loki said, watching the Bold Original tightly from his slanted pale eyes. "If you don't know what something is, it's an Earth thing."

Kobolev jumped to his feet. "You can't talk to me that way!" he bellowed, face purpling behind his beard.

"I can talk any way I please, *Standard,*" Loki said. "The

Universal Will has seen fit to make me corporal; you're subordinate to me." He laughed and spat. "Not that I need beg permission from a lump of ling shit to call it what it is."

Kobolev lunged at him, swinging a beefy fist for that thin high-cheekboned face. Loki threw up his left forearm and blocked the blow cold.

His right hand came up wrapped in the knuckle-duster grip of his battle knife. He raked the grip's studded bow across Kobolev's left cheek, laying it open to the bone. Kobolev roared and reared back, face pouring blood, tore out his own saw-backed battle knife, and lunged for Loki. The slimmer man evaded his charge, slashed him across the other cheek with his blade.

Without thinking, Mir found himself between them, with a hand on either man's chest. "Stop! Stop this! We're all alone on this world. We mustn't fight each other!"

Kobolev sneered and turned away, sheathing his knife. Loki emitted a shrill yip of laughter. "You have no understanding, *klad*-baby! He's closer to being one of *us* now. And I'll keep carving our likeness on his flesh until I reach his soul!"

Mir made his eyes meet the slanted pale ones, burning with strange fire. "You'll have to carve your way through me."

For a moment he thought he had pushed it too far. Loki's pale fine face looked scarcely human, cheeks flushed, eyes feral. But he laughed again, a rattling bright sound.

"Such things have happened, Junior Lieutenant," he said jauntily. But he put his knife away.

16

EXPLOSIONS WOKE MIR. He scrambled from his bedroll, rolled to his feet on cracked sandstone. He had his weapon in hand, without being aware of picking it up.

A trio of blasts, the distinctive muffled crack of blue bolts giving up their energy against a solid target. A crackling and crunching followed, climaxing in a crash of falling stone. The lieutenant looked frantically around. Landers who, like him, had been jarred conscious were popping from sacks and hunting cover. The already awake ignored them and the noises alike. They sat by their packs in apathetic slouches, rubbing their eyes and yawning.

One thing Mir had learned to trust infallibly was the death-bird instinct for danger. *It's not an attack.* Keeping his pulser ready, he moved off through the ruin to its southern end, where the hill fell away from the cement foundation in a sharp bluff.

A blue-green flash, a crash, ruination, and laughter. Cautiously Mir poked his nose and the snub muzzle of his pulser around a column.

In the midst of what had been some kind of broad terminal hall stood Eyrikson, white-blond hair seeming to glow in butter-colored dawn sun rays fanning across the tops of the trees. He was aiming his pulser at a rib which had once upheld long-vanished walls, and now was toppling to the yellow mat outside in a cloud of crumbled stone. He laughed uproariously, as if at some mighty joke. Around him in three directions stood the forest, a dense mist filling the spaces between trunks like murky water.

"What the hell are you doing?" Mir shouted.

The huge young transfer blinked at him. "Having a little fun, Junior Lieutenant."

"But this is vandalism! This is an irreplaceable cultural resource! Think of how *old* it must be!"

Eyrikson laughed. It wasn't a malicious laugh, merely disbelieving. "Aw, Lieutenant, get off it! It's just alien trash. Besides"—he shrugged a massive shoulder—"it's all falling down anyway."

He turned away, swung his weapon to bear on another ancient pillar. Reflexively, Mir raised the extended buttstock of his own pulser to his shoulder. The open battle sights lined up on the longish hair at the back of that thick neck; as his finger took up slack, the red dot of the coaxial sighting laser appeared at the base of the Lander's skull.

Eyrikson's head exploded.

Mir stood there frozen, his sighting laser a pallid finger reaching through the sky into infinity. For a moment he thought he had shot the youth himself, without being aware of it. The thought turned him cold; *Have I lost control?* He had seen it happen often enough in CLD.

Eyrikson's body slumped to the flagstones in a serial sodden thumping, the final contractions of his heart bubbling red fluid out the base of his violated skull, dyeing the remnant fringe of white-blond hair. Mir's second thought, more chilling than the first, was that the others would find him here, weapon poised over Eyrikson's corpse. . . .

He heard and felt the sound of a distant propellant explosion, as if invisible beings were blowing hard in both his ears at once. His focus shot past the half-headless body, downslope to the telltale ball of smoke, grey against a grey sky, that rolled up out of the sea of green.

"Rooks!" he shouted, turning away. As he did something cracked against the pillar beside his head. Stone chips stung his cheek. He threw himself flat on the sandstone, banging his right elbow cruelly.

"We're under attack!" he shouted, feeling naked without the helmet which lay beside his bedroll thirty meters away, remembering Poet's quiet prophecy of the night before. "Turn out and return fire!" He heard the sizzle of a Bitch fired full-auto from outside.

Holding his unstrapped helmet atop his head with one hand, Jovan tumbled down beside Rouen in one of the slit trenches they had all grumbled about when the lieutenant insisted they dig around the ruin before turning out for chow the night before. "How the hell did the bastards sneak up without anybody seeing them?"

"Fucking trees, fucking mist, fucking feathers," the sniper snarled, tracking his heavy shrouded barrel across the line of trees, a mere forty meters distant. "Bastards got no more heat signature than Kobolev's chilly needle dick."

They came gusting from the woods like bright confetti shot from a gun: hundreds of Rooks on foot, firing rifles. Their yellow beaks were wide-open, showing mottled orange-and-maroon tongues, and they gave off a terrible shrill cawing that rolled over the surprised Landers like hurricane wind.

Landers savaged the charging autocs with bolts and needles. Bodies smoldering or shredded fell meters upslope from the point they were hit, so fast were the bird-creatures coming. Their comrades vaulted them, keening hate, and came on.

When they closed to twenty meters—less than the blink of an eye—Kyov shut his eyes and triggered the Claymore mines chained around the hilltop. These had been placed sideways, so their blast axes paralleled the perimeter; the Landers knew from ancient bitter experience that enemy infiltrators, coming upon the devices in the dark, liked to turn them around in hopes the Landers would fill their own faces with steel marbles when they touched the things off.

Flashes and ax bites of noise: the Rooks blew away like autumn leaves on the wind, a wind that sighed and sang with tens of thousands of invisible pellets. Claymore thunder circled the hilltop, crashed back in echo waves from the woods, subsided to leave nothing but ringing in the defenders' ears and the sound of the morning breeze rustling through the forest leaves. At least two hundred autocs had been killed. They lay without moving, without moaning. The smell of alien blood, harsh as a shout in an unknown tongue, rolled over the defenders.

A breathless moment, and they came again, hundreds of them, fury undiluted by their predecessors' fate. Backup Claymores dropped another hundred like an unseen scythe. Survivors fled into the woods in a horizontal storm of blue bolts.

From the woods came single shots, aimed. Helmets and visors of bulletproof composite turned slow, heavy, soft-lead slugs, but their sledgehammer impacts snapped heads back on necks and dropped Landers stunned to the bottom of their holes.

The Landers' pulsers—Model 17 Directed-Energy Pulse Projector, Dispersed/Lightweight, Selective Fire, 2cm., made by the powerful Vorhiys Design Bureau on Novy Utrecht—had optical sighting scopes as well as iron sights and lasers for close-in work. The support electros had computerized scopes with IR and ambient-light enhancement capabilities. If the Rooks exposed themselves enough to aim fire, the human intruders could see them. And the first axiom of modern war was: *If I can see you, I can kill you.*

But there were hundreds of feathered shooters, thick in the underbrush between the boles, firing over fallen trunks, even perched in treetops with rifle barrels propped in forked branches. Even so the humans could put out more fire; but their fire was spread out around a wide circle, whereas the attackers could concentrate theirs. Flamer men Poet, Dieter, and Ovanidze tried to burn back the forest. So dense and water-soaked was the wood of the trees that the superheated plasma seared and charred them, rather than set them ablaze. The plasma jets could induce spectacular steam explosions that flayed any Rooks hidden nearby with splinter-shrapnel, and burn away the underbrush and flush autocs concealed within in screaming fireballs, but they could start no sustained blaze.

So the Rooks gained fire superiority, used it to drive the defenders deep in their holes or shrinking back among the cathedral's masonry bones. And when the Landers' fire slackened, the Rooks charged again.

Their onslaught blocked most of their own covering fire. The Landers popped up to meet them with a killing fusillade. But the Claymores were gone, and the autocs' clawed yellow feet tore up the distance between trees and defenses like wet paper. With breath-robbing speed they were among the defenders, stabbing, clubbing, clawing.

The technotoys were good, in their way, the infantry radars and tactical displays and energy weapons and night vision devices. Much of the time they even worked as intended. Now mature technology yielded to fury, primitive and primal.

But the Collective Landing Detachment fought constantly, and constantly on the ragged edge of battle, where all foresight, doctrine, and theory were reduced in the Universal solvent of hand-to-hand combat. The autocs were used to a primitive style of war, trained to fight with bayonet and rifle and their formidable natural weapons, beaks and claws. And they were filled with the oldest and most potent battle drug of all: hatred of a brutal unjust invader.

The Landers met them with the fury of betrayed children.

Loki threw away his grenade launcher, its hand-wound drum empty, drew his battle knife. A Rook with belts of waxed paper cartridges crossed over his purple-plumed chest raked hind claws across his belly as he came out of his hole. Black talons tore through the bullet-resistant tunic like cheesecloth. Loki went on his butt on the damp yellow mat, the front of his battle dress hanging in shreds.

He screamed so shrilly and so loudly that those nearby thought his guts had been spilled. The purple-feathered Rook did; cawing triumph it raised its foot for a killing slash at the man's face.

It kicked crosswise. Loki snapped his body back flat on the ground, so that the great splayed claw passed over him. Then, as if his body were a spring, he whipped himself up and at the autoc. The Rook tried to recover, to sweep its leg back. Loki smashed the studded knuckle bow of his knife against the side of the feathered face. The beak crunched with a sound like a giant eggshell being crushed. The creature toppled backward with Loki astride it, stabbing spasmodically at its brightfeathered torso.

A green Rook loomed above the blond man, with rifle held both-handed above its head, bayonet down, poised for a stroke and seemingly unconcerned that he would certainly skewer his comrade as well. Bellowing, Big Bori rose from his own slit trench, firing the last of a hopper of 2mm needles into the creature from two meters away. Its chest burst like a firecracker, and it toppled backward.

Another Rook drove at Bori with its bayonet. He side-stepped swiftly and met it with a roar and an overhand stroke from a sharpened entrenching tool. The e-tool was the humblest of implements in the mighty arsenal of the Engine of History: a simple spade with a half-meter handle. An Engine Regular wouldn't deign to consider such a thing a weapon. But the Landers, who found the holes those spades could scrape for them in alien soil far more consistent protection than all the marvels of Collective science, had also long learned their value in close-in combat, where they were brutally effective cut-and-thrust weapons.

The sharpened spade blade split the Rook's face and skull. Before he wrenched it free Bori had shattered the skull of a second Rook and broken its neck with a sweeping backhand blow of his other fist. Then he pulled the e-tool loose and dug it up under the rib cage of a third.

Lurking up among the ruins, sniping when he could pick a clear target out from the body seethe, Mir watched Balt rear up, hoist a Rook kicking above his head, and throw the autoc into its comrades' beaks while Hynkop crouched white-faced behind, guarding his abuser's back with pulser ready.

He saw Gollob go down, blood pennons streaming from a face laid open by a kick. He raised his pulser to kill the creature who had struck the boy, but there were Landers in the way. The Rook stooped to pick up a bayoneted rifle. Sturz scrambled from his hole and threw himself on the creature's back, arm locked around a white throat. The Rook dropped the rifle and raked the scrub's arms with taloned hands, easily tearing ballistic cloth and raising bright rills of blood.

Weeping, Gollob came up to his knees and plunged his knife again and again into a buff-feathered belly. The bird-creature belched blood and dropped to its backward-angled knees.

Color caught the edge of Mir's peripheral vision. Up among yellow masonry bones he saw Poet stalked by a Rook with a scarlet back and buff belly. The slight human had exhausted the Medurin Design Bureau power cell which powered his flamer—as the cans powered the pulse-guns and electros—and jettisoned the bulky backpack. The butterfly knife in his left hand looked pathetically small against the half-meter bayonet jutting from the barrel of the autoc's rifle.

Smiling his Zone half smile, Poet made a come-hither gesture with the fingers of his right hand, palm up. The Rook made a clacking sound and lunged. Poet ducked behind a pillar. The bayonet struck chunks off the stone.

Poet stuck his head out the other side of the pillar. Again the autoc jabbed and missed. Laughing like a happy child, Poet jumped out the opposite way, then dodged easily back from the creature's lunge.

Picking up the pattern, the Rook automatically tracked to its right, expecting the pesky human to emerge on that side next time. Instead Poet came flying out to the left again, hit the flagstones with shoulder tucked, and rolled past the autoc. His knife licked out. Hamstring severed above its left foot, the Rook squawked and fell.

Before it could recover, Poet leapt across its body. His left hand lashed downward as he passed over. When he hit and rolled away blood pumped bright orange from the autoc's slashed throat.

A Rook that had crept up under cover of a breast-high stub of wall launched itself at Mir with a scream. Mir hit it in the torso with blue bolt. Momentum carried it forward into him, knocking him backward and cracking the back of his head against a buttress. Despite his helmet, the impact filled his eyes with momentary stars.

As he lay with the Rook's body surprisingly light atop him and the stench of half-cooked guts filling his nostrils, he saw a fresh irruption of Rooks fill the ruins like a cloud of feathers blown in on a gust of wind. Numbers alone were about to overpower the human defenders. With arms from which the strength had fled he tried to push the dying autoc off him.

Black Bertold thrust a fist high, clutching an apple-sized sphere of shiny alloy. "Grenade duel!" he shouted, his deep voice ringing like a gong. "Hug the planet!"

As half a dozen Rooks closed on him from all directions he pulled the pin on the fragmentation grenade, dropped it right at his own feet, and hit the pale pink sandstone beside it, curling into a fetal ball.

The grenade duel was sheer mad desperation—and consequently a favorite tactic in CLD. Visor down and face tucked against his thighs, ballistic cloth covering his back, Bertold was reasonably protected against the grenade. It went off with a ringing bang, blowing a leg off one Rook and dropping the others into thrashing squalling feather-tangles, their legs and bellies filled with fragments.

Grenade pops rippled through the ruins. Flashes lit smooth ancient stone like fireworks celebrating some forgotten holiday. A pair of Rooks flanked Mir and charged him. He clawed a grenade from his own harness, pulled the pin and dropped it, lips skinned back from teeth in panic ecstasy. He coiled tightly about himself, hoping desperately that he had actually managed to turn his hands and face away from the bomb.

The explosion kicked him between the shoulder blades like a Santander mule. He heard a bird chorus of cries. When he dared pull his face away from his thighs one attacker lay unmoving on its back, huge eyes starting sightless at the turquoise sky that served the cathedral for a ceiling. The other sat clutching its right leg, which was missing from the knee down and pulsing blood from the stump. It made no sound, only opened and closed its beak in mechanical rhythm. Feeling horrid, Mir seized his pulser and killed it with a burst.

The little telltale light at the rear of the receiver went from green to red. His power cell was dry.

He looked around. Throughout the ruin Landers were finishing Rooks wounded in the grenade duel with blue bolts, knives, boots, even hunks of fallen stone. Outside, the surviving autocs were vanishing into the wood, pursued by the defenders' jeers.

He looked down at himself then. The front of his battle dress was slimy with alien blood, and bits of tissue and Universal Spirit knew what clung to his belly and thighs. He turned away and vomited.

The men on the perimeter slaughtered the wounded with methodical fury; Mir made himself not watch. Then they collapsed back into the ruin itself, seeking the greater protection the sporadic walls of stone provided.

"Casualties?" Mir forced himself to ask when Kyov presented himself.

The older man shook his head. "Pretty much everybody's cut or banged up.

"Fatalities?" Mir asked from a dry mouth that tasted like the dung heap outside the Rook farmhouse.

"None, sir. Only Eyrikson."

Mir felt knees go pliant, sat down hard on warm sandstone. "We pulled through again."

"This time, sir," Kyov said, with a faint, sad smile.

Mir nodded convulsively. "All right. Get the wounded tended to, and then we'll fort up here for when they come again."

"No sir."

Mir looked at him. He felt a surge of anger. "What do you mean, Section Sergeant?" he demanded.

"I mean we can't stay here, sir. We have them on the run; Starman and Rouen have picked up heat signatures from a large body of enemy, moving rapidly away through the trees."

"So? We've shown we can beat them from a strong enough defensive position. Where stronger than here?"

"Yeah," called Balt. "All we lost was a stinking scrub."

"Shut up," said Kobolev dully.

"We also shot up half of our ammo, shitcans, and launch grenades, between this fight and the dustup at the LZ," Stilicho said. "That's including the extra shit we humped from the joyboat. Two more fights like that and we're dry."

"What are we going to *do*, then, if we don't fight here?" Mir demanded. He felt panic fingers clutching at his throat, and fought not to let their marks show on his face.

"Run and hide like cowards," Kobolev sneered. "That's what he's saying."

"Run and hide and *live*," said Loki. He had a bandage wound around his middle. The Rook's talons had shredded skin as well as battle dress, but had not violated the body wall. "You're free to stay here and be a dead hero, if you like, you Circle Jerk hero."

"Maybe someone will compose a song," Starman said. " 'The Needle-dick's Last Stand.' Of course, no one will be allowed to *sing* it. We're deathbirds; it's forbidden to glorify us."

Kobolev looked death rays at him, but the Bold Original had no more energy to fight with. And he had seen those wiry black hands seize the thick neck of a Rook infantryman and break it, like a Collective-farm wife wringing a chicken's neck.

"We're forbidden to be heroes," Poet said. "Ask Gollob to look it up in his Book."

Gollob, whose face was a mask of off-color artificial skin, disinfectant ointment, and dried blood, raised his head and stared at him with pathetic eyes. He said nothing.

"We *did* only lose one man," Dieter said, rising from Gollob's side. "We beat the putes for not much cost."

Loki laughed, a high discordant sound that bounced around among the ruined columns and rattled in men's bones. "Don't you *see?* There's a whole world of hurt out there. Millions and billions of Rooks, a couple dozen of us. If we kill a thousand—fuck me with a flamer, *ten* thousand—of them and lose a single man, we've fucking *lost.* They can throw bodies and more bodies at us till we drown in orange blood, and never know the difference."

"It's like erosion," Stilicho said equably. "They just keep at us bit by bit until they wear us down."

Jovan held up his left hand, shrouded in a bandage that was already soaking through with blood. A Rook had nipped off his little finger with his beak before the Lander could get a blade in him.

"Only nine left," he said, dreamy with the painkillers and Max Nix he'd been hit with. "And then—" A shrug.

Mir covered his face with his hands, overwhelmed by the situation. *He's right,* he thought. *And so what? If we escape from here, they'll stay after us, they'll whittle us down through slow attrition. And we've got no more than a few weeks' food left on starvation rations.*

But he would not give up. He could not; if he had had that in him, he would have left his bones on the Meatgrinder practice fields.

He was aware that the Landers were staring at him. He wanted to shriek at them, to rage, to damn them for the pressure of their eyes.

Instead, he dropped hands to thighs, drew a deep breath, expelled it, and rose.

"You're right, Kyov," he said. "Assemble the men. We move in ten."

17

THE ROOK HAD a bright scarlet crest atop a green head. Its throat and bib were yellow, lower belly a white that seemed to glow in the midmorning sun. As it spread its arms, vestigial flight-feathers along the bottom extended, and pirouetted, Kyov could see that its upper back was slate grey, its lower back and tail green. To the veteran it seemed smaller than the beings they had faced in combat.

"Pretty," he said. "Maybe it's a female."

It reached out its right foot and scratched three times at the bare orange dirt. It was performing its dance in front of a tall, narrow frame building of what from the outside Kyov would guess to be one large room, its steeply pitched roof covered with grey sheets of what the Landers had discovered to be straw suspended in some plasticlike matrix. Twoscore beings that could only be juvenile Rooks—little fat puffballs of buff-colored feathers, with black beaks and tiny colored tufts atop their heads—sat on their backwards knees on the beaten soil and watched with rapt attention.

Kyov passed the glasses to Poet, who lay beside him on his belly. The two and Rouen were hidden in a stand of saplings whose bases were choked with brush, that nestled in the fold of a hillside overlooking the dance from several hundred meters away.

Poet gave the curious ritual a glance and swept the glasses around the horizon, looking for signs of the Rook mounted

166

patrol they had spotted just after dawn that morning. They could easily have bushwhacked the dozen riders and wiped them out, but in the past weeks they had learned to be wary of calling attention to themselves. Pulsers were quiet, but the blue bolts tended to sizzle and pop when they gave up their energy; and even if the riders were given no chance to fire off their noisy black-powder carbines, the Rooks could utter a piercing death cry audible for kilometers.

It was bad business to have the countryside roused against them. When not abandoned, the "collective farms" housed dozens or even hundreds of Rooks. When an alarm was raised the farms in the vicinity sent out parties ranging from half a dozen to twenty Rooks, armed with anything from farm implements to long rifles. With them came meter-tall featherless bipeds, with toothed jaws instead of beaks, and supple pebbled piebald hides. These served as watch and tracking beasts.

At first the men were contemptuous of the rural militia. A few blue bolts, or even a single sniper shot from Bitch or Starman's laser, delivered at a range which seemed impossible even to good marksmen armed with long-barreled but primitive rifles, would suffice to scatter any single band.

But once the Rooks detected the intruders the bands just *kept coming*, from all directions, gathering like a storm, striking unexpectedly as lightning. They lacked the suicidal collective courage which had impelled the main force regulars to hurl themselves into the teeth of horrific firepower at the landing zone and the ruined cathedral. But, like partisans the ancients had fought on a dozen other alien worlds, they didn't need it. Tenacious anger and occasional individual acts of mad courage were enough to make them lethal.

The intruders laughed less at the Rook farmers after one jumped from cover and rammed a pitchfork through Corporal Geydar's throat. Known as "Weepy" for his habit of crying at the least provocation, and often for no reason at all, the little noncom had died without uttering a sound. He shot his assailant dead, dropped to his knees, and just sat, bleeding out before the others, fighting off the ambush, had been able to reach him.

After that, when the biped hounds raised their yodeling, cackling call that sent prickles down every Lander's back, Section had learned to *move,* as quickly and stealthily as they could.

Kyov studied Poet covertly, from the sides of his eyes. The youth had left his flamer with Nau for this reconnaissance. He had a pulser slung across his back, which he would only use in an emergency; he disliked guns, preferring to dispatch his enemies with the horror and display of his Little Sister, or at close range, with a knife, where he could feel his victim's blood gush hot over his knuckles. His cheeks were shrunk to hollows beneath his cheekbones, and his light blue eyes were fever-bright, and not from Zone alone.

The men were down to crumbs a day; starvation waited just around some soon bend in the road, ready to beckon them with a croak and a crook of a withered brown finger. They had found no signs of human life since witnessing the destruction of the Regulars. Nor had the solar disturbance passed around the limb of the sun, as Ovanidze suggested it might; instead the interference had grown worse and worse, so that even their helmet headsets could scarcely drive a signal farther than fifty meters. By night the colorful auroral sheets had been replaced by great glowing loops, plasma channels created when the Rookery's magnetic field trapped high-energy radiation pouring in from the sun, which crossed the sky like monstrous tentacles, holding the humans to their fate.

The one blessing was that, inexplicably, the Strahn—or whoever—had not returned to exploit their victory over Kosmos. And even that advantage was questionable: forbidden barracks rumor said the Strahn treated their prisoners of war well.

The Section sergeant studied the young scout. He had known Poet much longer than Mir had; the boy was not as young as he looked, and had been Detached while still in mid-adolescence. Kyov was even more perplexed by him than the lieutenant was. Though he hid it behind sullenness and drugs, the boy was intelligent, extremely so—as bright as any man in Section, perhaps even the brilliant, mercurial, and lethal Loki.

Somehow the spectacle of this alien ritual, this Rook dance, must touch the youth; so it seemed to Kyov. There was an alienness to it, a wonder, that one with Poet's perceptiveness would have to be dead inside not to feel. Yet the youth spared scarcely a glance, as the small fat youngsters began, one by one, to rise and perform their own complex convolutions around their teacher.

Perhaps he is. Dead inside.

He saw Poet stiffen. "There," he said, and read coordinates the binoculars' processor wrote on the optical lenses: "Radial three-two-three, twenty-three hundred meters."

He handed the glasses to the sergeant. "By the trees."

Kyov aimed the glasses as indicated, adjusted the focus to his older, tired eyes. A line of feather-trees followed a watercourse, a ditch or canal from its straightness, though its banks were not built up. A party of fifteen riders, regular cavalry by the uniform yellow of the feathers sewn to their tunics, rode parallel to the trees and just inside them at an easy shuffle-foot trot.

Section had managed to keep clear of massed infantry formations since the cathedral fight. But fast-moving cavalry patrols were a threat, though the heat signature for a mount and its rider was hard to mask. The Rooks had quickly learned that the invaders had special sensory abilities, and had already grown adept at circumventing them. The lush, lovely vegetation and pleasant rolling hills of the Rookery provided wonderful natural cover, which the Rooks knew well how to utilize.

The cavalry even more than the militia had tormented Section with quick-converging attacks. They had inflicted the other fatality Section had suffered since fleeing the ruined cathedral, Henriks, lanced through the belly. Hemorrhaging too badly for the limited medical skills—and even more limited equipment—of Kyov and Dieter to stop, he had obviously been unable to keep up.

As it did at such times, it fell to Kyov to have a few quiet words with the boy, explaining the terrible stark truth of the situation. The dying transfer, not truly comprehending, wept and cried out for his mother. Kyov watched, pain stark as a brand on his face. Then he had rummaged in his own ruck, brought out a rolled blood-khaki pair of socks. He knelt and slipped them into Henriks' hand.

The scrub smiled. "Mr. Bun," he said. He rolled onto his

side, cradled the sock-roll against his cheek, and blissfully closed his eyes.

Tears streaming into his beard, Kyov aimed his pulser and blew the boy's head off.

The deathbirds distributed Henriks's gear among themselves. They left him as they had left Eyrikson and Geydar, booby-trapped—in his case, with a power can jury-rigged as an "overload grenade," set to give up all its stored energy in a single blue-green flash that would vaporize everything in a two-meter radius. They placed the smoldering ersatz sock-toy on his chest, folded his hands over it, and marched away.

"Do they act as if they're tracking us?" Kyov asked. That was another reason Kyov wondered at Poet's lack of response to the simple wonder of scenes such as the schoolyard dance. The boy displayed a marvelous sensitivity to the intentions and actions of autoc races, though their mental processes and body language differed as radically from one another's as they did from humans'. Some autocs' behavior was almost entirely comprehensible to the dullest Lander; others behaved in a manner no human could regard as anything but unpredictably bizarre. At one extreme or the other, or anywhere between, Poet had an uncanny gift for reading them.

"They're hunting us," Poet said. His hands trembled slightly as they held the heavy glasses, though his elbows were propped on bare soil beneath a bush. "But they're casting around. Don't have a clue."

"Hope they don't pick up none of them damn lizard dogs," Rouen grunted, tracking the squadron through the scope of his sniper-Bitch. The Landers had learned in particular to dread the beasts' weird hunting calls.

His face under normal circumstances was not fat, but had a full-packed look to it—not unlike Ovanidze's, but whereas the tech's cheeks were lumpy and looked scarred, even though they weren't, Rouen's were baby-smooth. Unlike Ovanidze's face, though, which remained visibly as unaffected by the situation as the tech himself was, Rouen's features showed the claw marks of hunger, exhaustion, constant dread, the growing conviction of hopelessness that nobody spoke of directly but everybody talked around.

"We'll be fine," Kyov assured him. "Let's go."

"Want me to waste them?" he asked, covering the Rook children and teacher.

"No."

Rouen's finger stayed on the trigger, taking up slack to the break point. No matter what outlandish shape his targets assumed, to his dark eyes all were Preservation Angels.

"We don't want to alert the patrol," Kyov said gently.

"Oh," said Rouen. "Right." He slid back down into the fold in the hill, drawing his Bitch after him. He capped scope and muzzle, slung the long, heavy weapon, and set out after Poet, who had already begun picking his way to the top of the hill.

Kyov paused, kneeling, taking a last look at the Rooks in the schoolyard. All the children were up now, some following the teacher in its—her?—dance, others following patterns that complemented the central dance, interlocking in a weird ethereal beauty. He felt at once an enormous warmth fill him, and contrarily an endless, aching emptiness.

With effort he tore the glasses from his eyes and moved out.

"Section Sergeant Kyov," the Dancing-Master said as they walked, with the mild afternoon sting fading from the sunlight on their faces and shadows stretching and darkening through shades of brown all around, "you mustn't take me wrong. You are a good man—none better—and solid as good Molotov armor plate."

Kyov smiled faintly. "I'm glad you feel that way."

"But—" the Dancing-Master was saying, without awaiting a response, "but—and this is the rub—it is just wildly inappropriate for you to be senior to me. Your military experience is vast, no question. But it's a question of training, and here's the crux: I am a trained professional, groomed by the finest *Akademiyas* in the Collective—

"If he starts on about his teaching days at *Akademiya Stahl,* Junior Lieutenant," Loki sang out sweetly, "Corporal Loki requests permission to slit his belly so he can vent all that pent-up bullshit without troubling the ears of the rest of us. It's only the communal thing to do."

The Dancing-Master frowned briefly at the interruption but otherwise paid no heed. He had grown adept at ignoring Loki.

"Truth to tell, I have wider training and experience than even Junior Lieutenant Mir, but the Stellar Collective has seen fit to leave his commission intact despite the fact of his being Detached, and it would be not just Particular but treasonous to question that."

"Why do you give a shit?" Jovan asked interestedly. "You're already condemned to death. Live a little."

The Dancing-Master stiffened. Like the others his cheeks had caved in and his eyes were fever-bright. It lent his handsome features a certain ascetic dignity. "I was born and bred to serve the Universal Will. I have disgraced myself, but I'll die before I will behave disloyally."

"More fool you," Jovan said. His words had an odd, slurred quality. A Rook farmer's beak had torn open a hole in his right cheek as big around as a forefinger-and-thumb circle. Jovan had refused to allow it to be patched over with artificial skin from the medical stores, and after the bleeding had stopped had taken off the dressing. He claimed he liked the way the breeze blew in his mouth and kept his tongue cool.

They were slipping through woods, following the border of vast fields of early-season grain ready to ripen, brown and inviting. It was torture to see so much food right there to hand. But, though Mir and Kyov had forbidden it, the Landers had tried to eat the local food—grains and nuts found in storage, flesh covertly butchered from a herd beast killed by Jovan, who blandly explained he thought he saw an enemy scout hiding behind it. Those who sampled the autochthonous produce said it tasted good enough—wonderful, sometimes, though hunger may have affected that perception.

But their bodies did not find it so attractive. As soon as the food hit human stomachs it was instantly ejected in wracking spasms, projectile-vomit barrages that endangered bystanders and left the victim quivering, sweat-wet, and too spent to move.

"I have the most experience of serving as an officer of any man in this Section, and there you have it," the Dancing-Master said. "But I do not begrudge Junior Lieutenant Mir his rank."

"He comes from a better family than yours," called Black Bertold, swinging along in command of the rear guard. His right arm was in a sling, broken by a rifle ball. He had also taken a lance through the left thigh. He had cut himself a walking stick of some black hardwood, and gimped jauntily along with it held in his left hand to help him. It was widely believed he had held a commission himself, in the Kosmos Marines, but even when he got drunk and expansive and talking about the old days he was always elliptical about exactly what role he had played.

The Dancing-Master scowled, because what Bertold said was true, and consequently a sore spot: the Dancing-Master came from a long line of Engine officers, some of whom had attained flag rank. But Mir was Ministerial; his father had held District-level rank in Values. Disgraced the Mirs may have been, but their former Service translated into current *klad*.

"But the matter of Section Sergeant Kyov," the Dancing-Master persisted, "is merely and obviously an oversight. He was, after all, a cargo handler at a spaceport, which I think any observer will agree will scarcely prepare a man for military command. Nothing against you, once again, Section Sergeant; it's merely that the facts do not support your being senior to me."

"You may be right," Kyov said.

The Dancing-Master nodded. "Of course I am. And I have taken steps to rectify the situation, as I'm sure you will not mind. I have written letters to the Ministry of Struggle. Not only that, I've dispatched copies to the ministries of Continuing Revolution and Values; they are responsible, too, after all, for maintaining the fighting trim of the Engine of History."

The White Rat had walked up close. He regarded the noncom keenly with his blue-white eyes.

"May I have your boots?" he asked. The Dancing-Master was proud of his boots, officer's boots, soft and supple. He had either contrived to keep them through the Grinder, or gotten his hands on another pair.

"What? I beg your pardon? Of course not! Why would I give you my boots?"

"When you die," the Rat said. "Can't be long; you obviously have a mighty death wish."

"What a fool!" yelled Balt from near the front of the straggling line. Landers turned to stare in irritation; they weren't aware of enemies nearby, but nobody was too comfortable about the stocky ex-felon trumpeting his bull bellow about the countryside. "Calling attention to yourself like that."

He took a bite from the tiny chip of suss bar clutched in his grubby fingers. At his side, little Hynkop tottered along under the weight of the Bitch-MG and ammo hoppers. His skin was pale as paper and seemed as thin, and he barely had meat enough on his bones to hold them together inside his battle dress.

Balt was treading a thin line here, if as everyone suspected he was browbeating his assistant gunner and stealing his food. Justice in the Detachment usually amounted to what you could secure with your fists—or the fists of any allies you might have the wits or *klad* to muster. Those who could not hold on to what they had got short shrift and shorter sympathy.

But down here in the dirt, everyone's ass was on the same line. Nobody expected great things from Hynkop, but the little scrub was becoming too frail to raise a pulser and too hunger-palsied to aim. When the shitstorm broke, the deathbirds got as defensive about unfitting a man for combat as the most anal-retentive red-ass personnel officer.

Then again, Balt was not a man who paid much heed to anyone's boundaries—except to obliterate them.

"What do you mean?" Dancing-Master asked, nonplussed.

"The will of the Powers-that-Be, the Brass and the Big Circuits, is the Universal Will revealed, of course; they'll all tell you the same," Loki said in a fleering mock-pedantic manner. "I'm surprised you weren't aware of that fundamental truth. Were you not an instructor of History and Moral Philosophy?"

"You know I was," the Dancing-Master said sullenly. "But oversights happen."

"And that works to our benefit, if you'd think about it," Jovan said. "We're the scum of the Universe. It only annoys the Brass to be reminded we exist. Seems to me you're calling down a world of hurt upon your shoulders by calling attention to yourself, brud."

The Dancing-Master sniffed. "What are they going to do, Detach me?" he asked. The traditional deathbird defiance mantra sounded feeble from his lips.

Balt rumbled laughter, stuck his hand down the back of his trousers, scratched his rectum, sniffed his fingers. "Ah! Officers, politicals, children of *klad*: all fools." He peered at the Dancing-Master from beneath densely forested black brows that grew together in the middle. "With all your school knowledge and your books and your classrooms, you never learned that things can always get worse. Ha."

The Dancing-Master lapsed into sulks. The rest of the Section straggled along, their movements showing the blurriness of men who are pushing the limits of exhaustion—but for whom that is familiar territory, territory they have long since learned to navigate. Looking at them, Mir knew they would go on as long as anything human could, and then they'd keep going. But even these men had their limits, and they were bearing down like a battlewagon in catastrophic reentry.

"One thing I'll say for this place," Jovan said. "It is beautiful. Gives a man a sense of peace."

"The only thing you know about peace is to piss on it, just like the rest of us," Starman said.

Jovan lacked the energy to glare at him. "It's good farmland here," he said. "The soil's so rich you can taste it."

"Don't think to fool us with your hayseed talk," Loki said. "We know what kind of plowing you have in mind."

"We all have it in mind," Black Bertold said, "so let's hear no more of it. Some of us care to be able to sleep nights."

"Not Chyz the Jizz," Florenz said. He was marching along as best he could hanging on to a strap passed through the back of Nau's belt. The upper half of his face was covered in bandages. He had survived the cathedral fight by huddling against the base of a fragment of wall. "He'll be pounding off all night, as usual."

The taller transfer, walking flank guard with the rest of Second Squad, hung his head and looked down at the ground.

"Bertold won't be able to sleep tonight for dreams of the boy brothels," Stilicho called from near the front of the procession. "Feathered rumps don't inspire him."

Bertold laughed. Van Dam, marching at Kobolev's side behind the Third Squad leader, perked his head up. He had been more sullen and withdrawn than usual since Eyrikson's death.

"Maybe you should take Hynkop away from Balt!" he said. His eyes had a feverish quality, and his voice was too loud, as if he were challenging the sergeant. Bertold ignored him.

The Section continued its march, spreading out when the

strip of woodland joined a larger forest. The men continued to banter in a distracted manner. Balt fell out to the side, kneeling down to fiddle with the fastenings of his boot, leaving little Hynkop to stagger on alone with his burden.

As Van Dam came walking past, Balt swung his fist at the transfer's crotch, hard enough to lift his boot soles from the crumbly mulch underfoot. Van Dam fell to the ground on his side and huddled around himself, moaning.

Kobolev shouted and started forward. He halted abruptly when he found the tip of Balt's battle knife pressing into his own groin. Balt grinned at him with his awful teeth until Kobolev held his hands out from his sides and backed away.

Balt straightened, went over, and kicked Van Dam in the kidneys.

"What's mine is mine," he said. "Remember that, dragon-breath."

18

"SIR," OVANIDZE SAID. He knelt in the leafy litter of a forested hillside where Mir had fallen the men out for a rest break. He religiously checked his communications set at every halt.

Which reminded the young lieutenant of Karl Marx's definition of religion. Religion was not forbidden in the Stellar Collective; all faiths were said to be worship of reflections of the Universal Spirit, whose cult in fact came close to being the established religion of Realized space. But Mir, like all Collective schoolchildren, had been exposed to measured doses of the thought of the great collectivists and communitarians who helped build the road to perception of Universal Truth: Marx, Lenin, Mussolini, Stalin, Galbraith, Hitler, Mao, McDowell. The specifics of their teachings had often been superseded, errors revealed, and discredited along the inevitable march of Historic Process; certainly they and their adherents had fought among themselves. Yet all had made vital contributions, played key roles in the Process, and were honored today.

Mir squeezed his eyes shut. *My mind is freewheeling again.* He had eaten his last scraps of rations yesterday.

He rose from where he'd been sitting. His joints ached, the walls of his stomach seemed to be rubbing together; he felt immeasurably old, though his body seemed light, so light it might just float up into the turquoise sky and keep going for-

ever. He walked slowly over to the tech with little bars and
patches of yellow afternoon light, filtered through trees, running over him like tiny creatures, and squatted down beside
him.

"I have something," Ovanidze said.

Mir swayed as if to a blow. His pulse accelerated so hard
it nauseated him. Just the briefest of human contact would
seem like rescue now.

"What is it?"

Ovanidze switched his unit to repeat the signal it was receiving over Mir's headset. The lieutenant frowned. He
heard . . . nothing. Just an occasional crackle of interference,
breaking through the slightest of hums.

"What is it?" he demanded. Disappointment flushed his
cheeks and made his chest feel scooped-out, and he swore if
the tech was playing tricks on him, that he would suffer for
it. He fought the impulse to grab the man by the front of his
blouse and shake him.

"Carrier wave, sir," Ovanidze said blandly. "Somebody's
broadcasting." He indicated the readouts on his set. "From
right nearby, too."

"Why don't I hear anything?"

"They're not broadcasting anything in particular, sir. Just
have a transmitter powered-up, keeping a channel open."

"Try to raise somebody."

As the tech bent to work Mir realized the fingers of his own
right hand were vibrating, making insect rustling noises among
the crumble of fallen leaves. He was quivering like Poet with
a fresh shot of Zone inside him. He drew his hand to his leg,
pressed it hard against the sun-warmed fabric to contain its
jittering. He did not want the others to see how excited he
was. It was a sign of weakness; and if this proved another
disappointment, they would fashion a cross of it to hang him
on.

The tech sat back shaking his head. "No joy, sir. Nobody
responds."

Mir squeezed his eyes shut and felt blackness open away
behind them. *So close! We seemed so close. . . .*

"The signal comes from *somewhere*, sir," Ovanidze said.
He tapped the lit displays flickering on the front of the set.
"And it isn't far away."

The deadly lassitude drained away through the soles of Mir's boots. "Up!" he shouted, jumping to his feet. "Everybody up! Get ready to move."

There was the usual grumbling in response to the end of a rest break. What was unusual was how slow even the ancients were to respond, as if they were all ancient as Narva in fact. It was not a sign of growing disaffection with Mir—or at least, not primarily. It was a sign that they were reaching the limits of their endurance.

Ovanidze slung the weighty commo pack across his back and consulted a handheld RDF unit. "This way," he said, pointing off at an angle over the hill's shoulder.

They began to climb, bent forward for balance, trying not to slip on the loose mat of debris that covered the forest floor. Mir had not entirely abandoned his desire to strike for *Tse-*745, the Rook city that now lay northeast of them. But near-constant harassment by Rook militia and regular patrols had prevented them from doing much more than circling around to the west.

They had worked their way into an area marked as mountainous on Mir's tac display. In reality their surroundings seemed mostly high hills, bare pink-and-ocher rock with most of the sharp edges worn away, maroon-leafed hardwood forests where small bright-feathered quadrupeds ran up and down gnarled trunks and castigated the intruders from sharp pink beaks. There was little sign of settlement in the area: the occasional tang of a campfire on the morning air, the thunk and rasp of a woodcutter's camp. The up-and-down going was rough on thigh muscles quivering from a long accretion of fatigue poisons and little rest, but the pursuit seemed to have forsaken them.

Perhaps that was a good sign in itself; perhaps it meant some substantial concentration of humans survived in the vicinity, to draw away the enemy's attention. Mostly Mir didn't know what to think, and tramped along in an ocher-hazed reverie, remembering childhood fields under bright Santander sun—unnaturally white in memory, in contrast to the warm and friendly saffron of the Rookery's star—or the gentle voice and dry soft-scaled cheek of Tsatchka, his nanny and nurse.

Even now, with the men coursing around Ovanidze like excited hounds as the tech trudged stolidly along the path his radio direction–finding gear indicated, Mir found himself phasing in and out, between present and nostalgia. Brutally, he forced himself to remember his arrest, the Meatgrinder, the time they broke his hands, the first time he was raped: the sense of tearing invasion, the pains shooting into belly and back . . .

The painful memories had the desired effect, of driving his focus back to the here and now. He made himself concentrate on the shine of sunlight between branches, the chatter of birds fluttering in the treetops overhead, the forest smell, even the exertion sting in his quadriceps. He was not daring to let himself think about what might be causing Ovanidze's signal. He feared some climactic letdown that would finally send him crashing over the edge.

Instead what they came to was a slope of a ridge that had slumped in a recent miniature landslide. Small maroon-and-yellow seedlings protruded from the burnt umber dirt.

"Here it is," Ovanidze said, standing in a dry watercourse that ran diagonally downward past the base of the slump.

"Wonderful," Kobolev said. "You've led us to a dirt pile." He raised a big fist. "I'm minded to make you pay for leading us on a trip to Earth, little man."

Ovanidze seldom showed much expression. Now he sneered. "This is where the signal comes from," he said with conviction.

Kyov dropped to his knees and began to pull away fistfuls of soft, moist, fragrant soil. "Let's dig," he said, "and see what we find."

Landers shed packs and fell to with their entrenching tools, the edges of some of which still bore nicks from Rook skulls. Even Florenz, caught up in the moment, dropped to his knees to scrabble at the dirt with his hands. In a few moments there was a thunk, and Nau sang out, "Hey! I've found something!"

Landers converged on the spot. A flurry of spades, and shortly a square half meter of hard surface, matte off-white, was revealed.

"That's molded Engine polymer," Stilicho said. "Kind they use for prefab buildings."

"Whatever it is they must've blasted a hole in the hillside to slide it into, then dropped the slope above to bury it," Loki said.

"What are we waiting for?" Jovan demanded. "There might be food inside!"

That got the Landers busy. Shortly they exposed the end of what seemed like a hemicylindrical tunnel driven into the ridge. There was a door in it.

Mir started for it. *Think like a combat officer,* he told himself sternly, and stopped. "Section Sergeant Kyov," he said.

Kyov nodded. "Poet, open it. Stilicho, cover."

Reluctantly the men backed away. Survival reasserted itself. You never knew what might be waiting behind a closed door. No matter how innocuous it seemed.

Stilicho disengaged the latch, gave the door a soft push inward, flattened his back against the wall as Poet aimed his Little Sister inside. The interior was brightly lit, white gleam and chrome.

"Faugh!" Stilicho exclaimed, as a wash of air from inside reached him. "Somebody's dead in there."

Showing no reaction, Poet pushed inside. Stilicho slipped in after. The others crowded around in a semicircle, eager to see, but unwilling to get too close to the smell.

The scrubs looked at the ancients, faces asking questions they dared not vocalize. "Smell of death is something you have to get used to all over again," Jovan said. "Every time."

A few impatient jostling heartbeats, and Poet emerged. "It's clear," he said. "Nothing alive in there."

The Landers crowded in. There was an antechamber, with a desk and two chairs, a shiny alloy examining table, white cabinets along the walls. Beside the desk lay the body of a man in BK Engine fatigues with patches bearing the open hand insignia of Medical Corps. His head was pretty much gone from the lower jaw up; bits of blackened dried tissue clung to the wall and the end of the desk, and there was a spray of blood dried maroon-black on the polymer face of a cabinet. A directed-energy pulse pistol lay near the corpse's right hand.

"Pute did himself," Big Bori said, touching the dead hand with the toe of his boot and snatching it abruptly back, as if fearing contamination. "Why he'd do that?"

"Why don't you go to hell and ask him, you great ape?" Starman said.

Bori turned a worried face to him. "Don't say that, Starman; please don't. I'm afraid of ghosts."

"That's all right, my friend," Loki said, reaching up to lap the giant's shoulder. "If you go to hell, you won't even spare a thought for ghosts."

"Really?" asked Bori, sounding vastly relieved.

"So what the in Planet Hell is this?" asked Jovan, staring back at a bulky mechanism, dominated by a cylinder two meters across and three long, surrounded by covered meter-high polymer vats, that filled the rear of the buried shelter.

"Come, now, comrades," Stilicho said. "Don't you recognize it? It's an R&R unit."

Loki snapped his fingers. "Of course! The deathbird's second home."

"And we don't have a first," added Poet.

Once past the unexpectedness of it, Jovan of course did. R&R was short for *regraf & regen*, regrafting and regeneration. Some called the units the secret weapon of the Engine of History; certainly, all the unit's veterans, Jovan included, had ample experience of them. From a tiny tissue sample they could regrow a man a lost limb, new guts, sheets of new skin to replace old burned away, all within a couple of days, thanks to cloning and forced-growing techniques that were the pinnacle of Collective medical science.

The deathbirds got little field maintenance in the main. But if they were injured in battle, the Stellar Collective was assiduous about scooping them up and pouring them into R&R units. They were valuable salvage, after all.

Starting at the hairline, a frown worked its way down Jovan's long face to his chin. "No food."

"Well," Dieter said, rubbing his hands together. "At least we can get patched up. Maybe we can get Florenz back his eyes."

"But there's no *food*," Jovan persisted. "Who gives a snake if we have all our fingers and toes if we all starve together? *I* don't care how good my corpse looks. Shit, I want you all to puke at sight of it, so at least you'll be sorry I'm gone."

He wasn't alone in his sentiments. A frenzied search of cabinets and lockers produced no food at all, only polymer cartons containing huge bags of not-quite-clear liquid.

"What's this?" Bori asked, hoisting a bag to eye level and peering through the contents at the fluorescent light overhead. "Booze?"

Kyov squinted up at the label printed on the side. "Nutrient solution," he said. "For the tissue culture."

Bori cocked an eye at him. "Nu—nur—nute—that word you said means 'food,' doesn't it?"

Kyov nodded.

Bori reached to his harness, pulled out his fighting knife from the upside-down scabbard, plunged its double-edged leaf-shaped blade into the bag. Then he held it up and let the clear fluid cascade into his open mouth and over his chin.

"Here, you great fool, don't hog it all!" Jovan shouted. He grabbed at Bori's arm, showing just how desperate his hunger was making him. You didn't *grab* Big Bori.

Instead of having his arm wrenched from its socket and used to beat him unconscious, though, Jovan was hit full in the face by a stream of clear vomit jetting from Bori's mouth. Surprise as much as impact knocked him on his ass.

"Gah!" Bori spat, dropping the bag to the synthetic tile floor. It burst, showering everybody nearby with the viscous contents. Gagging and retching, the giant cast red-eyed around the shelter, then seized Kyov by the front of the battle dress, hoisted him bodily into the air, and slammed him into a set of cabinets.

"You tried to poison me!" he bellowed, cocking an immense fist.

Stilicho pushed himself in between the two. "Easy, there, big boy," he said in his customary calm voice. He put his hands on Bori's fist and began to draw it gently down. "Kyov didn't do anything of the sort. You just went flying off in all directions again."

Talking to Big Bori like a gently reproving adult worked— sometimes, if you were the right person. At this moment Stilicho happened to be, so the giant allowed himself to be backed away. He let Kyov slide down the white front of the cabinets. The noncom rubbed his chest, shook his head, and uttered a sigh full of sadness for the whole universe.

"What happened to you, man?" Loki demanded, as Jovan

picked himself dripping off the floor tiles. "That was an impressive spew."

Bori scrunched his face up. "It was *bad*. It made me sick. Kyov said it was food." He started to glare red-eyed at the Section sergeant.

"Now, Bori, you know better," Stilicho said. Bori didn't; Kyov *had* said that, after a fashion. But Bori was in childsubmissive mode now, and accepted the calm voice of authority. He settled down.

Loki squatted down beside the bag, which Bori had cast from him to splat off one of the vats and lie gurgling its contents onto the floor. He dipped a finger in the fluid, tasted it, and spit.

"Fah! The great fool's got it right for once! This stuff tastes like Kosmos deck disinfectant."

"You're exaggerating," Jovan said. "Besides, you're just not serious about food; it's why there's no meat on that skinny frame."

"I've ample meat where it counts, pig farmer!" Loki said, grabbing his crotch.

"A man who's hungry enough can eat anything," Jovan said.

"Why don't you lick Bori's puke off your face and show us?" Starman said.

The lanky Lander grimaced. He wiped his mouth and environs carefully with the sleeve of his battle dress, checked with the back of his hand to make sure it was clean. Then he went to the fallen bag, picked it up, and took a hearty swig of the fluid leaking from it.

His geyser of vomit spattered the wall two meters away.

The Landers applauded. "Not as mighty an effort as Bori's," Dieter said, "but creditable, creditable."

Jovan, wracked by retching, staggered back against a set of lockers and slid down to his rump on the slightly resilient tile. He peeled lips back from teeth in a gesture of disgust and despair.

"Nobody could keep that shit down," he said. "It's like drinking benzine."

He looked up at his bruds, and all of hope and much of life left him in a sigh. "We're in the whiz jigger true. We're going to starve."

Loki had narrowed his eyes, which gave him a feral look. He studied the gleaming cylinder for a moment, then looked around at Ovanidze. "You, our noble technician of death," he said. "Can you work this thing?" He waved a white-spider hand at the R&R unit.

Ovanidze frowned. He prided himself on his ability to fix or operate anything mechanical; it was his utility to the unit, his shield against the physical abuse and most of the verbal that was the lot of practically every Lander, especially those as physically unprepossessing as he.

"I'm . . . not sure," he confessed. "I can fix it if it's out of order. But to get it to work—" He shrugged. "Likely some programming involved. More than I'm comfortable with."

Nau pushed forward, face shining with eagerness. As soon as Loki turned his eyes—now pale green—on him he quailed and seemed to sink into himself.

"Well?" Loki demanded. "Why do you call attention to yourself, scrub? Do you feel a pressing need for a beating? We'll certainly oblige you!"

"N-no sir!"

"Sir! He calls me *sir!*" Loki swept a long-suffering gaze around the circle of his comrades. When he looked back at the miserable transfer he snapped his right arm out to full extension, duster-hilted battle knife gripped in gauntleted hand, like a fencer about to lunge. "I am a *corporal,* you miserable sow's afterbirth, not an officer, not the Direktor's spoiled darling; I *work* for a living. Now tell me why you bothered us, or I'll cut some vents in your nose!"

Nau opened his mouth. Nothing came out.

Kyov stepped to his side. "Easy, son. He's mostly talk."

Loki twitched the knife aside to aim at him. "Don't be too sure, old man!"

"I—I have some programming," Nau said. "I think I could make it run, with help from Ovanidze."

Loki looked at him, cocked a brow. "Oh so?" The transfer nodded.

Loki frowned, but it was not an angry frown: thoughtful. He lowered his knife, tapped its tip against his teeth. Then he grinned a rabid fox grin.

"So then, my brothers," he said, "we shall eat like kings."

PART TWO

In the Kettle

19

THE WOMAN WAS of medium height, thin and pale. Blonde hair had been planed off flat atop her head, and hung around the back and sides in a lank fringe. She wore a grey dress that was little more than a tube sealed at the shoulders. The Book which hung down the front of it on a chain of polished-hardwood beads the size of her thumb joint was massive, nearly as broad as her rib cage.

Drink in hand, she leaned against a square-section column, allowing the light of Santander's setting sun through the floor-to-ceiling windows of the Citadel of Values, the Ministry's headquarters in Santander city, to throw her features into dramatic relief, and regarded her circle of listeners with deep-set eyes.

"Changes are due," she said throatily, "and they are coming. The Universal Will becomes clearer. A paradigm shift is in the wind."

Her audience, half a dozen males and females likewise dressed in the ascetic style popular among young Values personnel of Custodian class and Communality faction, bobbed their heads and made appreciative noises.

"For example, take the name: 'the Engine of History.' That's far too mechanistic. It should be changed to 'the Green, Growing Plant of History.' "

Standing nearby, skeletal at his own banquet, Albrekht Mir moved away from the muted approving hubbub with as much

haste as he could muster without showing it. His face was
expressionless, mirroring his emotional state. His thoughts
were bleak.

He cast his eyes about the great room. Its only furnishings
were the serving tables set discreetly against the far wall, with
solemn-stiff Dependents standing behind them like attentive
automata in high-necked white tunics. Square white-stuccoed
columns standing alone and human figures in groups cast bold
shadows across the floor.

Mir paused by a column to survey his guests. *Your power
base,* he thought.

For a moment he felt the future pressing down upon him
with planetary weight. The only heavier burden he knew was
the past. Perhaps that was what drove him onward, obedient
to the laws of fluid dynamics.

Another cluster of earnest molders of Collective opinion
stood nearby. Observing the nearness of the great man himself,
one pitched his voice to carry: "The Stellar Collective has
reached a crossroads," he announced. "The design bureaus
are out of control. Production shortfalls threaten our economy.
The recent disaster in Strahn space shows that Struggle has
been taken over by Devolutionists who haven't a clue."

He glanced slyly toward Mir, to make sure of the supervisor's attention, and then, with adolescent piping clarity, said,
"The solution is simple. Values must take over everything."

Mir traversed his spare handsome head to bear on the boy.
The young man took his stare for approval. He allowed himself a modest smile and nod and turned to accept the plaudits
of his listeners for making such a smashing, cogent, truly *Universal* statement.

Mir walked on. He was unsure of his destination, and that
was perhaps the part of this function, so trivial and so crucial,
which bothered him most. He had become a man who lived
for *direction.*

A door opened, and Natalya Mir swept into the room, followed by her retinue. At once heads turned. The crowd began
to gravitate toward her.

She still wore her hair cropped close, a silver-white cap.
The fit of her severe grey uniform showed how she had begun
to fill out, though not with excess flesh. She was working out
like an athlete, had actually been training with the Shadows,

Values' ultrasecret commando formation. The pulser pistol she wore on a plain web belt—in contravention of polite custom among Custodians—was not for show.

Above the herd she caught sight of her husband. Her smile of greeting was radiant, and so was she. He allowed himself a hint of smile and a nod, and she turned her attention back to her admirers.

From a behind-the-scenes producer she had turned into a media star. Her prime time "ValueShare" program—which the scurrilous called "Catch 'Em and Kill 'Em"—was the District's top-rated news sim. The Communal Courts were livid. Not only was she usurping their function, but her commando format—sweeping down on Devolutionists wherever they happened to be with cameras hot, subjecting them to a drumhead court-martial–style trial onsite and then executing them was a lot more action-packed than the static Communal Court simcasts. The only programs more popular were the Health & Fortune lotteries, which were unassailable; they not only offered authentic human misery, but a chance to *get something*. Chances like that weren't easily come by in the Stellar Collective.

Mir shook his head. Natalya had always been at least a handsome woman; they had made a highly presentable pair from earliest days, which helped further their respective careers. As Natalya had grown heavier, her husband's interest had wandered. He had taken younger lovers.

Now his wife, in her late forties, had become authentically beautiful, lit from within by the fire of her purpose. And by her demeanor she was more devoted to him than ever. Yet now he was beyond physical desire. He was not incapable; it merely struck him as irrelevant.

He could appreciate the irony of the situation. That sense had not been expunged by white walls or chromed tables.

A figure emerged from a side service door to stand like a gaudy rock among the esthetes and idealists, squat and balding: Sendak. Mir's pulse quickened. Mir would not admit he was the man Mir was *hoping* to see, or even whom he *wanted* to see. Sendak, rather, was the man it was *optimal* to see.

Seeing that he had caught the DVS's attention, Sendak smiled. It was a big smile, full of yellowed teeth, as out of place as a scream—as out of place as his bright red blazer and bright blue pants, among the muted voices and muted colors of the Values elite. Like the scars and pockmarks that ravaged the face around them like a battlefield, the stained, skewed teeth were a statement of defiance. In a day in which R&R medtech was readily available—to a man in Sendak's position—to retain such disfigurements approached autarky.

Mir nodded. Sendak bobbed his goblin head and withdrew. Mir started for the door.

"Supervisor."

It was the boy who thought Values ought to take over everything. He had not joined the migration to Natalya's circle. Perhaps he felt real power still reposed in the DVS. In which case he might not be the utter fool he sounded.

"Where is your Book?" the youngster asked. His own was so immense he had grown a hump of muscle at the base of his neck from holding it up. It was clearly the best-developed muscle of his body.

Albrekht Mir looked past the drawn cheeks and ascetic's pallor, through glass-empty eyes into the colors of what served the young man for a soul. He saw both the desire to curry favor and the desire to challenge. He considered squashing him like the small and crawling thing he was, decided that was not his optimum solution.

The supervisor himself wore a charcoal grey jacket over a white turtleneck, an ensemble which without conscious intent emphasized the *boiled-down* character of the man he had become, a being stripped of nonessentials. For all the very cogent work he had done gathering every scrap of information available on his own supporters, as on every bloc of the planet and Stellar District of Santander, he had not yet realized that the increasing asceticism his hangers-on displayed was merely his faction molding itself like plastic to conform to its leading figure.

Mir raised fingers strong and elemental as branches of a tree and touched himself on the sternum, between the dark lapels. "In here," he said, and moved on.

Values Citadel was a glass spike jutting from city center, charcoal black, austere, and imposing, as befit a Ministry charged with setting the spiritual tone for the whole vast Stellar Collective. Mir's office occupied the apex, a pyramid of polarized glass hundreds of meters above the herd grazing on canapés and local champagne in the reception hall. Its appointments were black and silver. The lights were dialed low. For color there was the sunset, indigo, mauve, and fire.

At one time the great black-gleaming desk had been surrounded by holo images of Albrekht Mir in his former life, dedicating a new Reorientation Camp for Political Unreliables, meeting the Direktor, gazing paternally down into the terraced pit of the CommuNews command center, from which his wife valiantly fought to counteract the Devolutionst lies promulgated by the networks run by Struggle and the ultimate enemy, the Ministry for Continuing Revolution.

The images had gone into the fusion bottles, along with the usual desktop mementos, not to mention the effects of the woman who had occupied the office during Mir's imprisonment, or indeed the occupant herself. The bric-a-brac had not been replaced, and would not be. Mir was bent on purging clutter from his life.

Without being invited, Sendak pulled a tube-framed chair to Mir's desk and sat. Sendak was not a man who asked permission, even of a District Values supervisor.

"Service," he said, smiling.

Mir touched his breastbone and made ritual reply: "Duty. How goes your work?"

"Well. Adequately well. As you know, I'm a man with quite the nose for human foibles." He tapped the organ in question with a forefinger. "And the heads of the minor ministries have their share of those, indeed they do."

"You acquire leverage?"

"We acquire leverage."

"Will they stand with us or against us? Or try to play the middle game?"

The scarfaced man shrugged. "By law and Universal Will we are a tribal people," he said. "That means conscience follows the bloodiest spear. If you move decisively enough, the minor players will fall neatly in line—not to mention the Deps in their masses." He smiled. "No one is eager to be either fertilizer or plasma."

"And the major players?"

"Struggle will never be a friend to Values, but since we're not on the frontier, they haven't much influence. With the

Universal war for Universal peace going full bore, they can't spare much by way of a garrison for peaceful Santander District.''

"And Revo?"

Sendak leaned back in his chair, crossed his legs, steepled his fingers before his beak nose.

"Your wife is a forceful woman, Supervisor."

"She is that. Do you disapprove?"

Sendak rubbed a fleshy cheek. "She's pissed off Revo righteously, stealing the ratings from the CC sims as she's done." The simcast Communal Court proceedings went out over the Universal Truth Network—which belonged to the Ministry for Continuing Revolution. UTN was the main bitterest enemy to CommuNews, as Revo was to Values.

Mir allowed himself the least of frowns. "In all our months of association," he said, "this is the first time I've known you to avoid a direct answer to a direct question, Sendak."

Sendak laughed. "I'm not now, either. I'm building a framework; I can't know what's favorable and what's not until I know about what game you care to play."

"What do you surmise?"

"A test?" The coarse man laughed again. It was coarse laughter. "All right, then. Revo focuses all their wrath—and their attention—on your wife's public persona. At the same time, they're drawn to dismiss her as no more than another fluffhead sim star."

He gestured as if weighing options in either hand. His hands were contradictions: large and scarred, yet fluid in motion, suggesting the capacity both for brutality and utmost sensitivity.

"On the one hand, anger, on the other, underestimation." He made twin throwaway motions. "I'd say you're setting yourself up to be attacked. And it's ever more politic to strike back than to be seen to begin the festivities."

A moment, and Mir nodded. "You are masterful at what you do."

"I'd be ever so much more masterful if you were more forthcoming. Then it's only our enemies' intentions I'd have to guess at."

"I'll take that under advisement," Mir said. "One thing: do not underestimate my wife."

Sendak grinned with horrible teeth. "If you suspect me of underestimation, Supervisor, I suggest you go ahead and neck me now, and save us both the suspense."

Mir studied the man, decided he saw in him what he had seen all along. "You're a tool adequate to the task at hand."

"Right." Sendak crossed his legs and clasped hands around one knee. "Now: I've found your boy."

Mir drew his head back.

"At least I've found where he was sent. The Rookery."

Mir squeezed his eyes shut.

The Rookery was the greatest military disaster in Stellar Collective history. At least, it was the greatest in recent memory. The Collective was not assiduous in preserving its memories of failure.

The Strahn were a race of compact centauroid beings who had used their own version of faster-than-light drive to forge a Hegemony of "trading partners"—actually subject races, conquered but not closely held—to spinward of the Stellar Collective. For two generations they and the Collective had been aware of each other. For the past ten years Universal they had actually been butted up against one another along a hundred–light-year frontier, while their diplomats wrangled in perfect amity and equally perfect bad faith.

The Engine of History was strong enough to crush the Strahn in short order—if it could devote its whole energy to the task. It couldn't. The Stellar Collective must keep expanding or collapse of its own weight. It was surrounded by enemies, and by races desperately—if not always consciously—hungering for Realization. The barrier of the Hegemony must be swept aside. Such was inevitable, the Historic Process.

It was, however, fundamental policy to expedite Process whenever possible. Accordingly, the Supreme Staff decided not to tackle the powerful Strahn head-on. Rather they would make a flanking move to a star system beyond the boundaries of both polities, hanging in a dwindling froth of Population II stars outside the galactic plane. It boasted a planet eminently habitable by human and Strahn alike, but which the Hegemony had not yet claimed or tried to garrison. Best of all, its population possessed such a young technology that they would be able to offer only the most cursory resistance to Realization.

A great war fleet had been assembled. Five million men would be landed on the planet's surface simultaneously, overwhelming the autocs by sheer force of awe.

The fleet had consisted almost entirely of the horde of transports necessary to move such a force and its moon mass of supplies. A mere handful of warships were sent along as escorts. Pulling too many battlecraft off the frontier might tempt the Strahn Navy into lunging across it. It also increased the likelihood of the end run being detected, and surprise was key to its success. And why waste the hulls to the losses inevitable in mass Lo-space Jumps? The Rooks had no fleet. Their gunpowder and draft-beast technology couldn't touch the transports in orbit.

The Strahn had learned of the plan. The Kosmos fleet had barely shaped orbit when a raiding force hit. Carnage was almost absolute. Ninety percent of the invading army was vaporized in its transports and landing craft. Ten thousand ships were destroyed by the sharklike Strahn cruisers. Only a few escaped.

They left behind almost sixty thousand men, virtually without supplies, on the surface of a world which produced no food the human body could metabolize.

"Your son's Section was in the first assault wave," Sendak said.

Albrekht Mir raised his head. He realized he had wandered away somewhere behind his eyes. He didn't know how long. *How do I feel?* he wondered. Do *I feel? Should I?*

"That probably gave him the greatest chance of survival," the scarfaced man continued, "at least of those Kosmos didn't carry away with them when they ran off with their tails between their legs."

"But it's been weeks!"

Sendak shrugged.

Mir rose and paced to the slanting window-wall. Night was complete but for a pool of sullen orange along the western horizon. The city was coming awake, a jewel scatter beneath his feet.

"What's Struggle doing about it?"

"Well, the Engine is clawing for Kosmos's throat, and the space navy is fighting to hold it at bay. The army's been presented with a wizard opportunity to dust off all its old demands that Kosmos be done away with, or reduced to a subordinate formation like the wet navy.''

''That won't happen.''

''Not bloody likely. But Kosmos is tossing sacrificial victims off the troika at a wondrous rate. Pretty soon every burg in the Octant can have its own patch of wall complete with the silhouette of an admiral to decorate its public square.''

Mir turned from the window. ''Surely they're going to mount a rescue effort.''

''Far from sure, Supervisor,'' Sendak said. ''To send a force strong enough to kick the centaurs off the Rookery could fatally weaken the frontier. And there are those in the Engine of History who feel that writing off the whole doomed affair is the best way to deal a body blow to Kosmos.''

Mir shut his eyes and took a long breath. ''Continue your work, Sendak,'' he said. ''And your . . . inquiries as well.''

Sendak rose. ''I'll do that thing, Supervisor. Shall I send in your wife?''

''No.'' Mir wasn't yet ready for her to meet his expediter. ''Have someone else do it.''

''As you wish.'' Sendak bowed and withdrew, leaving Albrekht Mir alone with the stars and his thoughts.

20

THE GOOD SMELL of roasting pork filled the late afternoon air. It had taken Haakon Mir several days to get over his nervousness that the Rooks might smell the cookfire in front of the still mostly concealed R&R bunker, or spot the smoke and hunt them down. But regular recon patrols swept the area in a wide radius, and reported no sign of Rook activity other than a camp of a half dozen woodcutters about four and a half klicks away. With the bulk of two respectable hills—not quite "mountains" to Mir's mind, but large enough—between them, the risk seemed small.

Chyz hovered close-watch over the hunk of meat sizzling on its spit, turning deep pink and beginning to blacken on the outside. The Coggies made much of insisting that the Mad Wanker—who was still assiduous in his hobby—wash his hands carefully in the nearby stream before handling their food. But he showed a definite talent for cooking, and did not seem to mind the chore. And of course his willingness to take on that unpopular duty won him a measure of increased acceptance from the ancients.

Fallen logs had been pulled together by the entrance to the R&R bunker and rudely trimmed with knives and sharpened e-tools to serve as benches. With no threat of overhead reconnaissance—except from possibly the Strahn, whose gravitic anomaly detectors and synthetic-aperture radar would pick out the buried facility from O as if it had a red-glowing ten-kilometer arrow pointing at it—they didn't have to worry about such markers betraying their presence. The ancients sat on the logs bickering cheerfully and gambling with Stilicho's dice, he and Narva being the only men in Section the others trusted not to cheat; Kyov, of course, would no more think of cheating than he would of raping a scrub, but he didn't gamble, either. He preferred long solitary walks in the wood, chewing on a twig in lieu of something smokable.

Ludicrous quantities of *klad* were constantly changing hands—favors, diverted stores, loot from alien worlds. At least in Loki's case Mir suspected it actually existed; there seemed little limit to what the man's errant genius was capable of. The ancients still spoke of a caper before Mir came to Section, when the 523rd had been stationed on the desperately polluted heavy metal mining world of Primus. Loki and Poet, with eventual half-unwitting help from the Master of Disaster— dead on Hovya, like so many others—had gotten involved with underworld dealings, and had, for a brief period, apparently controlled a measurable percentage of all property on the Stellar Collective's first planet. Then Loki, characteristically, had overplayed his hand. The whole scheme suffered catastrophic reentry; Loki and friends had been lucky to duck out alive, and the ensuing scandal had actually hit the Collective-wide media. Since his father's primary job was control of media for all of Santander District, Mir, who had been a cadet at the time, remembered the incident quite well.

Mir allowed himself a slight smile, and marveled that it didn't strain his face. The diverse pieces of Section, many new since Hovya took great bites out of it, were beginning to fit themselves to one another; if it wasn't a happy whole, at least it was beginning to function in a tolerable way, and one which increased everybody's chance of survival on what remained a very hostile alien world.

And maybe that's all false-optimism glow, now that the walls of my stomach no longer rub against each other, that ever-censorious part of his mind whispered. Another replied: *And what of it?* Life Detached had taught Haakon Mir to seize every moment of *absence from pain* as pleasure, to be clasped to his breast and cherished like a lover.

The food was monotonous, but there was plenty of it. And

it didn't taste half-bad. Just so long as you didn't dwell over-long on what it *was*.

A nerve-grating wail ripped the still mountain air. Mir looked over hurriedly to see Loki clutch his skinny breast and topple over backward, having lost again to toothless Narva. He would owe the Oldest Living something prodigious if they ever got back to Realized Space alive.

The thought caused odd currents to flow through Mir's belly, alternately hot and cold. Hardly anybody spoke anymore of rescue or return. They missed women, of course, even Balt, for whom Hynkop was no more than a convenient receptacle. And they missed alcohol and other mind-altering substances— not even Loki was mad enough to find out what effect fermenting the autoc sugars would have on the human metabolism. The foul-tasting nutrient fluid could probably have been turned into alk, but Mir had made Ovanidze responsible with his life for their stocks; it was their lifeline, and when it played out they were all dead.

Despite those lacks, the Landers seemed content here. So was Mir. They seemed to be living in a dream up here in the mountain quiet. No one was eager to awake. . . .

Mir drifted back into the half-buried shelter. In the back Ovanidze and Nau were fussing over the R&R unit like broody hens. Up front in the receiving and examination area Sturz was, as usual, on hands and knees next to a bucket of strong disinfectant, trying yet again to scrub out the stink of death— which hung yet about the place, floating in corners and lurking in gleaming mechanism crevices like a coy specter.

Ignoring him, the Dancing-Master held forth to an audience of mostly scrubs, using the office as his informal ET. Even CLD's deathbirds labored under an obligation of incessant in-doctrination. The Dancing-Master was the only one who took it seriously.

"Stalin and Hitler," the Dancing-Master was saying, in his finest lecture hall style, "were both great heroes of socialism, which was a main precursor to our Collective thought, though not yet fully in tune with Universal Truth and Will. They fought each other in a great war because of the machinations of the capitalists, who were Devolutionists devoted to a highly Particular and consumerist dogma; in extreme cases, they actually shaded into autarky."

He paused for gasps of horror from the scrubs, which were forthcoming. *Autarky* was a word dangerous even to breathe. Of course, as deathbirds they had less to fear than the Department in the factory or the vast housing complexes which seemed to begin crumbling before they were finished building. But even they could find themselves leaving their silhouettes on a handy wall, if somebody dropped the autarky bug in the ear of an MTJK or MET drumhead court-martial. Fear of being caught out as a deve was practically written in their genetic code.

"Hitler's great error," the Dancing-Master continued, smugly certain of his audience, "lay in his obsession with the Jews; he saw, correctly, that they had contributed to the rise of urban and industrial civilization which was man's original sin, but he laid too much blame at their door. Today, of course, Jews play an active role in the Stellar Collective, and Judaism is an acknowledged facet of Universal Truth."

"They still deny the Word of God," said Lennart, who leaned against the lockers with his arms folded, smiling sourly. "They deny the divinity of Christ His Son."

"Now, Lennart," the Dancing-Master said, "don't be doctrinaire. That's what got you into trouble in the first place. Christianity has a place in the Universal scheme as well; you simply took things too far."

"The Lord of Hosts will not be denied," Lennart said. "Not even the heretics who teach the false doctrine of the Universal Spirit are greater than he."

At this the scrubs twittered among themselves like frightened songbirds, but quietly, since Lennart was little more reticent about working out his resentments with his hard, scarred fists than the rest of the ancients. Florenz's cheeks flushed with guilty excitement at his sedition.

The Dancing-Master let Lennart's outburst run its course, listening with a slight superior smile. He and the zealot had an odd alliance, or perhaps symbiosis. Of all the men in Section, each was the only one who would consistently *debate* the other, instead of pounding them into silence. Kyov would talk, of course—he never resorted to his fists, to enforce discipline or his own sense of *boundary*—but he resisted their best arguments with such calm compliant obduracy that both men soon reduced themselves to sputtering frustration when they tried to talk to him. On the other hand, Lennart and the Dancing-Master squabbled like market women on an agro world, and enjoyed it all immensely.

"Sir?" Florenz raised a tentative hand. The bandage about his eyes was fresh and white, replenished daily. As predicted, the Landers had been able to heal most of their hurts with the regraf/regen unit. They had been able to do nothing to restore Florenz's eyes, however; Dieter and Kyov agreed that they lacked the expertise to remove the splinter from his head without endangering his brain. The young Lander had professed himself willing to wait for rescue. It was a symptom of the optimism that had taken hold of the unit in the two weeks since the discovery of the R&R bunker.

The Dancing-Master stood straighter. Unlike Loki, he did not object to being called by an irregulationary honorific. "Speak, boy."

"You said earlier that Hitler's greatest contribution was his recognition of urbanization and industrialization as humankind's original sins," the blind boy said. "But, uh—I come from an industrial world. Seems like there's a lot of industry and big cities in the Stellar Collective. I mean, isn't the Medurin Workers' & Farmers' Cooperative, where they make shi—uh, power cells, isn't that a whole factory *planet*?"

"A collection of factory planetoids, actually." The Dancing-Master clucked and shook his head: he was enjoying this. "Don't they teach you anything these days? Urbanization and industrialization are like the State: they shall wither away when Final Victory is achieved. They are a necessary evil, to be dispensed with as soon as feasible."

Gollob got a cagey look on his young face. "So you're saying the Stellar Collective is *evil?*"

A titillated gasp ran through the scrubs like an accelerated-time epidemic. Mir saw Lennart frown, and felt his own brow furrow slightly. Potential informers could be a problem—and how ironic was it, for a Ministerial-class child of Values, which relied on informers, to harbor such a thought? But it was a truth he had learned the way he had most truths of CLD, at the cost of substantial pain.

Perhaps the bitterest realization of all was that, even as a deathbird, you still had something to lose.

The Dancing-Master was oblivious. *"Necessary* evils," he

said grandly, "and so in concert with Universal Will. The Universe is far from a perfect place." He smiled. "That's why we fight."

"I thought we fought because we were bad, and sentenced to death." Florenz's earlier crisp interest had transmuted abruptly to gloom. He showed quicksilver mood changes since his injury.

The statement took the Dancing-Master momentarily aback. Lennart uttered a quiet raven croak of laughter.

The door opened behind Mir. The Rat came in, nibbling a chunk of roast meat with his shovel-shaped incisors.

"Food's ready, Lieutenant," he said. "Better come grab a share before it's gone."

"Thanks." Like Ovanidze, the White Rat got along quite well with the lieutenant—Mir acknowledged the Rat's supremacy as a scavenger, which was the albino's criterion for whether somebody was worth bothering with or not. Also like the electronics tech, the Rat was a specialist whose skills were bone-vital to Section's survival, and every man in it; he was immune to a lot of the strictures and intramural abuse the common Lander suffered. There was no risk of catching a jacket as an officer's bun-boy.

Chyz was carving chunks from the roast meat with his battle knife. Mir unshipped his mess kit and took his place in line. Bori, chewing a mouthful so huge his cheeks bulged like a squirrel's, pushed past on his way to collect Gollob, his assistant Bitch-gunner; it was their turn to spell Balt and Hynkop on watch.

Loki held up his chunk of meat, sniffed it daintily, wrinkled his nose. "Insipid. An insult to my very educated palate."

"Hey!" Jovan exclaimed. "That's *me* you're talking about!"

"I rest my case. You lack essential vitamins. It comes from having been raised a hayseed on a backwater world; you lack the life experience to give you real flavor."

"I should give you some lumps on the head for flavor," Jovan said sullenly. "I suppose you think your gamy ass tastes better?"

"Of course. What you call 'gaminess' is in fact character."

Hearing the exchange, Nau, who had emerged with Ovanidze, looked down at his own polymer mess kit and gulped.

"I can't get used to eating part of somebody's butt," he said.

Sitting on a fallen log, Stilicho chuckled. "It was never used for the customary purposes," he said. "You should know that; you grew it yourself, in those vats of yours."

The scrub made a noncommittal noise. "Think of it as ham," Kyov urged, chewing. "It's what it is, really."

"I was raised as a vegetarian," announced Gollob in a high, shrill voice. "It's the only way in true accord with Universal Will."

Lennart cuffed him on the back of his head, ejected him from the line, and stepped forward into his place. "Starve, then," he said. "That's all the sooner you'll come into accord with God's will—which is that you be cast into the Lake of Fire, unless you repent your sins."

Clutching his head, Gollob looked at the line. Those behind Lennart, including fellow scrubs Florenz and Sturz, presented a solid front against him. He teetered to the end, saying, "It's all right, he's right, I deserved that."

Bori glared at him. He followed the giant unfed up the hill.

The rest of Jovan's "ham", cloned and force-grown in the R&R machine, was doled out, leaving a portion for Balt and his A-gunner. The Landers settled down to eat as the peaceful evening settled in around them.

Poet, having fired his food down his throat without giving any sign of tasting it, squatted next to the fire, heating the tip of his butterfly knife and pressing it against the back of his right hand. Chewing the last of his own meal, Kobolev walked over to peer at what he was doing. The youthful-looking Lander was branding a flower into his flesh, using the blade's tip for petals.

Kobolev's nose wrinkled at the smell of burned skin and hair. "How can you stand to *do* that shit to yourself?" he demanded.

Poet shrugged. "Are you afraid of pain, man?" He looked up with a grin that was both shy and sly. "Pain doesn't hurt. I can show you."

The Bold Original shuddered and turned away. "He gives me the creeps. He does. The man is obviously insane."

Loki cocked his head, peering at him with the eyes-bright

gaze of a large malevolent bird, an impression reinforced by the way a cowlick stood up from his yellow hair.

"Aren't you?" he asked with some interest. "We're all insane here. Sane men never leave the Grinder alive."

Kobolev scowled at him. "What do you mean?"

Narva's strident caw of laughter made everybody jump. "To be living in hell, and still cling to life," he said. "Isn't that the insanest thing of all?" He cackled wildly.

Kobolev frowned, thinking he was being made fun of, and strode toward the Oldest Living, cocking his arm to backhand him.

With a clicking insect clatter of safeties, a dozen weapons were pointed at him. "Not wise, Standard," Rouen said softly. "Not wise at all."

Kobolev glanced around at his surviving sycophant. Van Dam squatted helplessly, frozen in mid-rise by the blank glass eye of Starman's laser, casually aimed at him across the sitting man's thighs.

The big man clenched his lips inside his beard, twitched his head, and turned away. He retreated to the vicinity of van Dam and sat. Behind him Narva's cackles crescendoed.

Balt came sliding and cursing down the ridge, followed by Hynkop carrying Bitch and ammo. As he cut himself three-quarters of the remaining meat, Balt glanced down at Poet, who ignored him. "Making yourself pretty, huh?"

Poet didn't even glance up. "His decorations are coming along nicely," Loki said. He raised a scar-vined forearm. "Almost as pretty as mine."

"Ha!" Balt spit in the fire, perilously close to the smaller man. "I had the most scars of any man in Section—any in Company! And I wasn't such a pussy to give them to myself. I earned my scars!"

The scrubs were staring at him in horrified fascination, which was not an uncommon response to Balt. "What happened?" Nau asked.

Balt showed him such a terrific snarl of rage that the boy almost fell over backward off his log. "Balt wanted Poet to suck his dragon for him," Starman said. "Poet shared a piece of his Little Sister instead. Scorched most of the skin off him."

Poet smiled.

Balt hunkered down well apart from the others and began

to tear at his food with his brown teeth. "I got him back," he said between bites. "Dosed his food with lye."

The scrub's eyes were getting too big for their heads. Even Florenz had his face fixed toward the burly, filthy Lander.

"How did you both *survive?*" Florenz asked.

"R&R," Poet said, adding a petal and holding up his hand to admire it.

"Maybe it's time I did something about those pretties of yours," Balt rumbled.

"If you try it now, there won't be a next."

Kobolev slapped his hands on his thighs. "Well, that's the most words I've ever heard him put together at a time," he declared. "Why do they call him Poet, anyway? He hardly speaks, and Process knows if he can read, much less write."

"Does everything have to make sense to you, Standard?" Starman asked, with a nasty knowing smile. "If so, your life in the Detachment is liable to be short, and crowned with disappointment."

Kobolev rose and stamped off into the woods. Van Dam scrambled to follow.

Inside Mir, something broke. Putting aside his own mess kit—from which he had just finished self-consciously licking the last few dabs of grease—he rose and walked toward Balt. The squat man glared up at him from beneath his single brow.

"Lander," the lieutenant said. "I think you've made a mistake."

"Huh?"

With a smooth facility that would have astonished the young cadet he once had been—who could literally never have imagined himself cultivating something so coarse as knife-fighting skills—Mir drew his knife from its inverted sheath, stabbed Balt's meat right off the plate. Holding it in his fingers, he cut what remained in half, let one piece fall back into the mess kit on Balt's lap.

"Your hand must've slipped," the lieutenant said, "while you were cutting."

He turned and walked toward Hynkop, who sat hunched several meters up the slope behind Balt. Balt just sat there staring at his back, mouth hanging open, a piece of Jovan's rump hanging out half-masticated.

Mir held out the piece of meat to the boy. Hynkop jumped back as if it were a damaged power can about to pull a cat.

"Here, boy," Mir said. "Take it. You need the nourishment."

White-faced, Hynkop shook his head. He held his hands protectively over his kit. Mir frowned.

He knelt. "Here," he said again. Gently he pushed Hynkop's hands aside and laid the meat in his kit. "Eat it." A pause, and then, "That's an order."

He rose and turned to walk down the slope, past Balt. Balt glared at him, but neither moved nor spoke. Mir went back to where he had been sitting before and lowered himself back to the bare trodden earth.

There was a brief gust as most of Section let a held breath go at once. "You ain't smart, Lieutenant," Rouen said, "but you got balls like a Tagore Gromdrache."

Mir felt a light coat of sweat pop into being across his forehead. It was suddenly very cold in the forest. The birds seemed to have quit singing, and his own bit of Jovan got up and began to dance around in his stomach as it came to him exactly what he had done. Balt was the most violent man in Section, and compared to him, Poet, Loki, and Starman *adored* officers.

Hynkop squatted there staring down at his mess kit as if Mir had turned him to an ice sculpture. He broke into frantic movement, snatching up the meat and scrabbling forward on all fours to thrust it at Balt. Balt looked at him. Hynkop shook the meat pleadingly, then placed it gently into Balt's kit.

Balt lashed out with a thick arm that sent kit, meat, and scrub flying. Hynkop rolled over on his side and curled into a knee-clutching ball. Tears drew snail tracks of shine down his cheek.

Mir started to rise. A sense of presence at his elbow made the young lieutenant jump. It was only Kyov, hunkering down next to him.

"Save your energy, sir," the sergeant said quietly. "You can't make it better. Just worse."

Mir settled back down. "What do you mean?"

"You've earned Hynkop a beating. If you press the issue, you'll only make it that much harder on the boy."

"Why didn't he take the meat?"

"Because he knew Balt would blame him. He tried to make amends." A sidewise bob of the head. "You see how that worked."

Mir frowned, opened his mouth, shut it, shook his head. "There must be *something* to be done."

"No, sir." Kyov looked in his eyes. "It's how a lot of us were raised, anyway, Lieutenant. I was luckier than that; I judge you were, too. But most of these—" he looked around and shrugged—"they know how the game goes. As far as Balt's concerned, anything that happens is Hynkop's fault. Hynkop understands that."

Everything's his fault. . . . Mir understood, too, now that it was cast in those terms; it was the way his life had turned, after he was Detached. Under arrest, awaiting a *pro forma* trial and then transportation to the Meatgrinder—not to mention the Grinder itself—everything that happened was his fault; if a jailer's testicles itched, he could expect a boot in his own on that account. But to be *raised* that way—

"Life in hell's nothing that new for a lot of Landers," Kyov said. "It's one of the reasons the ones who live do."

Feeling like a bag of sick despair, Mir shook his head and sighed. He felt an overwhelming need to *do* something—and an overwhelming lack of anything *to* do.

"Don't worry about Balt, by the way," Kyov said. "On your own account, that is. He won't try to get back at you."

"Why do you say that?" Balt had a reputation for outstanding vindictiveness.

"If he was going to do anything to you, you'd have had his knife in your kidneys the second you turned your back, sir."

Mir swallowed.

"As it was, he was too shocked to act. And after that—" Kyov shrugged again. "You're an officer, even though you are a deathbird; he can't touch you without taking risks, and for all his bluster that's not something he enjoys. And you're . . . *accepted* by the men, for the most part, sir. You don't make too many mistakes, and you treat us like men, and that's more than most officers do, Detached or no. And the ones who love you least—"

"Let me guess," Mir said. "Loki, Starman, and Poet."

Kyov nodded, smiling slightly. "Exactly. They're the ones

who'd most dearly love an excuse to withdraw Sanction from Balt and close his file for good and all. Fragging an officer who hadn't earned it would do it, especially one who's Detached like the rest of us. You have Sanction too, you know.''

"I understand.''

The older man shook his head. "In any case, he's transferred his anger to the boy. *He'll* bear the brunt—and if you or I interfered, Balt would kill us, and the rest would watch and never lift a finger.''

Mir looked down at the backs of his hands. The sun had vanished behind the surrounding hills, and the evening breeze stirred the fine pale gold hairs on the backs of them. The ghost glow of the aurora began to tinge the northern sky in pink and blue. The great tentacular display of plasma channels following the lines of the planet's magnetic fields had vanished; the aurora sheets were shrinking day by day. Whatever unthinkable storms had wracked the primary were subsiding; Ovanidze had begun to spend more time with his commo gear, trying to reach other humans—if other humans remained alive on the Rookery.

Thank you, Section Sergeant, font of wisdom and true backbone of this unit, Mir thought bitterly. *Now you've cast a cold and merciless light on my own cowardice: the fear—the certainty, if you will—that if I try too hard to* lead *my men, they'll kill me.*

"What do you think would happen to us without you, sir?'' Kyov asked in a voice scarcely louder than the rattle of the breeze in the leaves overhead. "We're still marooned on a little lump of dirt in the middle of cold space, alone and friendless. Without you holding us together as you've done, how long would we last?''

Mir looked deep into Kyov's eyes. They were hazel, bottomless, and sad, as always. Instinctively Mir wondered if his subordinate were flattering him, seeking to lever himself a little bit of *klad* with the unit commander; it was the way of the world, and not just inside the Collective Landing Detachment.

But Mir saw no sign of advantage seeking. Kyov was comforting him, as he comforted all the men—when he could.

He stood up, stretched. It felt as if the muscles of his shoulders had turned to iron bands, brutal-tight. There was one more detail to see to, ridiculous as it was.

"Lander Hynkop," he said. The boy didn't react. His flanks and shoulders continued to shake with silent weeping. "For disobeying a direct order, you are sentenced to"—he threw his hands out from his body in a helpless gesture "—to go without food the rest of the day."

Without looking anyone in the face, he walked up the slope, past the bunker, and into the trees.

Kobolev slammed the base of his fist against a tree. A few fragments of bark rained down on him, and a bright-feathered climbing quadruped stuck its beak over a branch to chitter complaints against him.

"It's *intolerable,*" he exclaimed.

"It sure is," van Dam agreed.

"That Lieutenant is a whey-faced fool, with no more backbone than a *lushcha.*" A *lushcha* was a kind of slime mold, an iridescent shapeless mass about as large and active as a small dog. The life-form appeared on at least five planets within the Stellar Collective, and some scientists from Progress theorized it was native to none. How it got there no one knew. "That mewling old woman Kyov is no better."

"Smacks, the lot of them," van Dam agreed.

"Well, things are overdue for a change around here. And we're just the men to change them."

"You got that right."

Kobolev rasped his palm across his beard and looked at his companion. "It was the lieutenant who got Eyrikson killed," he said. "If he wasn't stupid and weak, our brud would be alive and standing here right beside us."

Van Dam's hazel eyes watered. The three of them had all grown up together, running crushed-coral streets among the coquina houses, all different colors vibrant in the blue-white sun, scattered across the steep hills of Crescent Bay on Fanon. They had gone into the Engine of History together, been Detached and pulled through the hell of the Meatgrinder together, had—thanks to a little last residual *klad* adhering to Kobolev from their former life—managed to be assigned to First Section together. Van Dam was not a man with a lot of room for feeling in him. But he missed his old brud Eyrikson.

"He can't get away with that shit," he rasped. "He can't. It ain't *right*."

Kobolev smiled. "He won't, my brother. I promise you that."

Vibrating with loss and the lust for retribution, van Dam took three steps forward and three steps back, then slammed a punch into a tree. "Ouch!" he exclaimed, and bent over, clutching his bruised knuckles.

Kobolev slapped him on the back. "Don't worry. We shall take our rightful place at the top of this dung heap we've been dropped into, and then you'll see some fancy payback."

Van Dam looked up at him. "When?" he asked, in a voice still taut with pain.

"I don't know," Kobolev admitted, "yet. But our time will come."

He grabbed van Dam by his brown hair, dragged his head up. "Have I ever been wrong yet?" he demanded.

The Lander managed to give his head a small shake. "Never."

Kobolev nodded and let him go. "All we need," he said, "is the proper moment. And, my friend, that time *will* come. Never fear."

He let his comrade go. "I won't permit you to fear."

21

"SIR," OVANIDZE SAID, "I'm getting something."

Mir tried to rub the sleep out of his eyes. The time since they had found the R&R bunker was the most restful time they had known since they hit the Rookery, and for a long time before. In truth, not since his arrest had Mir known such a sense of peace, or security. Of—did he dare even think the word?—*freedom.*

In the pit of his belly a many-legged beast began to crawl: *It's all about to end.*

Here among the trees atop the ridge the air was crisp to the edge of cold, but not beyond. An earlier storm had passed; stars shone out bright as lasers in a clear black sky. The aurora was nothing but a pallid shine at the base of the northern sky.

"What have you got for me, Ovanidze?" the lieutenant asked, with a trace of reluctance.

The tech nodded his round head as if he'd been put a yes/no question. "I might have gotten results for you earlier, Junior Lieutenant," he said, "had you permitted me to take a patrol up to one of the higher peaks after the solar disturbances calmed. These mountains tend to block transmissions."

"I didn't want to split us up, Ovanidze," Mir said. "We've been through that. Now out with it: what have you got?"

"Transmissions on a standard battalion-level command frequency. Your TD, sir?"

Mir had left it down by the bunker. Sensing that something

was up, the Landers were awakening and drifting up to the ridgetop in dribs and drabs. Mir pointed to Gollob, blinking and shivering in his undershorts, to run down and fetch his tactical display.

A few moments later he was back, pale skin glowing almost blue in the light of a rising moon. Ovanidze opened the cover, which was also the screen, linked the TD to his communications set.

"They're located here, sir," he said, pointing a knobby finger at a flashing white square in the midst of the display. The surrounding terrain looked unfamiliar to Mir.

Ovanidze touched a key. The square became a steady outline, surrounding a city symbol. "That's a provincial capital," Mir said, "250 to 500K population." He looked up at the tech. "Just where *is* this city, Senior Lander?"

The tech tapped more keys. The square shrank as scale increased. Eventually a yellow dot appeared in the screen's lower right-hand corner, marking their current position.

Someone emitted a low whistle over Mir's right shoulder. "Five hundred klicks," Stilicho said. "A righteous hump, Junior Lieutenant."

"Piece of cake," said Dieter, rubbing his hands together. "We've all done 80K quick marches in a day in Grinder, right? And fought a mock battle afterward to boot. It should take us less than a week."

There was a general rumble, like the mutter of distant artillery. "Come join us in this fucking *solar system,* Dieter," Jovan said disgustedly. "That's 80K in twenty-four Universal *hours,* over flat country and no opposition."

"When I was in the Grinder," Poet said through clenched teeth, "we did 80K as a graduation exercise. They used it to kill off half of us; they'd been taking it too easy on us, they said."

Unlike some of the men, Poet was still sleeping in his clothes and boots, paranoia being as fundamental to his being as oxygen metabolism. Nonetheless he was shivering, arms wrapped around his chest as if to contain the vibration of his skinny ribs. On the other hand sweat stood out along the roots of his dark hair despite mountain night chill.

Is he going through withdrawal? Mir wondered. Sooner or later Section's supply of Zone had to run out. Perhaps it had.

"It's fifteen days' march, easy, you blind fool," Lennart said to Dieter. "And that's if we drive ourselves, and the Lord holds out his hand to shield us from our foes."

"Surely not!"

"First of all," Stilicho said, dropping a broad forefinger to the display, "we got a good 30K more of mountains to cover. If you run up and down even that much in one day, best leave your Dirt turned on, so we can find your stiff before the birds do. Once we clear the mountains, we're going to have to snoop and poop to keep clear of autocs. We'll be lucky to do that in fifteen days *local*."

"And of course," Loki murmured, "where a battalion of us is, there the birds will flock."

"Like fucking vultures," said Balt, scratching his testicles. Hynkop stood behind his shoulder, keeping his face down. Mir saw the boy's right eye was swollen almost shut, and his stomach turned over with guilt.

"Can you make out what they're saying?" Mir asked Ovanidze.

The tech's shrug provided the answer. *Security*. The transmissions were scrambled, and not only did Section not have the key to the distant unit's commo, the distant unit would not be able to decipher theirs.

"Can we push a signal through?"

"Not from here, sir. Our set's strained to push a signal a hundred klicks under good conditions. Which I doubt we'll ever have on this stinking planet."

Mir blinked at his characterization of the Rookery. *Have to take his filters into consideration:* a planet whose primary interfered blatantly and incessantly with communications could never seem pleasant to Ovanidze.

The lieutenant grinned. "It seems to me our equipment isn't rated to do a *lot* of the things you can make it do, Senior Lander."

"Yes, sir," Ovanidze said, showing no reaction to the blatant flattery. "But not under local conditions. When we get out of these mountains, get a little closer, maybe I can punch something through to them, at least let them know we exist. Unless the blighted sun acts up again."

Mir nodded. "Very well. Everybody who's not on watch,

back to your racks and grab some sleep. We move out at first light.''

"No," Loki said.

Mir stared at the corporal. Loki's handsome face was tilted up, emphasizing the way his eyes were set on marked slants above his high cheekbones. His expression was no more readable than usual.

In a Regular outfit, for a corporal to defy his Section CO that openly would likely result in *both* being Detached, if there were any witnesses on hand who also happened to be informers, for the military brass or the civilian secret police of Revo or Values. In the Detachment, things went differently.

I must walk carefully, Mir knew. *Mines here!*

"What do you mean, Corporal?" he asked carefully.

Loki looked at the others gathered around like insects drawn by the tiny flickering lights of the commo set. "We've got it good here, right?" he asked. "Our stomachs are full, even if Jovan's sorry ass tastes like old boot soles, and Process protect us from ever having to eat anything at all of Balt's!"

Balt growled. Loki plowed on, heedless. "We may feel the lack of the tender little darlings, but we can always date the cousins of Chyz the Jizz's sweetheart, Rosy Palm and her five sisters. Or we can go off in the woods together; it's nothing new. The important thing is, nobody is *shooting* at us.''

"He's got a point," Stilicho said.

"On top of his head!" Dieter exclaimed. "These are our *comrades*—"

Loki did a quick shuffle-step sideways and side-kicked Dieter in the pit of the belly. The dark-haired man sat down hard.

"Where was I? Ah yes. Most of all, there is no one with his boot upon our necks. No red-ass noncoms to make us crawl for kilometers under heavy packs in the mud, for the sheer joy of seeing us suffer—and to slam us in the shocks or cells if we flag! We are''—he paused and swept his comrades' faces with eyes that took fire from meek pilot-light shine—''*free.*''

Gollob sat down and covered his ears with his hands. "You're saying bad words!" he wailed. "This is—this is *autarky!* I won't listen. I, Lander 234-444-523-115-11111, affirm and apologize for my crimes—

Ignoring him, Loki spread his hands as if to encompass the men gathered atop the ridge, beneath the stars and the blackboughed trees. Mir noted the sullen slump to their shoulders and thrusts to their jaws. With a shock he realized most were unwilling to see their forest idyll broken.

"These *are* our comrades," he said in a voice he hoped was calmly assertive. He kept his hand on the pistol grip of his slung pulser in case Loki was minded to side-kick him. Such an act would destroy any pretense he had of commanding this unit; if Loki tried it, Mir would shoot him down and take the consequences as they came. "They're our fellow men."

"Are they? *Are* they our comrades?" Loki asked with fine contempt. "Do you call those who spit on you in barracks, and on the line hang back to let you do the fighting, and never raise a little finger to aid you if you're wounded, even if it's in saving their miserable lives—do you call such 'comrades,' Junior Lieutenant? If these are your *comrades,* let's see you go into a red-ass officers' mess and get them to stand you a drink from their allotment!"

Mir breathed through clenched teeth. There was nothing to say to that. To go into a Regular officers' mess would be to invite a savage beating at the least. No military court would convict a Regular for punishing a deathbird for such presumption, and he'd get no sympathy from the Landers, who'd reckon he'd paid the price of his own stupidity.

"This is absurd!" bellowed Kobolev, who'd turned up late on the scene with van Dam in tow. "These are our fellow soldiers, our brothers in arms! We've got to go to them!"

Starman laughed, a jagged screech that put the night birds to silence. "You haven't got it, have you, Standard? *They're not your brothers anymore.* They'll knock your teeth down your fat throat if they hear you refer to yourself as 'soldier'. You're a deathbird now and forever."

"Little as I like to admit it," Black Bertold said, "our Bold Original is right. We've duty to consider."

"What duty's that?" Loki demanded. "To die?"

"What if we get gigged for dereliction?" Dieter asked. He had struggled to a sitting position and sat holding his belly. Loki threw a glance toward him. He held up a warding hand. Though slender, he was heavier set than Loki. But he was no match for the blond madman, and knew it.

The others started to share uneasy glances. Dieter's point hit meat. Deathbirds enjoyed a certain degree of license: they were *already* under sentence of death, and it would embarrass the Collective to have to preempt the court and carry out the sentence with a firing squad. Also it tended to defeat the whole purpose of CLD.

But deathbirds were not *immune*. Open mutiny, desertion from the battle line, refusal to fight—these were called "dereliction," and punished instantly with firing squads. Under the doctrine of collective responsibility a whole Squad or Section might die for the acts of one or two members—and that wasn't all. If the Big Circuits were feeling especially vindictive, surviving family members on the outside could also go to the wall.

Accusation of dereliction was one of the few dreads Collective justice still held for deathbirds. That was one thing the Stellar Collective excelled at: finding out what you still had to lose, and taking it away.

Loki made no move toward Dieter. "Dereliction, how?" he asked, voice silky-quiet. "Junior Lieutenant, have we orders to link up with this formation? Do we even know what it *is?*"

"No," said Mir, as though through a throat half-full of ash. It was a blow to his military academy pride to be debating orders with an outlaw like Loki. Yet this was CLD; if there was a different way, no one had bothered to tell him of it.

They gave no classes in commanding deathbirds at the *Akademiya*.

"We can't even *talk* to them," Loki said. "How can they call dereliction on us for failing to join them?"

"They may be in trouble," Kyov said quietly.

That made Stilicho raise his head. "If they're on this world," he said, "they're in trouble."

"And so are we," the Section sergeant said. Even in the darkness, the lines on his face seemed to the lieutenant to have cut deeper. "Sooner or later the Rooks will find us. Sooner or later we'll run out of nutrient. And while for now we have food in plenty, it's not exactly ideal."

"We're starting to taste pretty monotonous," Jovan admitted. "Besides, all this eating our own meat's starting to give everybody the shits."

"A larger formation," Mir said, "a battalion or a regiment, might have food. They have to; how have they stayed alive so long, otherwise?"

"The same way we have, maybe," said Poet through chattering teeth. Oddly, Zone shortage was making him more talkative.

"I think they have better things to do with their R&R units," Ovanidze said. The tech sat with a headset on and the phone pulled away from one ear, listening to the debate and the distant signal simultaneously. "Listen."

He switched the set's output to speaker. The voices were unintelligible, but unmistakably excited. Above the background sizzle was a deeper, more distinct rattle, like hail on a composite roof.

"It's those chem guns the autocs use," Stilicho said. "Fighting going on."

"So they have food," Loki said. "So what? I suppose they'll be eager to share it with convict scum."

"That's a big city," Jovan said. "If they got birds on 'em, likely they got a *lot*. Don't think they'll turn down a couple dozen new pulsers."

"Red-ass putes never do," Starman said. "It's after the shitstorm stops howling about their ears that they remember they're too good to have us underfoot."

"So you think we should plunge into the shitstorm with them?" Loki demanded, with a ferocious glare for Starman, a usual ally. Mir tensed; battles between those two—like battles between one of them and Poet—tended to be nasty, with plenteous overkill.

But most of the venom had drained from Loki, who had obviously lost the upper hand. Starman just sneered and shook his head, Loki balled a fingerless-gloved fist, punched himself savagely in the jaw, and stamped off into the night.

Mir vented a giant sigh. "Right. Now, let's get some sleep. Tomorrow—"

"Sir," Kyov put in. "What about food?"

The lieutenant stopped dead. Their own cloned flesh turned bad soon after it was removed from the forced-growing unit, despite the lack of local microorganisms to attack it—unless, of course, that was another point their briefing had gotten wrong. Nobody in Section knew any means of preserving fresh meat except refrigeration, which they didn't have.

"What about the nutrient solution?" Nau asked. "We could carry that along."

"Nobody could hold that shit down, you idiot," van Dam said. "That's why we're eating our own butts."

"What about IVs? There's equipment in the lab."

"Doesn't exactly fill a man's belly," Jovan said.

"We wouldn't be able to feed everyone off drips even if we stayed here," Ovanidze said. "Take too much time."

An idea began to infiltrate Mir's mind. His first reaction was to try to drive it off; it was just too grotesque. But the more he thought about it, the more workable it became.

But not more attractive. He sighed.

"I know what to do," he said.

22

POET SHOOK LIKE a wet dog. "There, Lieutenant," he said sullenly, lowering his binoculars to point. He did not offer the glasses to Mir, who had struggled up into the crotch of the tree beside him. "See for yourself."

This better *be important*, the lieutenant thought. He kept it to himself. Poet was off the Zone now, and oscillated unpredictably between sullenness and savagery.

The very night they caught the signals from the unknown unit, the youth had gone into convulsions. Mir hadn't seen this happen to him before, but apparently it was nothing new to those who had been in the unit longer. Big Bori had stunned him with a blow behind the ear, and the others rolled him in sheets from the medical-bunker locker and taped him so he couldn't move. He'd been left stacked against a wall during the several more days Section lingered at the bunker to put the lieutenant's plan into effect. Whenever his moans of withdrawal agony got too nerve-wracking, somebody bashed him in the head again, or tossed him outside to frighten the birds and the feather-squirrels.

Now he was even paler than usual and shook incessantly. Still, the lieutenant had to admit that even in the grip of whatever demons Zone hid him from, Poet was unlikely to call false alarms.

Ignoring the itch where his new "food" arm was attached

to the left side of his rib cage, Mir raised his glasses to his eyes. Almost at once he pursed his lips in a silent whistle.

They were most of the way to their goal—maybe fifty kilometers away from the larger unit, which was forted up in some kind of compound on the city's outskirts. The journey had been blunt easy, at least as far as opposition went. The Rooks seemed to be devoting their attention to the known large concentration of invaders, to the exclusion of all else.

Just once, early on their journey, had Section brushed up against autocs. Three days out from the bunker, with the landscape falling away into foothills around them, there had been a rustle in thick brush clustered with three-lobed scarlet berries, and suddenly a short, plump, yellow-feathered Rook was standing practically in the middle of the strung-out column. It opened its black beak wide in a squawk of surprise and fled.

The whole Section gave chase, crashing through scrub up the flank of a long finger pointing down from mountain into lowlands. Everybody seemed to be shooting at once, blue bolts causing eruptions of steam from berry-laden bushes, Bitch needles rattling like rain among stiff purple leaves. Grenades were cracking off in quick succession, so that the fleeing autoc seemed to be bouncing like a pinball from one eruption of smoke and debris to the next. As he bellowed fruitlessly for the men to cease fire, Mir marveled that nobody—including the Rook—was hit.

It couldn't last. The terrified autoc topped the slope and ran down into a fold on the far side. That put it in the open—the brush ended at the crest. After five scurrying steps blue bolts converged on it from all directions. Lavender steam erupted from it, and it fell smoldering, one outflung claw actually falling into a low fire built beneath a large slate-colored pot.

A bright cluster of Rooks looked up in surprise from their various tasks. The men stopped where they were and hosed them down. The birds barely had time to cry out in alarm before grenade blasts and needle storms and directed-energy pulses knocked them down, or a flamer's kiss dropped them to the ground cover as stinking smoking black dolls, like giant fowl left too long in the oven.

It was over in about the time it took Junior Lieutenant Mir to shout, "*No!*"

They found no weapons, searching the blood-splashed remnants of the camp. As near as Mir could figure it, Section had come upon a family; most of the corpses were small, several no more than half a meter tall. Only three, from their height, seemed likely to be adults, even accounting for sexual dimorphism.

By appearances they had been gathering stalks like tall jointed lemon yellow reeds or attenuated bamboo which grew in stands nearby. These, it seemed, they chewed in their beaks, stewed in the pot, and then chewed again. Sheets of material like grey plastic stabilized with a generous proportion of the masticated reed were found stacked, some dry, some still moist. Nau guessed that something in their saliva served as a sort of adhesive, evolutionary relic of nest-building days. With that as a foundation stone for their materials technology, it might explain why they were so unusually advanced in synthetics, like the polymers that made up their gun barrels.

Most of the Landers ignored the young scrub's speculations. In between bouts of vomiting, Mir found himself intrigued, in an abstract kind of way. Eventually Stilicho cuffed the boy without force and told him to make himself useful policing the camp.

They blew a hole in a comparatively bare patch of earth a way downslope from the camp, tumbled the bodies inside, and covered them up again while Lennart muttered prayers. It was not an *obvious* mass grave, unless the Rooks had as much experience of them as the veteran Landers did; and the unexplained disappearance of the reed-chewing party was much less likely to bring the countryside out in force to hunt intruders as the discovery of a bunch of burned and blasted bodies. The other visible marks of slaughter were eradicated as well as could be, and Section moved on without a backward glance.

In the nine local days since no one had referred to the massacre, at least in Mir's hearing. He was getting so he could sometimes close his eyes without seeing those tiny charred bodies.

Now he opened his eyes wide and lowered his electronic binoculars to peer over them across tawny fields of man-high ripening grain. Then he put the glasses back to his eyes.

"It looks like an entire *army*," he breathed. "How many are there, would you guess, Standard?"

"How the shit should I know?" the scout snarled. "Ten thousand? Twenty? Too snaking many."

Army seemed a good call to Mir: bright parallel columns on at least three roads, and stretching back as far as the junior lieutenant could see. Now that he knew they were there, he could *hear* them: the distant-thunder susurration of their footfalls, attenuated and low as the sound of the planet's heart beating away down in the molten core; a mutter like a faraway flock of migrant birds, like wind rattling the leaves of a wood in middle distance. A sound indistinct, and anything but loud. Even straining to spread his hearing netwide, it was hard to seine that murmur from the light midday breeze.

Still, it hit him like a fist in the gut. He was a seasoned fighter, deep in death-ground—as deep as a suffering cog dog could get. The Engine of History could deploy a stupefying array of sensors, from satellites and warships in O to in-atmosphere craft to instruments on and under the ground. But for all that one of the bitterest lessons any combat soldier learned—if he survived first contact with the enemy—was that all he could *really* depend on was the keenness of his own senses, eyes/ears/nose Mk I. The need for keen senses was cubed by their utter lack of assets on the smiling, sunlit death trap that was the Rookery.

I should have heard *them,* he told himself bleakly, *should have noticed an entire* army *before Poet called me on the Dirt.* Despite the respite at the R&R bunker—or could it be *because?*—he was wearing down.

He made himself focus his glasses on an artillery unit, slate grey gun barrels trailed and mounted on limbers drawn by the round-billed herd beasts. Artillerists in straw hats rode wagons with white fabric covers that came to points at either end, like arcades.

"Nasty great howitzers, Lieutenant," Poet said with something like gloomy satisfaction. "Long-barrel direct-fire tubes, too. Everything for a party."

Mir nodded, skinning lips slowly back from his teeth. He had learned respect for the primitive Rook firepower—which was nowhere near as primitive as they had been led to believe. Still, impressive as the artillery train was, it would not survive half an hour engaged with a single battery of Engine tube or rocket artillery, with radars and computers to direct counter-battery fire.

But does the besieged battalion have *heavy artillery*? If they didn't, those primitive rifles with the polymerized-ceramic barrels represented a world of hurt.

"We'd better shake it loose," Mir said. "We want to get where we're going well ahead of this lot."

He shinnied back down the tree, dislodging many leaves and painfully cracking his knees twice and his elbows once. Just before he jumped down he caught his remaining vestigial arm, a sort of handless wing hanging in a sleeve sewn beneath his real left arm, in the crotch of a branch. While he had no motor control over the arm, his nervous system was wired to it. It gave him an odd, dislocated twinge, a feeling of almost sexual pain. He dislodged the wing, and let himself back down.

Section had dropped into a loose circle in the underbrush of a little wood tagging along beside a stream. Squads One and Two dozed while Three, on alert, bitched about their increasing diarrhea and the discomfort of the "field rations" some of them still had sprouting from their bodies. Mir and his noncoms had decided to have one man in three grafted with spare limbs speed-grown from his own tissue; Kyov and Dieter were concerned about the possibility that the extra limbs would upset the human metabolism in some unpredictable way. Also, there was a limited number of the limbs that could be grown at once in the R&R vats; to grow enough for each man would take more time than Mir was willing to hang on at the bunker. Now that the decision to move to join the other humans had been taken, morale could only suffer from lingering in false home-comfort.

They carried along some nutrient bags and IV drips. Kyov and Dieter insisted the graft carriers needed extra nutrition, and while it would have been impracticable to feed a whole Section entirely from the drips, a single Squad's worth could obtain supplemental nutrition from them readily enough. Mir did not entirely catch the logic of that—there was something off the mark and incestuous about feeding off parts of your own body anyway, even if he'd thought this new wrinkle up himself. But the two ersatz medics were insistent, and in

CLD—so different from the rest of the Stellar Collective, where formula and hierarchic rigidity ruled—those with the most knowledge carried the most weight in council. At least in units that wanted to *survive*; so Mir deferred to their judgment.

Kneeling by the stream to splash cool water on his face, Mir told Ovanidze to convey the latest intelligence to the battalion besieged in the Rook city. They had established communications two days ago, when Section got within a hundred klicks, using bursts of noise in an ancient binary code that long predated the flight of the Originals from Earth at the beginning of the twenty-first century. Communications specialists like Ovanidze still learned it, possibly out of guild pride. It still came in handy, as events were proving.

Communication with the other humans had not been exactly free and easy. The old dot-dash code was cumbersome and slow, and the larger unit, from paranoid reflex perhaps, had not been very forthcoming. Of course, Mir had to admit that a battalion under attack from an estimated ten thousand Rooks might have other things to do than chat with him.

He was troubled in an obscure way that the trapped unit refused to reveal its identity. But the security reflex was deeply ingrained, and not just within the Armed Forces. He, on the other hand, had authorized Ovanidze to admit straight-up that they were CLD; better, he reasoned, that their prospective hosts not be surprised when the newcomers came within reach of their guns. He hoped he had made a proper call.

"Battalion has a query, sir," Ovanidze reported from beneath his headset. He had not been selected to carry the unit's very special "field rations." He tried not to act smug. "They want an ETA for the Rook reinforcements."

Mir rubbed his chin with his left hand. Beneath his armpit the wing itched abominably. It did all the time, really, but usually he could suppress it. The tug he had given the "field ration" vestigial limb still throbbed, making its presence known.

Rooks marched at a quicker pace than humans could sustain. But while sporadic rain had not mucked up the dark red-orange dirt roads badly enough to inconvenience Section much, the road-bound Rook army was struggling. Tens of thousands of taloned feet and narrow wagon wheels churned the roads into swamp—and the roads weren't much to begin with, more scarcely improved parallel tracks across flat farming land than the highways Mir's tac display claimed they were.

"I'd guess at least two days for the Rook main force to reach the cantonment. That means they should start looking for them anytime from"—a quick mental calculation, based on the Rookery's rotation period of just over twenty-eight Standard hours, a "standard" itself based on the rotation of a world no man or woman born in the Stellar Collective had ever laid eyes on—"about midnight local tomorrow night to three days from now. I doubt they can get there any sooner than forty, forty-five hours."

Ovanidze relayed that, nodded, and hummed to himself as he translated the response in his head. "They want to know when to look for us, sir."

Reflex was to tell them a time later than he expected to reach the cantonment. That surprised him: *They're our comrades. We're coming to aid them.* He wrote it down to Detached paranoia. There was a reason for honesty far more compelling than the brotherhood of humanity: anybody approaching the perimeter before Section was expected—and especially if Rook-sized blobs started popping up on IR scopes—was liable to be greeted with a horizontal energy-storm comprising everything the besieged battalion had left.

Mir surveyed his men. They were gaunt, and the brightness in their eyes might have been fever or madness or both. But they were CLD. They knew how to cover ground, even under the beaks of an alerted enemy. And now, for the first time since they had been abandoned on the Rookery, they really had a place to go.

And the days are long here, he reminded himself. "Midnight," he said. "Tell them to expect us at aught-aught hundred local, with bells on."

23

THEY BEAT THE deadline by fifteen minutes.

It was surprisingly easy. The grain ripening in the fields raised purple-and yellow-fronded heads higher even than Big Bori's. Section followed roads and irrigation ditches, hidden from view. Minimal caution kept them clear of the field-workers.

They encountered no patrols. The Rooks evidently thought they had all the invaders in the vicinity trapped in the cantonment. Their military attention was firmly fixed on its walls.

Section hit the suburbs, actually small villages centered tightly on a large central structure with high stone walls—palace, town hall, or cathedral, no one could say. Unlike the farmhouses, which in this region were mostly wattle-and-daub, the dwellings were walled and roofed by panels of plasticlike reed-stabilized mats, possibly synthetic, possibly products of the foothill camps like the one Section had wiped out. Like the farms, they seemed built to accommodate a dozen or more Rooks each.

Like the country-Rooks, the suburbanites turned in at sunset, or gathered in plazas before the gates of the central structures to perform convolute torchlight dances. Either way they left the streets pretty much to the heavily armed ghosts of First Section.

The Landers could tell when they reached the city proper: they ran up against large stone apartment blocks, three and four stories tall, with outer walls of great yellow blocks which seemed to Mir to have once been part of an encircling city wall. Beyond them rose the city skyline, all spires and towers and zigs and zags.

Most of Section were urban scum, who knew how to alley-crawl and dodge the pokes before they were out of diapers. Even the confirmed country boys like Rouen and Jovan had learned the hard way how to snoop and poop city streets, both against the Collective's enemies and the more particular enemies of the Collective Landing Detachment: the pokes—PO-CAs, civilian police—shore patrols, Engine military cops with white gloves and golden gorgets. Deathbirds seldom got leave . . . officially.

The scrubs—none of whom seemed hardened criminals, or even low-echelon Deps who might be expected to have had street wisdom ground into their faces—and the high-Custodian Mir and the Dancing-Master were weak links on urban creeps. But they all had been through the Grinder, and junior lieutenant and senior sergeant had survived many a street patrol in a combat zone. And even the Dancing-Master was not too proud to defer to the skills of wise human rats like *the* Rat and Poet.

The apartments were brightly lit from within, presumably by oil lanterns like the ones Section had found at the deserted stone farmhouse a lifetime ago. They passed several blocks from an open square in which several hundred Rooks were gathered in eerie silence for some torchlight ritual. Mostly they had the narrow streets, cobbled here with smooth stones, to themselves.

There were foot patrols, customarily four Rooks each armed with stub-barreled weapons that were probably shotguns, metal breastplates, and pole weapons with two-meter hafts, hooks for heads, and spiked tips. The point Rook of each squad had a bull's-eye lantern, whose dim yellow beam he shone importantly into pointed door arches and alleys as they tramped past. It gave the urban Landers twinges of nostalgia for the flywheel-powered torches carried by beat pokes back home.

But the alleys were deeper than the feeble lanternlight would pierce. And there were the usual crates of refuse in the alleys, and the tall, crowded-together buildings were richly supplied with buttresses and odd crevices and doglegs. Rooks seemed to savor a degree of clutter in their surroundings. For the snoop-and-poop experts of Section it was playland.

"Scan *this*," murmured Jovan, peering cautiously over a masonry lip at the cantonment in which the Collective battalion was besieged. He knelt on rubble behind what had been a window. One side had been extended in a fused-edge circle, evidently the work of an overload projector.

The building had once been three stories tall. Now it was about a story and a half. At that it had fared better than buildings closer to the cantonment. Collective direct-fire weapons and forays by demolition parties had leveled every structure within fifty meters of the walls. It had undoubtedly been horribly costly in terms of lives and munitions, neither of which could be replaced. But a kill zone was as vital as air; the besieged needed a buffer to keep the fast-moving Rooks from swarming over walls and defenders in one of their screaming heedless mass attacks.

They had tried, anyway. The grey dust and masonry chunks of the kill zone were practically paved with still lumps of feathers, dark in darkness, that fluttered wanly in the breeze.

The smell of Rook dead rotting was different from human decay. But it still had that quality of tweaking the nose, of getting into the stomach and tickling like the fingers of a swallowed hand, of adhering to the skin like greasy film.

"Lemme see your glasses, Poet," Jovan said, reaching out.

"Fuck you," Poet said.

Jovan frowned at him. Then he dropped it. Poet didn't like anybody touching his stuff.

It wasn't as if you needed vision enhancement to scope all you needed of the situation. The cantonment walls were finely fitted stone, two and a half meters tall, forming a square about three hundred meters on a side. The outer face was pocked like a lunar surface with myriad bullet craters, and here and there the larger gouge of a cannonball strike. There weren't many of these. Even if the battalion lacked heavy support weapons, there was simply no way for a Rook direct-fire tube to survive the first shot it fired, especially at such close range.

The number and clustering of the bigger craters indicated that they kept trying anyway. There was even a three-meter stretch where the wall had been beaten down, a little to the

right from Section's lie-up. Evidently the Rooks would keep
manning a piece until the invaders rendered it unworkable—
not that easy with a simple tube. It bespoke suicidal courage
born of the screaming hatred the Rooks felt for the violators
of their homeworld. But that was old news; every man in
Section knew the birds knew how to die already.

More alarming was the damage to the top of the wall and
the buildings beyond. Beside a large cleared space stood a
large central keep featuring the usual stone walls, arches, and
buttresses. A starred green Collective flag hung from a standard at its peak, illuminated by a single small shitcan-powered
spotlight in pathetic defiance. Single-story brick structures
stood next to it, some with flat roofs, some peaked, that might
have been storage buildings. Around three sides of the yard
stood ranks of buildings made of the plasticlike mats, whose
order and slapped-together transience screamed *barracks*.

All the buildings showed artillery scars, especially gaps torn
in roofs. That meant slanting fire from weapons out of line-
of-sight. The Landers well knew Rook rifled guns seriously
outranged their grenade launchers; unless the besieged battalion had mortars or other big indirect-fire weapons of their own,
their fancy counterbattery radar would do zot for them.

As if to emphasize the fact, from away off to the left a
scream ripped the sky's clouding face. Section heard the hard
slap of the shot half a heartbeat before the shell flashed white
in the midst of the parade ground.

"I wonder what it was?" Nau whispered, as the report blew
over them like a gust of wind.

"Who gives a shit?" Balt hissed furiously. Nau's head
ducked into his collar like a turtle's.

"It's your grave, my bright-eyed boy," Loki said cheerily,
"unless Kosmos finds something in its pants except ID cards
and comes back for us."

"Thanks for reminding us all, Loki," Jovan said sourly.

Loki grinned his death-jester grin. "My pleasure," he said.
"You may all think of me as the reality fairy."

"Fairy, anyway," Balt grunted.

Loki laughed, a ringing sound, despite being pitched low to
keep it from the ears of the besiegers in the buildings to either
side. "Don't you wish, you brute? I'm not for the likes of
you."

Anger kindled at the backs of Balt's small eyes. "Are you saying I'm queer? I'll kill you, you mincing little—"

"Why don't you two clowns put a rag in it?" Kobolev snarled. "You'll have the birds down on all our necks, with us in sight of safety."

Silently Loki mouthed the word, "safety," and shook his head. His grin was wild, and edged like broken glass.

"They must be dying to see us," Dieter said. "And for me, it'll be a relief to finally see human faces other than your grimy mugs!"

Jovan sat back on his haunches and sucked on his lips. "They'll have food, surely. These red-ass battalions get rations for like forever." He held his slung pulser with one hand, rubbed his belly absently with the other.

"Who knows?" Dieter asked in a voice bright as a fresh copper ingot. "Maybe they'll have women!"

Stilicho sighed in disgust. "Dieter, you've truly Departed on us at last." *Departing* was the generic term for what happened when a ship made a probability-drive transit through Lo-space and didn't come out. It could mean catastrophic deresolution or catastrophic superimposition, or just going *away*—as in, to the other end of the Universe, or Process knew how many billion years into past or future, or some combination of the above. It happened about once every ten thousand jumps, which added a certain spice to space travel. "Do you really think the brass dropped a field brothel along with a bloody battalion?"

Dieter's eyes shone. "Why not? The red-asses stint themselves nothing."

The stocky man shook his head. "For my part," Stilicho said, "I'll be glad to get shed of these wings. They itch me worse than all the lice this world doesn't have."

That got a chorus of assent. Their march cross-country had been so little opposed that it took days less than anticipated. Just over half the "field rations" had been consumed.

"At least we'll be in a strong position," the Dancing-Master offered. "Strong walls with strong backs to hold them until Kosmos Force comes back."

"And here we have proof positive that higher education rots the brain," Loki declared. "Kosmos isn't *coming* back, my fine child of *klad*. They have run far away, and are busily planting their probes and hoping the rest of the Universe has forgotten us as finally as they have.''

"Corpor—'' the sergeant began. Then he noticed that Loki was looking at him with a queer little smile. "Loki, I don't care for your tone.''

"Why should things change now?'' Loki asked, and turned to peer through a fist-sized hole melted through the wall by blue bolts.

Florenz sat with his back to a half-standing interior wall with his arms around drawn-up knees, and his face lifted so his bandaged ruined eyes could gaze out into infinity. "Maybe I'll get to go home soon,'' he said dreamily.

The others flicked glances at him. They showed mostly pity. A Lander never went home. Dead men got no leave. And they had no homes to go to, even if they did: such relatives as survived whatever transgression got them Detached would be mortally shamed by having a deathbird in the family, and Collective guilt by association made it insanely risky to so much as *talk* to someone who had been condemned.

An unspoken part of Tradition was a measure of tolerance for crack-up due to combat fatigue, since most every Lander had his bouts with it, soon or late; there was no dustoff of psychological casualties from CLD. The thickness of that tolerance was based largely on how likely a man's behavior was to get his bruds killed. Florenz had some margin yet; he had begun to ramble the last couple of days, but that was all.

Not everyone felt the same, though. Balt glared at the wounded scrub and growled. He had promised repeatedly to kill Florenz if the boy got within reach. More unsettling to Mir—usually if Balt talked he didn't act—was the fact that Poet had been giving the youth hooded glances the last two days. The little scout and flamer man had perhaps the finest-honed survival instincts in Section, and very few compunctions about acting on them. If he decided Florenz was a liability, there would be very little Mir or Tradition could do to save him.

Shaking his head, Mir slipped bent-over through the doorway next to Florenz into the room adjoining. Here Bori crouched by an uneven two-meter hole that might or might not have begun as a window, peering at the buildings surrounding the cantonment through the computer-enhanced scope of his Bitch. The machine gun stood propped on its bipod behind him, resting on a sturdy hardwood table which had somehow survived. Bori may have been simpleminded, but he was a proficient Bitch gunner. He knew well that you didn't hang the fat barrel of such a prize target as an infantry-support weapon out the window for every enemy in sight to zero in on if you could help it. If the muzzle was a meter or so inside your embrasure when you shot, you still had a good field of fire, and Anton had the Devil's own time picking you up. It was a vintage deathbird trick, part of the oral tradition of passed-on lore that went so far toward making the Collective Landing Detachment such a formidable fighting force.

Beside the table a Rook foot soldier lay on his back, big eyes wide, beak and eyes alike agape. The plumage of his chest was matted-dark with his blood. Bori, who had stolen up upon him from behind and looped a wire garrote with chunks of human thighbone for handles around his thick neck, was likewise soaked and a-reek with Rook blood. Even Mir barely noticed the stink. A-gunner Gollob sat next to the table with thin shoulders slumped, visibly trying not to look at the corpse.

A platoon of twenty-some Rooks had held this building. Their eyes and rifles had been fixed immovably on the pocked cantonment walls. They died without a sound.

Hard lessons of combat and evasion had taught the Landers a lot about their opponents' sensory packages. Rooks saw much better than men, but did not hear as well; their sense of smell was no keener than a human's. It stood to reason that those great golden eyes, which in the daytime looked as if they ought to glow with a light of their own at night, should also have served to collect a great deal of light at night. But the Rooks did not seem to see well in the dark, and they hated to operate under its cover, preferring when possible to bivouac under steep-sided tents. When deployed on sentry duty they huddled in lumps, their body language and the positioning of their crest feathers, which better served to express emotions than their largely immobile facial muscles, suggesting sodden self-pity even to alien eyes.

A Bitch could be tuned to fire projectiles at just below local speed of sound, so that they created no sonic boom—the amount of noise made by a minute metal sliver traveling around Mach 10 could be pretty startling. Fired single-shot, a subsonic needle made no noise at all, and even on full-automatic the weapons were soundless except for the faint whine of the ammo-blower and the skitter—like miniature robot mice in an air vent—of needles being blown through the flex hose into the receiver. The trefoil-section needle shape of the fléchettes gave them great sectional density and an excellent ballistic coefficient; it took them forever to lose speed to air friction, and they penetrated like evil rumor. Up to a good two hundred meters, you could count on dropping a still target with a brain shot—at least, if their braincases weren't armored better than human or Rook ones were.

At close range the Bitch's unwieldiness made it a problematic weapon for silent killing. That left *mano-a-mano* murder, and the ancients were adepts. Some of them, like Poet, liked it better that way.

One way or another, the fight for the building had been over in less than fifteen seconds.

"Getting anything?" the lieutenant asked.

"Oh, yes, sir," Bori said in that clear child's voice, eager for approval. "Lots and lots of hot spots."

Mir nodded. If the Rooks held their positions long enough, their bodies' heat signatures would eventually seep through walls.

"Use your light enhancer for more detail," Mir directed softly, "and scan for anything that looks like it might be an artillery piece." From history classes at the *Akademiya* he knew that even muzzle-loading artillery could fire shotgunlike munitions like modern beehive rounds, with devastating effect against infantry in the open. If the Rooks had smuggled fieldpieces up under cover and not fired them yet, they might have escaped the defenders' eyes and sensors.

It was unlikely Section would spot anything the besieged battalion had missed. The defenders would know to the millimeter the position of every Rook on the perimeter. But where ammunition resupply was chancy—not to say *nonexistent*—a protracted siege meant a sort of *modus vivendi* evolving between besiegers and besieged.

Even if they had no support arms at all left, not even rocket launchers and overload projectors, the humans could dig the Rooks out of their fighting positions readily enough. A hail of blue bolts would erode the stout masonry walls like rain eating away a dirt clod. But it was an expensive way to fight.

So evolutionary pressures had produced a simple accommodation: the Rooks had learned that if they inconvenienced the humans individually, they died in a blue energy-storm. If they just hunkered behind their walls and watched, they were fine—until their own commanders launched them in another desperate mass charge.

"Check the high points, too," Mir said. "Mark me down anything that might be a sniper."

Big Bori grunted assent. Mir opened Dirt links to the other snipers and machine gunners, as well as Poet, Starman, Black Bertold, and the Dancing-Master, all of whom had scopes or glasses, and gave them similar orders. When the time came to move, he wanted to be able to neutralize any unusually dangerous enemy firepower at once.

Footing in the kill zone was as treacherous as it could possibly be without mining—which the defenders assured them they hadn't done, and which the lieutenant believed, since it would have been both costly and useless. Demolition had churned the ground to mounds of loose khaki dust, concealing odd-sized chunks of masonry ready to turn beneath a boot and trip you up, and little pockets that could suck your foot down and snap your ankle for you before you knew what was going on. Ironically that was less of a problem for the Rooks, whose lesser body weight and wide splay-toed feet gave them much less ground pressure than booted human feet, than it would be for Section.

It was going to be a desperate dash, with no stopping and no going back. Mir wanted all the edge he could grab.

The bars of light serving as "hands" swept around the dial of his watch. Military chronometers were programmed to imitate ancient "analog" clocks, since they were easier to read in the dark. His men reported nothing that suggested a hidden fieldpiece, but picked up five likely sharpshooters, on roofs and in spires. Their scopes transmitted these images to Mir's TD, which in turn forwarded them over the Dirt net to his snipers and grenadiers. The images were painted on helmet faceplates by tiny lasers, color-coded as to target priority.

Starman, whose laser would point infallibly back to their position like a brilliant blue finger, had his rifle slung. Only the five whose grenades and invisibly small fléchettes could not be sourced by the naked eye would fire.

Mir gave the order to stand ready.

"Ah, well," Black Bertold said, rubbing hands together with his usual jock heartiness, "who wants to live forever?"

"We do," came a hissed chorus from the dark of the ruin.

Mir watched the second hand seep toward the apex of the circle and midnight. "Time," he nodded, and drew a stubby flare launcher to announce their arrival to the defenders.

"*Get down!*" shrilled through the net. Then Loki tackled him.

24

Mir spit corpse-flavored dust and glared at the blond Lander. "Corporal, what the *hell* do you think you're doing?"

"What? What is it? What's going on?" blind Florenz demanded in a half–held-in squeal. Mir heard the thunk of a fist hitting meat. The ancients had laid off physical abuse of the wounded boy, since, with the maybe exceptions of Balt and Poet no one was eager to kill him by poking a splinter of the piece of wood lodged in his head into his brain. But nobody was feeling patient just now.

Loki's face was half a meter from the lieutenant's. He had snapped up his clear visor. His breath stank like a corpse. Mir quailed, but thought, *Maybe we all smell like that. We've become ghouls, haven't we?*

"That flag, Junior Lieutenant," Loki said. "Do you see anything odd about it?"

Mir felt his eyes bug. Loki wasn't what any man would call *stable,* or any doctor sane, but he was one of the last the lieutenant would expect to somersault over the edge in a combat situation. "What?" he managed to blurt.

"The flag," said Loki, calm but insistent.

"What of it? It's the Collective flag." The Stellar Collective's flag was a five-pointed green star in a black circle with a red border, against a green field. The flag atop the central building lay limp in a rare windless sky, but even in the light of the single defiant spot the green was evident, and a bit of black.

"The *star*," Loki said. "Look again. Look *close*."

For a moment longer Mir stared into Loki's eyes. They were almost water-pale. He turned, lifted his head to peer through a break in the wall.

There, gouging into the black: a point of red. Mir felt his heart jump into his throat.

The others had dropped to their bellies in the rubble and were gazing madly over their sights in all directions, not sure whether the Rooks were about to burst in on them or what. The nearer men were listening to the conversation. "*Revo!*" somebody hissed.

The insignia for the Ministry for Continuing Revolution—Revo—resembled that of the Collective. But Revo's flag had no border—and its star was red as blood.

As was the star on the flag that flew from the distant standard.

Somebody groaned. "Fucking *scabs!*"

Revo was not only the proprietor of the more widely feared and hated of the Collective's two chief secret police organs. It also operated a paramilitary arm that, while not on a scale to rival Kosmos or the Engine of History, made up a significant portion of the Collective's armed might.

"The Stellar snaking Guard," Stilicho said in disgust. "We should have known this was too good to be true."

"Now we know why they let the Rooks trap them like mice in a cellar," Starman said. "Cowards and fools, the lot. Can't hit a target—unless it's the back of someone's neck they have the muzzle of their pulser pressed against!"

"Not always," Kyov said. "On Wau'patshi the Stellars knew how to die."

"I wish more would practice," Starman said.

Rouen shook his head. His eyes held a hunted look. "We can't go in there. They'll neck us all sure."

The words turned like a knife in Mir's gut. Rouen was one of Section's steadiest men. If he started to deresolve, the unit might just come apart here in sight of what Mir still believed in his marrow was sanctuary.

"Why would they neck us?" he asked, striving to sound calm. "We're all in this together."

"They're our comrades!" Gollob exclaimed. He tried to keep his voice down, resulting in a steam whistle squeal of outrage. "They are the guardians and protectors of Universal Will! It's treason to doubt them." He struggled to his knees. "I, Lander—"

Somebody grabbed the strap of his ruck and yanked him down.

Mir realized his lips were peeled back, forced them shut. Foul grit had covered his teeth. It rasped the sensitive membranes. He fought his own feelings of unease: Revo were deadly—sometimes literally—rivals to Values. He had been raised to regard MCR as a nest of treason and Devolution, autarky even. And that was before he came into the Detachment, where Revo was *really* hated.

Still—*We're marooned here together, men fighting for our lives. That has to override everything.*

"Come on," he commanded, rising to his feet. "We've got to move. They're expecting us. The Rooks might stumble on us any second, and there's a whole fresh army about to land on us like an avalanche."

"All the more reason," Loki said, "not to walk into that rat trap. Which is indeed well stocked with rats!"

"Apologize to rats!" Starman snarled with seeming fury. "Apologize!"

Loki had gotten to his knees, where he performed a mock bow. "You have the right of it, my friend. Rats are our brothers, outlaws and survivors all. We have no more kinship with the creatures in front of us than we do with the ones behind us."

"That's ridiculous, Loki," Mir said in exasperation. "They're men. We're men. We all have to stand together against the Rooks, or die."

"We can still do a fast fade," Loki said. "Back into the streets and alleys, all the way back to the mountains if we choose." He was beginning to sound near-desperate. "Listen: either Kosmos will come for us, or they won't. If they don't, we die here, sooner or later. But at least we can die without stinking Revo boots on our necks."

"We've got no more time for this. Snipers, grenadiers, on my signal, take your targets down. *Now*!" Mir raised his flare launcher and fired. A magenta meteor arced across the sky and fell toward the Revo flag.

The savage crack of Bitch projectiles outbound at full velocity split the air like sword strokes. Grenade launchers made their ax-on-wood *thunks* as Stilicho and Black Bertold fired on predesignated targets.

Mir tried to push his will into Loki through the eyes. The lanky corporal snapped down his faceplate with a weird piping cry. He spun and fired a single grenade without aiming, toward what Mir hoped was his assigned target. Then he pulled back the trigger and held it, cranking out half a drum of grenades while turning his skyward-tipped muzzle in a semicircle.

"Go! Everybody up! Run!" Mir ordered.

Loki stood as if rooted, staring at him. "This is on your neck, Haakon Mir!"

"Fine," Mir said, "just go!" The lieutenant was running, obedient to his own command, but he kept eyes fixed beyond the cantonment walls. He felt sick conviction that Loki had decided to drop a burst of grenades in upon the Revo battalion.

But no. If Loki was a creature of chaos, he was also its master; he plied it with the skill with which Poet used his blade, or Starman his sniper's laser. The grenades cracked off among the shattered buildings surrounding the kill-zone in a firework flicker. Instead of just being alerted, the additional blasts ensured that the Rooks would be disoriented and confused, and, with luck, terrified: where was this new bombardment coming from? Had a relieving army of invaders somehow crept up behind them?

Mir wasn't watching where he was going. His foot crashed into a hidden pocket and he fell headlong, gashing open his forehead on an edge of fallen cornice. Fortunately the fall levered his foot free. Still, his ankle throbbed, and felt as if it were held on by badly stretched elastic bands as he scrambled up to run on it once more.

Just in front of him he could see Florenz stumbling along, one hand wrapped in the straps of Stilicho's backpack. In the corner of his eye he saw the flash of a Rook rifle. Belatedly the besiegers were catching on to what was happening.

From the rampart ahead flickered a hail of blue bolts. Mir flinched, expecting despite his earlier brave words to be blown backward by a superheated stream from the tissues of his own chest as directed-energy pulses took him. But they sizzle-sang over the heads of the running Landers, raising the hair on the back of his neck and leaving a tang of ozone.

The deathbirds raised a hoarse shout, more like the cawing of infuriated Rooks than a human sound, began to fire blindly toward the dark encircling buildings. The loose dust seemed to suck Mir's feet into itself at every step. It was such a short distance from their covert to the breach. Yet the yielding soil held them to a slow-motion forward stumble.

They've got to get the range eventually, he thought. And a hammerblow struck him under the right armpit, above the half-healed wound left by the amputation of a food wing. White light flashed behind his eyes, and he fell headlong.

He felt boots thud by. He raised his head in time to see Loki's gangly form wolf-lope past. The corporal glanced down at him, faceless behind his visor. He ran on.

Mir shook his head, tried to rise. Pain filled the right side of his body like incandescent gas. It left no room in his chest for air. His arms felt as weak and worthless as the vestigial stub wing that dangled from his left side to the rubble, sending weird random sensory jangles through his neural network, signals his brain had not yet figured out how to process.

His men were passing him by. *They're leaving me!* he thought. "Wait!" he tried to cry, but his dust-desiccated croak would have been inaudible over the rising firefight roar even if anyone had been listening.

His arms gave way. He fell with a whump and a fresh pain-blossom from his stub arm, trapped between his body and a block of masonry. He lay there trying to gather himself, trying to lever some breath into his lungs, some strength to his limbs. He doubted the soft-lead Rook projectile had penetrated his battle dress, but blue streaks of sharper agony lancing through the white pain-cloud made him think some ribs were cracked.

The birds had good marksmen; it was only a matter of time before a sharpshooter zeroed in on some vulnerable part of him. Or they could simply plink away at him and pound him to bloody jelly held loosely together by chammy armor-cloth; Mir had seen that happen to a man before.

Of course, he might just stay where he was and feign death. *Till I die from dehydration, or the Rooks overrun me in their next wave-attack.*

Footsteps Dopplered toward him. He gasped. It was like inhaling broken glass. He tried to bring up his pulser, irrationally convinced it was a Rook, though the impacts were human-heavy and came from the direction of the cantonment walls.

A hand, grabbing the harness of his rucksack, hauled him to his feet, draping his arm over a broad shoulder. "Come on, Junior Lieutenant." Kyov's voice in his ear. "I've got you now. Can you run?"

He could. Not well, but relieved of the chore of keeping himself upright, he could at least drag his legs across the evil rubble. Blue flickers danced like static discharges all along the wall top; the breach before them was edged in fire. Bullets moaned overhead, but the Rooks were still shooting by reflex.

They reached the breach. Men stood or knelt to either side, hosing fire at the buildings behind. Mir tried to lift a boot over the bottom of the hole, banged his shin instead. He stumbled forward and skinned his palms on the dirt inside the compound. Rough hands reached out to drag him inside.

An angry squawking rose from the buildings surrounding the cantonment. The Rooks were screaming their rage at being cheated. As he crawled farther into the cantonment, aided by Kyov's steady workingman's hand, Mir glanced back to see a company of Rooks burst out of the building they had just left, brandishing half pikes and bayoneted rifles.

The men of Section were jumping up and down, cheering and jeering at the birds. Some of them dropped to a knee and opened up on the belated pursuit. Still in the line of fire, Kyov had to let go of Mir and flop down on his face next to him.

The lieutenant hoisted himself on an elbow and turned to look out the breach. The Rooks were closing the gap with frightening speed, hooked beaks open in screams of hate. Blue-green fire gouged great chunks from their ranks, but they came on as if they meant to burst the stone walls asunder with the force of rage alone.

When the nearest was within five meters of the breach, double thunder crashed. White light flared, and clouds of tiny steel balls from two command-detonated Claymores set flanking the hole shredded forty of the man-high birds in an eyeblink. Mir fought to his knees and added his hoarseness to his men's cheers as the survivors turned and tried to flee, only to be dropped smoking to the rubble by blue hemispheres sprouting from their backs like brief parasites as blue bolts gave up their energy.

The moment of elation left Mir with the air from his lungs. He slumped forward, dropping hands to thighs, feeling suddenly ancient and sad.

A blow to the back of his head knocked him sprawling to the hard-packed dirt.

25

"COME ON!" A harsh voice cried. "Up, you scum! Over here! Do it now, or die where you lie!"

A boot slammed into his ribs, right where the bullet had taken him. Orange pain drove like a Rook lance through his torso right to the top of his skull. He gasped. All the strength fled his body, and he fell facedown.

He waited for a blue bolt in the back of the neck. Instead strong fingers hooked the collar of his battle dress tunic, and Kyov was dragging him farther into the compound, onto the hard-packed ocher soil of the parade ground. He felt other hands strip his pulser away.

By force of will he managed to coerce air into his lungs. He fought upright, swayed, waved his Section sergeant away.

Almost at once the butt of a pulser slammed into his kidneys. He lost his hard-won air, dropped to his knees. By some miracle of levitation he kept from going all the way forward onto his face.

Most of Section was already there, disarmed and kneeling with hands behind heads, surrounded by laughing, jeering men with red patches on the sleeves of their battle dress. "What's going on?" he demanded.

A backhand slap rocked his head on his neck. "Shut up, scum!" someone yelled. Blinking at tears, Mir saw he wore the single white lozenge of a Basic—a bottom-echelon cog, what the Engine called "Soldier" and CLD "Lander." The man must have noticed he had struck an officer, because he hawked and spat. Mir felt something slimy-wet strike his cheek and begin to roll down toward his jaw.

"So they call you junior lieutenant," he sneered. "That cuts no steel here! We're the Stellar Guard, and don't care where one turd ranks among the others!"

A pack of half a dozen Guardsmen were chivvying young Gollob as he walked toward his mates, arms raised and tears streaming down his cheeks.

"Here's a nice tender one!" a Guard called. He caught Gollob behind the head with his fingers, drew the scrub's face to his, and kissed him on the mouth.

Then he clamped down with his teeth and wrenched his head back, tearing a flap away from the corner of Gollob's mouth. The Lander reeled away with a scream, clapping a face to his ruined spurting cheek.

"What are you doing?" the boy cried. "I've admitted my fault! I am Lander 234-444-523-115-11111! I apologize for my crimes—*what are you* doing?"

Mir's eyes followed the Guard who had bitten Gollob. In horror Mir saw his blood-smeared jaws work briefly and then his Adam's apple bob.

Guardsmen swarmed over Gollob like hounds, clawing at him, grabbing his arms and pulling as if trying to wrench them from their sockets. They converged on him by dozens, gaunt and burning-eyed. Six armed Guards stood watch over the kneeling Landers, dancing and sidling with the agitated desire to join their fellows.

Roaring, Big Bori rose to his feet. Blue bolts instantly blasted the ground before him. Dust wreathed the giant like martyr's smoke. Loki lunged, made an arm, caught the hem of Bori's pants leg, and yanked a foot out from under him so that he toppled with a crash.

"We don't have a chance!" Loki hissed. "Don't give the putes the satisfaction!"

"Bend the neck!" Kobolev whispered, hoarse, and desperate. "Bend the neck!"

Cheeks burning, eyes streaming, Mir bent the neck. It was a reflex he had learned well.

Gollob was lost to view in a seethe of shouting, laughing

Guardsmen. Mir heard his voice cry, "Mommy, mommy, *please!* I'm a good boy, Mommy! *Help me!*"

There was an awful sound like canvas tearing. The cry became a bubbling shriek, that rose higher and went on longer than any sound Mir had heard a living being make in all his time in Hell.

From somewhere off in the night, a voice repeated the cry: *"Mommy, mommy, I'm a good boy!"*

Another answered: *"Mommy, please!"*

"I'm a good boy!"

"Mommy, help me!"

"Mommy! Mommy!"

The screams became a chorus, a tumult of Mommy-cries, like the cries of a flock of shorebirds taking flight. Mir turned his head to stare at the Guard nearest, the one who had struck him and spit on him. The man was fidgeting, hopping, rolling his eyes with the lust to join in the feast. An erection tented the fly of his trousers.

He caught Mir's attention and laughed wildly. "That's the birds," he said excitedly. "They're wizard mimics." He danced in and slapped Mir again. "Now keep your filthy eyes to yourself!"

Mir looked wildly around, hoping to see his men rising from their knees in a vengeful rush. It would be suicide, of course; the Guards' pulsers would smoke them all within five steps. But at least they'd die on their feet . . . and quickly.

But no. Kyov wept openly, his whole upper torso shaking as he kept his hands clasped behind his helmetless head. Puke slopped over Jovan's lower lip, though he didn't dare double over. Lennart prayed in a ragged whisper: *Yea, though I walk through the Valley of the Shadow of Death . . .*

Poet took Mir's eye. "Max Nix, Lieutenant," he said. "Makes nothing."

Gollob's shriek rose to a crescendo, broke into a turbulence of gurgling sobs, and stopped. Then there were only the sounds of frenzy, and of rending, and the mocking hateful Rooks celebrating an invader's end.

"Listen up, Lieutenant!" Mir heard Loki cry. A Guard stepped quickly in to club the corporal in the back of the head with his pulser. Loki fell onto his side, spilling his blood in mustard-colored dust. "It's all your work, Lieutenant! *His blood is on your neck!*"

Loki set his jaw in lordly disdain, then, as the Guard systematically began to piledrive his boot into his kidneys.

Hardly feeling the pain from his ribs or his knees, Mir knelt in a dull red haze shot through with slurping sounds, and brutal arguments punctuated by blows. After a life sentence or so he became aware of a presence nearby.

He looked up. A man stood near him, bareheaded, regarding the Landers with a faint sneer. He was tall, with broad shoulders and big knuckly hands and the wound-wire build of one who has had all excess burned out of him long since. Iron grey hair was cropped close to his head. Knots of muscle worked beneath the tanned tough hide of his cheeks, as if he were constantly chewing. At the base of his corded throat he wore the simple golden ring of the Circle of Life, the Stellar Collective's highest award. His bearing was that of a man in command. Two enormous Guard noncoms stood behind him with pulsers in their hands to enforce that command.

Grenade launchers must have opened up from within the cantonment, because explosions flashed white among the buildings, and sharp cracks chased light-echoes between battle-scarred walls. The chilling cries of "*Mommy! Mommy!*" subsided.

"Filthy animals," the officer said. "They should be exterminated. They cannot possibly be brought into accordance with Universal Will!"

For some reason that made Mir furiously angry. "Our mission is to uplift pre-Objectives, to Realize them, not destroy them."

The officer stared down at him. His eyes were pale in his dark face, and seemed to burn like beacons. "Your mission is to die, Junior Lieutenant," he said in a voice like the clash of gears. "I am Storm-Colonel Tigrosian, commanding the 212th Battalion, Stellar Guards, and I shall certainly see that you do so."

Storm-Colonel was Revo for Lieutenant Colonel. "Why?" Mir croaked, not caring if the Guard struck him again—and more than half-hoping the man would simply shoot him.

Tigrosian glanced toward the churning crowd, who seemed to be directing their attention to something on the ground in their midst. "My men hunger, Junior Lieutenant," he said quietly. "Most of our rations were lost, along with our heavy weapons."

He spread his big hands. "What would you have us do? Eat each other, like animals? My men are the cream of the Stellar Collective."

He shook his head and chuckled. "Of course, we've been doing just that. You can't *imagine* how pleased I am to see you, Junior Lieutenant."

"You mean you brought us here—?"

"You brought yourselves here," Tigrosian corrected briskly. "Of course, we weren't going to *discourage* you." He smiled.

"You can't just slaughter us like cattle!" Mir yelled.

"Why not? You're sentenced to death already. That makes things much simpler, really."

"But—but we're sentenced to die at the hands of the Collective's enemies!"

"And so you shall, if things are traced to their proper causes. We're besieged here by the Rooks—and before that, we were abandoned on this dung heap planet by sniveling traitors from Kosmos. *They're* the ones who will cause your deaths, Lieutenant. And they'll pay. Universe damn them, they'll *pay!*"

He finished in a red-faced scream. Then his expression broke like a clay mask and he chuckled.

"Just look at it as giving life to your comrades, ah"— he gestured at the vestigial wing hanging from Mir's left side— "in arms. An ingenious use of an R&R unit, by the way, Junior Lieutenant. You are to be commended."

Men were beginning to drift away from the pack surrounding whatever was left of Gollob; rubbing red smears from their faces. They wore dark shiny bibs of wet, and Mir saw that beneath the bibs were other stains, dried crusty.

Storm-Colonel Tigrosian gestured. "Lock them away," he commanded. The Guards keeping watch on Section kicked and cursed the Landers to their feet.

Mir rose with the rest, started off with them toward a rambling single-story brick structure with a low peaked roof. "A moment, Junior Lieutenant," Tigrosian said.

Hard hands clamped Mir's biceps. He looked frantically left

and right; the colonel's two goons had him. A pulser in the kidneys put him back on his knees with tears leaking from the corners of his eyes and him hating himself for the weakness.

"Don't worry, Junior Lieutenant," Tigrosian said. "We're not going to kill you yet. We've learned to ration our meat most carefully. We lack refrigeration, and spoil rapidly, you know: it's the microorganisms we brought with us."

Mir looked at him through layers of exhaustion and hopelessness and pain that swathed his eyes like dirty gauze. "Then what?"

"My officers and I have yet to dine today," he said, "and as selfless servants of the Universal Will, we reserve to ourselves the choicest cuts."

Mir's stub arm was seized, yanked cruelly taut. His brain danced with semiprocessed neural impact. He saw moonlight skitter the length of a large knife blade, felt pressure as the tip was worked between the tough polymer threads of his battle dress. The ballistic fiber gave less protection against sharp implements than bullets, which were comparatively blunt; once the blade's tip had made a hole, the edge sawed quickly through, huggling a semicircular tear, baring the pallid base of the food arm.

Mir saw teeth drawn back in pack-predator grins. Blades flashed. Blood sprayed, black in the night, and a red bomb of pain burst in his brain, and he screamed until it seemed the tissue of his throat hung in ribbons.

26

THEY CAME AT two hours after midnight, when the human body is supposed to reach its lowest ebb. Three skimmers floating silent on contragravity fields, black stealth composite hulls driven by columns of electrically charged air, using the hills to mask their approach. Aboard rode thirty-six picked Stellar Guard commandos in black armor cloth, masked and sealed; lethal gas was one of many options at their disposal.

They emerged over cultivated land, dropped to two meters, sweeping silent by the dark of the moon, rising now to cross a windbreak line of bilondras, lowering again for final approach to target.

According to official history, the Originals had fled Earth to escape a civil war between two great computers which had come to life and were warring for control of the planet. Though official history was of course Universal Truth, the more sophisticated—such as Albrekht Mir, himself a guardian of that Truth—regarded it as *truth* of a metaphorical kind, and the story as apocryphal.

Nevertheless it remained an unbreakable, almost obsessive, policy of the Stellar Collective to ensure that computers—software, actually—didn't become *too smart*. One of the Collective's most prestigious occupations was that of Special Designation Systems Analyst, colloquially called *terminator*. These were the secret police of the cyber realm, constantly monitoring the Collective's myriad data-processing systems,

civilian and military, for signs of self-awareness. The termi-
nators could go anywhere and poke into anything, regardless
of security classification, and their powers were wide-ranging.
It was known that they could blank any database, or even
physically destroy a computer or network of computers, purely
on suspicion. Rumors spoke of research facilities neutralized
by thermonuclear devices for dabbling with artificial awareness—even entire planets sterilized, on the chance that a system *might* have achieved consciousness, and spread its
infection worldwide.

This consuming fear of a Cybernetic Stalin had consequences. Among them was that the expert systems processing
sensor input had some holes in them.

A metallic mass the skimmers' battle computers had IDed
as heavy farm equipment revealed itself as a gravitic anomaly
detector-guided EM antiaircraft weapon. The flak-Bitch threw
out a thousand needles a second, and could sustain fire for a
full minute. The lead skimmer fell from the sky in pieces.

The second skimmer squirted frantic directed-energy pulses
like luminous blue-green feces, by luck more than targeting
silenced the AAA Bitch. The skimmer slid to a landing on the
hilltop garden that formed the roof of DVS Mir's residence.
The third craft flew over, stopped, turned, dropped toward the
main entrance. Its chin-pulser sprayed the front of the great
house, raising horizontal glass-fragment sprays.

On a monitor screen in the residence's well-armored under-
belly, Albrekht Mir watched three overload projector charges
converge on the skimmer in the front yard like poles of blue-
green light. It crashed onto the lawn. Trained to the razor edge
of frenzy, half a dozen black-clad assassins managed to spill
out onto their feet, weapons flaring.

Two heavy flamers in pop-up turrets concealed as planters
flanking the entrance hosed them with white-and-yellow brilliance. They became torches, performed brief whirling dances,
and went out.

Sendak shook his ugly head and clucked mock-
sympathetically. "Poor stupid putes. Did they really think
Revo could scratch its discharge-chute without Values getting
smelly fingers?"

It wasn't that simple, of course. Values, ever-subtle, worked

constantly at infiltrating its major rivals such as Struggle and
Revo; and would lay groundwork across generations to get its
sleepers emplaced. But it had taken prodigies of resourceful-
ness and effort for Mir and his chief expediter to ensure they
would receive advance warning of Revo's attack on the DVS.

Mir called for a monitor to show the garden-terrace. In
enhanced-light shadow play he watched the final squad of
Revo killers, apparently undeterred by their comrades' fate,
blowing in the armored skylights with shaped charges. They
slid down into the master bedroom and an exercise room on
slim black cords.

Where they were promptly hacked down by Shadows waiting in shadow, led by Natalya Mir herself.

"Gone to be soldier-boys," Sendak said, chuckling. "And
girls. Not for me, not for me."

Mir looked at him. "Are you afraid?"

Sendak laughed delightedly. "To tell you all the truth, District Supervisor," he said, "I'm simply too old for that shit."

27

"Our Father, Who art in Heaven, hallowed be Thy name...."

His father, Values supervisor for Santander District Albrekht Mir, was there, speaking his dry, demanding way over the dull prayer mutter: "It is of course inappropriate that the practice of relic religions be permitted today, especially religions so intimately caught up in the cultures of colonialism and exploitation. The only religion the Collective should countenance is direct veneration of the Universal Spirit, which personifies Universal Truth and Will. This constitutes an oversight by Direktor and Praesidium which we of Values hope to soon see rectified...."

It grieved Mir to see his father this way, a once-robust man gone all gaunt and ascetic. From somewhere came a rhythmic rustling, like metronome mice. Mir's eyes, working against gummy residue, opened. His father's voice faded and was gone—as he recalled with a jar his father himself was.

The prayer continued. With a much worse start, like a fresh boot in the belly, Mir remembered where he was. And he wondered if he wished his father *were* still alive—because he could not bear to think of him trapped in such a hell as this.

It was humid, dark, and close, but from the vagrant shine of a lantern placed somewhere outside his field of view Mir could see that the proximate hell he occupied was a cell about eight meters square, with yellow brick walls and moldering straw on the floor. An astringent reek invaded his nose, not quite familiar but suggesting excrement. Section's survivors were crammed into the cell. They stood leaning against the walls or sat in tight huddles. In one wall was a sliding door of heavy planks shod in tarnished brass. Its upper half was vertical metal bars.

His chest felt as if it were on fire. He looked down at himself. His chammy blouse hung open in front. Beneath it a pressure bandage was held by tape wound around his ribs to the site from which his vestigial arm had been amputated.

"They didn't want you to bleed to death before they were ready for the rest of you, Lieutenant," Rouen said.

Ignoring the agony that ate like a cancer at his side, Mir jumped up and flung himself at the door. It failed to budge when he threw his strength against it. He tried to squeeze his head out through the bars, but they were too close-set.

He was looking across a brick-paved runway about three meters wide at the similarly barred door of another cell. A lantern hung from a sconce on the far wall gave off what illumination infiltrated Section's cell. None seemed to make it into the cell across the way.

We're locked in a stable, he realized. There were differences in detail from the riding stables he had known on Novy Utrecht, and the ranch house ones on Santander, but the similarities were unmistakable.

A rush of pallid motion from across the way. A great pale blur suddenly filled the barred window opposite. A black hole opened near the top of the mass to emit a titan scream.

Reflex jerked Mir back. He stumbled over someone and sat down hard. Rouen gave him a harsh look as Mir took his leg off his shoulder. Narva broke into pealing cackles.

Mir thrust himself back at the bars. The pale thing was gone from the window opposite.

"So somebody's awake in there, eh?" a voice dried and cracked like ancient pottery said from up the runway. Mir turned his head, managed to wedge a bit of his forehead between bars so he could see to his left. A tuft of dark hair hung from what he guessed was yet another barred window.

"New meat," said a voice from the vicinity of the tuft. "And I do mean meat." The voice laughed.

"Fuck," Jovan said in disgust. "Pute thinks he's a real comedian. Let me get my hands on him; *I'll* teach him some real thigh-slappers."

Mir moistened his lips. "What—what's in there?" He nodded his head at the cell across, not sure if the gesture could be seen.

"A mutant. A monster." Another laugh. "The scabs could feast for days off him, but they're afraid his madness taints his meat. They don't know what to do with him."

Dizziness washed over Mir. He reeled backward toward the spot he had occupied before, collapsed at the foot of the wall. The impact of tailbone on the straw-covered brick stabbed pain through his side. That woke aftershocks, remembered pain slamming peristalsis through his body. He closed his eyes and gritted his teeth to keep from crying out.

When the tremors passed he became aware of that shuffling noise again. It seemed to be picking up speed, and was accompanied by little plosive groans. When his vision quit spinning so fast Mir glanced down. Chyz lay facing the wall with his feet toward Mir, working one hand rapidly. Mir turned away.

"If you come on me," muttered Jovan, who sat near the scrub, "I'll kill you dead. I swear."

"It's an abomination!" Lennart shouted from near the door. Mir must have almost trod on him when he rushed to look out. "It's an affront to the Lord to defile himself like that! We should—"

Big Bori came up off the floor, grabbed Lennart by the throat, picked him up, and slammed the back of his head against the bars so hard the door shook. Lennart's eyes rolled up into his head, and he went limp.

"Your constant gibble-gabble at Jesus bothers me more than his pounding off!" Bori yelled. "Stop it now!" He shook the quiescent form.

"Let him go," Jovan said. "He *has* stopped, if you haven't noticed."

"Oh." Big Bori released the Christian, who dropped right down into a boneless heap. The giant slouched back to where he'd been sitting.

Mir started to his feet. "Save your joules, Lieutenant," Jovan said wearily. "He isn't dead. Lennart's head is mostly bone, and the rest is stuffed too full of Jesus to hurt."

A splat of a heavy body hitting the bars across the runway, and a shrill gibbering scream. Mir jumped. The other Landers fidgeted and bitched.

"What *is* that?" Mir demanded, cat-tense, as the noise subsided to blubbering.

"What the joker down the hall said," Jovan replied. "The biggest son of a sow I ever saw."

"He must be three meters tall!" Nau said. "He's bigger than Bori!"

"Two and a half, anyway," Stilicho said. "Big and crazy."

"Human?" Mir asked.

Stilicho shrugged. "Looks human," he said. "Least as much as Bori does."

"Hey!" Bori said. "I don't like it when you say bad things about me!" He began to cry.

"Scabs found him wandering just before they fought their way into town," called the voice from the cell up the runway. "Rumor says he's some kind of supersoldier bred on some backwater world. Can't talk sensible now, if he ever could. Mostly he just screeches."

Mir made his way back to the window, hung on the bars for support. "Who are you?" he called.

"Just another cog from the Engine of History," the voice said affably. "Thirty-two hundredth Battalion, 75th Light Infantry. Got separated from my bruds, and the snakin' scabs trolled me in. They called me a deserter, and here I am."

The voice chuckled. "They were about to call me lunch, when you boys came strolling in, innocent little lambs." And he laughed uproariously at calling a passel of deathbirds "lambs."

A shattering crash. The bars vibrated in Mir's hands. Dust fell from the rafters and got in his eyes. He let go and fell backward onto the crowd of his men.

This time nobody glared at him. They were busy making love to the straw as an incoming artillery barrage smashed down outside.

The shelling went on for what seemed like hours. Mir knew that was unlikely; he had extensive firsthand experience of how the awful helplessness of being under bombardment stretched time. But he had never actually been imprisoned *and* shelled at the same time before.

Even for a man who had been arrested for treason, Detached, and gone through the Meatgrinder, it added a new dimension to the plenum of *powerlessness*.

At last the bombardment stopped. Mir felt continuing tremors, realized the arms he had folded over his head were shaking uncontrollably.

He picked himself up from the mass of sprawled bodies. Florenz sat with his back to the wall, screaming in a constant high note, broken only by pauses at improbable intervals to suck down a fresh breath. Bloody tears squeezed out of ruined ducts to blaze red trails from the bandage down his cheeks.

The air was full of dust and mold and pungent chemical-explosive smoke. Nobody had been allowed to go outside to use the latrine, and as usual many sphincters had been shaken loose along with the other debris by artillery bombardment, adding a certain wet lushness to the cell's stink. Mir flailed to his feet, staggered to the door.

"What was that?" he shouted, his own voice far away through the ringing in his ears. He could hear besieger voices rising like a windstorm outside the walls, bird cries mingling with that uncanny mimicry of human distress: "*Mommy, mommy!*" "Are the Rooks attacking?"

"Probably not," the voice came unflappably back. "They do this every night. Sleep deprivation, you know, just out of hate. Makes the scabs act even nuttier than normal."

Mir turned and slid down to the floor, next to the still-inert Lennart. He didn't even have the energy to check to make sure the zealot was still breathing. Florenz's cries had ceased; somebody had beaten him to silence, driven by his nerve-tearing screams beyond caring whether he drove a wood fragment through the scrub's brain or not.

Mir felt his eyelids transmuting to iridium. His heartbeat was still jackhammered from the protracted adrenaline surge of getting shelled, but suddenly it was all he could do to stay awake. And more than he had the energy to do; he surrendered and let the black rise up over his head, and at the last let go of consciousness with a drowning man's relief.

If the Birds shelled again that night he didn't know it. He was rattled back into awareness when the heavy door was slid out from behind his back and a boot landed in his ribs.

"Up, Junior Lieutenant Deathbird," a harsh voice commanded. He opened his eyes to see one of the storm-colonel's bodyguards looming above him, backed by a pair of Basics with leveled flamers.

The bodyguard's face folded in tectonic disgust. "Or should I say shitbird? Faugh, you stink even for CLD scum." He gave Mir another kick in the ribs. "Now, on your feet and look smart about it, our we'll drag you on your face. If any of the rest of you turds with legs make a move, we'll cook ourselves breakfast *right now*."

His backups laughed. Their cheeks were hollow, and most of their teeth were gone.

Painfully, like a building falling down in reverse motion, Mir got himself upright. Sitting with his back to the far wall, beneath a high arched window through which gruel-colored dawnlight dripped, Starman raised his head and his black eyes met Mir's.

The dark man smiled. "Looks as if you're the main course, Lieutenant."

Loki snickered. "Perhaps Lennart is right after all," he said, "and there is a God."

"You're a brave and resourceful man, Junior Lieutenant," Storm-Colonel Tigrosian said. He turned from the narrow window of his office in the large central structure. There was no artificial lighting in the small stone-walled room. Against the sunlight blazing from the window the Revo officer's head was a blur of blackness, yet from the sudden flash of teeth Mir could see with surprise that he grinned.

"Have you ever heard a joke that ended with the line, 'you don't eat a pig like that all at once,' Junior Lieutenant?"

"No, sir," said Mir.

"No matter, no matter." Waving a big hard hand Tigrosian sat behind the desk. Aside from being chevron-shaped, with the point toward Mir, it was a fairly desk-looking desk; all things taken with all other things, the Rooks were quite manlike for autocs. The Storm-Colonel's chair was a crude construct of dark and lustrous-finished wood that had evidently been knocked together from pieces of Rook furniture to better accord with knees that bent backward instead of forward.

The officer gazed at Mir with near-white eyes. "You have

done well to bring your men so far, Junior Lieutenant; I commend you. It's too bad you are a condemned traitor.''

He shrugged. ''Still, I have to admit your status
... simplifies things.''

''You really intend to kill us all and eat us?'' Mir asked.
His muscles quivered with weakness, but somewhere he found
the will to remain standing at attention.

''Oh, yes, Junior Lieutenant. No help for that. It's all a
matter of survival. Of the fittest—very deep-ecological, you
know.''

He jumped up, paced back and forth before the window, a
surprising fidget for a man so filled with force.

''We're in a desperate spot here, Junior Lieutenant, and no
question. No heavy weapons, few rations, subsisting on water
from the sewers below us, that tastes foul no matter how we
filter it.'' He shook his head. ''We can't hold out much longer.
We've eaten all our own dead, and were reduced to drawing
lots to see who'd go into the kettle next.''

He stopped and fixed Mir with a beacon eye. ''You can see
how providential your arrival is for us, Junior Lieutenant? Like
a sign that the Universe means for us to survive until help
arrives.'' He slapped a hand on a desk. ''The Universal Will!
That's why we fight!''

''It doesn't look so providential from my angle, sir,'' Mir
murmured.

Tigrosian frowned. ''What's that? What? What?'' His two
guards, who stood flanking the door at Mir's back, shuffled
their feet on the stone floor as if bracing to give the young
officer a beating for his insolence.

Tigrosian waved a hand. ''Never mind. You have a smart
mouth. But that's CLD; what can we do, Detach you, right?''
He shook his head. ''If sanity prevailed, we'd simply shoot
you for your crimes, not arm you and set you loose upon a
suffering Universe. But politicians call the tune we all dance
to. Politicians and civilians, right?''

To Mir, who after all had been trained as a regular officer
of the Engine of History, Tigrosian and his men *were* civilians,
secret policemen playing at soldiers. And not very bloody *well*.
They had gotten themselves trapped where the Rooks could
concentrate against them, and fired off all their mortar rounds

in panic so they no longer could respond at all to the besiegers'
artillery, primitive though it was.

He didn't say so. Not because he feared the consequences,
but because he lacked the energy for debate.

"Besides, you're thinking, we're going to eat you anyway."
The Storm-Colonel sat abruptly, leaned forward over hands
clasped on the desktop. "Am I right?"

Mir said nothing. "Am I *right,* Junior Lieutenant?"

"Yes, sir."

"But maybe not." Tigrosian studied Mir's face closely, and
laughed at the involuntary hope he saw take shape beneath the
dried blood and grime.

"Ah, so you're listening to me now, Junior Lieutenant; very
good. I have a situation here, you understand, that goes beyond
the fact of being marooned and under siege. Now my men are
loyal to me; they love me; any man jack of them would jump
to take a bolt or bullet for me, am I right?"

This was fired over Mir's shoulder at the guards. "Yes,
Storm-Colonel!" they both snapped in unison.

"You see?" Tigrosian said. "Their loyalty is absolute. But
they've been *through a lot,* my men, understand. And your
arrival poses problems. It's got them . . . stirred."

He held up his hands and shook them slowly, as if to clear
away water droplets from washing after he'd had a piss. "The
fact is, good policy would be to keep you alive as long as
possible, ration you out. But the men are hungry. If I didn't
watch them, they'd turn on each other in an instant, snarling
dogs that they are."

He struck the desktop and jumped upright. "Snarling *dogs,*
do you hear me, Junior Lieutenant? Snarling dogs!"

Mir stood stiffer and fixed his eyes on the brightness of the
window past Tigrosian's shoulders. The Storm-Colonel released a breath that was almost a sob.

"But they're good boys," he said, "solid at the core.
They've been through a lot, you know."

For a moment he just looked at Mir. The younger man was
trembling uncontrollably, and thought he must pass out any
moment from the strain.

"You can help me, Junior Lieutenant," Tigrosian said in
as smooth a voice as his rough vocal cords would pass. "You
can help me a lot, and in turn maybe I can help you. Give

you a chance to eat rather than be eaten, so to speak."

"What does the Storm-Colonel mean, sir?" He found his eyes focused on the golden circle at Tigrosian's throat. Death-birds called that medal the Circle Jerk or the Golden Sphincter, and above all else dreaded the officer who lusted after one.

"Cooperate," Tigrosian purred. "It will be easier . . . for all of us, I assure you . . . if things proceed smoothly, with minimal resistance."

He stood with one forearm across his sternum, the elbow of the other arm propped on it, palm cupping square jaw. "Let me see—ah. We can be *debriefing* your men, shall we say by pairs? Your men would never accept such coming from us; men of the Landing Detachment are famous for their distrust of anything to do with the Ministry for Continuing Revolution; after all, if they didn't have an unhealthy disregard for authority, they wouldn't be convicts, hm?"

It seemed to be a rhetorical question. Mir stood stiff at attention and let it float past him in the mote-heavy deadly still air.

"But coming from you—after all you've been through together, after you've brought them so far—well, they're much more likely to accept your reassurances that nothing untoward is going on." He smiled. "So what's it to be, Junior Lieutenant?"

Mir swayed from the effort of holding himself upright, of holding his mind in a conscious state. He was aware of sedimentary layers of filth coating his body, his face, even his eyelids, aware of the trickle of sweat from beneath his armpits, aware of the itching-burning-salt-stinging from the spot where his food arm had been amputated. Most of his bones ached from kicks and blows. He had filled his pants somewhere during his bouts with fear and unconsciousness, and was aware that he filled the office with a stupefying reek of grime and human grease and stale sweat and shit; was aware of the lumpiness, cold and clammy like obscenely familiar corpse-fingers, of the excrement pooled in the seat of his trousers, as if he were some derelict swept up sleeping in an alley to be shipped off to a labor battalion.

There was nothing left of himself, it came to him, to remind him of the days when he had been freshly commissioned Junior Lieutenant Haakon Mir, a youth with a promising future, a child of Service, a *man*. The promise was a lie, the privilege revoked, and his manhood had been fucked and beaten out of him a hundredfold. He was, as near as his fogged brain could calculate, sentenced to death three times over: by the court on Santander; by the Rookery itself, through starvation or the claws of its autochthons; and by Tigrosian himself, since the next promise an officer of Revo kept to a deathbird would also be the first. He was what sensory impressions indicated: a reeking lump of offal, nominally alive, and that through some Universal oversight.

He felt his mouth form a strange stupid mechanical-man grin, hinged at the corners. *They're afraid of us. The mighty Stellar Guards with their numbers and their guns, and us deathbirds disarmed and locked in a cell you can spit across . . . and they fucking* fear *us.*

"Come now, Junior Lieutenant," Tigrosian said smiling. "Your men surely cannot begrudge sharing flesh with us. It's the communal way!"

Mir's smile just kept getting larger. It felt as if filth cracked like gesso around his lips and flaked away. It felt as if his head were in danger of splitting in half. He sucked down a deep breath.

"Fuck *you,* Storm-Colonel!" he shouted.

Tigrosian's face expanded in surprise and then collapsed in a look of demon rage. His face was too suffused with blood to permit the passage of words; he gestured with a fist instead.

Haakon Mir had the last laugh. The first hammerblow to the kidneys tripped the circuits of his central nervous system and dropped him to the floor, out cold.

He had drifted by unhappy chance back into something like consciousness when the door of the stable-cell creaked open and he was flung bodily in atop his own men. They moved aside to let him roll on his back on foul fly-buzzing straw.

As the door groaned shut on its metal track again, Loki gazed down his nose at him disinterestedly. Yellow shine from the window turned Loki's hair to an ironic halo.

"So the kitchen sent you back, Junior Lieutenant?"

28

Vague awareness of conversation, a buzz of sullen passion that slowly resolved into words.

"One thing you can count on, my children," Loki was saying. "Colonel Coprophage won't eat us right away. Or as a wise man—myself—is wont to say: political power flows from thrusting one's dragon—or reasonable facsimile thereof, in deference to certain ladies we've all known—up another's rectum. Our storm-colonel's consuming vice is power. He will, therefore, fuck us before he kills us."

Sitting with his back to a wall and only Hynkop daring to sit within a meter of him for his body stench, which was majestic even by the standard of a prison cell filled with diarrhea-ridden troops, Balt scowled. "What if he has to kill us first to get hard?"

Loki peered owlishly at him. "It must be rewarding, Balt, to know with utter confidence that, no matter what the gathering, you can lower the moral tone."

Balt glared at him, then smiled and nodded.

"I just want to know if he's *kidding*," Kobolev said peevishly.

"There you go," Starman jeered, "lusting after certainties again. It'll be the death of you yet, Standard." Kobolev gave him a red-eyed look of hate. Van Dam muttered darkly. The Bold Original held up a hand.

Sturz gasped and sidled away from Narva, batting air with

a hand that was almost black with dirt. "I can smell your farts!"

"You can?" asked Loki with a dreamy expression. "Wave some this way. Even the Oldest Living's peculiarly noisome brand of flatulence would smell like spring blossoms in here."

Sitting cross-legged, Jovan struck himself on a skinny thigh. "It isn't *right!*" he exclaimed. "They just can't hold us down and shit on us like this."

"Payback is a mother," Black Bertold said, nodding. "The Mother of All."

"There's got to be some way out of this," Nau piped up. "We just have to think of one." He stopped, looking horrified at his own temerity, looked wide-eyed around the cell and then slumped in on himself as if preparing to ward blows.

But the other Landers were nodding as Mir rolled over and tried to reassemble the broken parts of himself into something vaguely manlike. Broken metaphorically, with the exception of his left hand, which seemed to have been stomped on and busted with some thoroughness—he knew the feeling well— his most recent drubbing had added only aches and bruises to his varied and splendid collection.

"Perhaps you're right, lad," Loki said, nodding judiciously.

"We're survivors, aren't we?" the White Rat asked. "We've all been through hell before—a dozen hells. At the easiest, only one in four survives the Grinder, and that's before we see the battle line!"

Stilicho sighed. "We've been through some tight places together, and there's fact."

Dieter jumped to his feet, jostled his way to the window, grasped the bars. "We can get out. Of course we can!" He turned. His cheeks were flushed, his blue eyes bright. "Does anyone have a knife? We can dig at the mortar holding the bars in. It's only that plastic stuff."

"No," Stilicho said. "The putes searched us thoroughly. Didn't leave us so much as a spoon."

As if by common accord all heads turned to bear on Poet. He was a knife lover, and notably cunning. If anyone had held out a blade, it was he.

But the young-looking Lander only shook his head and held out his hands.

"Come *on!*" Dieter exclaimed. "There must be something."

"Yes," rumbled Bori. "Get us out of here. Then I'll find that storm-colonel and teach him a few good lessons about letting his men hurt that dribble-chinned little pute, what's his name?"

" 'Hurt' him?" Jovan said. "Bori, they *ate* him."

Bori's brows crawled up his face. "They did?" He covered his face with his hands in terror.

"Revo filth," Starman said. "They're what I called them: cowards. If we can get out of here, they can't stand against us!"

"Yes, I think we could arrange some choice diversions for our storm-colonel," Loki said. "And in exchange he'd sing us some pretty tunes, for many an hour."

"Do not forget Kosmos," said Lennart, raising his head from his knees. His eyes burned like cigarette-embers in darkness. "They ran off and abandoned us in this Gehenna."

"It's true," said Starman. "We've many accounts to settle."

"And we're the men to do it!" Dieter said enthusiastically. "We're CLD. Everybody fears us—and they're right to!"

In a corner sat Kyov, where he could keep his eye on all his men at once. Now he sadly shook his head. "We might as well go to the root of the problem," he said, "and lay plans to travel space to Praesidium and bring the Direktor and the Executor to account. They're the ultimate source of our pain."

Everybody hesitated, as if waiting for one of Gollob's patented outbursts. Then the Dancing-Master frowned.

"Now, Section Sergeant, I understand that we are all condemned traitors, and perhaps morality therefore no longer has meaning for some of us. But I must admit I'm shocked to hear you, of all men, voice such irresponsible sedition."

Kyov looked at him. "I *meant* that we were as likely to do that as bring Tigrosian or any of his men to account!" he snapped.

The Landers yanked their heads back as if he'd slapped them every one. For Kyov, who bore the suffering of all in stoic silence, to raise his voice was almost unheard-of.

"We all talk high and wide and free about how we *will* do

this, and *would* do that. Yet when they come for us, we'll bend the neck again.''

Dieter dropped to his knees before the sergeant, tears streaming from his eyes. "Kyov, Kyov, don't *say* that!"

Kyov shook his head. "It's true. You know it's true, every one of you. Who raised a hand when they tore poor Gollob limb from limb before our eyes? Only Bori, and he caved in quick enough. The rest of us stayed on our knees and *watched.*"

Tears cascaded down his own cheeks now, matting trails through silver-tipped beard hairs that poked through his own filth-coating. "We've been schooled well. We are *victims,* all of us, taught to accept punishment as our due. It's why we fight for them rather than against them. And we can no more change that than we can change our need to eat and breathe and shit.

"We talk big, we're all outlaws, all heroes of our personal fantasy-sims. But when they crack the whip, we roll onto our backs. We bend the neck to their command, and we always will!"

One by one the Landers dropped their faces, until only Mir remained looking at the noncom. Kyov met his eye, shook his head, and lowered his own face to his knees.

So this is how it feels when hope dies, the young lieutenant thought. In an odd way it almost cheered him; he had long since thought all the hope burned out of him.

He let his gaze wander up among the rafters, where a pair of small birds were weaving bits of straw into a nest, with no thought for the enmity their larger cousins bore the occupants of the space below. They came in through small ventilation holes let through the stone high up under the roof pitch; even had there been a way for the Landers to get up there, they could not have enlarged the hole wide enough to pass even the Rat or Poet.

But still . . . the thought that *something* was free to come and go from this hellhole, without a thought for politics or war or death, cheered him. It was all he had.

They spent the long morning expecting at any moment to be hauled out, singly or *en masse*, to be devoured by the hunger-crazed Revo Guards. The Landers dozed or spoke in harsh murmurs as a thin wash of cloud seeped across the sky and turned the normal friendly light of the primary glaucous and unhealthy.

Mir phased in and out of awareness. Mind and body were near breakdown—and not for him alone. For each of them, stress had been accumulating steadily until it had achieved planetary mass.

Even during the time at the R&R bunker, which now seemed an idyll of the most perfect peace he had known, still there had been the stress, omnipresent but unacknowledged, of abandonment; of the certainty of eventual discovery or starvation. On top of that lay the stress that every entity in CLD knew at every hour: of being under suspended sentence of death.

What's the difference? he tried to tell himself. *If it comes now or by some miracle is held off a day, a year, ten years— what difference does it make? The end result will be the same: sentence executed.*

Yet he found himself laboring through black depression like a man stuck in tar. The wonder was that he found himself unwilling to let go and simply sink, to allow the blackness to seal eyes and nose and mouth forever. In blackness there was rest; yet he would not yield.

At noon, the mutterings began from outside.

The scrubs started kicking each other and squabbling about who was putting whose feet on whom. The dispute ended in choking sobs. Mir became dimly aware of Loki and Poet conversing in tones that sounded perfectly normal.

"Do you remember the time on Primus?" Loki asked. Poet nodded. The dark down on his upper lip looked like the ghost of a moustache. Beneath it he showed the ghost of a smile.

"I remember."

Loki laughed. It was a brittle sound, a desiccated husk of his usual strident bray. Like the self-shaped shell left behind by an insect in molt. "Ah, Primus! There's a place. Thousand-story arcologies rising from swamps of toxic muck. Belts of factories in O that glitter the sky even at midday! Where criminal gangs rule the elevated walkways, with spaceships overhead for support."

The Dancing-Master frowned. "That's ridiculous," he said.

"Criminal gangs don't have spaceships. That would never be permitted."

Loki crowed. "Aha! There speaks a man too resolute to be swayed by mere facts! Was that one of the command skills you taught at the *Akademiya?*"

"Don't be foolish," the Dancing-Master said. "It simply makes no *sense* that mere criminals would have spaceships."

"Ah, but there's your folly: the Universe makes no sense, and all your learning's shit." Loki ostentatiously turned back to Poet. "Where were we? Back on Primus, where we came so close—*this close*"—he held up thumb and forefinger, separated by a sliver of dank air—"to wealth beyond dreams. Yes, I dare to use the forbidden word: wealth!"

Jovan raised his head from between his knees and showed a grin. "Somebody yell for Revo," he croaked. "Good thing they're right close to hand."

"What couldn't we have done, Poet, if we'd succeeded?"

"Bought our way out of CLD."

Loki blinked at his sometime partner. Poet had a way of surprising even Loki, the master of surprise. "Perhaps, perhaps. But there are ways to disappear—among the billions of Primus, among all the worlds of the Collective. A man with sufficient *klad* can find them."

"If we could run," Poet said, "we would have. Long ago."

Loki looked at him a moment longer. Then a corner of his mouth quirked, and he laughed, and snapped his fingers. "*That* for your drab practicality! If you're minded to be such a spoilsport, then, let us recall the ladies in their penthouses, glittering and fine, and ready to go quivering-moist at the touch of someone with the delicious taint of Down Below!"

The White Rat cackled, sounding almost like Narva. "Go on! None ever got moist at the thought of *my* touch, and I was born a Downy."

Loki sniffed. "Perhaps your approach lacked a certain savoir faire."

Balt stirred, scratched his crotch. "Don't talk about women," he growled.

"Balt, if we take the sensibilities of your misshapen dragon to account, we're barred from discussing anything with a hole in it," said Loki.

Starman lifted his head. "Shut it a tick," he said. "I hear something. Outside."

The White Rat grabbed the bars over the narrow window. He wasn't quite tall enough to peer out, even standing on tiptoe. With unlooked-for strength he hauled himself up to look.

"Scabs," he said. "Clot of them standing about the parade ground. They're talking and looking this way."

Mir sat bolt upright, trying to swallow the column of fear that rose up his throat. They had almost exhausted the water in their canteens. His tongue felt swollen huge.

The crowd grew larger. The inmates could hear the murmur of debate, rising to angry shouts, but it took some time to make sense of the words.

"Tigrosian's turned up with half a dozen bodyguards," the Rat reported at length. "The storm-colonel wants to ration us out. Some of the men want to just haul us out and eat us now."

The clamor rose outside, a raw chorus of rage and hunger. Florenz sank down small and covered his ears.

"Hey!" Rat sang out. "A fight's started now. Two men going at it—one's down. Pross!"

He yanked his head back, lost his grip on the bars, and dropped to the floor. "They all just jumped on the man who went down. They're doing him like they did poor Gollob."

Screams were clearly audible above the mob rumble outside, rising impossibly high in stair-step leaps, then cutting off. Starman jumped up and took the White Rat's place at the window.

"They're all going at it now," the dark-skinned man reported with a wolf grin of satisfaction. "Falling on each other like dogs."

Scream echoes chased each other around the rafters like bats. Sturz rolled into a ball and began to sob. Even Nau, most stable of the scrubs, showed whites all around his eyes.

From across the runway, a steam whistle–scream. Everyone in Section jumped as if they'd been shocked. Mir leapt to his feet and stared out the window above the door.

The far cell's occupant was clinging to the bars of his door and shrieking terror. It was the loudest sound Mir had ever heard a human make. As he watched, the monster flung himself away out of sight into the gloom of his cell. From the recesses came wild cries, interspersed with a banging that vibrated the stone walls.

"What's going on outside?" Loki shouted over the tumult. "Are the scabs eating that wiry pute Tigrosian yet?"

"No joy," Starman reported. "A bunch of them made a run at him, but his guards brought four or five of them to Now, and the rest backed off." He shook a fist out the window. "That's it, you ling shits! Cease to exist!"

"That'll give them something else to sink their teeth into," Dieter said brightly.

The racket from across the runway reached a jarring crescendo and stopped. Guardsmen ran into the stable with pulsers ready. Section shrank back toward the cell walls, staring fearfully at the door. Shaking, Mir held his ground.

The Guards hadn't come for them. They fumbled at the lock which secured the cell across the way, hauled the door open with a metal-on-metal squeal. A moment later six of them emerged, half-carrying, half-dragging the limp form of the giant. He was naked, blue-pale, and his face was entirely obscured with blood. The front of his skull was dented in.

"Yes!" the unseen fellow prisoner exulted. "The monster bashed his own brains out. *He'll* keep the scabs off us for a while."

It was the wrong thing to say. One of the Revo Guards dropped the hamhock wrist he was holding, snatched up his slung pulser, and fired at the Engine Regular's cell. Blue flashes lit the high-ceilinged runway. There was a scream, a thump. The scab let his weapon hang on its sling, took up his burden again, and helped his bruds scrape the body the rest of the way outside into light drizzle that had begun to slobber down from the sky.

Mir expelled a breath he hadn't been aware of holding. He felt a certain sorrow for the passing of a man whose face he had never seen.

"It's a battle royal out there," Starman reported. "They're falling on the dead monster like Wolfram tigerfish. Ripping chunks out of him with their teeth. They're killing each other to get to him now."

"It's a feeding frenzy," Jovan said, unconsciously rubbing his own belly. "How much longer is it gonna be before they decide to break down the doors and really grunt down?"

* * *

The Bold Original was deeply, smolderingly angry. Things were not to his liking, not at all. Lesser men had brought him to this, and by rights should suffer.

His remaining companion-of-youth van Dam was squatting in a corner, mashed down to a barely vertebrate lump of misery by the terrible sounds from outside. Kobolev patted his shoulder, which flinched from touch like a horse's flank from a stinging fly. Under such circumstances it was Kobolev's instinct to assert himself, to seize control of the situation.

To *command*. It was why *he* was the only one fit to lead, especially such a collection of sewage filtration as this. Accidents of rank notwithstanding.

"Here, now," he said, pitching his baritone voice low to soothe—and not to carry. "Get hold of yourself. Eyrikson would want that, wouldn't he?"

Van Dam made a whuffling sound that might have meant anything. "It's cowardice that got us into this mess," Kobolev said, "cowardice and folly. They put the wrong men in charge. But we have a *chance*."

The man's shaking seemed to subside. "The others are blind fools," he said. "They don't listen to us, even yet. Kyov is a weakling, an old woman; *he* hasn't the stuff in his sac to stand against us when the time comes to assert our rightful place. It's that mewling pute of a junior lieutenant. Do you hear me?"

Van Dam nodded. Kobolev patted him on the back. "We shall have our chance. This I promise you. Have I ever been wrong?"

Slowly van Dam raised his head. Face and eyes were red. He shook his head.

"Well, then," Kobolev said. "I—we—are the only chance any of us have for getting out of this whiz jigger alive. It's the lieutenant who stands in the way. Do you understand what I'm saying to you?"

Van Dam looked at him. The riot roar without ebbed and surged like surf in a storm. The stone outer walls passed the impacts of wrestling bodies.

"Yes, Kobolev," van Dam said. "I understand."

"Good man," Kobolev said. He felt warmth spread through him.

He knew he wasn't meant to die like a miserable herd beast, torn to death by a pack of beasts. He was intended for greater things, as he had known all his life.

It was simply the Universal Will.

"There must be three hundred of them out there, mad as zongs," Starman called. "Hey! That fucking coward Tigrosian and his boys are backing off! *They're giving in.*"

Somebody moaned. Mir hoped it hadn't been him. *We've come so far, endured so much. . . .*

And part of him said, in a voice much like Loki's, *We're deathbirds. And you expect us to be treated* fair?

The stable doors burst open. A mob flowed in, smashed into the door to Section's cell with a violence that drove Mir back. Twisted faces leered between bars, fists seized the bars and shook, and pounded futilely on stout brass-bound wood. Rioters shouted for guns or a pry bar, to take the door down. Their voices sounded less human than the Rook mockery. Mir could smell their hot breath, rank with rotting human meat. On their hides lay the chalk pallor of corpses.

The men of Section climbed to their feet. None would look at any other.

A long metal bar was brought. Cursing, pummeling each other, the rioters thrust the tip into the latch, put the weight of many bodies on it. Metal groaned in duress, broke with a musical sound.

As if a ringing aftershock, another sound arose. It had something of a whistle to it, something of a scream, and something of the juddering sound Mir associated with rural railroad trains on Santander, where expensive hard-to-maintain maglev nets were found only in the cities. It quickly grew louder, while the rioters froze in the act of throwing open the door.

A bang like the earth splitting open. Mir was hurled to the floor.

29

THE CELL WAS filled like a balloon with reeking chemical smoke. Through the ringing in his ears Mir could hear no more clamor from the cell door. He crawled back to it, painfully winched himself up.

The runway was clear of all but curling tendrils of smoke.

Men were shouting at his back, demanding to know what happened. Starman picked himself up and looked out the window. "Shell hit," he said. "Big one. Left a huge crater in the middle of the parade ground. Bodies *everywhere*."

"Those siege guns we saw," Poet said. He sounded calmer now than Mir could remember ever hearing him. "Rooks must have gotten here quicker than we thought they could."

Again the freight-train scream. Mir threw himself on top of somebody too concerned with becoming one with the floor to protest. This explosion made the stones groan around them, and dropped a rain of dust and straw and old feathers on them.

Another ringing blast, farther away, then a fourth, farther still. The men lay on their faces, bodies tensed, waiting for a 30cm-shell to come crashing down on their heads. But no more explosions came.

"Battery of four," Stilicho said at length, sitting up and dusting himself off.

"Dropped a few in on us to let us know they were there," Black Bertold said. "Now they're probably waiting for their spotters to report how well the shells fell."

273

"The cell door!" Loki shouted, leaping to his feet. "Scabs broke the lock!"

Before anyone could move the door was flung open. Four Guards stood there, three with leveled flamers.

"Out!" snarled the fourth, who held a pulser in one hand. "Now!"

The Landers were beaten out onto the parade ground to stand in a ruminant huddle, blinking into cloud-filtered light that dazzled after cell gloom. A faint drizzle misted down. Work parties hauled off bodies in plastic sheets. The feeding frenzy had apparently been sated, or at least scared out of the scabs.

Twenty armed Revo Guards moved to surround Section, weapons aimed. "See," Loki said brightly. "I told you this would happen: he's decided to fuck us first."

Tigrosian stood near a crater-mounded ejecta-ring, looking as if nothing unusual was happening. He nodded as Mir was prodded up to him at the point of a pair of pulser muzzles.

"Fall your men in, Junior Lieutenant," he said.

Mir blinked at him, uncomprehending. "Do as you're told!" snarled one of the bodyguards.

Dubiously Mir turned, called for Section to form up. They did so, slowly, not so much from recalcitrance as reluctance of their bodies to respond. Revo Guards with guns surrounded them. Mir looked back over his shoulder at Tigrosian, who nodded.

"Section Sergeant Kyov," Mir said in a croak, "call the roll."

"Yes, sir." Kyov turned, stood to attention. "Balt!"

"Here," Balt said, voice barely audible.

"Bertold."

"Here."

"Bori."

"I'm here."

"What's this?" one of Tigrosian's flankers asked. "I didn't know these dirtbags were allowed names?"

The storm-colonel waved him to silence. Kyov continued through the roll until he hit the name "Eyrikson."

Without hesitation the White Rat shouted, "FD, Section Sergeant!"

Kyov kept calling names. When he hit Geydar, Stilicho sang

out. "FD!" Next came Gollob, and Ovanidze answered the same.

The storm-colonel pushed himself forward past Mir. Balt stood nearest to him, but Balt on his best day did not invite contact, even from a haughty officer of Stellar Guards. Next to him stood Bertold, who even gaunt and befouled carried himself like the soldier he had been.

"You, Sergeant," Tigrosian asked. "What does 'FD' mean?"

"Fucking Deader!" Bertold shouted into the rain. "Sir!"

The storm-colonel frowned, sensing perhaps he'd blundered into an ancient trap. He stepped back and let the roll continue. As he did so, scabs were carrying out crates with BK polymer sheets thrown over the tops and setting them on the ground nearby.

When the roll was done—with a lusty, "FD, Section Sergeant Kyov!" by Loki, on Zorich's behalf—Kyov turned and saluted Mir. "All present and accounted for, sir."

"Very impressive ceremony, Junior Lieutenant," Tigrosian said. Mir wasn't sure whether he was being sarcastic or not. He didn't much care. He was exhausted, and his body felt like a giant bruise, and his broken hand throbbed, and the drizzle was making his battle dress feel stiff and clammy and was beginning to run down the back of his neck besides. He wished Tigrosian would order them butchered and get on with it. Or maybe that the Rooks would be satisfied with their ranging and drop another heavy barrage on their heads.

The storm-colonel gestured to him. "Come close, Junior Lieutenant."

Mir hesitated, then obeyed before one of the bodyguards could move to batter him into compliance. Tigrosian reached out as if to drape his arm around Mir's shoulder, then thought better of it.

"The Rook reinforcements arrived sooner than we thought possible," he said in a conspiratorial voice. "They have some of their siege train emplaced already."

"We noticed that, sir."

Tigrosian's pale eyes narrowed. After a beat he went on, "Our infantry radars are useless with the buildings in the way, but directional microphones and seismic sensors indicate the Rooks marched in along roughly the same route you took, and are concentrated to the south, between the cantonment and the outskirts of town. They have begun to move troops around left and right to reinforce the units surrounding us. When they're satisfied with their deployments, they'll bombard us in earnest, and then overrun us.''

He shrugged. ''Obviously, we can't hold here. We're therefore going to break out. We shall make our move in the direction they least expect it: due south.''

Mir didn't know why he bothered to hide his reaction, which was *Typical Revo tactical genius: assault straight into the teeth of the greatest concentration.* But the reflex of concealment had been well ground into him.

''You and your men,'' the storm-colonel continued, ''will create a diversion by breaking out in the opposite direction—north, toward the city center.''

Scabs twitched the covers off the crates. Inside was piled Section's gear: weapons, helmets, Ovanidze's commo set.

''You may order your men to recover their weapons, Junior Lieutenant.''

Feeling very strange, as if his skin was a spun-sugar shell he had been poured into, and which might rupture if he moved too decisively, Mir complied. Passing puzzled looks from eye to eye the Landers moved forward and picked up their arms. They seemed subdued, and their eyes tracked ceaselessly side to side, as if they feared that once they had weapons in hand, the Revos would scream, ''Escape!'' and mow them all down. But the armed Guardsmen did no more than keep them covered with their own weapons.

''What happens once we break through the enemy lines, Storm-Colonel?'' Mir asked. *If we do.*

''Why then, Junior Lieutenant'' the officer said, ''you're free to do as you see fit.'' And he smiled at Mir's look of incomprehension.

''This is never going to work,'' Jovan said as they huddled by the wall at the cantonment's north end.

''What's not to work?'' asked Dieter with a serene smile. ''We shoot our way out, and we blow where we please. Just like the wind.''

''With only a hostile autoc city all around us,'' Jovan said.

Dieter laughed. "So what? We're charmed. Nothing can touch us now."

"Are you pukebags ready?" asked a storm-lieutenant with a bandage over one eye. Mir nodded. "Then stand clear."

Section moved to either side of the seven-meter-wide stretch of the compound's north wall the Revo sappers had wired with explosives. They turned backs and pressed hands over their ears as shaped charges cracked off, blowing a breach in the wall.

Before the shrill-sharp blasts finished echoing off the surrounding buildings, Section's three grenadiers were up, firing looping bursts into the nearest buildings across the kill zone. Mir shouted the order to move, then jumped over a stub of wall through swirling dust and charged out into no man's land.

The Rooks were caught on their heels. Even slogging through the deep dust and debris with legs that felt like lead, he had covered half the distance before muzzle flashes bloomed from the structure he was running toward, and fat soft-lead slugs moaned past his head.

He didn't dare to look back, for fear no one would be following him.

He carried a grenade in his hand. Without slowing his pace, such as it was, he pulled the pin and pitched it into a black doorway right ahead of him. Then he hauled up his pulser and charged through into dust and blast-echoes.

A Rook was rolling back and forth on the floor almost at his feet, clutching the spurting stub of an arm and squawking. Mir had to vault the wounded autoc. Another stood against the far wall, face feathers streaming blood, trying to aim a rifle at him. Mir shot him twice.

A blue bolt flashed by him. Too late to evade it had it been aimed for him, he pirouetted to the side. The blast excavated the stomach of a Rook that had just rushed in the door with a bayoneted rifle. The creature sank to its knees vomiting blood. Reflex more than mercy caused Mir to blow its head off as Stilicho kicked the Rook with the amputated arm out of the door and finished him with a shot of his own.

A sound as of giant footfalls. Grey dust seeped down from the ceiling of the gutted room. Coincidentally or in response to the breakout attempt, the Rooks were firing their new heavy guns into the cantonment.

Stilicho showed teeth in something like a smile. "We're better off out here," he said, "than back there under *that*."

"We'll see," Mir said, without intending to.

First Squad crowded into the room with him. Kyov and Poet squatted by the far door, securing it against the Rooks. The Dancing-Master and Black Bertold reported that their men had all made it into flanking rooms intact.

From there it was a smooth machine, in which even the scrubs did their part as if from long practice—which they'd gotten, in the almost-combat of the Meatgrinder. Toss a grenade into a room, follow its blast with pulsers flaring, finish the wounded with shots to the back of the head or quick strokes of knives across feathered throats, do it over again. The Rooks were quicker, men stronger. Surprise, grenades, body armor, and most of all brutal practiced professionalism gave the humans a decisive edge. They slashed through the half-smashed building like living blades.

At the far end Mir stopped, looking out narrow foyer windows to the street. The building across the way showed him a blank face, without window or door, only seemingly random scatters of darker stone blocks among lemon yellow ones.

From behind him rose the ululating mimic call: "*Mommy! Mommy!*" bringing his hackles along. He almost missed the scrape of talon on the grit covering the hardwood landing above. With a freefall sense of coming late to the dance, he pivoted and fired through a broken-out segment of floor, dropping a Rook drawing a bead on him from above with a carbine.

"Junior Lieutenant!" his headset exclaimed in the voice of the White Rat, left behind as rear guard. The scavenger rarely showed emotion; now he sounded near frantic. "The birds are pouring out from everywhere! They're already over the cantonment walls! They're coming this way!"

"Is their surprise ready?"

"Yes, sir!"

"Then move! First Squad, hit the street and cover!"

He threw himself through the window, tucked his shoulder as he'd been taught in jump training, hit, rolled. His training hadn't exactly covered landing on cobblestones, but he didn't think he'd broken anything.

The Rooks were bursting from the buildings to either side.

He shouted a warning, sprayed the street to his right with blue bolts. Birds squalled and fell.

Poet stepped from a doorway to Mir's left, sent a white incandescent spike wreathed in yellow flame roaring up the street. The Rooks hit by the plasma jet were dead before their bodies fell wrapped in flame, and their terrible shrieks the product of superheated air venting from their lungs, not intolerable agony. The survivors in that direction were terrified anyway, and dived back into the buildings they'd just left. The rest of First Squad rushed out and dropped into position to fire both ways along the street.

Mir came to his knee. A bullet split a cobblestone where he'd lain an instant before, tumbled away with a weird whine. He looked up and saw gunsmoke puff from the roofline of a building across the street.

He assessed his tactical situation: it sucked. His Section had the firepower of a Rook regiment, but the advantage was mostly illusion. The autocs held the high ground, the low ground, and most spaces in between, and the stone buildings gave them excellent cover and concealment.

A cavalry unit seemed to be massing down the street to his left. A mounted charge against autofiring energy and projectile weapons would normally be suicide. But Rook snipers in doors and windows and on rooftops would pick Section to pieces while they concentrated fire on the feathered riders.

Second Squad burst into the street. The men quickly sought such cover as the doorways and building facades offered—with one exception. As casual as though on promenade in the park Loki, rod-upright, walked out, firing a stream of 25mm grenades from the hip. Yellow-beaked mounts reared, screamed, fell in thrashes of color.

Thunder rolled out of the cantonment. The Rook heavy guns were weighing in again, and this time they weren't firing for practice. The building Section had come through shook to the impact of a long round as the White Rat raced forth, holding his helmet on his white-haired head. "*Here they come!*"

Mir's officer training had discouraged *initiative*. Experience—with Kyov for an assistant—had taught Mir a radical lesson: when it all came crashing down, it was better to make a wrong decision *now* than hesitate.

"Come on!" the junior lieutenant shouted. He turned and

ran to the right. No Rooks visibly blocked the street that way.
That was enough, in the millisecond he had to decide.

Shrilling their raptor cries and their taunting human calls of
"*Help me!*" Rook infantry poured from the kill zone into the
ruin. Behind them their clutch-sibs were swarming over the
walls of the enemy-held compound like their tiny winged
cousins flocking to a ruptured seed-grain sack.

In their eagerness to be at talon grips with the hated intruders, the infantry—infertile females leavened with smaller,
drab-plumed males who had been passed over for breeding—
lunged into the smoky, death-stinking gloom, not caring
whether the naked-pale drab-voiced things were waiting in
ambush.

They weren't. The structure was deserted. One large room
emptied through a single door in the far wall to the interior of
the structure. Twenty warriors lunged ahead, crowding and
elbowing each other for the right to be first to stoop on the
prey.

The swiftest Rook, beating her clutch-sisters and the drones
by a full three steps, won more than the honor of being first
in pursuit. She also won life. Her right foot hit a wire that
crossed the narrow corridor at shin level, half a meter along.
She fell headlong, incurring the disgrace of accidentally dis-
charging her rifle.

The Claymores mounted to either side of the entrance tore
the rest of her squad apart like the claws of a giant bird of
prey.

As Mir ran, the building to his right, whose far side faced
the cantonment, was four stories tall, as near as he could guess.
The Rooks did not go in much for regularity; windows were
scattered across the facade as randomly as the droppings the
clouds of blue-and-purple urban birds that went rushing up
into the sky at the invaders' approach spattered on the cobblestones. Every window seemed to have a Rook in it, firing
as fast as it could ram a new charge home and prime and wind
the firing mechanism.

Mir tried to look ahead and blast back with his pulser at the
same time. He was grateful the energy guns had no recoil—
and were light enough to shoot one-handed, sparing his broken

hand. As it was, if he hit anything it was sheer luck. In his peripheral vision he saw Third Squad hit the street and follow Second, while First found its feet and pulled rearguard, concentrating fire now on the cavalry formation. The riders were mostly shot to pieces, dead or fled, but Rooks were still gathering down there, beginning to snipe around corners.

With Second Squad around him, Mir hit block's end, angled across the street, and rushed left around the corner.

Halfway down this block Rook infantry blocked the street. The first two ranks—front kneeling, second standing—already had their aim.

A huge black-feathered Rook with a scarlet head shrieked an order. Fire stabbed from muzzles even as Mir and Second Squad, skidding on slick-worn stones, tried to reverse direction and dive back to cover.

A bullet struck Mir in the chest. Pain blazed through his right thigh. He fell hard, seeing his men go down around him.

30

THE STREET SEEMED filled with silence, though that was surely an illusion, aftereffect of the volley's crashing noise. Mir's right leg didn't seem to respond. Around him the men of Second Squad lay sprawled.

The tall Rook stalked forward. It held a long curved sword with a hooked back in one talon. Mir looked frantically around, saw his pulser lying just out of reach. He stretched an arm for it. The leg wound blasted agony up his spine. The Rook officer raised its sword.

Its scarlet head exploded in black-and-purple steam.

"Ha-ha!" cackled Narva, who had risen to one knee to fire an aimed shot from his pulser. "Not dead yet, you feathered reactionaries! Not by half! Ha!"

Second Squad was picking itself up from the stones, punishing the ranked Rooks with fire. The birds, believing their volley had killed their targets, were taken totally by surprise and fell into confusion. The rear ranks with weapons still loaded, were unable to make their way forward as the front ranks bolted away from Second Squad's guns, as Third came pounding around the corner to add their energy.

Before Mir had struggled to his knees the Rooks had fled, leaving dead and wounded strewn like leaves on the street. Blood was pumping from his right leg. As Third Squad advanced along the street, weapons ready, he pulled a self-adhering patch from a blouse pocket, stripped the seal, slapped

282

it against the wound. A sting told him the medicated patch was in contact with the wound. He pressed harder, to ensure the patch sealed itself to his skin and the fabric of his chammy trousers.

A hand on his shoulder. He jumped, tried clumsily to pivot on his down knee, almost fell. The hand caught fabric, steadied him. It was Kyov, the lines of concern etched deeper into his face than Mir had seen them before. "Can you walk, Junior Lieutenant?"

Would even you help carry me if I couldn't? Mir shook off the internal question, not sure he wanted the answer.

"Yes," he said, determined to make it so.

First Squad rounded the corner on the dead run. There was a sound like the wind through a thicket, and then, with a terrible clatter, masonry dust erupted in a cloud from the faces of the buildings to their right.

"What the hell?" Mir demanded in a cracked voice.

"Beast-pulled arty, Junior Lieutenant," Kyov said. "We got the crew of the first, but there were at least two more."

Mir shook his head. *And we thought these primitives would be a cakewalk.* The "primitive" canister round from the field-piece would have shredded his entire Section as effectively as the giant Claymore it functionally was if it had caught them on the street.

Every man from Second Squad was up on his feet now. Except one. Dieter lay on his back, arms outflung, in the midst of a pool of dark red. A slug had nipped between the lower rim of his visor and the collar of his battle dress and severed the carotid. Big Bori and Chyz were spattered with red from the arterial spray like paint from an aerosol can.

Despite the need for speed, Mir limped to the fallen man's side and, holding his right leg stiff, bent the left to reach fingers to his neck.

"Don't bother, Lieutenant," Stilicho said. "He's FD."

"He'll not be going home after all!" shrilled Loki with a wild laugh. "There's what looking on the bright side buys you."

The White Rat squatted beside the fallen Lander, tucked a pin-pulled grenade into dead hands, and rolled the corpse on top of it.

"With luck he'll take some souls with him to Planet Hell,"

the scavenger said, rising and slinging the compressor pack of the fallen man's flamer across his bony shoulders, "buy himself some *klad*."

"Surely he's bound the other way," Kyov said, panting softly. "We've all been through Hell already."

"You talk like him," Poet said. "There isn't any heaven. It's Hell or nothing."

"Not for the likes of us," Lennart said, eyes hollow behind the smoky polymer of his visor. "What is the Lake of Fire prepared for, if not to receive the likes of us?"

They progressed along the street by rolling over watch, one squad covering while the other two dashed ahead. *Where* they were going was an open question. Bound to the surface of an alien world, with every being's claw turned against them and nothing they could eat, was one place any better than another?

Tactically, at least; ahead of them Mir saw one of the looming many-windowed structures with the spindly buttresses and point-arched windows he thought of as *cathedrals*. Its spiny towers represented the highest ground around, its walls strong protection.

Mir was deadly aware of the danger of being trapped, as the much-stronger Revo battalion had been inside the cantonment, where grotesquely superior numbers would overwhelm them soon or late. But for now the cathedral would do for a goal; perhaps they could draw breath there, momentarily safe from the sniper fire that pounded them through helmets and body armor and pitched them bruised to the cobblestones on every fifth step. Perhaps that would give them leeway to come up with *something*.

There's always something. Isn't there? His mind still refused to come to terms with absolute hopelessness, with a void of options far more complete than the supposed vacuum of space; with a situation in which optimum decisions could only defer death, and that, likely, for minutes at most.

You're abandoning the Guardsmen, a voice said from the back of his head, as if to perfect his despair. He could still hear the horrible cries as the Rooks stormed the cantonment and their heavy artillery shook the cobbles beneath their boots like an endlessly protracted earthquake. *They* are *men*.

And another part of him wondered if that were so; and yet again, whether it was any more true of himself and his outlaw command. The old refuge offered itself: *We were ordered to break out. We've broken out. And now we're on our own.*

He was too sophisticated to swallow that rationalization whole—and perhaps he was too sophisticated for his own good, and so always fated to land here, among deathbirds, even if his sister hadn't been framed for treason? But a Collective cog perforce grew used to makeshifts, and none more so than the souls lost in CLD.

"The tall building, the cathedral," he called over the Section net. "We'll make for there."

Behind them a tumult of angry bird voices broke out like gunfire. The "Mommy" calls from the cantonment had lapsed into the turbulence of distance, were no more clear than the words the wind spoke. These cries erupted right behind the running humans, as hundreds or thousands of the man-tall birds joined the pursuit.

For all their awesome firepower, the Landers were gripped by fearful urgency, hot as the packet of air riding before a flamer's pulse. With their instinct for the high places, the birds were finding the rooftops and sniping them like hail. Soft-lead bullets shattered cobbles or raised dust flowers off stucco facades and tumbled away with ricochet whines. Sometimes one found destination on a cloth-armored body or limb, and then a curse, a thump and rolling clatter of arms and arms and legs over smooth-worn stones as a running Lander fell. Before his momentum quit rolling him over and over he was wrestling himself to his feet again, with maybe a grab at a pack strap from a passing comrade to aid him.

Long-legged Loki was first up the steps to the triple-arched door of the soaring asymmetric structure. Big Bori fetched up with his back to the wall at almost the same instant, bulky Bitch held like a carbine in his hands. Nodding to the giant to cover him, Loki kicked the door open with a heel, wheeled around inside, and stepped quickly right, hurdy-gurdy ready.

The raptor screams were getting closer. When Loki did not cry them off, Mir and the rest came pounding through the door, desperate for the stone walls to stop the lead hail from beating them to pieces.

Inside was cool grey dim, shot with beams of amber light that swarmed with motes like midges. There was a smell of cool stone to the place, and varnished wood, and the lingering not-unpleasant body smell of the Rooks themselves. Mir limped along, dragged boot scraping on parquetry hardwood floor, gazing up and around in wonder. Above him soared a great vault of void, filled with shadow and footstep echo, but mostly with *peace*.

There were no pews, to Mir's surprise. His family, belonging to Values' cutting-edge Communality faction, professed a belief in the unadorned Universal Spirit, though they had not been observant. As a youngster, though, he had explored Santander's quaint hinterland Catholic churches, and had an idea what such were like. Instead of pews the Rook cathedral—if cathedral it was—had soaring structures of polished wood, racks of perches rising rank on rank up to the distant ceiling. And high up on them were bulky, shrouded figures, silent and still, like—

—Like Rook soldiers, stationed or perhaps meditating within the great communal structure, momentarily frozen with surprise at this intrusion. From twenty meters above the floor the fire blossom of a rifle going off filled the cathedral void with reverberating noise and Mir's soul with a sense of confused betrayal as the bullet gouged ancient colored wood at his feet.

From the slanted perches overhead muzzle blasts flashed like lights on a random chaser circuit. Loki raised his hurdy-gurdy, then cursed and let it fall to the extent of its waist-length sling, unwilling to risk dropping the roof on their heads. He snatched up his slung pulser and hosed blue brilliance into the heights as the rest of Section, fanning away from the doorway, opened fire on the scores of startled birds above them.

Mir's attention was fixed on the Rook who had fired first. He could see the creature working away up there in the dim, ramming a paper cartridge down the barrel of its rifle with a long brass rod. Its great yellow eyes were aimed straight at the lieutenant. It raised the cover on the primer pan, poured a dollop of powder from a flask, and suddenly the rifle's length was interposed between it and Mir, and the human was staring into a black third eye.

He came out of his trance, fired. A blue sphere ate out the bird's belly like speed cancer. It fired. The shot plucked at Mir's collar like a friendly bid for attention, and the creature fell, trailing smoke and blood like festive streamers.

Bori and Balt stood back to back, roaring counterpoint and firing their heavy Bitches from the hip. Needles chipped dust from ancient stone and dropped birds from their perches like feathered fruit. As Mir looked Bori's fléchette stream sawed through the supports of a perch almost twenty meters high, spilling three Rook sharpshooters with despairing croaks.

Through the peaceful ancient space moved Section, killing as it went. With a whoosh and a roar, Poet's flamer sent a dragon's tongue licking at the heights, turning a complex conjunction of perches into a torch and the Rook snipers perched on it to shrieking comets. The flaming perch threw orange-yellow light broken by writhing bands of shadow down to the floor, overriding the frantic strobing of blue bolts. The cathedral was a seethe of smoke and dust and stink: burning feathers, scorched flesh, smoke, blood, feces, varnish, mold, the sharpness of burned propellant. It was stone desecration, and Mir felt like a rapist.

A feathered tapestry hanging along one wall was swept aside and clot of Rooks rushed in from some side passage. Poet's flamer set the hanging to a reeking, leaping blaze and dropped three Rooks as shriveled puppets. Another, somehow dancing sideways past the plasma jet, side feathers flaring into blue flame from its passage, struck at Poet with a saber. The hook-backed blade severed Poet's left hand, which gripped the flamer's pistol grip, just above the wrist. Final random neuron firings clenched his fingers on the firing stud, vomiting a blinding yellow-white jet.

With his right hand, Poet turned the plasma stream on his assailant, cindered the creature from the waist up. His stump spurted blood, dead black in the hideous backwash light. Without hesitation he thrust the wound into the flame gush, cauterizing it in a microsecond. Then he staggered and went down. His Little Sister spent her fury against the thick base of a perch, making of the structure a tree of roaring fire.

Somebody kicked at the severed hand; from that or the power cell's exhaustion the fire geyser cut off, dropping the cathedral like a stone into what seemed, for an eyeblink, like darkness. Then the blaze of many fires reasserted themselves, turning the dark into Hell's high noon.

Mir limped toward Poet, wondering why he bothered, wondering if it would be a favor to save the boy even if they had

any prospect for survival. Stilicho got there first, square and
solid as one of the stone blocks that made up the walls. He
stooped, slung Poet across his back in a fireman's carry, rose
up with the flamer nozzle dangling on its hose past his shoulder, holding Poet in place with his left hand, firing a pulser
with his right.

And then it was all over but the burning. Mir found himself
staring up, into spider traceries of flame against the groined
arches of the ceiling fifty meters up. No one was shooting at
them any longer. All was silent but for the fire's angry self-
absorbed mutter, and the pop of a few final blue bolts donating
their energy to stone or wood as the Landers realized they had
won. Again. For whatever it was worth.

"We lose anybody?" he asked. The words hurt his parched
raw throat coming out, as though they were burrs.

"Rouen's FD, sir," Jovan reported. "Round took his helmet off, and another caught him smack above the eye."

Mir closed his eyes, seeing the quiet former rancher,
perched in the loft window of an alien farmhouse watching
alien lightning sear alien sky. *Men die,* he told himself. *It's
war, and it's our lot.*

*And we'll all of us leave our bones behind, before the sun's
full down . . .*

A figure loomed up before him, head bare to show a square-
cut silver-grey plush of hair. "You boys had better keep moving," said Storm-Colonel Tigrosian in a conversational rasp.
"The street back there's filling up with birds. I barely got in
here with my hide intact."

Mir's first reflex was professional, which gave him a twitch
of inappropriate pride: *I'm still an officer of the Stellar Collective.* He looked round, caught the eye of Ovanidze, who
had lost his helmet and stood by oblivious to a fallen shard of
wood smoldering in his mustard-colored hair. The lieutenant
gestured back toward the door they had entered through. The
tech turned and loosed a flamer jet. The wood, shaped centuries ago by meticulous hand, polished and preserved and
cherished over years, caught fire at once and burned with a
breathy hissing roar. Ovanidze swept the plasma stream left
and right, making sure to involve the bases of the pillars near
the door and the feather tapestries, showing gorgeous-plumed
Rooks engaged in ritual dance, that flanked it, erecting a bar-

rier of fire behind them. If he felt the mass of his profanation, his round, fist-cheeked face didn't show it.

Mir stared at the storm-colonel. The Guard officer's face was smudged with char, and a burn glowed red on one cheek, borders glistening with melted human fat. It must have been hideously painful, but Tigrosian grinned.

"You stare at me as if I'm a ghost, Junior Lieutenant," he said.

"What are you doing here, sir?" Mir asked in a voice that cracked like glass beneath a boot.

"Breaking out," the storm-colonel said, "along with you."

Mir stared at him. His eyes felt peeled and raw. *We never were a feint, were we?* he wanted to scream. *We're the real breakout, as much as will ever be. It was the doomed resistance of your battalion that was the ruse—a cover for your own escape.* The words were too heavy to push up the column of his throat from his churning belly.

He felt the weight of the pulser in his tired, burned, abraded hands, longed for the courage to raise it and fire right into the scab's astonished look, to put a blue bolt right into that mouth and see perfect white teeth flying back at him, shrapnel driven by brain steam. But he could not. Bending the neck was too ingrained in him, it was wound in his very DNA. He ached that one of his men, his desperate wolf-jawed outlaws, would have the sheer antisocial stuff to burn the colonel down. But they wore the victim's yoke as much as he, and it dragged their heads down like the mass of an invisible planet.

"Let's go," he said to his men. "We can't stay here."

"Sir!" Chyz screamed, spinning from the far door, the one they had been heading toward. "They've got a fucking cannon—"

The door blew in. The six-kilo cannonball snapped the scrub's spine and caved in his rib cage just in shouldering him out of its way. It hummed past Mir and struck a perch's pillarlike support with a splintering crack.

A chunk of heavy wood filigree dropped right on top of them. A beam as big as Mir's thigh missed him by the width of three fingers, shivering hand-rubbed wooden tiles by his boots. He barely registered it, staring in horror as Loki, prowling along a wall with his grenade launcher in hand, was struck

down by a falling support, then hidden behind a curtain of
flame as a burning section dropped.

Overhead the remaining perches were beginning to sway
and break with splintering sounds, fire-involved tops waving
like palm trees in a gale. The whole faerie structure was going
to drop on them at any second.

He gave a last glance toward where Loki had fallen. The
corporal was completely surrounded in flame; no way to help
him. Mir felt odd emptiness: Loki was a monster, in his way,
yet he was also somehow Section's twisted soul, its best as
well as its worst.

What does it matter? he asked himself as his mouth filled
with bile. *Now or in a matter of minutes, we're all meat.
Tigrosian's a bigger fool than I thought if he thinks his treach-
ery's won him more than a handful of heartbeats.*

Just inside the blown-down door, Black Bertold knelt,
hurdy-gurdy shouldered and making a ponderous chunking
sound as it cast grenades into the street. The 25mm blasts
would do no damage to the beast-towed light fieldpiece unless
they blew off a wheel, but they plucked its crew to shreds like
giant fingers.

A moan brought Mir's head around. The storm-colonel lay
pinned to the parquetry under a nest tangle of heavy timbers.
Flames were already running the beams like brightly plumed
Rookery rats.

Tigrosian lifted a pain-twisted face to Mir. "Help me!" he
gasped.

Landers stood around the trapped Revo officer, staring
down at him. "You can't leave me here!" he cried.

One by one they turned away.

A groaning creak swelled around them like an organ chord.
The rest of the network of perches, well alight, was about to
go. "Everybody out!" Mir shouted. "Quickly, before it all
comes down on our heads!"

And he looked down deliberately to meet Tigrosian's gaze.
The storm-colonel's steel-colored eyes had turned to water. As
though he were breaking glass rods that stretched from eye to
eye, Mir jerked his head aside and ran. His brain would not
allow him to make sense of the frantic cries that followed him,
but some snakelike thing that coiled in his gut, whose tail ran

round the base of his cock and curled up the cord of his scrotum, relished their pain like a feast.

Outside dusk air tasted cool and sweet despite the clouds of propellant smoke. Mir reeled down the steps, turned right on instinct. "Come on! Follow me!"

He glanced back, saw Stilicho coming after, Poet still slung over his back, saw the Dancing-Master, bareheaded, towing Florenz behind him with one hand wrapped in a strap of his ruck.

From the front a desperate wail: "*Oh, God, my God, why hast Thou forsaken me?*" Mir snapped his head around to see Lennart go down under the talons of a troop of Rook cavalry sweeping around the corner.

The sight struck Mir like a shot. His smoke-burned eyes stung with the unfairness of it: *Can't we have a moment to rest?*

He raised his pulser, as if through some thick colloid. And a real, physical blow struck him high in the chest.

He looked down. The ball had found a gap torn in his battle dress by hungry scabs. Blood dyed the filthy bandage wound around his torso. He felt blood turbulence bubbling in the base of his windpipe.

On the steps of the cathedral Kobolev stopped to fire a burst from his Bitch at the onrushing cavalry. Nothing happened, except the whine of his blower fan seemed to take on a higher, angry pitch. A needle had gotten crosswise in the flex feeder hose, blocking it.

With a curse he tore the ammo backpack straps from his thick shoulders, dropped the pack to the pavement with the now-useless electro atop it. As he reached for his slung pulser he saw the junior lieutenant go down. On all sides Landers flopped to steps and cobbles to pour desperate fire into the charging beasts.

He glanced at van Dam with a gleam in his blue eyes. His shadow stood by his shoulder, ready to do his bidding, right where he belonged.

Kobolev slapped van Dam on the biceps. "There," he said, nodding a black bearded chin at the fallen officer. "He killed Eyrikson. Make sure of him."

Van Dam gave him a loose-lipped grin and ran.

*   *   *

Mir never really lost consciousness. It was just that for an unknowable space of time the world was all red and black and roaring in his ears.

And then he was aware of being on his back, looking up at a yellow-green near-evening sky, and against it a darkness he recognized as van Dam.

The burly brown-haired youth grinned down at him. ''This is for my brud,'' he said in a hoarse whisper. He aimed his pulser at the center of Mir's forehead. A grimy finger tightened on the trigger.

Half a meter of needle steel lance head poked through the front of his throat with a sound like paper tearing. Instead of a blue bolt, a hoselike stream of blood hit Mir in the face. The lance was ripped back out of the Lander's neck as the cavalry-Rook swept past. Van Dam folded to the cobbles like an abruptly vacated suit of clothes.

Mir pressed a hand to his chest. It came away all blood, and he could hear the bubbling whistle, actually feel the air pulsing in and out of his side to the ragged rhythm of his lungs. Blood filled his mouth. Its taste was hot copper. His other hand groped like a blind animal, seeking his pulser.

The Rook riders were in among his men, stabbing with their lances, chopping with their swords. He saw Bori standing amid a whirl of riders like a bear at bay, ignoring the lance heads that pierced his battle dress to impale his great chest, bashing Rooks from the saddle with two-handed swings of his Bitch. He saw Starman reeling, clutching at a lance stuck through his belly and laughing through the blood cascade from his mouth, firing a pulser one-handed. *The Section's dying,* the junior lieutenant knew. *This is the end.*

The slow heavy stutter of a hurdy-gurdy laid itself with deceptive calmness across the chaos sounds. Grenades began to burst among the ranks of riders pressing up the street toward them, spraying flame and smoke and body parts. Mounts screamed through great yellow beaks, turned and fled despite the efforts of their riders to control them.

Loki was striding down the steps of the burning cathedral, wreathed in the smoke of his own smoldering body. His helmet was gone, his hair burned away, the skin of his head charred black. He fired off the rest of his drum of grenades at the now-retreating Rooks and dropped down to sit near the lieutenant. To his horror, Mir saw that his battle dress had melted itself to his ribs, become new skin, become chitin, hard and black and shiny. His hands had been charred to calcined claws immovably fixed to the weapon.

It was unbelievable that his muscles, dried and contracted by the burning, should still have the flexibility to keep him upright, much less the strength to extricate him from the weight of blazing rubble that had fallen on him.

That he still lived was unendurable. Mir puked blood and sour.

Loki gazed down at the officer. Red cooked meat showed through fissures in the charcoal that covered his face. His eyelids had been burned away.

"What's the matter, Junior Lieutenant?" the apparition asked through a lipless mouth. "It's only skin."

Mir let his head fall back. They had, at least a few moments to themselves. To die in . . .

A noise as if the sky was a bowl, and had just cracked clean across.

"What was that?" he managed to ask. His voice seemed to come from light years away—from the palatial house on Santander, perhaps, where Tsatchka waited in a bedroom packed with all the lost toys of his childhood, to enfold him in her soft-scaled arms and cuddle and croon to him and make all right again.

She would wait in vain. He knew. A tear rolled from the corner of his eye and down his cheek, a last kiss of coolness.

Loki laughed. "A sonic boom, Junior Lieutenant."

"A sonic—" Speech failed while his mind struggled with the concept. It could mean only that high-tech intruders had returned to the Rookery in ships of space. Was it the Strahn, come back to claim the fruits of victory? Or could it even be—

"Junior Lieutenant! Look! A *Franco*-class battlecruiser, right above our heads!" Ovanidze chattered like an excited Rook as he swung his commo pack off his back and knelt to work it with fumbling fingers.

Mir looked up. A shadow shaped like a blunt barbed lance head was settling from the evening sky right on top of them.

"They've come back for us!" he heard the Dancing-Master shout hoarsely. "We're saved!"

Haakon Mir had just enough strength left for a slight smile of appreciation for the irony of it all. "Yirina," he whispered.

Then he let his head fall back to the smooth hard stone, and closed his eyes.

EPILOGUE

Universal Will

Epilogue

ALBREKHT MIR WAS watching a CommuNews simcast of his wife, pulser in hand, leading the Chief District administrator, ruler of Santander District, down the steps of Collective House with his wrists wrapped before him in polymer restraints when the communicator hummed for attention.

"Send," he said. The face of Sendak appeared like an asteroid above the black marble desktop.

"Service," the face said. "Supervisor, I have news."

News had been plentiful the last few days. A mighty Kosmos Force fleet, assembled in secret, had fallen from Lo-space into Rookery orbit like a sword of Universal retribution. It had struck decisively—

—Against nothing. The Struhn had killed and run.

Natalya had been bubbling over with hope since word was released of the return to the Rookery. Never mind that the decisive act of vengeance had tumbled into the chaos of another fiasco—nor that in their rage at being cheated of killing centaurs, certain ship commanders had opened fire on Rook cities with orbital weapons, in the process destroying an as-yet-undetermined number of human survivors. Natalya was so excited that she found room to enthuse about her growing certainty that Haakon still lived even while finalizing plans for the stroke that would deliver the District into her and her husband's hands.

"What have you learned?" Mir asked.

"Your son died on the Rookery."

Mir's soul vibrated as if struck by a hammer. He just sat. His eyes felt as if they had grown sticky in their sockets.

"Fortunately," the pitted face said, breaking into a smile, "he was recovered within minutes by a lighter from the *Petain*, easily within the margins of full recovery, without loss of function."

Without loss of function. A quaint way of saying that Albrekht and Natalya Mir's sole surviving child survived in fact, was a person, not a vegetable.

"I shall speak with you later," Mir said, and broke the connection.

The door to the lift opened. Natalya Mir strode into the penthouse office, all in black, sweeping a gleaming black helmet from her head. She carried a pulser slung across her back.

Mir rose. "Natalya! I thought you were still at Collective House—"

She grinned at him, looking decades younger than her years—looking younger, perhaps, than he'd ever seen her look. "That was a delayed cast. We wanted to make sure the images showed exactly what we wanted them to."

She ran to him, cheeks afire with triumph. He held her off. She went stiff, eyes hurt.

"What's the matter?" she asked. "Albrekht, why won't you let me hug you?" The elation fled her face, and it was like the disorderly evacuation of a town, leaving desolation.

"It's Haakon, isn't it?" she asked in broken tones.

"He's alive, Natalya. He was . . . badly injured . . . but he lives."

She wrapped her arms around his neck and kissed him hard. "Oh, *Albrekht!* Surely now we can get him out! Our son will be free!"

Gently Albrekht Mir disengaged her arms from his neck, marveling at their newfound strength.

"Perhaps," he said.